The Great Big Doorstep

The Great Big Doorstep

A NOVEL

E. P. O'DONNELL

With an Introduction by Bryan Giemza and an
Afterword by Eudora Welty

LOUISIANA STATE UNIVERSITY PRESS · BATON ROUGE

Published by Louisiana State University Press
Originally published as *The Great Big Doorstep* by
Houghton Mifflin Southern, 1941

Louisiana Paperback Edition, 2015
Manufactured in the United States of America
First printing

Library of Congress Cataloging-in-Publication Data
O'Donnell, E. P. (Edwin P.), 1895 or 1896–1943.
  The great big doorstep : a novel / E. P. O'Donnell ; with an
introduction by Bryan Giemza ; and an afterword by Eudora Welty. —
Louisiana paperback edition.
    pages ; cm
  ISBN 978-0-8071-6029-9 (pbk. : alk. paper) — ISBN 978-0-
8071-6030-5 (pdf) — ISBN 978-0-8071-6031-2 (epub) — ISBN
978-0-8071-6032-9 (mobi) 1. Families—Louisiana—Fiction.
2. Depressions—1929—Louisiana—Fiction. 3. Louisiana—Social life
and customs—1930–1939—Fiction. I. Giemza, Bryan Albin. II. Welty,
Eudora, 1909–2001. III. Title.
  PS3529.D535G74 2015
  813'.52—dc23

                                                      2014049748

The paper in this book meets the guidelines for permanence and durability
of the Committee on Production Guidelines for Book Longevity
of the Council on Library Resources. ∞

To

GERTRUDE B. O'DONNELL

CONTENTS

INTRODUCTION

YOU MIGHT say that E. P. (Edwin Phillip) O'Donnell's life was writ on the iron roads and on the water, making him truly a son of New Orleans. Rail and river, the tides of broken family, economic scrabbling, and forced migration conspired to carry E. P.'s parents to this southern port city. He was born in New Orleans on March 25, 1895, to Edward and Alice O'Brien O'Donnell. Alice was a native Louisianan whose parents were born in Ireland. Edward, born in Indiana and later orphaned, was a locomotive engineer in an industry that opened to human hands wetlands where ivory-billed woodpeckers still flitted. Edward's father was an Irish American contractor whose career busted on the Brooklyn Bridge. Soon after, he vanished into American anonymity, leaving his offspring to the goodwill of relatives, a brokenness that would be reprised in E. P.'s own life.

By 1900 the Edward O'Donnell family was living at 1331 Lafayette Avenue in New Orleans. The 1910 census lists the family— including E. P.'s sisters, Claire (ten) and Nettie (seven), and Alice O'Donnell's brother—residing in a shotgun house on St. Ferdinand Street near the railroad corridor (the house no longer stands). The teenage E. P., "Pat" to his friends, had by that time already finished his schooling and was working at odd jobs. A 1912 New Orleans city directory lists E. P. as, simply, a "clerk." A pattern of off-and-on employment for shipping companies played out in the years that followed. The year 1916 found him working as a clerk in the audi-

tor's department of "NO T&M RR" at 610 Poydras Street. By July
he was employed as assistant purser on United Fruit Company's
SS Coppename, spending his summer shipping to Belize.

Even as E. P. took to the seas, the country was facing a dramatic
and precarious period. The following year the United States entered World War I, and in 1918 the plague of the flu pandemic com-
pounded the plague of war. In later interviews, O'Donnell claimed
to have driven an ambulance for the Red Cross during the flu out-
break, which is possible (if very reminiscent of Ernest Hemingway,
his literary hero).[1]

One of the earliest photos of E. P. to survive shows him and
his future spouse in 1919. Gertrude Blanche Barangue was born
on February 3, 1899. Her father named his parents' countries of
origin as Spain and France, and her mother's parents were German born. In the photo, E. P. and Gertrude are dressed in Sunday walking clothes but perched with the odd delicacy of two log-
rollers, near the interlaced skeins of whitecaps hissing off of Lake
Pontchartrain. Today we might think of the photo as depicting a
young couple, but E. P. had already reached the meridian of his
life. Pneumonia, flu, and tuberculosis were the leading causes of
death in O'Donnell's birth year, and the life expectancy was forty-
seven. E. P. would squeak out forty-eight. Gertrude would live to
be ninety-seven. At the moment of the photo, though, the two are
forward looking, and the future is bright. It is the only picture of
the couple that was passed down to their grandchildren.

In the photo, E. P. stands almost as if alone, jaunty, perhaps not
altogether pleased to suffer the intrusion of photography on life.
We're reminded of his contemporary Ernest Hemingway, who also
walked log-strewn shores, as ecological frontiers closed suddenly all
the way from the deep swamps of Louisiana to the lakes of Michi-
gan. It's possible that O'Donnell, who had once given boxing lessons, crossed his arms to conceal the three fingers missing from his

E. P. "Pat" O'Donnell and Gertrude Blanche Barangue, Kenner, Louisiana. 1919. *Photographer unknown. Courtesy of Maureen Selby.*

left hand, noted on his 1918 draft registration. The loss of those fingers might well have spared him from the action of the century's first great war.[2]

In 1920 E. P. still lived with his parents and siblings at the corner of Marais and St. Roch Avenue. Prohibition began, and William Faulkner would claim, rather outrageously, to have been a rum runner around that time, but it's far more likely that O'Donnell had some experience in that area.[3] From December 1921 through February 1922, E. P. was launched on the crew of the steamship *Cartago,* which, in its heyday, was used by United Fruit Company to ferry workers from the West Indies to the banana colonies. He would have heard the patter of many languages, since the crew typically required about ninety-five souls, of which about a third were Americans and the rest foreign-born.[4] O'Donnell started as a shipboard checker and eventually became barman. The Puritanical strictures of Prohibition were a world away.

Meanwhile, in 1921 Gertrude was listed by her maiden name in a New Orleans city directory as a clerk for the Southern Railway System. But in Soards' 1922 City Directory, she is listed as "Mrs. Edwin P. O'Donnell," working as a stenographer and living in a shotgun house at 926 N. Salcedo St. (Another city directory from that same year lists Mrs. Edwin P. O'Donnell as resident of Gulfport, Mississippi.) Though a marriage record has yet to be located, these facts suggest that E. P. and Gertrude took on married status, formally or informally, around the time of O'Donnell's three-month stint on the *Cartago*. A son, Patrick Albert ("Pat") O'Donnell, was born to the couple on November 13, 1922, and another son, Daniel Edward O'Donnell, was born on January 17, 1924.

It was during this period that the new father tried to make a settled life for his family. He had perhaps a middle-school education but had made his way through trades and eventually worked his way up to the position of advertising manager at the Ford Plant on the outskirts of New Orleans, a job that he would credit with honing the concision of his writing. On the cusp of finding a footing in the middle class, by 1927 he and Gertrude were living on Cleveland Avenue in New Orleans. It's possible that around this time he first met on a factory tour Sherwood Anderson, who, it is said, encouraged O'Donnell to try creative writing.

Quizzically, perhaps against all expectation, E. P. did just that. He was one of those rare men equally at ease with the working poor as with the leisured class of New Orleans's moneyed arts boosters. By summer of 1928 he had joined the Poetry Society of Louisiana, whose members included Cleanth Brooks (then on fellowship at Tulane), Hodding Carter, and Bonita Godchaux. O'Donnell's poetry was published in their chapbook, *Calas Tout Chauds: A Book of Verse by Members of the Louisiana Poetry Society*. A critical mass was

forming among the creative class in New Orleans, and in the headline of February 5, 1928, the *Item-Tribune* might fairly call New Orleans an "Artist's Mecca—Nearly All Reside in Quarter."[5]

In mid-November of that year, O'Donnell's bohemian nature
openly asserted itself. Newspaper accounts corroborate this as a
time when E. P. took a legendary three-week stroll (he would de-
scribe it as merely cashing in his accumulated vacation at Ford) on
the levees all the way from New Orleans to land's end, some seventy
miles away, around Boothville, Louisiana.[6] O'Donnell had found
the setting for his work, and what would ultimately become *The
Great Big Doorstep*. Boothville would be the place where he felt most
at peace, and his point of retreat in later years when his relationship
with Gertrude faltered. His rambling partner for the long walk was
a radical artist named Douglas Edwin Brown, only recently arrived
to the Quarter arts scene. Brown apparently enjoyed the company
of a natural-born raconteur, and the artist sketched scenes from

"Church in the orange-growing section, Boothville, Louisiana. September
1938." *Photograph by Russell Lee. Library of Congress.*

life along the levees as they walked. He would later travel to Haiti, and come to know Diego Rivera in Mexico, before teaching art at Dillard University in New Orleans. Today some part of his work is preserved in the Smithsonian American Art Museum.[7]

The two continued to collaborate and move among the New Orleans bohemians. In February 1929 O'Donnell joined with Brown and other organizers to establish the Provincial Gallery on Jackson Square, a place intended to showcase local artists. It opened its doors with an exhibition of watercolors by Brown and Myron Lechay. With Irish insouciance, O'Donnell found himself drifting among a remarkable company of artistic innovators.[8]

Nineteen twenty-nine was an important year for O'Donnell, as he took his first deliberate steps toward becoming a full-time writer (though he did not yet relinquish various day jobs). He published his first work in a journal, a piece called "Transfusion" that appeared in Mississippian Charles Henri Ford's avant-garde little magazine, *Blues: A Magazine of New Rhythms.* But if O'Donnell had set himself to the task of becoming an artist, he had chosen a uniquely inauspicious time for it. On October 29, 1929, the stock market crash announced the onset of the Great Depression, and for O'Donnell, a period of lean living. Writing to Bennett Augustin years later, he would reflect back on a time of "depending on my people for tobacco and carfare."[9] The 1930 census would find E. P. and Gertrude renting 610 N. St. Patrick Street in New Orleans. Gertrude's profession is listed as stenographer at a steam ship office, while E. P. continued to work as a bookkeeper at the automobile plant.

For the next several years, he published with remarkable success. In May 1931, "Like a Man!" appeared in *Collier's Weekly.* The story, set in in the mountains of North Carolina, was E. P.'s first national commercial magazine publication. In October he published "Fragments from Alluvia" in *Scribner's,* a premier venue for emerging American writing. By 1933, E. P.'s short story "Jesus Knew" would be included among the twenty-seven short works to receive *Scribner's* narrative prize. Collected in *Scribner's* "Life in the United States," O'Donnell would appear alongside such authors as Carl Carmer and Marjorie Kinnan Rawlings. He placed "Potent Delta, A Story" in *Harper's Monthly* in March of 1933, and December saw "Three Delta Romances" published in *Story* magazine, with Sherwood Anderson's work in the same number. In publishing his stories in the major journals he might well have benefitted, as did Thomas Wolfe and Ernest Hemingway, from the literary patronage of Sherwood Anderson, who in correspondence referred to him as "the immortal Pat."[10]

Even as O'Donnell quickly built up a story portfolio, and the Depression was eroding his finances, he was broadening the scope of his ambitions. By 1932 he had begun planning what would become his first novel, *Green Margins*. He would spend the next three years writing it.

The year 1935 would be another watershed. In April "Jesus Knew" was published in *Harper's* and later nominated for the O. Henry prize. But O'Donnell's big break came when his entry for *Green Margins* was chosen "from 800 manuscripts" to receive the Houghton Mifflin Literary Fellowship Prize. The Houghton Mifflin prize would soon be established as a springboard for major talents; in subsequent years recipients included Robert Penn Warren, Philip Roth, and Alice Walker. O'Donnell would be represented by famed agent Maxim Lieber, whose clients included Erskine Caldwell, John Cheever, Langston Hughes, Carson McCullers, and Thomas Wolfe. Lieber promised to make arrangements for translation and international publication. O'Donnell's writing career wasn't merely launched; it was suddenly soaring.

Yet his correspondence shows that he worked that year from the "one-room shack" he had purchased in Boothville. He wrote frequently to his friend Bennett Augustin, who was trying to start up *Menagerie,* a little magazine in New Orleans. The print run went from July 1935 until May 1936, with O'Donnell as a regular contributor. Sometime during 1935, Mary Paula King, who would become O'Donnell's second wife, arrived from Texas. If O'Donnell had drifted away from his young family, he was apparently still married, as he mentioned in one letter that he would prefer not to ask his wife to make a donation to keep the *Menagerie* afloat. He continued to take odd jobs, splitting his time mostly between Boothville and New Orleans, trying to make ends meet with various seasonal truck-farming enterprises, including raising lilies and oranges, with interludes as a waterman, harvesting shrimp and oysters. If he had hoped to transition to full-time writing, it was becoming clear that his objective remained elusive.

Yet the muses, it seemed, were singing. In October 1936, *Green*

"Creole girls, Plaquemines Parish, Louisiana. October 1935." *Photograph by Ben Shahn. Library of Congress.*

Margins was published. E. P. appeared as the featured writer on the front page of that month's *Saturday Review of Literature,* and the novel was promoted on splashy two-page advertisements. It sold 88,000 copies in its first year, about half as many as that year's best-seller, Margaret Mitchell's *Gone with the Wind.* The book was widely and favorably reviewed, drawing praise from critics as far-flung as Julian Huxley, brother to Aldous.

O'Donnell was stepping up. A 1928 *Times-Picayune* profile called E. P. a "ferryboat bootblack turned writer,"[11] and a later profile confirmed that one of O'Donnell's first jobs was shining shoes on the ferry from New Orleans to Algiers. Eight years later, on the crest of gathering fame, a *Saturday Review* photograph captures O'Donnell, freshly arrived at Times Square for the National Book Fair, having his shoes shined.[12] Sanguine about his prospects, he wrote to Augustin, "[I]n this country I have sufficient following to insure a good living."[13] O'Donnell's friend Carl Carmer said that the Book Fair portended the end of the age of the "book snob."[14]

The Fair was hosted in the Rockefeller Center and designed to showcase the complete life cycle of a book to the public. In a recognizable forerunner to the convention center of today, but still a novelty at the time, booths of "striking and original design" provided positions for all the major publishers of the day.[15] Mayor La Guardia was there to cut the "symbolic ribbon of book-binder's tape" that stretched across the main aisle.[16] Attendees who paid their thirty-five cents could marvel at the original manuscript of *Gone with the Wind.* A miniature paper machine burped out pulp and made paper before spectators' eyes; the fifty-two-inch-wide device had just barely cleared the fifty-three-inch windows.[17]

Sixty authors read from their work, including three Pulitzer Prize winners. James Weldon Johnson, Norman Rockwell, Archibald MacLeish, and James Farrell all made speeches over the course of a two-week exposition that drew more than 80,000 attendees.[18] A cage of lizards, on loan to accompany a book on the subject, watched with unblinking eyes over a reading given by seven poets, including Edgar Lee Masters and Carl Sandburg; "Lizards Find It Dull," the *Times* headline reported.[19] There were ongoing children's exhibits, and in the "the second speech I've made in my life," Pamela Travers, author of *Mary Poppins,* would explain that she tried to capture the "essential magic which lies in reality."[20] To read about it gives the impression that magic hung over it all; the whole thing was suffused in a festival atmosphere, according to the coverage, with overflow crowds singing and making jokes while they waited in line.

Perhaps O'Donnell passed the time signing his books, but if there was one session that he almost certainly attended, it was "Regional Literature." The speakers included his friends Carl Carmer and Sherwood Anderson, as well as George Jean Nathan, editor of *The Smart Set* and longtime paramour of Lillian Gish, whose sister Dorothy would later star in the stage adaptation of *The Great Big Doorstep.*

After the remarkable gathering at the Book Fair, O'Donnell styled himself, foremost, as a writer. The following year, 1937, novelist Thomas Wolfe chanced to meet E. P. "and wife" at the Roosevelt Hotel bar, the closest thing to the Algonquin in New Orleans. He would write of them in his journal, dismissively: "Young, phony, fast."[21] But things were moving fast, for the moment: in the same year, *Green Margins* was published in German under the title *Das große Delta: Roman (The Big Delta, A Novel)* by Bermann-Fischer Verlag, and Robert Penn Warren would include O'Donnell in his anthology, *A Southern Harvest.*

O'Donnell had started work on his next novel, *The Great Big Doorstep,* sometime during this period, when a misfortune broke his pace. A heavy smoker and drinker, he suffered a "heart ailment," more than likely a first heart attack, and developed the habit of composing "lying down on an army cot with a typewriter canted up on a self-patented contraption in front of him." Still, he wrote, and continued to eke out a small income. His shack must have been stuffed with books, so many, in fact, that used-books vendors still routinely encounter O'Donnell volumes *ex libris,* inevitably spotted from the hot damp of southernmost Louisiana.[22]

O'Donnell is hard to track for the next few years, but presumably he spent a good deal of his time working on the novel in Boothville. In November 1938 he spoke up for orange farmers in the Louisiana Farmers Union, who were embroiled in a dispute with the French Market over "speculators" and other issues.[23] When census takers found E. P. in his Boothville shack in 1940, they listed his marital status as "M?," and gave his profession as a writer, albeit one with no income from his work to declare. Meanwhile Gertrude was renting at 117 N. Genois St. in New Orleans with their teenage sons.

"Residents at Boothville, Louisiana sitting on dock. September 1938." *Photograph by Russell Lee. Library of Congress.*

O'Donnell was trying to spark a second courtship, a second life really, with Mary King. By June 1939 she, too, had received the Houghton Mifflin Fellowship to support her novel-in-progress. In the summer of that year, Jon and Louise Webb arrived in New Orleans and were shown hospitality by a circle of Sherwood Anderson's friends, including Marc Antony and—as a couple—O'Donnell and King. (By June of 1941, King was writing postscripts on the bottom of E. P.'s letters, referring to them with a wifely "we.")[24] For their part, the Webbs would later start Loujon Press and establish their beatnik magazine, *Outsider*, publishing Ferlinghetti, Kerouac, and Bukowski. Jon Webb remembered Pat O'Donnell for his "giant smile with the deep grooves lining his face." Those grooves had been etched by tobacco, strong drink, light reflected from water, and assorted hard lessons.

If O'Donnell was coping with the fallout of a failed marriage, there remained moments of transient jollity, as when, for Mardi Gras in 1941, he was granted the honor of taking the lead as the head of 120-foot long dragon (he had the ill-advised idea of shooting real fire from its nostrils). He worked as an occasional reporter for the *Times-Picayune*, covering, for example, the November LSU-Tulane match, a 19–0 washout. Though O'Donnell wryly noted that "the game was full of things that almost happened," he was interested in what did happen at the end, especially the donnybrook that culminated in the tearing down of the goalposts. There were other milestones to celebrate, too: On May 29, 1941, E. P. wrote to Gordon Lewis to say that he was "putting finishing touches on my MS now and will finish next week."[25] The next month, Mary King's *Quincie Bolliver*, a novel of hardscrabble life in East Texas, was published to solid reviews.

In the autumn of 1941, *The Great Big Doorstep* was published at last—and dedicated to Gertrude O'Donnell. But for all its pleasures, the year also brought hard news. In the spring, Elma Godchaux, doyenne of the New Orleans literary scene, and Sherwood Anderson both died, leaving O'Donnell and King feeling "lonely at times."[26] And the nation was once again under the cloud of war, just at the time when O'Donnell had hoped to clinch his place as a writer of reputation. The singularly inauspicious timing of what should have been O'Donnell's breakout book meant that it was lost to the tides of war.

O'Donnell found himself once again at the home front, this time taking up the pen for the *Times-Picayune*. The connections between petro-chemical agriculture and war industries are made explicit in his series titled "Plowshares Are Swords." "No traveler studying America fails to call us the most wasteful people on earth," he observes in an article showing how a seventy-year-old cotton gin might be transformed into an antiaircraft gun. Over the span of eight articles that ran from January to March 1942, O'Donnell demonstrated the importance of canning, poultry, milk, and every sort of thrift to the war effort.[27]

He also became something of a champion of the southern poor. Maxim Lieber, O'Donnell's pro-labor agent, was connected to the likes of Richard Wright, James Farrell, and Leon Trotsky, and his implication in the Alger Hiss affair would eventually spell the end of his time in the United States. It is perhaps unsurprising, then, that O'Donnell's *Times-Picayune* profile, "I Was Robbed by Hitler," tiptoed past the issue: "For Pat is labor, and there is not an ounce of self-pity in him," the newspaper claimed.

If E. P. was for labor, he was also an entrepreneur of sorts, and 1942 brought some fresh prospects. On January 15, the *New York Times* announced that Broadway producer Herman Shumlin had commissioned Albert Hackett and Frances Goodrich to dramatize *The Great Big Doorstep*. Dashiell Hammett was backing the play.[28] Dorothy Gish and Louis Calhern, screen stars in their own time, were on the marquis for the Broadway adaptation. On June 8, the

New York Times reported that *The Great Big Doorstep* "will be filmed by Warner Brothers if negotiations between the studio and Herman Shumlin . . . are completed."

Meanwhile, consistently positive reviews of the novel started to arrive. In a *Saturday Review of Literature* piece titled "What Deep South Literature Needs" (September 19, 1942), Cleanth Brooks cited O'Donnell as an example of a promising writer who pushes back against the "national clichés" directed toward southern literature. (In the same piece he named Mary King, Peter Taylor, and Eudora Welty as among the "most promising" proponents of a regional style.) One reviewer of *The Great Big Doorstep* pointed out that second novels are notoriously difficult, but this one, it was universally agreed, was better than the first.[29]

On November 26, 1942, *The Great Big Doorstep* debuted on Broadway at the Morosco Theatre. Reviews were mixed-to-favorable, and although Calhern was reputedly drunk for every show, his performance drew effusive praise.[30] Just a few days later, on November 28, the *New York Times* announced that a third novel by E. P. O'Donnell, *Delta Country*, was "in preparation" for Dell, Sloan & Pearce's American Folkways series, edited by Erskine Caldwell.

To outward appearances, O'Donnell's luck was running high, and yet there were signs of trouble ahead. In December 1942, Charles B. Driscoll published a portrait of O'Donnell in his nationally syndicated "New York by Day" column.[31] Driscoll interviewed O'Donnell approximately "three weeks" after the *The Great Big Doorstep* opened on Broadway. The "dark, black-haired, nervous Louisianan" was passing the time attending the play and riding the buses, making conversation with strangers. "Despite every attempt to be natural and to take part in the general conversation," Driscoll wrote, "O'Donnell was strained, tense, absent-minded. He was thinking about the boxoffice. Authors are that way."

The play closed abruptly on December 19. The war hung over everything. "Christmas Eve tomorrow!," Driscoll wrote in the same piece. Then, morosely, "Undoubtedly the darkest Christmas Eve in the lives of any of us now living."

O'Donnell, even though strained and in failing health, pressed ahead with his second act. On February 28, 1943, a marriage license was issued in New Orleans for E. P. O'Donnell and Mary P. King.

He would be dead within two months.

* * *

"One goes abroad, surely, when one crosses State lines," Carl Carmer told his audience at the 1936 National Book Fair, pointing to the exoticism that was associated with local color writing.[32] Today local color connotes artlessness, in every register of that word; local color is synonymous with *dated*, and unfortunately, O'Donnell was largely consigned to this category. Erskine Caldwell, who also spoke at the Book Fair, would cede his critical ground to William Faulkner after being deemed a colorist. It was said that his books were too melodramatic, that they made caricatures of southerners. These criticisms might be levelled at O'Donnell, too. Indeed, the Broadway adaptation of *The Great Big Doorstep* would be likened by some critics to an unfunny version of Caldwell's *Tobacco Road*.[33] On the other hand, Arthur Murdock, reviewing *The Great Big Doorstep*, maintained that the novel established O'Donnell "in the tradition of the American humorists of another era, the era of Ward, Twain, Harte, and Billings."[34] One is reminded of the various Louisiana sketches of Kate Chopin, too. Of course, O'Donnell belonged to his own time as well, at his worst resembling Roark Bradford, and at his best, favoring Faulkner and other heirs to the southwestern humor tradition.

In a newspaper column of 1941, the *Times-Picayune* editors refer to the territory of O'Donnell's novels as the "Teche country" of Lafourche and Barataria, and says that the area is peopled by "Slaves,

Filipinos, Negroes, Indians, and native whites."[35] It should have been given "Slavs," not "Slaves," but given the real-life condition of blacks in the Delta at the time, the typo seems a kind of Freudian slip. Barataria is a community in Louisiana, and it also happens to be the name of the imaginary island (from *barato*, "cheap"), awarded by noblemen as a practical joke to Don Quixote's Sancho Panza. O'Donnell plays another little joke in naming it "Grass Margin" in *The Great Big Doorstep*.

In this period of local color in southern writing, color, not cotton, is king. The palette clashes with our time. Even the names can get under our skin; in the opening pages of the *Great Big Doorstep*, a slingshot is referred to as a "nigger shooter." Caught stealing books, a feckless bluesman nicknamed Shoepick is coerced into retrieving puppies from under a porch. The comic payout, culminating in his injury, is about as subtle as an Amos 'n' Andy sketch. The scene evokes long traditions of minstrelsy, and the conventions of Shoepick's day in court can be traced to the nineteenth-century stage. In using Shoepick as the butt of the joke, O'Donnell's novel is a reminder that the pie-in-the-face traditions of southwest humor are based in physical and racial cruelty.

Without exonerating O'Donnell, we might say that there's more here. "If a book is any good," intoned Roger Burlingame, one week into the Book Fair, "it will leave a great deal for the reader to do."[36] We are not permitted to forget that Commodo Crochet (his name riffing both on the grandiose "Commodore" and the musical notation meaning "at a relaxed speed") is scheming for property rightfully belonging to Shoepick and his half-sister, who are the scions of a family that has endured unimaginable losses. O'Donnell likely had in mind the hurricane of 1918, which killed thirty-four Louisianans, as the prototype for the storm that killed Shoepick's father. He "had worked like a slave to make a fine house for his big family," only to find his life washed away with his efforts.

"Negro musicians playing accordion and washboard in front of store, near New Iberia, Louisiana. November 1938." *Photograph by Russell Lee. Library of Congress.*

The mixture of pride, sarcasm, and outrage ought to be boisterously familiar. It's hard to imagine that John Kennedy Toole could have written *A Confederacy of Dunces* without reading *The Great Big Doorstep.* Shoepick is a precursor to *Confederacy*'s LeRoy Jones, and like LeRoy, he talks back. Hailed before the Justice of the Peace for the theft of schoolbooks, Shoepick says, in a quick aside, "Dishya ain no cote." When a well-intentioned librarian imposes her charity on Shoepick, even Evvie, still a child, notices that "The librarian used the same tone . . . [she used] when speaking to children." But Shoepick knows how to play more than his guitar, and he manages to subsist without any obvious income.

Eudora Welty noted in her 1979 afterword that the only dated feature of the novel is in its expression of a prevailing attitude of the time, that the poor are passive victims. Of course, this is an attitude that O'Donnell enjoys skewering. Welty was too polite to say, directly, that O'Donnell wrote from within about a dignified under-class, more poor in money than culture. Ultimately, the documen-tary nature of *The Great Big Doorstep* might offer its best claim to posterity, for O'Donnell wrote about the lives of ordinary people struggling at the end of the road with less condescension and more familiarity than many of his contemporaries.

The New Orleans Little Theater first staged *The Great Big Door-step* in 1944; the Hackett and Goodrich adaptation of the novel would appear on Louisiana stages and throughout the country in every decade that followed and was twice produced for television during the 1950s. The book was brought back into print in 1979, as part of Matthew Bruccoli's Lost American Fiction Series, and in September 2009 the novel appeared on the *Oxford American*'s list of most underappreciated southern books.

Echoes of the world and provenance of *The Great Big Doorstep* are still very much with us. As Antonio Benítez-Rojo imagines the plantation, it is an "extraordinary machine . . . [that] repeats it-self ceaselessly."[37] Aboard the banana boats, O'Donnell might have glimpsed the repeated pattern of banana workers' longhouses, set about soccer fields and elevated on stilts. Calling in at Cristobal, O'Donnell would have seen the conjoining of American industrial might and the banana empire in the Canal Zone—not terribly dif-ferent, in its way, from certain cane fields and orange groves of home. So little has changed from the time of plantation culture that Shoepick's ravishing half-sister Juarelle must either submit to the concubinage of designing townsmen or else find a way to ward them off. The problem of *The Great Big Doorstep* is the problem of the plantation after the Civil War: who will occupy the Big House, so referred? In Faulknerian terms, will it be a come-lately Snopes? Or a latter-day Sutpen? Juarelle's eventual employment as a do-mestic by the Crochets provides the final proof that the family are indeed heirs to the plantation. That Arthur, one of the Crochet's sons, joins Juarelle in the garden should not be overlooked. Read *The Great Big Doorstep* carefully, and you will see that it is indeed a plantation novel.

Finally, consider the senses in which *The Great Big Doorstep,* for all its local specificity, is an *American* novel. The book's original jacket is all-American. It's a homespun article from the Delta cane, done up in red, white, and blue. The patriotic colors are a reminder that the Second World War is underway. The blue strands are braided through the red field, and shading enhances the optical allusion that the novel has a wicker bottom. That's how it was floated, in fact, on the jacket blurbs: "It took the Mississippi draining half the continent to produce the richness of this book," writer Sterling North says.

One might say that it's a trickle-down economy, without much

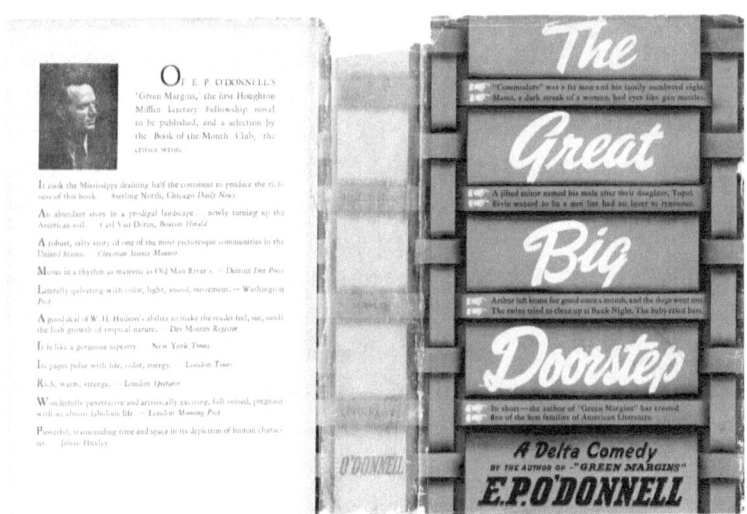

The jacket of the first edition of *The Great Big Doorstep,* published in autumn of 1941. *Reproduced by permission of the O'Donnell family.*

trickling. O'Donnell lived as far down the Mississippi River as possible without actually being over water, in a place where the gift of good land was appreciated. Consider the scene where Evvie goes along on a midnight visit to her mother's illegally planted lily patch, the waist-high stalks "stately, bristling wet" in the moonlight: "Evvie smelled a pinch of the earth. The harsh black soil had been laid down here in the Delta by the river. The river had brought it from the states of the North, laid it here like a present for those who would come."

Indeed, the Crochet family lives on the *batture,* a squatter's zone where alluvial soil builds up between the waterline and the levee. Contested ground where precarious shantytowns had formed even before the Depression. Land for anyone who was willing to brave its inevitable loss.

The era of resource extraction is in full gear. It's a time when the rural poor live alongside the soaring derricks of petrochemical industry, as seen in the strange tableau of the classic documentary film *Louisiana Story* (and like the boy of the film, the Crochet family keeps a pet raccoon). Dave Tobin, the lanky Texan hearththrob who saunters into the novel, arrives on transfer from the Freeport Sulfur Company to Port Sulphur, reeking of the infernal stuff. He more than likely works at the Lake Grande Ecaille mine, where the Frasch Process—injecting superheated water to liquefy sulfur—is being employed. The largest sulfur dome known to the world lies ten miles to the west of the port along the Mississippi, under a tidal estuary at land's end. The mosquitoes are so bad that the company purportedly uses airplane propellers, powered by Model T motors, to keep them away from workers. At the outset, the sulfur mine earns a reputation for being unbuildable.

Yet they built it. With her mother's help, Evvie writes a school report on the resources of Louisiana, drumming up a proud list of state commodities: molasses, oil, sulphur, salt, Easter lilies, oranges, seafood, rice, cotton, perique tobacco, fur. Cypress, orangewood, pine, magnolia, cottonwood, oak, ash, elder, rosewood, duck-wood, poisonball tree, myrtle, cedar, sycamore. Oyster shells, too: "They mash them up for chickens up north to eat, them shells," Mrs. Crochet says.

In her words there is an awareness of what it means to be economically colonized in a place where the country's president would visit only on a hunting trip (the spot where Teddy Roosevelt's horse was hitched is dutifully remembered in the text).[38] The Crochets are small links in a supply chain that provides out-of-season produce to markets as far away as Chicago. The folks at the end of the road who "have no ills that a dollar won't cure" are part of an American tapestry, too: Indian, Filipino, Caribbean, Cajun, and Croatian. Each a reed in the basket of a cast-off culture. Each of them the effervescence, the flotsam of empires that have broken apart on land and water.

All of which is to say that the book reminds us that the American economy has always been a global economy. It already lives on these pages, where the locals know the sound of every visiting boat motor plying the waters, and they scavenge goods from ships calling in from every corner of the world. Thus the paradox of the novel, which is at once intensely local and global: there are many blessings of place, and many reasons to escape them.

The obvious place to go, to get away from land's end, is to the cities, as Topal intends, or onto the water. By his mid-twenties, E. P. O'Donnell was launched on those waters, on the crew of the steamship *Cartago*, which, in its heyday, was used to ferry workers from the West Indies to the banana colonies. O'Donnell's world lies on the broad expanse of this echoing, deeper South, stretching across the Gulf, and to the Caribbean. In the story of human migrations and the exploitation of workers, you could say that he's a citizen of the global south, of the plantation south, broadly conceived. Call it the Meridional South of the Republic of New Orleans. Or the Maritime Zone of the Southern Wilds.

Its participants don't necessarily see themselves as actors on the field of history, or as pawns of American imperialism. They see connections, relationships, action, the hard facts of geography. "Evvie liked geography," O'Donnell writes.

> Unlike history, geography had a shape and a color that could be seen from the window. . . . The Delta winds and vapors belonged to geography; the big dunes of oyster shells; the clotheslines leaping like colored puppies; the bearded waterspouts; the naked willows heavy with birds; the rumbling truckloads of oil-pipe; the foggy sun bare as a skull. Geography made strangers strangers, such as the ones from Texas, or the passengers leaning on the rail of a white ship in the river.

Soon, U-boats will come to those shores. Soon, another world war at the Gulf's doorstep, another war to end regionalisms. Another

Batture Shanty at Riverbend, 1956. *Oil on canvas. Clarence Millet. Courtesy of Ogden Museum of Southern Art.*

war pitting the local and indigenous against the global. Geography is destiny, yes. And there is no novel quite like *The Great Big Doorstep* for taking us to that place and moment.

* * *

One wonders how many of O'Donnell's artist-friends were among those standing by to offer "transfusions" as he lay dying in New Orleans Charity Hospital. According to *Times-Picayune* coverage, his death came at the end of a "long illness," on April 19, 1943.[39] It was during Holy Week, on the day after Palm Sunday. He was interred at St. Roch cemetery on April 21, 1943.

Not long before his death, O'Donnell paused to remember his years on the artist's wandering path. Accompanying Alberta Kinney's painting of the bayou country in *The Saturday Review* (September 19, 1942) were O'Donnell's "Lines to Jules Petit," the *ubi sunt* in which he reminisces,

Let us remember we were younger . . .
Together we gambled money, Jules, and it was noon everywhere,
And afterwards our debts were forgotten like schoolbooks.
Who would not remember that plentiful bayou, and warm as a
    heart?
I can close my eyes and remember that often we fought, two
    friends embracing in the mire.
It was always without knives, but with good hatred, for the wine
    was stern.
But the lightning no longer strikes in the day
And the rushes are not heard.[40]

O'Donnell had a habit of seeking, or perhaps being driven to, the end of land. Such is the flotsam of a life. The cliché for it, *washed up,* doesn't really do it justice. O'Donnell never realized his ambition to start a "model farm" somewhere around Boothville. With his death came an end to an unfinished novel, envisioned as the third work in his Grass Margins trilogy, concerning "the building of a big, white highway through the marshes and sleepy river villages," and depicting "the impact of the automobile and electrical technics on the Delta people. . . ."[41] The highway has come, but the book is a lost lane-end.

Though he would be eulogized by the *Picayune* as a "quiet and reticent man," other accounts paint O'Donnell as gregarious and brash. In the end, like some of his ancestors, O'Donnell was lost even to his family in a restless country. His son Daniel settled on the West coast, and there a branch of the family remains. His other son, Patrick, married a New Orleans woman and settled near Baltimore, another port town with southern roots and a Catholic history. Gertrude did her best, but the sons inevitably endured a childhood clouded by unhappiness. One of the sons would remember, during one of E. P.'s infrequent visits, finding twenty dollars in his father's coat pocket at a time when his mother was struggling to make ends meet.[42] One of the sons seemed overtaken by E. P.'s baggage and would become an absentee father, too. Both sons would take to the water—Patrick to the Navy, Daniel to the Merchant Marine—as if the voice of a lost father might be found there. E. P. O'Donnell's name would become a subject to be avoided by family, so much so that his grandchildren would come to know little about him. Eudora Welty, in her afterword, regrets never knowing him, or anyone who did. It was the beginning of anonymity.

"I've the great fault of the Irish," O'Donnell said in one *Times-Picayune New Orleans States* profile. "I can't stand a slide rule existence." He could not abide a carefully calculated, legalistic morality, in other words. By contrast, Flannery O'Connor suggested that the fault of the Irish was precisely their adherence to a "slide-rule mentality." She explained the attitude that prevailed among

American Irish when it came to sins and sinning in a letter to Cecil Dawkins dated July 16, 1957: "They operate by the slide rule, and the Church for them is not the body of Christ but the poor man's insurance system."

One appreciates the situation of a former altar boy from a slide-rule culture who cannot lead a slide-rule life. *The Great Big Doorstep* offers a portrait of a family struggling with the same irreconcilabilities. If O'Donnell ran out of insurance over the years, his real-life family might find buried in the verses of these pages a better, or at least more shaded, man: a man who dedicated the book to his estranged wife, and who loved his sisters well enough to model characters on them. A man with a deeply spiritual bent, hidden in bygone novenas and devotionals and in the secret awe of nature. A man who would use pig Latin to slip a banned word past censors in *The Great Big Doorstep*. A man who gathered friends from every walk of life for the sake of feasting on *fruits de mer* and sharing a joyful story. A man, ultimately, who could not resist a joke, least of all the larger jokes that life plays on us.

So here is a paper flower, a lily for the lost, miscast, and forgotten. A lily, that most inconstant and miraculous flower, the one designated for Easter, weddings, and funerals. A lily for E. P. O'Donnell, one born of American soil, waters, images. Cast it on the Mississippi. Float it. Let it bloom again.

Bryan Giemza
January 2015

NOTES

This edition could not have come to print without the kindness and generosity of E. P. O'Donnell's grandchildren: Charleen Campagna, Kathleen Hughes, Daniel P. O'Donnell, Kelly O'Donnell, Michael O'Donnell, Mike O'Donnell, Maureen Selby, and Lisa M. Stanton. Additional support and help came from Julie Hebert, Justin Lacour, Tom Peyser, and M. Thomas Inge. For permission to reprint the afterword, gratitude goes to the Eudora Welty estate via the Russell & Volkening Agency, and for permission to reprint Clarence Millet's painting *Batture Shanty at Riverbend,* thanks are due to the Ogden Museum of Southern Art, gift of the Roger Houston Ogden Collection.

1. Lou Van Sicklen, "'I was Robbed by Hitler,' Mutters Pat O'Donnell," *The Times-Picayune New Orleans States,* November 8, 1941, sec. 2, 8.

2. World War I Selective Service System Draft Registration Cards, 1917–1918, National Archives and Records Administration, Orleans Parish, roll 1684920. In the 1930 census he would claim to be a veteran, which remains to be corroborated by military records. In the Van Sicklen interview he mentions that he served "the adjutant general's department during the [first] World War."

3. Joseph Blotner explains the origins of Faulkner's claim, and its likely false-hood, in *Faulkner: A Biography* (New York: Vintage, 1991), 143. For O'Donnell's career on the water, see Crew Lists of Vessels Arriving at New Orleans, Louisiana, 1910–1945, National Archives and Records Administration, series T939, roll 58. Within those records, see *Cartago* entries of Dec. 5, 1921; Jan. 16, 1922; Jan. 26, 1922; Feb. 6, 1922; Mar. 20, 1922; Mar. 27, 1922; and *Coppename* entries of Jul. 10 and Aug. 21, 1916.

4. See the *Cartago* crew manifest of Dec. 5, 1921, for a typical tally.

5. Susan Saward, "Clarence Millet," in ed. David Johnson, *KnowLa Encyclopedia of Louisiana* (Louisiana Endowment for the Humanities, 2010), http://www.knowla .org/entry/1127/.

6. Jacket copy for the first edition of *The Great Big Doorstep* erroneously states that this walk took place in the 1930s.

7. Askart.com, citing Clark Marlor, *The Salons of America* (Madison, CT: Sound View Press, 1991); Peter H. Falk, *Who Was Who in American Art* (Madison, CT: Sound View Press, 1985); and Derek Coursen, the artist's great nephew.

8. For more on the flowering of the arts scene at the time, see John Shelton Reed, *Dixie Bohemia: A French Quarter Circle in the 1920s* (Baton Rouge: Louisiana State University Press, 2012).

9. Undated letter, E. P. O'Donnell to Augustin, Bennett M. Augustin Collection (MSS 15), Louisiana and Special Collections Department, University of New Orleans.

10. Sherwood Anderson to Gordon Lewis, June 26, 1939, Albert and Shirley Small Special Collections Library, University of Virginia, Charlottesville.

11. K. T. Knoblock, "Painter and Poet."

12. Robert Disraeli, "Fair Days in New York," *The Saturday Review* 25 no. 3 (November 14, 1936): 12.

13. Undated letter of 1936, E. P. O'Donnell to Augustin, Bennett M. Augustin

Collection (MSS 15), Louisiana and Special Collections Department, University of New Orleans.

14. "Peril to Writers Seen in Book Flood," *New York Times,* November 13, 1936.

15. Eugene Reynal, "The Forthcoming New York Times National Book Fair," *New York Times,* November 1, 1936.

16. "Mayor to Open Book Fair At Preview on Wednesday," *New York Times,* Nov. 1, 1936.

17. "Paper Machine Put in Place at Exhibit," *New York Times,* October 30, 1936.

18. "Authors' Programs for Book Fair Set," *New York Times,* October 25, 1936; "Book Fair Closes," *New York Times,* November 20, 1936.

19. "Book Fair Throng Hears Seven Poets," *New York Times,* November 9, 1936.

20. "Book Fair Visitors Pass 50000 Mark," *New York Times,* November 15, 1936.

21. *Notebooks of Thomas Wolfe,* eds. Richard S. Kennedy and Paschal Reeves (Chapel Hill: University of North Carolina Press), 2:862.

22. This fact was confirmed by Terry Halladay, the literature manager of William Reese Company—Rare Books and Manuscripts.

23. "Orange Growers Protest Actions of Speculators," *The Times Picayune,* November 9, 1938, 11.

24. E.P. O'Donnell to Gordon Lewis from Boothville, with postscript from Mary King, May 29, 1941. Albert and Shirley Small Special Collections Library, University of Virginia, Charlottesville.

25. Ibid.

26. Ibid.

27. The "Plowshares" series ran in the *Times-Picayune New Orleans States* weekly from February 15 to April 19, 1942.

28. Dashiel Hammett, *Selected Letters of Dashiell Hammett, 1921–1960* (Washington, D.C.: Counterpoint, 2001), 194.

29. See, for example, the review by Herschell Brickell, "Delta Country," *New York Times,* November 2, 1941.

30. David L. Goodrich, *The Real Nick and Nora: Frances Goodrich and Albert Hackett, Writers of Stage and Screen Classics* (Carbondale: Southern Illinois University Press, 2004), 147.

31. The text of Driscoll's column was retrieved from *The Palm Beach Post,* morning edition, December 23, 1942.

32. "Throngs View Book Fair Exhibits," *New York Times,* November 6, 1936.

33. See "New Plays in Manhattan," *Time* 40 no. 23 (1942), 57.

34. Arthur Murdock, "The Delta," *New Masses* (March 17, 1942): 24–25.

35. Van Sicklen, "'I Was Robbed.'"

36. "Peril to Writers Seen in Book Flood," *New York Times,* November 13, 1936.

37. Antonio Benítez-Rojo, *The Repeating Island: The Caribbean and the Postmodern Perspective* (Durham: Duke University Press, 1992), 11.

38. In fact, Roosevelt's well-publicized 1907 bear hunt took place in northeastern Louisiana.

39. "Records of the Day," *The Times-Picayune New Orleans States*, February 28, 1943, 22.

40. *The Saturday Review,* September 19, 1942, 26–29.

41. Albert Goldstein, "Literature and Less," *The Times-Picayune New Orleans States,* December 25, 1942, 7. O'Donnell provides a verbatim description of his intended third novel to Bennett Augustin in an undated letter. Bennett M. Augustin Collection.

42. Maureen Selby, phone interview with the author, January 27, 2014.

The Great Big
Doorstep

1

A DOORSTEPS
OUGHT TO SHINE

AT THAT time there was a late frost in the Delta. In the morning the grass far behind the levees was crusted with frost. The tops of the orange trees, all blurred and stiffened, cradled in a furry mist the fruit that remained, where the blackbirds, the boat-tailed grackles, noisily devoured their fill. The blackbirds, with shards of black sunlight glinting off their wingtips, sailed from grove to grove in jubilant flocks, avoiding the river. The Mississippi was foggy through the morning. On such ships as ventured to navigate the fog, pilots blew the whistle and waited to hear which of two echoes came back first, so as to judge which shore was closer. People ashore saw nothing of the ships, only heard the muffled pounding of engines, the sloshing of propellers, an occasional whistle blast, or the tapping of chipping-hammers in the hands of seamen knocking the paint off the iron plates. In the vast marshes through which the river wound its final miles to the Gulf, the gun of a hunter thudded now and then. The geese had fattened themselves for their return to the Far North, and the deer were prime for mating.

Opposite the house by the levee on Grass Margin where the Crochet family lived, a ship anchored in the fog was banging its warning bell every few minutes. The bell had been ringing all night.

The two Crochet sisters lay raised on their elbows in the cold grass, looking up into a pear tree. Topal, the elder girl, took a pebble from her mouth and put it in the slingshot. Evvie, the younger girl, nudged her sister, whispering, 'It's a mocking-bird! Don't!'

'Mind your business!' Topal hissed.

After Topal released the pebble, the mocking-bird was still there, very pert against the sky, surrounded by white pear blossoms. In the rising sun he was drying his feathers, puffing them out and pecking at his underwings. Topal aimed another pebble. It flew past the bird. It curved over the levee and into the foggy river. Pear blossoms fluttered down. Topal loaded again, and shot. 'God dog it to hell!' she whispered.

'Let me try!' Evvie whispered. 'Give me the nigger-shooter!'

'Here, you little mealy-bug! It's all right for *you* to shoot a mocker, eh? Get him! Pi-yi him, Evvie!'

'Yes!' Evvie's eyes were hard as coins. Aiming, she clenched her teeth. The singer's gray breast was a plump target, exciting against the blue sky. A frayed veil of mist coiled about the bird, then passed. Evvie opened her fingers. The pebble slapped through the leaves and grazed the bird's tail, dislodging feathers that spun downward. Evvie closed her eyes. 'I killed him! Did I kill him?'

'Dirty little white-head witch, he's gone!' Topal cried. She pummeled the rows of bones in Evvie's crouched back. 'You missed him, you little ——'

'Mama! Maaa-maaa!'

A voice from the house called, 'Stop it! Stop beatin her! I see you! Topal! How many time I'm gunna tell you for God sake, for God sake to come and rench out the diaper before T. J. wets the other one? *You hear me now?* Mon Dieu, mon

Dieu, I wish I was in the gravy-yard. I could jump in the river, me!'

'Jump in with the diapers,' Topal muttered.

'Mama! Mama! She said ——'

Topal leaped upon Evvie and stopped her mouth. They wrestled. The vapors of their breath floated about them. Topal, who was twenty, was much the heavier; but Evvie was wiry and supple, with joints like rubber. Evvie was nearly fifteen. Presently she stopped struggling, having no more breath. Topal rubbed her head in the freezing dew.

'Shh! Look the blue-jay!' Evvie whispered. 'Let me get him!'

Evvie put a pebble in the slingshot and, still lying on her back, brought down the jay. He hopped away, wounded, and fought viciously when retrieved. She rapped his head sharply against a tree.

'That's twenty-nine,' said Topal.

They were collecting birds for an old crab fisherman back on the shore of the bay, who used the birds as crab bait. In exchange for the birds, he gave them coffee coupons. At the village store, the coupons were redeemable for premiums.

The sun was high when they crossed the rear drainage canal. They wriggled through the dense canebrake with the newspaper package of dead birds. The brake was alive with red-wing blackbirds that set up a din of sound like hundreds of rusty door-hinges. The girls waded gingerly over the sawgrass marsh, avoiding the tall graceful blades which could inflict deep cuts if brushed the wrong way.

They entered a cypress thicket. The motionless water was dark as coffee. In the cold green gloom the ancient trees were gigantic, and everywhere vines thick as a fist climbed high

toward the light. The movement of the girls' feet set up loud
musical splashes. Slow, wide-eyed, shrinking, they forged
through a wide area of fallen bark floating. Topal was angry
at the floating bark-mats, which might conceal moccasins or
snapping turtles. She kicked spitefully at the water.

'Listen, why do you want to get mad?' Evvie asked.

'Better be mad than scared any day.'

They stepped through a deep coulee whose surface was
covered with a scum of pale green seeds, and soon they saw
the vast blue sky of the open bay. From far out in the Gulf
there came the busy concerted roaring of the engines of the
shrimp trawling fleet.

'You go talk to him,' Topal told Evvie. 'If I smell him, I'm
going to throw up. And if he pinches your go-go, you haul off
and push him in the bay.'

The houseboat was anchored a little way from shore, far
enough to keep off ants. Old man Marigny on deck was squatting by a charcoal furnace dripping coffee with a rusty spoon.
Mink and otter pelts were tacked on the cabin to dry. The
dancing water was sprinkled with floating water-hyacinths.
Two turtles rolled off a log and sank. Topal waited for Evvie
in the low water, holding up her dress. Evvie waded with her
feet well ahead of her, feeling for sharp shells. The old man's
eyes watching her were cloudy as a sky, filmed over and dulled
by the good vigils of his past hunting days. 'Eh, la bas!' he
croaked. 'Come up, chérie! Mais how many bird you god
now?'

'Twenty-nine from yesterday and today.' Evvie dropped
the bundle on the deck and backed away from the man's
musky odor. His feet were shrunken, wrinkled from salt, the
toes very wide apart, the nails blackened by the juices of the
bogs. His quaking hands rummaged in the newspaper package.

'Me, I done ax you a tousan time to not bring me hummin-
bird, chérie. Loog. I say them is too zmall and tender for
baits.'

'You don't have to give us any coupons for them,' Evvie
said. 'We had them and we brought them. There's twenty-
nine other kinds. Those blackbirds are worth three coupons.'

'Wait, I gunna see, me.'

'Hurry up!' Topal yelled across the water. 'The green-
heads are biting like ole hell!'

Sniffling, scratching, grunting, humming part of an old
tune nobody had ever heard, the old man went to work on
the pile of birds. He squeezed them and smelled them and
parted the feathers to look. He arranged them into piles according to size. The humming-birds were thrown into an old
crock where Marigny's pet box-turtle lay. The turtle was so
fat that when he closed the front window of his shell, the
fleshy parts of his body would puff out of the other end. The
redbirds, blue grosbecks, larks, robins, grackles, and blue-jay
went into one pile. In the other were placed the smaller birds
— indigo bunting, scarlet tanagers, sparrows, an orange-
crowned warbler, and a goldfinch. Then Marigny crawled
into the cabin and brought out a fruit jar full of green coffee
coupons. It was his habit to wheedle coupons from the crews
of the shrimp trawlers that tied up along the shore each night.
He counted the coupons into Evvie's hands — three each for
the large birds, two for the small.

'Daz de moze coupon I ever give you so far, sweedart,' said
the old man. 'Whad kind premium you all gunna ged diz
time, eh? A welcome-rug fo yo Mama new doorstebs?'

'We got a welcome-rug for coupons a long time ago, but
Ma-mama is saving it in the loft.'

'Eh bien! A welcome-rug in de loff!'

'Till we get a better place to live in some day. Do you want more baits tomorrow?'

'Mais non, I done god some lips and ears from de new butcher. I dunno, me, ef I wunt no mo bird fo a while, because loog.' He reached behind him and uncovered a hamper full of salted cattle lips and ears the local butcher had given him. 'Daz de bezz kind of bait, yes.'

Evvie jerked her gaze away from the bloody cattle organs. Marigny plucked at her sleeve and looked up at her with a rheumy squint. 'Well, now you can ged a Blessed Mudda, eh? Nize big Blessed Mudda, eh? Mais you ought to ged you a loogin-glazz, chérie, to see yo pretty faze, eh? You god a beau yet, chérie? You gettin to be big gull now. Who's yo beau?'

'Nobody.'

Evvie and Topal went to the little general store on the levee. With those they had been saving, they now had more than enough coupons to get a statue of the Blessed Mother. The statue was about two feet tall. There was a gilded crown on the blonde head. The Blessed Virgin wore a blue robe, and stood on a crescent moon set among some clouds. The Child in her arms was asleep.

'Let me carry her!' Evvie said. 'I killed most of the birds.'

'Nobody wants to carry her, you little feen. And I'm quitting this business, killing birds for premiums to fix up a damn shack that's falling to pieces.'

'Oh, Tope, let's pass and ask Father Pennygrass to bless her!' Evvie cried.

'Go by yourself. I'm tired.'

Farther up the levee road, the girls parted. Evvie carried the statue through an orange grove. The tall ferns brushed her knees. She emerged on the rear road, and went to Father

Pendergast's residence beside the little church. The priest was on his front lawn practicing with his rod and reel, casting a fly at a handkerchief spread on the turf.

'Watch something, Evvie!' he called. With a deft motion of the wrist he flipped the fly through the air, and it landed a few inches from the white target. 'Holy cow!' he cried. 'That was a close one!'

'Do it some more, Father!'

The fly on the line was jerked backward, the steel whistled, the fly streaked through the air and fell just short of the target. Evvie smiled approval, the statue in her lap forgotten. A door in the house opened and the old housekeeper's voice called: 'Dog gone it, you come and eat, now, Father! Breakfuss been ready, and I got things to do, you hear me?'

The priest winked at Evvie. He threw the fly once more.

'What you got there? A Blessed Mother?'

'Yes, Father.'

'How's Mama? I've got a Missal for her.'

The voice from the house complained, 'Ef that ain a shame! To fix a lovely broiled eel, and . . .'

'All right, all right! Soon as I bless this statue!'

The girl held it in her arms. She watched the priest. Saying the old Latin words in a sober tone, he lowered his eyes, and with his thin nervous hand drew a cross in the air — two lines, one drawn through the middle of Evvie vertically and the other across her chest. Then he turned and ran whistling inside. Evvie carried off the statue under her arm. She felt the two lines still there, dividing her body into four parts.

The statue of the Blessed Mother was placed on the mantelpiece of the front room of the Crochet house. They occupied a rented house at the upper end of the Margin, near the rice fields. The house was in two parts, the main dwelling of two rooms, and the kitchen, which was only twelve feet by twelve, but was several feet higher than the front two rooms. The kitchen leaned over in the shape of a problem in long division. To prevent it from falling, the landlord had placed a horizontal timber high up along its side, shored up by a second piece of timber, an old schooner-boom, running obliquely to the ground and held there by a stake.

In front of the house was a great tall cypress, dark and brooding above the gaily flowered orange trees, with a single strand of Spanish moss hanging from a limb. The house had a magnificent front doorsteps of ornamental cypress, the finest doorsteps in Grass Margin.

There had been a time when Mrs. Crochet, sitting on the front gallery, would complain, 'Ef the landlord don't fix us a front steps so my lil Indians can crawl down in the yard without pestering the hind leg offa me, I bet I'm gunna take it out the rent.'

'I could scrub it white on Saturday!' Evvie would say.

'Ef my Papa could see me now in his grave! Jiss as well no house as no doorsteps to get in and out.'

'A doorsteps is a handy thing,' said Commodo, her husband. 'It ain in the house and it ain out. A fellow comes that you don't wunt him in and you don't wunt him out neither, you keep him talking on the steps unless it's rainin.'

'Me, I like a shiny doorsteps. Let the chirren mess it up all day, but in the evenin it oughta shine.'

Then one day during high river, Arthur, their eldest son, had found a doorsteps drifting down the river among some logs. With considerable risk and difficulty, Arthur had recovered the doorsteps and towed it home in the skiff. It was an enormous affair, almost as wide as the Crochet house itself, with decorated cornices and panels, meant to grace one of the big plantation houses up the river that were always falling apart these days. But it was low enough to fit the Crochets' front gallery, which was set rather high on old piling butts.

'Sacré nom!' Mrs. Crochet laughed. 'That's what you can call a front steps, yes! How many rich people didn't squat there to catch some sun nobody knows, all in their graves now, or living in town. What we gunna do, we gunna surprise your Papa tonight. Wait when he sees it. Wait! Don't nail it. Jiss lean it there. Anything a person nails on a house belonks to the landlord, they say.'

Topal snickered, 'We got us a doorsteps. All we need is a house.'

When Commodo Crochet came home and saw the handsome doorsteps, he said, 'Before hell, it's grand! Listen what I'm sayin, you all! Some day we gunna have a house to go with that stupendable doorsteps. I arready made up my mind.'

Mrs. Crochet said: 'Arthur, him he nilly got drowned untanglin it from the logs. Now I guess you gunna expeck him to find a house floatin down.'

Thereafter, mosquitoes and sandflies permitting, the family spent as much time as possible on the beautiful front steps. Sewing was done there, hair dried, peas shelled, afternoon naps taken, funny papers read. Evenings during fine weather, the whole family gathered. A pleasant time of day in the Delta — clouds over the Gulf turning to rosy foam; weary sea-fowl crossing the sky to roost; people passing darkly on the levee road, slack-shouldered and mindless as though strolling off somewhere forever; or young mulatto girls going to look for mail, with faces powdered as far back as the jawbones.

'I hear a ship!' Commodo, sprawled on the bottom step,

would announce without opening his eyes or budging one of his pudgy limbs.

'Norwegian!' Fvvie cried.

'American,' Arthur guessed.

All of them watched the open place in the willows of the shore. The ship appeared. Its smokestack showed the emblem of a Brazilian coffee line.

'I coulda tole you,' said Commodo. 'I remembered the knock in her engine.'

Mrs. Crochet waved her thimble at a pair of girls passing on the levee. One of them was rolling a baby carriage piled high with unopened oysters from the store. 'When a ugly girl goes with a pretty girl,' she said, 'bote of them is satisfied. The ugly girl likes the other one because she's pretty, and the pretty one likes her because she's ugly, I think. Ugly girls don't like to be together much. Two pretty girls likes to walk together sometimes because it makes a lovely span.'

'Can I ask Root and Juanette to eat?' Topal asked.

'I said no and it's no,' said the mother. 'The frogs ain't done bleedin. Ask Arthur. He caught the frogs.'

'Arthur, can I, huh?'

'It's up to Mama.'

'Heck. Twenty some-odd frogs hanging on the clothesline and can't ask in a friend to eat! Can I ask Root? Just Root?'

'You got a plate and a fork and something for company to sit on besides the floor? First you wunt frogs, now you wunt company!'

'If I ever get my own room I bet I'll have in a friend for coffee and stuff. We live in the lousiest shack on the Margin.'

'Tell that to your father that he loss two days' work with the pains and sour stummick.'

Then Mrs. Crochet dismissed the subject by tapping her foot and singing a song of her girlhood:

> A bole bumble-bee idly roaming o'er the lea
> Met a sweet clover blossom wet with jew . . .

Evvie said: 'Papa, how come everybody else owns a home and we don't? We keep getting bigger and the house stays the same.'

'We gunna own one,' Commodo said, slapping the sweet tawny surface of the front steps. 'You wait one day. I done made up my mind.'

'To match these steps?'

'Nothing different.'

'I guess it'll be a lovely house, then.' Evvie examined the texture of the rich glossy wood. 'Mama, it does shine!' she announced. Streaks of blue from the sky played over the surface of the boards.

Mrs. Crochet looked at the doorsteps sternly. 'That doorsteps is our property,' she said.

Commodo Crochet in the past had made several efforts, some of them physical efforts, to start a fund for the down payment on a home to match the doorsteps. The last physical effort he had made, a few months after the finding of the doorsteps, had resulted in his becoming a ditch-digger, or 'drainage expert,' as he called it.

Commodo and Arthur were fishing shrimp that time in Federation Bay with a cast-net. Commodo stood in the bow of the skiff. He placed one of the lead sinkers between his teeth, gathered the big net in his hands, and swung his body for the cast. The net opened and pancaked out beautifully, but the sinker left Commodo's mouth too late. It jerked out his false teeth. Arthur went overboard and, directed by his father, soon recovered the dental plate. But he also found something else.

'Oysters!' he yelled. 'Oysters down here, Papa! One cut my foot!'

Oysters in Federation Bay? And the beds not marked? Had someone planted them without telling anyone else, then left the country?

Arthur and Commodo brought home a skiffload, and there had been great rejoicing. The Crochets filled their shrunken stomachs, and gave a mess to the sewing-machine agent. For three evenings, the father and son returned to the bay. They owned no oyster-tongs, so they dug their booty from the low water with an old potato fork. It was a large reef. The oysters were fat and salty. Commodo peddled oysters in the mornings from a wheelbarrow to the families living among the orange trees on the narrow winding strip of dry soil behind the levee, and Mrs. Crochet hid the money. Almost six dollars for two hours' work in spare time! At this rate, they would save up the down payment for a house to fit the doorsteps in a short time.

On the fourth day, while they were digging in the bay, a man came in a blue lugger, a Slavonian. He was very amiable.

'Hey! You buy oyshters, eh?' he called, grinning.

Commodo stood erect in the waist-deep water. He rubbed his sleeve across his mud-speckled face. The sun was bitter.

'These your oysters?' Arthur asked the man.

The Slavonian nodded and drew a square in the air with a forefinger dark as a club. 'Me and my podna got tree acre here. You know? Is cheap, dem oyshters, because you come fish them yourself, cull them yourself. Is hod work. I make them cheap for you.'

'You mean money?' Commodo asked.

'Ten dollar. Is four skiffload.'

'Eh?'

The Slavonian reached behind him in the pilot house. He brought forth a pair of field glasses, and showed them to Commodo. He smiled only with his mouth.

'My boy, him he nilly cut off his ankle on your oysters,' Commodo said.

'I'm sorrit.'

'These foreigners come plantin oysters all over our bays. I got no money. I got six chirren to feed, me. Before hell, I never heard of such a thing so far. My bruddin-law's a lawyer.'

'Five children you will have next week when your big daughter get married,' said the Slavonian. 'I know you. You Commodore Crochet, one time captain on *Blessed Trinity*. I tink you got no bruddin-law.'

'She's not getting married, my Topal. It's all off.'

'I'm sorrit.'

'God dog it, I had to buss up that ingagement. You know something? That man, that Tayo Delacroix, come to find out he's got anudda woman up the road. Me, I had to buss up the weddin. And now, for spite, what Tayo went and done, he went and named his mule after my Topal. You think I ain got trouble, you? I say I got six of them to feed.'

The Slavonian said: 'I tell you. I see you dig nice. Maybe you like to dig ditch on my orange grove in Venice, eh? Pay for the oyshters you owe me.'

'Me, I'll do any livin thing to cancellate a honess debt!'

Commodo had never dug a ditch before, but he knew a lot about the properties of flowing water, because he had spent many youthful years plowing with oxen in the flooded rice fields. The ditch he dug for the Slavonian was so fine that it caused comment all up and down Grass Margin. Commodo had been pleased and excited. No one had ever praised his work before. Other people came to him to have ditching done. So he had become a drainage expert.

The house to match the fine doorsteps had remained a family dream.

Into this household the statue of the Blessed Mother was brought. Evvie was given charge of the statue, and on Saturdays she dusted it well. The mantelpiece was not level. Along with the remainder of the house, it vibrated badly whenever a ship with a big propeller passed close to the dwelling. The vibration caused the statue to move toward the edge, and Evvie had to watch it constantly and to slide it back into place every now and then. Sometimes she would find it turned around, facing the wall. 'Some day when three-four big ships passes here,' said Commodo, 'that-there Blessed Mudda's gunna dance around tell she gunna fall and mash one of these chirren that's passing under its head in. Jiss anudda worry layin on my mind.'

2

YOU CAN'T DIG A DITCH

ON STRAWBERRIES

FREQUENTLY, when going off in the morning to do a job of ditching, Commodo Crochet would forget his dose of bicarbonate of soda. When this happened, Evvie would be sent to bring it to him.

'Sweedart, take the levee,' Mrs. Crochet said one morning, 'and carry Papa this invelop where he's working by Mr. Bob LaRoque's. Tell him Mama say dump it in a glass of water like a good girl and drink it after they gunna feed him the ten o'clock breakfass, and hurry back.'

'Mama, I'm starting to get hungry.'

The little twins, Gussie and Paul, were on the floor drinking cups of black coffee. Mrs. Crochet poured a cup for Evvie. Evvie said, 'This don't stop me from getting hungry any more.'

'We gunna have a turdle for breakfass, darling, and Mama's gunna iron your drawers so you can go to school at twelve. You oughta be glad.'

Evvie went out thoughtfully. Topal was on the front steps with the baby. She was patiently trying to teach T. J. how to suck his thumb, so that he would be easier to take care of. Evvie dragged her feet through the front yard dust. Clouds of blackbirds crashed upward through the orange trees before her. Huey, the Crochets' rooster, followed her until she threw an orange at him. Topal called after her in a sweet voice, 'Hurry back, darling, because we've got roast turkey and stuffed aigplants and floating island for dinner, you hear?'

Evvie raised up the back of her dress toward Topal. Walking up the levee road she hunted blackberries. She found certain bushes she had been watching for weeks. The berries were not ripe. She ate some green ones, wondering how sweet soil could produce sour fruits, or how the sun could sweeten a berry at last.

A big ship was coming up the river. There were passengers, early risers, spotted people with flapping scarves among the lifeboats, a fat boy with a balloon, a woman aiming a camera. Evvie waved and smiled. Two men dumped a can of refuse over the side. The ship was leaking, trickling red water through a hole in its swollen belly.

Evvie saw the pilot. He was leaning over the bridge rail trying to attract her attention. He was Dewey Crochet, her father's brother. Uncle Dewey leaned out and waved at Evvie, and she answered with the same gesture.

Then Uncle Dewey with both hands drew a big curve in profile, starting at his chin and ending at his hips, and pointed down the road with his thumb. Then he put his palms together and lay his head on them sideways, as on a pillow. Then he pointed to the sun, after which he grabbed his own sleeve and shook it. He was telling her to go home and awaken her father, because it was getting late.

Evvie extended her palm toward the ship and shook it from side to side. No siree. Then she drew the profiled curve of her father's big belly, pointed up the road, spit on her hands and rubbed them together, drew her thumb across her forehead and flipped away the imaginary sweat. Uncle Dewey threw up both hands and looked upward.

In the LaRoque orange grove, Evvie followed the main ditchbank toward the rear, looking for her father. Commodo was engaged in widening this ditch. Evvie did not see him anywhere. The ditch was a fine, precisely straight cleft in the blue clay, its water reflecting curds of drifting cloud. Fiddler crabs fled before Evvie's shadow.

A Negro woman came from the chickenyard carrying some eggs in her apron. She frowned at Evvie's skinny legs, and spat a thin curved thread of snuffjuice.

'My Papa,' Evvie said.

'Yeah.'

'Where is he, well?'

'Ain studden bout yo paw. Reckon he eatin in de house. Ah done cooked de grub, das all Ah know. Unch. Unch. Go see aft him. Ahm behine in my wuk accounta yo paw, missy. Evva time at man come heah to wuk Ah godda cook three-fo extry dishes an dey expeck me to wosh besides. Wosh dis an wosh dat untel Ah don know mass fum a hole in de groun accounta yo paw. Unch. Gimme fo bits a day an ain paid me sense tomorrowll be two weeks. How come we godda feed yo paw extry dishes alla time?' The Negress limped off, her lips high in the air and her buttocks bouncing spitefully.

Evvie glanced around her. Gloomily she studied her father's shovel lying on the ground, polished like silver, and the handle rubbed to a brightness — the implement that was supposed to feed eight mouths in the Crochet house. She liked the shovel. She had never been allowed to touch it. 'Hands off! Hands off!' her father would tell the children. 'That shovel's to feed you all with!'

Evvie went to the residence by the levee and stopped beneath the kitchen window. She smelled the kitchen's breath, savory and cruel. Mrs. LaRoque was feeding her family the big ten o'clock breakfast. Evvie climbed on an overturned bean hamper and peeped in a corner of the window.

Commodo sat with his back toward her, his denim jumper spattered with patches of various shapes and hues. His plate was piled high. He did not talk. The food on his plate was arranged like an engineering project into careful dams and sluices, and he loaded the stuff into his mouth with the practiced diligence of a man working on contract.

'Twenty cents a pound by the butcher in Lacroix that steak cost,' Mrs. LaRoque was saying.

'I betcha!' Commodo replied. 'It ain everybody on this river can have beef-meat and times is so hard. I know that much.'

Evvie's thoughts hovered between piety and desire. A mound of snowy rice was on her father's plate. He opened one of his dams, and she watched the rice slowly absorb a thick brown pool of meat-juice.

'Us, we believe in eating, Mr. Crochet,' said Mrs. LaRoque.

'You believe in something I believe in, Miss LaRoque.'

'I always say thang God there's more than we need here, and you know it's true, because you work for plenny people on this Margin.'

'Eh bien, I worked for most everybody but myself sense I started following drainage work, and sampled most everybody's table.'

'Go look once in my ice-box what's there for tomorrow, and go look by my garbage pile what we throw away. The dogs knows it. Everybody's dogs on the river nearly is getting fat by my garbage pile.'

'This is a feedin house,' said Commodo.

Bob LaRoque spoke. 'It won't be feedin long if the swimps don't sell better pretty soon like you see them out in my boat.'

Mrs. LaRoque said, 'Somebody says you said the Durots feeds you the best of all when you dig ditch for them, Mr. Crochet.'

'Who, me?'

'Yes, sir. I'm sure, me, you couldn't say that. This meal costed two dollar and eighty cents without the swimps.'

'Let me taste them swimps, please mam. Listen, I hope I never move from this spot if I said that to anybody.'

'Figure it up. Six pounds steak, twenty cents pound. Lovely butter from town. New potatoes. Strawberry jam. Tell me something, did you ever had strawberry jam, you, by the Durots for breakfass? I bet you never. My grampaw was a pilot.'

'Me, I never said nothing like that to nobody.'

'The pilots got to have their jam. They want their pickles. Melba toast. They get them habits on the ships when they eat at the captain's table. Pickled walnuts. Chutneys. Sauté this and sauté that. We was raised to eat. How could anybody say the trashy Durots that they mix spaghetti with red beans and oysters and potatoes in the same pot could feed better than me when you dig for them, if you said it, which I don't believe you did.'

'I hope I may never move from this spot!'·

'Eat meat, Commodo!' said Bob LaRoque.

'You got your salad and berries yet,' said Mrs. LaRoque.

'Leave him eat meat, Mama,' said one of the daughters. 'You can't dig a ditch on strawberries.'

'Take that piece with the bone!' suggested Bob LaRoque. 'Give him more beans! What the hell!'

Evvie went hesitantly around to the back door and knocked.

'I want to give this to my Papa,' she told Mrs. LaRoque, and shifted her big ravenous eyes toward the dwindling food.

'Come in, darling!' Mrs. LaRoque urged.

Evvie handed her father the envelope. 'You forgot your cooking-soda, Pa.'

'Oh, I had cooking-soda for him!' Mrs. LaRoque said. 'Look it waiting for him on the zinc!'

Commodo, grinding away at a mouthful, stopped to pull Evvie's ear. He pressed his greasy lips against her cheek. 'That's a good girl. Now run home and tell Mama thank you for me.'

Mrs. LaRoque watched Evvie walk out the back door. 'But that's a sweet little girl, Mr. Crochet. So pretty. You ready for your berries? Here, take plenty!'

On her way home, Evvie passed a field where dandelion greens grew in thick glossy clusters. She sat there and ate leaves until her hunger was gone. At home, she curled up in the crotch of an orange tree by the kitchen window where the greedy bees filled the air with a thick humming.

The Health Nurse had come on her regular visit, and was talking to Mrs. Crochet in the yard. Miss Nellie was oval and rosy, dressed in white, a large blur in the sun.

'It's a disappointment, Mrs. Crochet,' she was saying as she plucked an orange from a tree.

'We can't help it, Miss Nellie.'

'A disappointment. I thought the Crochet family would be off the Book ages ago. Still, I guess you're really co-operating with me, striving to get off the Book.'

'Yes mam. Evvie got her teets fixed, her, on the Dentist Trailer, and I'm taking T. J. to clinic regular to go on the scale.'

'Well, I'm sorry for your vicissitudes, but you can appreciate the Crochet family gets on and off my Book oftener than any other family, white or black.'

'Take us off the damn book, and leave us off!'

'Now — now ——'

'Nobody axed you to get on your book! Throw the book in the river, all I care, me.'

'What!' Miss Nellie clutched to her huge bosom the brief-case with its loose-leaf family progress record. Then she smiled indulgently. 'Please don't be offended, Mrs. Crochet. I mean after all. You see, I just want you to shun defeat. Shun defeat. Pray. Pray for help to use your effort only in directions that produce results. It's a hard life.'

'Are you working for the church or the state, Miss Nellie?'

'The state. My feet right now are aching, yet I must go on and on, because, you see, we must shun defeat!' She took Mrs. Crochet's soap-shriveled hand. 'I mean after all. Picture me. I walked in here glowing with hope, expecting, if I couldn't take you off the Book, at least to be able to move you up among the green tabs, to Somehow Improved.'

'Things you tell us to eat they coss too much, and my husband making two dollars a day when he works. Yesterday, me, I gave Topal one of my Grammaw Ernestine's lovely lace curtains for a crawfish net, and she brung home three handfuls crawfish.'

'Of course. Of course. We can only try. Where's the budget sheet I gave you?'

'Gussie, him, he used it to make a kite when I was in the tub.'

'Here's another. Listen, don't aim too high at first. Let's forget what I said about the gold tabs. Let's shoot for the green, Somehow Improved. Simply the green. Later we'll talk about the gold. Shall we?'

'It's awright with me, Miss Nellie.'

'Wonderful! Tell Commodore tonight. Gather your family together and drink your orange juice all together. Thank God for all these oranges. Drink a toast to health!'

'Our landlord, he owns the oranges.'

'Tut-tut! Mr. Dupré won't mind. A toast to health! Tighten your belts and grit your teeth. Just think! The Belchers are among the green tabs since Wednesday! The Pasquals, too, that sweet young couple in Dutch Scenery! Think what nice company you'll have up among the green tabs! Oh, my poor feet!'

'Low heels is what you wunt.'

'Perhaps so.'

'You pretty heavy for the high. Look the fat hanging over the sides of your shoes.'

'Dreadful, isn't it? I'll never get rid of these mission bells. Look!' She pulled her skirt tightly over her thighs to show the bags of fat hanging in the rear. 'My sister calls these my mission bells, one on each side swinging when I walk.'

Commodo Crochet walked into the yard. His body had the appearance of a figure fashioned out of dough and baked brown and puffy. He wore a leather jacket over his denim jumper, which could not be buttoned over the swell of his belly. He had on an old green derby hat. His lips were badly chapped, peeling all over. His face was creased with pain.

'What you say, Miss Nellie,' he said. 'You come see us again?'

'When duty calls, Commodore, when duty calls.'

'Why you ain working?' Mrs. Crochet asked.

'New potatoes, I guess,' Commodo replied. 'I got the burning and can't liff the shovel a inch.'

'Gall bladder,' Miss Nellie pronounced. 'Eat vegetables.'

'A man can't pitch dirt on vegetavles and cooking-soda. I'm going the doctor. Get me a clean shirt.' He went to his wife. He bulked largely over her. He squeezed her to him. 'Now don't worry, Duck. I be all right. Is my radio working?'

Mrs. Crochet followed him into the house. 'Misère, I don't know nothing about the ole radio, me.'

'Don't allow nobody burn up my battery while I'm out working, Duck. That's only the pleasure I got, the radio.'

'I don't know nothing about the ole radio.'

'Bring me some vaseline for my lips.'

'Vaseline grows on trees. I got none.'

'Well, send Evvie for two cigarettes. Here's two coppers.'

'Evvie's restin. Pass on your way.'

'I wunna smoke now. Can't she run to Zhule's?'

'Pass the store on your way.'

'Where's Topal?'

'Minding the baby. Her dress is toren. The neighbors can see all she got. Now hush and pass on your way when I'm busy with the Helt Nurse.' She kissed him and handed him a starched shirt.

Commodo sat in the office of Doctor Wall. He continually picked at his chapped lips. After a while the doctor came in, wearing hip boots and carrying a pirogue paddle. He had been on a confinement case out in the marches. He introduced Commodo to another doctor who was with him, a visitor from New Orleans.

The doctor, wearing a white smock reaching down to the hip boots, pressed his fingers into Commodo's abdomen. The visitor, sitting in a corner, watched him idly.

'Where's the pain?'

'Right here, Doctor. It's starting to go way now.'

'When did you eat?'

'Ten o'clock by Bob LaRoque's.'

'What did you have to eat?'

'Steaks. Strawberries. Red beans and rice. Potatoes and gravy and salad and stuff.'

'Get up and stoop over. How many helpings did you have?'

'I dunno. Two or three, Doctor.'

'Sure. I see what the trouble is. Your alimentary channel has only one terminal. Put on your clothes. Don't worry. This is a common condition. From now on, eat about one-third as much as you're eating now.'

Commodo dressed himself.

'Doctor, I like to have some medicine,' he said.

'We'll see later on. You come see me when your clothes fit you. They'll begin fitting you in a few weeks if you follow instructions.'

On the way home, Commodo decided to have his wife alter his pants so they would fit. 'If I thought I need a tailor, would I go to a doctor with the pain?' he asked himself. 'I bet if I went to a tailor, he'd send me to a damn doctor. They got you comin and goin these days.'

Mrs. Crochet stood at the steaming wash-boiler, and the Health Nurse sat on the kitchen steps.

'Thank God in a way your husband is so well-fed,' said Miss Nellie. 'If only the rest of you were. He weighs more than all of you put together. That makes it look pretty bad for me, Mrs. Crochet.'

'Yes mam.'

'I told my Chief yesterday, "The day will come," I said, "when the state might give us boatloads of organs like kidneys, liver, brains. Organs and organs, whole tanks of codliver oil and give it out like the church gives holy water." Evvie and the twins are so pale. The only twins I've got, and paler than any children on the river, and we're powerless to help, in a way. Even yourself, if you don't mind. You could use some calories and vitamins.'

'God knows I don't mind.' Mrs. Crochet poked at the boiling clothes with a broomstick. 'I got a fine stummick, too. I'll put my stummick up against anybody's.'

'*Did you instruct Evvie about babies?*' the nurse asked in a whisper.

'Not yet, Miss Nellie. She ain axed me, and I been so busy.'

'Start with the flowers and the little crawfish riding on their mother's tail. Do it soon, Mrs. Crochet. Don't let me down on the sweetest little girl I've got on this river.'

'Yes mam.'

'So the Chief said to me, "But look at the husband of that family, with the classic obesity!" So I had to explain it's the people he works for that overfeed him.'

'Eh bien!'

'Yuman pride! Trying to outshine one another. Doctor Angew can't understand the classic obesity.'

'And the chirren needs meat!'

'And the children need meat! I was at Durots' one day when Commodore was digging for them. They're having a war with the LaRoques, trying to feed Commodore better than the LaRoques right now. Give a guess what they had for dinner? Lovely veal pocket from town!'

'And always they mostly live on robins and grocery soup!'

Miss Nellie sighed. 'If only Commodore could bring home some of those lovely meals, you'd make the gold tabs like nobody's business.'

Mrs. Crochet paused in her washing. Her lean dark face froze into hard wrinkles as she gazed over the levee into the vacant fog. 'Yes mam, yes mam!' Her laughter was brittle and hollow, like the sound of castanets. 'Or else stop talking about what he had to eat when he comes home. Like yestiddy. Topal, poor chile, was licking her lips when that big ole rangatang come home talking about the roast deer-meat and black duck and all like that on LaRoques' table, sayin the deer-meat was too juicy and the gravy had a lil bit too much thyme. Him, he don't like thyme.'

The nurse nodded, swallowing the saliva in her watering mouth.

Evvie climbed out of her tree. Roused by the jarring of the leaves, a great cloud of the white-flies that infested the grove whirled about her like a swirl of snow. She wandered about among the trees. 'I'm bored,' she thought. She wanted to be alone. Nobody in this house could ever be alone. She went to the riverbank outside the levee, but her sister was there with the baby. Topal was secretly smoking a cigarette. Evvie stole off. She was sorry for Topal. Since a man had named his mule after Topal, and it had become known to everyone in Grass Margin, Topal had changed — grown more sullen and belligerent than before. She could not get along with any-body. Topal was a handsome girl with a face dark and brood-ing like her mother's, burning with resentment. But she was round-shouldered, and her chest was flat. 'She pretty like the mother used to be,' the women of the settlement would say, 'but she ain got no tiddies. Twenty year old, and not a tiddy to her name.'

Evvie went into the house, idly climbing the big front steps and thinking briefly, as she usually did, of a house to match them, with gables and casements and many retreats where one might be alone. She went into the little front room. Gus-sie was there. He was standing over the pallet that was used as a bed by Evvie and Topal. Paul, his twin brother, just awhile ago had taken a nap on the pallet. When Evvie came in, Gussie quickly hid something behind his back.

'What are you doing?' Evvie asked. 'Let me see.'

'Paul, he cut the tails off my lizards. I'm getting even.'

Evvie took hold of Gussie and turned him round. In his hands was an old tin can containing water. He had been pouring water on the bed in the spot where Paul had taken his nap. Evvie laughed and grabbed Gussie. She dragged him out to the porch. Now both of them were giggling. While the boy struggled, Evvie poured the water down his back, then pushed him off the porch. Gussie ran off, laughing and kicking his heels.

Evvie sighed. 'I wish I was disappointed in love,' she thought. The fine warm morning hurt her — the ground coming alive everywhere, the sky full of glad birds migrating from over the Gulf. She went around to the side yard to play with the pet raccoon. All day and part of the night the raccoon would walk back and forth at the end of his chain tied to the guava tree. Evvie stroked the animal, passed her chin lightly over the soft tail. The collar had worn the hairs from his neck. Even after they fed him each day on fiddler crabs, he would continue his restless pacing, trying to pull away. It was an indignity for him to live so close to the odor of his droppings, but nobody thought of that.

Evvie lay on the cold ground and dreamed, until she saw her father coming up the levee road. Commodo turned in at the front of the dwelling. Evvie in one movement slid under the house. The raccoon had stopped his pacing, and was watching her, the two live eyes glittering out of their black mask, the quivering nose pointing at Evvie under the house. Commodo passing saw the raccoon's fixed alert gaze pointing, and he stooped to peer under the house.

'Hello, Pa,' Evvie said. 'How do you feel?'

'Terrible. You going to school this evenin, darling?'

'Yes, sir. Mama's ironing my pants after while. It's my turn to take down the flag at three.'

'Mmmmm! But you like that, eh?'

'The flag pops and pops in a wind like this.'

'Mmmmm!'

'It almost smothers you when it wraps around you. You've got to be careful it doesn't touch the ground.'

'I say you learnin good in school, you. The importantess thing is to learn plenny, because you wunna be a Little Sister of the Poor some day. Them sisters is gotta be smart.'

There were humming-birds working around a wild salvia bush in the grove. These were newly arrived migrants, and they streaked back and forth in their angry colors, squeaking like mice. Evvie sighed, stared through the trees, and pursed her lips. Before going to the convent, she intended to fall in love, to have a lover to leave behind. Through the trees she saw the top of the big cypress rising high, and dark as a throne.

3

I MADE A SONG

ONE DAY, when Evvie, Gussie, and Paul were going home from school, there was a blow of wind. They crawled under an overturned yawl on the river shore, and huddled to wait for the rain to pass.

'Look the fiddler crab, Evvie!' Paul cried.

'Hush up, Toe-cheese!' said Gussie. 'I'm listening for thunder.'

'The rain's nice under a boat,' said Paul. 'I'm burying the fiddler, Evvie!'

'I'm listening for thunder so I can say, "Jesus, Mary, and Joseph,"' said Gussie. 'It's not a curse when you say it for lightning.'

'Ain't the fiddler cute, Evvie?'

'Yes, he's cute,' Evvie answered. 'Don't let him pinch you, darling.'

'Evvie, where does fiddler crabs come from?'

'Nobody knows,' she replied. 'Nobody knows.' She liked the sound of the words.

A burst of lightning came under the boat, and the thunder sputtered and growled. 'Jesus, Mary, and Joseph!' Gussie said. He crossed himself. Paul was left-handed, and blessed himself the wrong way.

'Evvie's worried,' Paul said presently. 'Looka! She's worried.'

'She's worried because she spilled ink on her dress.'

'She's worried because she's gotta wash the dishes.'

'She's worried because she's gunna get a bad report.'

Evvie said, 'I'm worried because my new beanbags are in the corner in Mama's room where the roof leaks.'

When the rain slackened to a soundless drizzle, the big drunken fog rolled in off the river and lay there blurring all the naked willows and the huge piles of contorted driftwood along shore.

The twins crawled out and made off in the fog, followed soon by Evvie. In the misty drizzle they climbed the heaps of driftwood and leaped from log to log. They dodged in and out of the willows, up to their ankles in the sandy mud. Evvie allowed them to go ahead while she walked thoughtfully, searching the scrawled sands for whatever interesting things the river might have brought from up North. But this day she found nothing worth keeping.

She found Paul and Gussie playing in a dome-shaped shelter some older boys had made of driftwood and willow branches. Her brothers had dug a sloosh-hole in the mud floor. Every day the children passed here. Evvie would play with them, or lately she lay on a log and waited for them to tire. Sounds of another world came to her from a ship anchored somewhere out in the fog, the soft muttering of machinery, the gurgle of bilge-water pumped from a hold, or the voices of men. This side of the levee was masculine. Men worked on boats, paddled their pirogues. Young girls only occasionally went near the water; adult women never. Evvie was never able to locate the exact direction of the ship-sounds in fog.

'Awright, take it easy!' a voice called from the far white depths. It was a watery voice, out of great wet depths, strange and lonely.

Evvie climbed over the logs. She removed her shoes, cautiously waded a little distance from shore. The water about her flowed heavily, like liquid soil. She gazed long into the heavy fog to locate the direction of the voice. It had seemed very close.

'Wait, hold it!' the voice yelped. Then: 'Awright!'

There was a rumbling crash, a great weight striking a hollow metal deck and bouncing. Then more voices, and a peal of gruff laughter. Then, amid a series of lesser sounds, tapping, scraping, dragging, a gay popular song was whistled. Such sounds always were exciting to Evvie. The hidden visitors soon would be gone with their ship. Sometimes there would be the quick beat of unseen heels walking on metal. A piece of running tackle would croak. The fog washed over her face and throat, chilling her lips, collecting in beads along her eyelashes.

Suddenly the ship's bell burst into a succession of startling bangs, very close. Her heart stopped, and she felt as if she had swallowed her throat. She jerked around, facing the sound's exact direction. She then looked for the shore behind her. It was lost. She called her brothers. No answer came from the shore.

'Paul! Gussie! Where are you?' she yelled.

Evvie remained where she stood, up to her knees in water. The current bore heavily against her legs, and a shrimp collided with her flesh, pricking like a hot needle.

'Oh, Gussie!' a voice on the hidden ship called. 'Oh, Paul!'

Evvie smiled.

'Where are you, Gussie dear!' another male voice called.

'You shut up!' Evvie cried.

'Who are you?' a voice asked.

'A shepherdess!' she answered.

'What's your name, baby?' the first voice called presently. The ship's bilge pump worked on, saying words. Heck, dunk a fish too! Heck, dunk a fish too! Heck, dunk a fish too!

'Evvie Woolworth!' the girl called.

'Can't hear! Say it again!'

'Evvie Woolworth!'

'How you spell that, baby?'

'What's the address, sweetheart?'

'How old are you, darling?'

'Hey, how about a date?'

'Hey, how old are you?'

'Fourteen going on fifteen!'

There was a silence. Then the voices began to speak to one another, words and laughter mixed. Then all the voices broke into a song:

> I do not know
> It may be so
> But it sounds like crap to meeeee!

She turned her back on the burst of laughter that followed. She liked the men, the hard carelessness of the laughter. She could feel them gathered under the bell, with their short hair and many pockets, their uncouth ways, their swaggering in a straight line toward the things they wanted. She saw herself as an ungainly crane wading, with her dress gathered behind as a tail. The ship's bell banged again, without startling her. Soon it became only another of the bells she had known, in the day or at night. The ship would go away. She had been

listening to hidden bells since she had been a child who be-
lieved the purpose of a ship was to carry a flag. She could see
the willows, their pale skeletal tops reaching. She waded
ashore.

Her mother was standing there.

Mrs. Crochet's spine was straight as the back of a pew.

'Is this how you mind your bruddas?' she asked.

'I was minding them. They dashed off.'

'And don't dodge every time I move my hand.'

'I'm not dodging.'

'Didn't I tell you a hundred time to come right home from
school?'

'There's no room inside to play when it rains, Mama.'

'Come here. What was you doin while ago? If I can hoe my
Easter lily ten minutes that the grass is taking charge of the
whole patch without the chirren runnin home scaring me to
death their sister is drowned in the fog ... What you wunt in
the fog?'

Evvie lightly vaulted a log lying waist-high in her path.
She ran to another and sailed neatly over it. Mrs. Crochet
crept under the first log, following Evvie, grabbing a stick.
Just then a voice from out in the river called: 'Oh, Evieeee!'

'So *that's* it!' Mrs. Crochet said. 'Who is it?'

'I don't know, Mama. Some fellows. I don't know.'

'Some durdy sailor of a sassy bum out there, eh?'

'I don't know.'

Evvie dodged her mother's swishing stick. 'You gave him
your name for what?'

'Mama, I didn't give him my name!'

'How did he get it?'

'I didn't give my name to anybody.'

'Before hell! You *tole* him your name!'

Mrs. Crochet overtook Evvie scrambling up the levee slope, and hit her across her pointed backside. 'Maybe I ain gunna straighten the poker on your ear, me, when I get you home, chasing durdy sailors from Liverpool and I-don't-know-where with their durdy beards and tellin them your name in the fog. Jiss wait!'

Mrs. Crochet saw a man coming down the road driving a mule dragging a sled loaded with beanpoles. Furtively she dropped the stick behind her.

Evvie said, 'I can't understand why I shouldn't talk to a man.'

'Because you gunna be a Little Sister of the Poor, you skinny little hipplecrite.'

'Why can't I be a Little Sister and talk to a man too?'

The fellow driving the sled had passed. Mrs. Crochet rapped her wedding-ring finger on the side of Evvie's head. 'Because you supposed to be thinking about Jesus, you little witch! About *Jesus!*' She swung her hand at Evvie's ducking head. 'About *Jesus*, you hear? Now you gunna come home and sit in your tub of cole water for chasin men. I'll fix your clock!'

Evvie went ahead, pouting. 'A person ought to be able to ask a decent question,' she grumbled. She did not mind sitting in a tub of cold water, but she did not tell her mother that.

'When the Sister come here beggin oranges for the poor in town, did you tell her you wunna chase men? No! You tole her you wunna be a Sister and go to the convent when you graduate.'

'I know. I keep praying to be worthy, but suppose I didn't want to be a Sister. You'd still fuss if I looked at a man.'

Mrs. Crochet stopped on the road. She placed her fists on the place where her hips had been when she was young

and plump. She hissed: 'Mais non! Mais non! I wooden
fuss! I'd laugh, me, and tell you go head and get married.
Live in a rented house! Get you a trapper and skin muskrat
the ress of your life and a band of kids pullin your skirt off
with bellyache from eatin kidney pills the sample man threw
in the yard. Get married and turn your back on Jesus on the
cross that he's beggin you to give up your life to the poor!'

'Ouch! I don't even know why people get married.'

'Broadcass it! Broadcass it on the road! They get married
to drip coffee through a undershirt sleeve.'

'So far I don't know anything about a man hardly.'

'Ain't you got a father and a brother? Sure! Take a look at
them! Smell your father's breath with the raw garlic! He's
too big for his pants, your father, and Arthur's pants is too
big for him!' Mrs. Crochet shook her fist under Evvie's nose.
'Listen, starting tonight, you gunna review your catechism,
you hear? You gunna start where Almighty God blew on a
hunk of mud tonight, you hear?'

'Ouch!'

Later, while Evvie was sitting in a tub of cold water in the
back shed, she called to little Gussie: 'Honey, go get me my
beanbags like a good boy!'

Gussie brought the four beanbags to Evvie. They were not
wet. The roof had not leaked on them. 'Catch!' Evvie said.
They played this game until the mother called that Evvie
might get out of the tub.

The next day after school Evvie led her brothers along the
riverbank, and for a long while they played in the shelter made
of sticks and bushes. Evvie rolled up her skirt and put her legs
into the sloosh-hole with theirs. The mud, the rich silt brought
down by the river from Arkansas, or maybe from Iowa, was

the color of milk chocolate coating their legs. The children standing in the hole embraced one another, and stamped their feet to produce the thick plopping sounds.

'This is our hole!' Gussie said.

'It's for the three of us!' Paul said. 'We're in podners!'

'It's a hole in the world,' Evvie said.

'Yeah! We made us a hole in the world!'

'We're Eskimos! This is our tent!'

'Yeah! Lil bitsy ole Eskimos!'

'I'm a walrus! I'm a seal! Looka me! I'm a seal!'

While they played, Evvie heard a twig break behind her. She turned. Near the ground, something was furtively squirming through the twigs and leaves that formed the wall of their shelter.

'A rat!' Paul whispered.

'Shh!'

The thing was brown. In the dimness it was shaped like a rat. It was stealing noiselessly toward Paul's schoolbooks which lay there in a pile.

'Get a stick!' Paul whispered.

'Shh! It's a man's hand!'

It was a Negro hand, dark brown or black, four long fingers and a curious thumb, wide and somewhat flat. They all stared at the strangely shaped thumb. Evvie had seen the hand before, on the road, in the post office. The hand reached the books, gently closed on them like a slow mouth biting, and jerked them through the leaves. Evvie jumped from the hole, ran outside, looked over the top of the shelter. The man had made off through the fog. She heard the snapping of twigs.

The boys ran excitedly home ahead of her; and before she reached there her father met her on the road.

'Start at the beginning,' Commodo told her.

'The hand was Shoepick's. That nigger up the road, Papa. I saw the thumb, and ——'

'I know. We done practically got him under the jailhouse. Papa's proud you seen that thumb. We'll get him today for sho, darling. Schoolbooks is state property. I'll fix him. Shoepick. That's the nigger don't pay taxes. Got a big-big house his father leff him, and don't pay taxes.'

'Papa, don't hurt him,' Evvie said.

'He gunna remember this day!'

'Papa, what makes Shoepick's thumb so wide and flat?' Gussie asked.

'Shoepick sucks his thumb, they say, darling. Got it all outa shape. They say he sucks it all night. That's what happens to lil boys that sucks their thumbs.'

'Papa, they won't hurt him, will they?' Evvie asked.

'Start at the beginning. Tell Papa. Is this the place?'

'This is where his hand came through, and he took the books.'

Commodo folded his arms. 'Listen to Papa! Was you all botherin anybody atall?'

'No, we were playing, Papa. I wonder what he wants with the books.' Evvie went down on her knees. 'This is the way he went. We thought it was a rat.' She stuck her arm far into the hole. Commodo held his derby hat behind him, and rocked back and forth on the balls of his feet.

'That's all I wunna know,' Commodo said. 'Tie your shoes and come.'

Oliver Legendre, the Justice of the Peace, operated a poolroom. It was built on the riverbank. On the other side of the levee near his residence was the old renovated packing shed where the cases of disturbers of the peace were tired. In this room was a desk and some benches, and two duck-boats hanging from the ceiling above the Justice's desk.

Evvie sat between her mother and father near the center of the room. They had been waiting nearly half an hour. The Justice of the Peace sat at his desk, a tiny man with a dark round face, large ears, black bangs on his forehead growing down to the eyebrows. His hands were folded. He was looking out of the window, motionless as a man sitting for a portrait.

The constable finally appeared with the accused, a small Negro carrying three schoolbooks. He had a cigarette behind his ear. Following Shoepick and the constable was Shoepick's sister Juarelle, a young quadroon with big restless eyes. Juarelle took a seat near the desk and put her hand behind her ear. She was deaf. When she was young, her mother had taken her to visit a neighbor whose children had the measles so that she would catch the disease and get it over with. This had brought on ear trouble.

Trappers, oil scouts loafing after night duty, fishermen, and other loungers from the poolroom now began to arrive and take seats. Everybody waited, without a sound except an occasional whisper or the scrape of a boot. Legendre, taking a paper from the constable, wrote in his book, sticking out his tongue and clamping his teeth on it. His pen made a sound like a gnawing mouse. Commodo shifted his weight in the creaky chair and took from his pocket a book of cigarette papers. He undid the elastic band and passed it through his lower teeth to remove a bit of food.

'I got rabbit to cook yet,' Mrs. Crochet complained to her husband in a voice meant to be soft. Without looking up, the Justice of the Peace frowned and rapped his knuckles on the desk. Mrs. Crochet pulled down her reddening face and became very small. Commodo turned and glared at her.

A tall reddish man wearing loudly squeaking shoes came in, tiptoed up to Legendre's desk and laid down a nickel for a game of pool. Then he sidled over and sat facing the Crochets obliquely. His face was rather young, but the front of his head was bald and emphatically white. His bony knees, thicker than the upper legs, came apart widely, showing a gap in the front of his trousers where the pants were unbuttoned. Evvie's big eyes watched him as he nonchalantly opened and closed his pocket-knife. He began to shave the hairs off the back of his hand. Evvie studied his shoes, which were sandals woven from strips of red leather. Everybody in the room watched the shaving of the hand. The man raised his eyes to Evvie, and smiled. She lifted her chin, turned her face away, threw him a glance from the corners of her eyes.

Suddenly the Justice of the Peace closed his book with a loud thud and bellowed at the ceiling: 'It's two years since anybody robbed anybody on this Margin!' Then he glared at everybody in the room, one after another. Then he leaned back and formed a little cage with his hands by joining his fingertips, and spoke very softly to the prisoner, his lips close to the cage and his voice traveling through it:

'Shoepick, why did you want to go and steal the little boy's books? What for? Can you read?'

'Assa. Ah din mean no harm.'

'Give me them books and let me see them.'

Shoepick handed over the books, then backed off and stood alone. His big lips hung loosely. The light from the dusty window showed prominently the pale trapped balls of his eyes, the hard black outline of his skull tilted slightly backward on his massive neck. Juarelle, the sister, sat holding her ear, frowning painfully, trying to hear the reason for her brother's arrest. Outside a mocking-bird was amusing itself dropping camphor-tree seeds on the metal roof overhead. The hard round seeds every few minutes would roll down the roof and strike the rain gutter. Bung.

The Justice looked over the books. 'Speller. Language. Dictionery. Come on and talk. Hold your tumb up. Is this the tumb you saw reaching, Evvie?'

Commodo nudged Evvie. She nodded her head.

'Shoepick, you better come tell us the reason why you did this,' said the Justice.

'Ah needed um,' said Shoepick.

'Do you steal everything you need?'

'Nawsa.'

'Hurry up.'

'Ah godda wride a ledda.'

'Who? What letter? To some woman? We want the truth in this court.'

'Dishya ain no cote. Ah swedda Gawd Ah godda wride a ledda. No wummun ledda. Godda wride a bidness ledda, and Ah wunda see how to spell good. Ah wunda spell good so dey pay 'tention to de ledda.'

'Who?'

Shoepick frowned. He looked from face to face among the brown visitors with their bright eyes roused. In the poolroom over the levee, loud talking mingled with the clatter of pool balls.

'You stole the books to see how to spell good to write a business letter, and what else?'

'A private ledda. A bidness ledda.'

'Tell us.'

R-r-r-r-r, bung. Another seed dropped on the roof.

'Ah made a song. Lashyea.'

'Last year or this year, you always making songs, or else you might could pay your taxes. Hurry up.'

A man sitting in a window took his cigar from his mouth and said, 'The Drainage Board gunna buy his property soon for taxes, yes.'

'That's enough!' said the Justice, rapping his knuckle.

'All I got to say, he ought to steal book from nigger chirren. C'est pas ——'

'That's enough, Octave!'

Shoepick went on: 'Ah made a song. Issa good song, Mist Oliver. De bess song Ah evva made. Ah written out de music an Ah sen it off. Ah sen it to Mist Synoground at de concern in Chicago. Dat concern had a piece in de race newspapa, say, "Be a song wrida." Ah sen it to um. Mist Synoground nevva written me back. Ah waided a long time. Nen de yudda day Ah was passin Chippy's Saloon up de levee an dey's playin a piece on de reckid. It was jiss lak mah song — on a phonograph reckid. Ah swedda Gawd. Dey tak alla mah words and mos all mah music. Dey got anudda man's name on de reckid. Ah swedda Gawd. Mah Chilblain Stomp. And dey ain paid me a cent. So I jiss wunda fine out how come dey ain paid me.'

'You mean to tell me you written that song, Shoepick?'

'Assa. I swedda Gawd. Dey jiss changed it a lil bit in one place.'

'A good lawyer's what you want.'

'Ah been to see Jedge Soniat. He say Ah godda have proof Ah sent de song to Mist Synoground. Ah ain got no proof.'

'Why?'

'Nobody seen me sent de song. Nobody heard me play it.'

'Why?'

'Ah din wunt nobody to steal it.'

'Some white man could write your letter. I could have done it for you. That's no excuse for stealing books from children.'

'Ah dunno what to say yet. Ah godda git some words.'

'You can make a song and you can't make a letter?'

'Nawsa.'

'Well, damn it — I — write him a song, then. You expect — listen, I've got no jurisdiction.' Legendre looked at Evvie Crochet.

Commodo Crochet raised his hand and shook it. He squirmed in his seat, and like a school pupil, he waved his hand at the Justice of the Peace.

Just then a barefooted fisherman entered the room and signaled to Commodo: 'Psst!' Evvie looked at the man making a noise like a snake, and nudged her father. The fisherman clumped over to where the Crochets were sitting. He leaned toward Commodo, whispering: 'Your boy over in the pool-room. Him, he got a pool ball in his mouth, and we can't get it out.'

Mrs. Crochet grabbed the man's denim sleeve. 'What?'

'A pool ball.'

'Jesus, Mary, and Joseph!' She knocked the man's arm aside and sprang from her seat. Commodo followed. Evvie tripped behind him. 'Mama, pull your dress out!' she whispered. Mrs. Crochet reached behind and pulled at her dress. The three hurried through the windy sunlight, and into the poolroom over the levee.

One by one the audience left the court for the poolroom, until only the prisoner and his sister, the constable and Legendre, were left.

'See what's the matter out there,' Legendre told the constable.

The constable left, and presently returned. 'Arthur Crochet tried a trick wid pool ball,' he said. 'He pud pool ball in his mout. It won't come out.'

'You can go, Valsin,' Legendre said to the constable. 'I'll call you by and by.'

Shoepick said: 'I swedda Gawd, Mist Oliver. Ah wunda fine out about mah song.'

Legendre closed his book and took off his eyeglasses. 'Shoepick, I'm going to turn you loose this time,' he said.

'Assa.'

'I've got a little job of work for you, Shoepick. Now you come on. Hurry up.'

He led the way out. Juarelle followed them, skipping to keep up. They went through the fig trees in Legendre's yard.

'Whut kinda jawb you got fumme to do, Mist Oliver?'

'I'll show you. It won't take you long.'

Legendre's residence was built close to the ground, about eighteen inches. It was dark under the house. Legendre stooped and pointed. 'My dog's got pups under there,' he said. 'Four pups, I think.'

'Assa.'

'She's a gentle dog, never bit anybody. But she won't come out. I want to put the puppies in the back shed and tend to them. Got a nice bed fixed up.'

'Sho.'

'She won't come out. Here, Gloria!' He snapped his fingers. 'Come out, Gloria! You see? She's afraid.'

'Ah don see no dawg, Mist Oliver.'

'Way back under there. Gloria! Gloria! No use. Shoepick, you're a little man. Crawl up under there and get the pups for me. Don't mash them, now.'

Shoepick looked into Legendre's eyes. His face broke into a big white grin. He scratched the top of his head. Juarelle stood looking from one man to the other, trying to understand what was going on.

'Get under there and get them, Shoepick. Then you can go home. I'm doing you a favor, and you're doing me one. Don't tell anybody. The people don't need to know.'

'Assa.'

'Step on it before the people come from the poolroom.'

Shoepick crawled under the house. 'Gloria!' he called softly. There came the sound of his back scraping the floor timbers. 'Come, Gloria!'

'What he doin?' Juarelle asked. She stooped and peered under the house. 'Where he goin?'

'Over toward the front more!' Legendre called to Shoepick. 'Gloria . . .'

Shoepick could be heard creeping over bottles and tin cans. 'Gloria!' There was the dog's gurgling snarl. 'Gloria!' Then came the noise of thrashing among the trash, snarls and yelps and curses, and a bumping against the floor joists. Shoepick slowly wormed his way out, walking on knees and elbows, pushing ahead of him the bitch, which he held firmly by the legs and muzzle. 'Here!' he said. 'Take yo dawg! Take her!'

Legendre backed away. 'No! Come out! Bring her out and take her to the shed! Never mind about the pups!'

Shoepick wriggled out. He dragged the squirming dog quickly to the back shed, threw her in, and closed the door. He limped to the cistern to wash his hands. One of them dripped blood. There were cobwebs in his hair, and on his forehead a large lump was forming. His sister followed him, holding her throat.

'Wait, Shoepick,' said Legendre. 'I'll get some iodine. I'm going to whip Gloria good for that. The idea! I'll get the puppies myself.'

Legendre hurried into the kitchen and brought back a bottle of iodine. He stood looking around the yard with the bottle in his hand. Shoepick and his sister had gone. Legendre heard them walking through the canebrake far behind his orange grove.

In the whitewashed poolroom, the village loungers and some of their wives stood around looking at Arthur Crochet. Arthur, a boy of eighteen, was sitting on a pool table with his jaws gaping and a portion of the white pool ball protruding from between his tightly stretched lips. He was breathing with difficulty, the breath coming in snores.

'Darlin,' said Mrs. Crochet. 'Darlin.' She stood beside him with an arm around his shoulder, and her eyes searched the faces about her for some hint of aid.

'It's all right, Mama,' Evvie consoled, as she patted Arthur's knee. Standing next to Evvie was the fellow with the red woven sandals. He was an employee at the sulphur works up the river. He gave off the smell of sulphur so strongly that Evvie's eyes smarted and ran water.

An old Cajun with a wet cast-net slung over his shoulder pushed through the group and squinted up into Arthur's face, examining first one side, then the other. He opened and closed his own toothless mouth, revolving the lower jaw. He turned to Mrs. Crochet, wagging his head vigorously. 'Tell him to go bommit,' he said through his gums. 'Go oudside and bommit, son. Ip you can bommit, duh ball come out and you won't peel it.'

'Hush up, vieux!' somebody said.

'Get a spoon,' said a big Negro woman. 'Big tablespoon. Put goosegrease on it, and work it aroun behine . . .'

'A doctor'd hafta slit back open the corners of his mouth,' another onlooker said. 'Don't tell me. Like a mullet's belly. Don't tell me!'

'Leave him alone,' Mrs. Crochet complained. 'Leave him ress. Ress, darlin.'

'Leave him lay down, he can't hardly breathe,' another woman said.

'You wunna lay down, darlin? No, leave him ress. Gimme a handkerchief, somebody, to wipe off the presperation.'

A blue bandana was produced with a lot of coins tied in one end of it. Mrs. Crochet passed it over Arthur's face. He cried out when she touched his jaw: 'Ah!' He pointed frantically to the aching jaw muscles. 'Ah-ah-ah-ah-ah-ah-ah!' A small boy among the onlookers giggled. A man's hand slapped his head and he squirmed off.

'Cancha push it out with your tongue?' somebody suggested. 'Push hard with your tongue. It's bound to come out.'

'Leave him ress,' said Mrs. Crochet. 'His father, him, insteada helpin the boy and tryin to do something...' She pointed over to where Commodo was leaning in a window studying the river. 'Looka there!' she called loudly for Commodo to hear. 'Look the ole rangatang! Him, he don't care if Arthur swallows the god-dog ball, and nobody can't do nothin! Like if I ain got enough trouble arready.'

Commodo turned, tilted his derby hat down over one eye, and glared defiantly at his wife. Commodo and Arthur had been angry at each other for some weeks, not on speaking terms. After an altercation, Arthur had left home, and was living from place to place with various friends. 'They big enemies now, him and the father,' Mrs. Crochet explained to a neighbor, 'over the father don't wunt Arthur's hunting dogs in the house, and he abuses him, and this one sasses him back. But Arthur's a good boy, I tell him. What can I do? Look him suffer.'

The crowd pressed closer. The sulphur man with the sandals was pressed against Evvie, and she could hear the ticking of his watch.

'Can't he push it out with his tongue?' someone asked.

'You need fishing-cackle to fish it out! Big shark hook!'

'Why don't he grab it and jerk? Jerk hard, Arthur!'

'Ah-ah-AH-AH-AH-ah-ah!' Arthur shook his head and looked appealingly around him.

Commodo walked disgustedly out of the place. He sat on the steps of the poolroom. A bird lit on the wire above him, a bright red summer tanager, singing a song like a robin's. Summer was on the way to pester him — sweat, the dreadful green glare of hot weeds, sandflies, cistern water turning warm and tasteless, and the heat on the tin roof of his ramshackle house beating down through the ceiling and warming the very furniture and floors.

He thought of Shoepick's fine big house which was to be sold for taxes. Shoepick's father had worked like a slave to make a fine house for his big family. During the World War, when the price of pelts went to record heights, the old man had trapped more than fifteen thousand dollars' worth of skins in two seasons. Two years later, the whole family except Shoepick and Juarelle had been lost during a hurricane in a little camp-boat in the marsh. Although the land was not worth much, having a large bog on it in the rear which left only some five acres for cultivation, the house was still in good shape, and more than big enough for the Crochets. Commodo wondered how much the delinquent taxes amounted to, and when the property was to be sold at auction. Then he remembered that the Sheriff had tried to auction the property a few months before, but nobody had bid on it because it was located in the Negro section of Grass Margin, and Shoepick's father was buried in the front yard.

Just then Oliver Legendre came through his front yard, stuffing a little bottle into his pocket.

Commodo got up and approached Legendre excitedly. 'Listen, Oliver, when is the Drainage Board gunna pay Shoepick's taxes and git his place?'

'When the river goes down. The Board can't pay the taxes until they hold a meeting. They can't hold a meeting until Emilien Perdu, the chairman, comes home from the marshes down by the Passes. Perdu can't come back until he gets his cattle out of the marshes. He can't get his cattle out until the water goes down. That will be a fine big place for the Drainage Board to fix up and rent out to all the oil company office people when they start drilling oil down here. It won't cost them much.'

'How much?'

'The interest and all is sixty dollars.'

Commodo's heart was beating rapidly. His stomach was turning sour. Walking beside Legendre, he looked at the river. The water would not be going down for some weeks. Shoepick's house would just about match the big cypress doorsteps. . . . But sixty dollars! There was no use thinking of the possibility . . .

He turned to Legendre and said angrily: 'You went and turn Shoepick aloose, I guess!'

'I got no jurisdiction, Commodore. We don't want to waste a day or two taking him up to the Parish Court, do we? He's a pretty quiet little nigger, and it's his first offense. I'll watch him from now on. But I can't get over him making that song. Right here in Grass Margin! No wonder he ain't worrying about taxes. I'll watch him from now on, hear?'

'You damn right! Me too, I watch him. Ef he go near my chirren again, I'll shoot the daylight outa him!'

'Leave him alone,' Legendre counseled. 'Leave him work on his songs. If it's true about that Chilblain Stomp, he'll be a rich nigger one day.'

'I'll knock him from here to the Ural, he plays aroun my chirren any more. Mock my words.'

'How's your boy? Is the ball out?'

'I dunno and I don't care, me. Stupid ass, settin up there eatin a pool ball, playin tricks and oughta be scratchin the marsh or something to get ahead. Leave him suffer. He ain under my roof any more, I tell the world.'

Legendre slouched into the poolroom. The women straightened their hair, the men stood aside to let him pass and walk up to Arthur Crochet. 'That's the cue-ball,' he said.

'It hurts him,' Mrs. Crochet said, beginning to weep. 'His jaw been open since I don't know when.'

'I see. It won't go down and it won't come out. Sit still, sonny. I ain't even touching you.'

A young trapper lying on the table lifted himself lazily and pointed. 'He can't swallow it,' he explained. 'It's too big. See what I mean? Me and him, we passed a good. time playin pool, and he bet me a nickel he could get the ball in his mouth. I wooden bet him, because ——'

Legendre leaped ferociously at Arthur and grabbed him around the neck. Mrs. Crochet screamed. Arthur fell back with the other man on top of him. 'Ah-ah! Ah-ah!'

'Hold his legs!' Legendre shouted.

As they struggled, Legendre forced his finger into the side of Arthur's mouth. Arthur writhed around the table. With Mrs. Crochet pulling at his coat, Legendre held on. He got his finger into Arthur's mouth, rammed it behind the ball and jerked it out. The ball rolled over the table.

Arthur sat up, holding his jaw, looking at the ball. He

glanced around with a shamefaced smile. He worked his jaw round and round. The crowd broke into laughter and excited comment.

'Looka his mout!' Mrs. Crochet cried. 'His mout got big from the ball. Maybe it's gunna stay that way!'

'Aw, hush up!' Arthur grumbled. 'I'm gunna try it again sometime.' People were slapping his back.

Mrs. Crochet swung her open hand at him. 'You durdy trash!' she cried happily. 'Trying to worry me!'

For a long time Arthur, ordinarily a shy boy with few friends, remained among the people and enjoyed the distinction which was his. Presently he fell in with a shrimp fisherman who bought him a drink and gave him a job on the trawler.

The three Crochets walked homeward on the levee shell road. With them was the sulphur man who had stood next to Evvie in the poolroom. He walked ahead with Commodo; Evvie and her mother in the rear. The man's name was Dave Tobin. He was tall and very thin, bent forward in the pelvis, and he dragged his feet, his long slow steps almost shaving the ground, the new sandals squeaking behind him. Tobin was a boarder with the Stavelkovich family, Dalmatians who lived near the Crochets. Even here outdoors, the sulphur smell trailed behind him in the fog, and Evvie Crochet's nostrils picked it up, lost it, found it again.

Commodo was telling his companion about fishing in the Delta: 'When a sheephead get aloose from your hook, young fella, he might come right back and bite again, yes.'

'A brave little devil or stupid one.'

'Like ef he wuntsa get caught. Sheephead got a little bitsy mout, and teets like rows of gravel in the mason. Hard to hook. Leave him swallow the bait. He nibbles like a crab. He pulls it down soft. And watch out you handle him caffle, yes! You talk about he's mean! Before hell, he can read you like a book, and he's libel to smack your face crooked, prog a fin between your ribs, or bite a helpin of gristle outa your hand any day, if you wunna know it.

'Now, irregardless what you go after, it's bess to mash up plenny-plenny clams and fling them aroun where you gunna fish. Now a redfish grabs and runs and fights. A bull-red gunna give you plenny fun to land. The bull is the she-male, and that's a funny thing. Winter time the bess for catching plenny fish, but they don't fight, because they cole. Plenny meat, but no fun. Summer time, take you along a heavy hunk of ice, because the fish gets soff quick. When fish-eyes is cloudy, throw them away. Eatin a cloudy-eye fish is injurial. The same all over the world, I think.'

'Hell's far!' Tobin exclaimed. 'Less us go fishing. I'm fool about hunning and fishing.'

'I got a pullin-skiff,' said Commodo, 'but can't pull accounta my livers and gall bladder gets upset.'

'I could learn to pull if I was showed once.'

They were near the Crochet house. 'Sweedart,' Commodo called to Evvie, 'why don't you take Mr. Tobin in the river and show him how to pull skiff? She can pull good as me any day.'

Evvie hung her head, moved closer to her mother, dug at the clamshell road with her toe.

'I mean it,' said Commodo. 'She was good as born in a boat.'

'Shonuff?' The lean man's reddish eyes would not let her alone. He had prominent teeth. Evvie thought of a school-room joke about a boy who was said to be able to eat corn off a cob through a knothole in the fence. 'I'm game,' Tobin said. 'Say, I got a little sister just like you. Come on, Sis. I'll let you be my sweetheart.'

'Your pants are open in front,' Evvie replied, skipping away to join her mother.

Several times thereafter Tobin dropped in to see Commodo to learn how to row the skiff, or to talk and sip the sherry wine he would bring as a kind of reason for the visit. He would knock timidly; and when he entered the house Commodo would bellow: 'Eh, là bas! What you say, bruddin-law!' Commodo hoped very soon to be friendly enough with Tobin to ask him for the loan of the sixty dollars he needed.

Tobin's voice issuing from between his great projecting teeth was soft, his words ordinarily few, so that when he spoke he was usually listened to. Evvie, dawdling at the dishpan, would listen to Tobin and Commodo warmly discussing momentous questions: Is a man who commits suicide cowardly or brave? If a Jew can become a Christian, why can't a Christian become a Jew? Is it worse to be deaf, or blind? If you inherited a million dollars, what would you do first? Occasionally Mrs. Crochet would chime in with a remark. 'Me, I dunno which shoe in the morning I oughta put on first sometimes, the right or the left.'

'I kilt many a man in the World's War,' Tobin said sadly, 'every one a stranger to me. We used to cut them down with the machine gun, crawling up and down the Argonne. My brother Evon stayed home and worked in a munition factory for a dollar an hour, nearly much as I made in a whole day. He bought him a barbecue stand in Houston, and he's prosperous today. It's curious a man gets paid more for making bullets than he gets for stopping them. I guess it takes a little bit more sense.'

Commodo said: 'Me, I got everything the matter with me like you see me here, from bunions to dandruff and back again through the sinus, the teets and tonsils, gall bladder, livers, stummick, and the hernia from when I was a boy I pushed a heiffer off the cattle-boats on a Ash Wednesday, it was like a purple balloon popped out by my nabel between the large and small intessments of the bowels. The pain variates. The curse of my life is gas.'

And Evvie would see Tobin walking the road alone. He was a lonely man, very courteous, especially toward the women, whom he seemed to regard as objects of reverence. But he did not fit into the younger female circles along the Margin; and among the older women there were none for him to seek. The girls of the settlement called him Ballhead Tobin. One day, after he had received his mail and left the post office, Evvie heard some Indian and Filipino girls discussing him in tones of flippant ridicule, and one girl mimicked his shambling gait. He was very shy in the presence of Topal Crochet, who never troubled herself to do more than answer his obliquely genial greetings.

When among the family, he would tease Evvie. 'Hurry up and grow! I want you to be my girl.'

'Don't bother me,' Evvie would say, then retire into a corner to watch the man furtively, and to wonder why it was not possible for one to hasten the growth of the body, as a plant is hurried by manure. But meeting her alone on the road next day, Tobin was amiable and shy. Evvie liked him because he was the first man ever to have linked himself to her, even jokingly. His eyes were bloodshot, irritated by sulphur dust on his job. Sometimes they were red and puffed as if from weeping. And he knew a lot of things, being thirty-two years old.

Evvie began to pay more attention to the Negro Shoepick and his sister Juarelle. She thought of the word Juarelle as a verb. To juarelle would mean to cry out or sing in long, kind of waving sounds from the top of a peak or tower. It was a strange and wonderful thing to her that Shoepick was black, and his sister almost white. She saw them walking the levee together, yet separated by several yards, Shoepick in the rear. It was said that Shoepick did not want his sister to go anywhere alone, because white boys might insult her. Juarelle always smiled admiringly at Evvie when they passed. Shoepick had no time to notice Evvie, but went past her with his white eyes, small as aspirin tablets, fixed on the ground ahead, thinking his black thoughts that no white person would ever see through. Juarelle walked without effort, her head raised high, as if looking over the heads of other people.

Once Evvie walked the road alongside of Juarelle from the post office. Juarelle was eating a cake. She offered Evvie half. 'No, thanks, I'm doing without cake in Lent,' Evvie answered. This was the first cake she had been able so far to do without.

Juarelle did not hear what Evvie had said. 'Dis is good cake!' she urged, smiling.

Evvie drew nearer and shouted: 'No cake in Lent!'

They walked on. A passing ship blew several blasts to warn a little boat crossing the river, and Evvie could feel Juarelle looking right at the balls of steam jumping from the whistle, and hearing nothing. Juarelle turned and looked at Evvie. Her nose was slightly tilted, very pretty. She spread her hands and looked about her.

'Spring gunna come soon,' she said in her curious, faraway voice. Evvie nodded her head vigorously and smiled.

'You're prettier than me,' Evvie said in a low, experimental tone. Juarelle walked on, looking straight ahead. To Evvie, it was like talking to a flower.

'Your name is a verb.'

Juarelle pointed over the river, where a square livid curtain hung from the clouds and a great upsurge of wind was kneading the stagnant heavens into a froth. 'Rainin there!' Juarelle said.

Evvie nodded. She looked the other way. 'The whole world is an island,' she said. In a tone even louder she spoke again. 'I haven't got any underclothes on. My mother and father had a big fight last night. My mother has nightmares. I want a lover to leave behind when I go to the convent.'

They were nearing the Crochet house. Juarelle said: 'Well I hope the rain dawn come here! I got plenny blankets to wosh. Miss Dupré, she gimme a dudden aigs to wosh her blankets.'

Evvie turned her head and said: 'I know why you're almost white. The sewing-machine agent kissed your mother.'

On another day when the school bus stopped on the back road near Shoepick's field, Evvie saw Juarelle trying to drive the mule over a ditch. The mule would not jump the ditch. Juarelle jerked at the reins. 'Hum up, mule!' she cried.

Shoepick was running across the field with a stick. Reaching his sister, he handed her the stick and cried: 'Hit him! Crack him!' The mule turned his big head and eyed Shoepick. Juarelle shook her head and dropped the stick. She jerked the reins. '*Hum* up there, *mule!*' The mule danced.

Shoepick reached down for the stick. 'To hell!' he shouted. 'Don leave im bluff you! To hell! Hit him! Hit him!' He shoved the stick back into Juarelle's hand. '*Beat* him!' Shoepick yelled. Juarelle struck the mule's flank a dainty blow. 'Hum up, Ranse!' The mule danced.

Shoepick saw another stick on the ground. He picked it up and whacked Juarelle across the back. 'To hell!' Juarelle

began to dance. Shoepick struck her again. She struck the
mule, and while Shoepick belabored her, pulled on the reins
and screamed at the dancing mule. 'Hit him hard!' Shoepick
yelled. 'You godda learn! You godda learn!' Juarelle,
crouched under her brother's blows, took the stick in both
hands and brought it down across the mule's back. A hoof
flashed past her face. She dropped her stick and ran.

All of the children in the bus were screeching with delight.
As the bus drove off, Shoepick took the reins and drove the
mule over the ditch. He did not hear the splashing of the
children's laughter.

At this time, Shoepick was being widely discussed in the
Delta by those who learned that a man had been arrested on
the Margin for the first time in two years, and by others who
heard his stolen song on the juke-boxes. One of those who
heard about the stolen song was a Negro band leader called
Plush Boardman, whose band on Saturdays played dances
in the larger Delta villages.

Plush Boardman went to see Shoepick, and heard some of
Shoepick's songs. Thereafter, Plush spent his Sundays at
Shoepick's house. Negroes would gather in the little packing-
house behind the residence that Shoepick used as a studio to
hear Plush, accompanied by Shoepick on the guitar, play his
famous trumpet. There would sometimes be dancing and
drinking. Plush's body was brown, emaciated, burning from
a fever. A story was told along the river that once, in competition with another trumpet player, Plush had made blood
come out of his instrument.

Plush encouraged Shoepick to quit worrying about the
forthcoming sale of his property, to stop messing with the mule
and going to the swamps for beanpoles for his sister's beans,
to devote all his time to making songs, because one day he

would produce a hit that would earn enough money for ten orange groves. Plush criticized all of Shoepick's songs, played them on his trumpet, and promptly discarded them as being not yet good enough to send off for publication. 'Go haid and make some mo songs,' he would tell Shoepick. 'Git happy! You ain made a real good song yet! Fine you three-fo wimmin livin far apart! If you git put out yo house, yall come live wid me in town. I git you a job in a bann! Quit thinkin bout yo propitty! Quit thinkin bout de song dey stole. It wudden such a good song, nohow, an you didn't make it all. Ain no way you kin colleck, nohow.'

Shoepick continued his efforts to write a successful song; but despite his friend's advice, he tried over and over to write a letter inquiring why he had not been paid anything for the Chilblain Stomp.

4

I WANT ME A CEDAR COFFIN

FOR a while Evvie found employment after school hours to help pay for a dress for her graduation from high school next year. She worked in the rice field of Mr. Willy Stanjovich, a rice grower. She reported each day after school, and remained until dusk, relieving the Filipino boy who helped the cook with dinner. Evvie's job was to stand on a tall platform made of saplings in the rice field with a long rawhide whip, and to crack the whip whenever a flock of birds descended on the field to pluck out the recently planted grains of rice. The sharp report of her whip would rouse them, and they would circle and fly into the big hackberry trees that lined the irrigation ditch, and there wait until Evvie fell to thinking and her vigilance waned.

Dave Tobin came by one evening. He was trudging the ditchbank on his way home from the marshes, carrying a .22 gun. He found Evvie lying face downward, with her hair dangling over the edge of the high platform. They talked a little while. He showed her a bird.

'Look what I shot,' he said. 'Do you want it?'

'Sure. Thanks, I like marsh-hens.'

'The clapper rail's its real name,' he said. His red head was flung back to look up at her. He was a funny-looking fellow with a red bony face, blood showing through the skin, a tuft of red hair sticking out through the open shirt-collar. His projecting teeth made him seem to be always smiling.

'I used to belong to the Campfire Girls,' Evvie said. 'We roasted some marsh-hens one night. They were good. We did it at a girl's house. We had to make out the kitchen stove was a campfire. The girls wouldn't go out in the woods.'

'Shonuff?'

'I got disgusted and quit. The girls were afraid of the woods.'

The sulphur smell was mixed with the brackish odor of the marsh. The sun shone into the red cavern of his talking mouth. Looking down, Evvie could examine every part of the cunning mechanism that shaped his drawling words.

'By rights I'm a athalete,' he was saying. 'I went to Texas A & M, a right good school down in Texas. I was a athalete, a pole-vaulter, if you know what that is.'

'Sure, I know.'

'Texas A & M. A fally good school, but too strict for me. My ways was too sloppy for military school. And I didn't like geology. I told them. It like to broke my daddy's heart when I quit. So I went to Freeport and got some work in the sulphur. Then I transferred to the sulphur company here. This is a lonesome place.'

'Are you a rough-neck?'

'Yes. I'm in the bull-gang so far. I'm trying to get in the office. Maybe I'll switch to an oil company when they start drilling here.'

Evvie stood up, swung her whip and cracked it, then lay down. 'I don't like oil companies,' she said. 'They don't give any good jobs to our boys around here. They give the good jobs to Texas people.'

'Some say Cajuns don't work steady,' said Tobin. 'Always wanting to lay off. I dunno. Soon as winter comes, they tell me, they want to go trapping in the marshes.'

'I don't blame them. Who wants to work for a boss if he can work for himself?'

'Are you a Cajun, your folks?'

'Sure. Cajuns are good people. You've got to study your history to know it. Ignorant people don't know it. Evangeline was a Cajun, and General Beauregard.'

'I know the girls are pretty, some of them,' said Tobin. 'I mean! I don't have to study history to know that. Looks like none of them wants anything to do with me. Not that I blame them much.'

'Aw, some of them are silly ... The oil companies want to take the oil from under our marshes, and not leave anything here, my father said.'

'I leave all my money here. Most all the girls are pretty, and some are sure independent. They won't dance with you.'

'Nobody around here gets any benefit from the oil except broken springs from the roads torn up.'

'Texas and Delta people are sure different, and hard to agree. We're mostly old Americans in Texas. Most Delta people are Catholics that wear medals and play Bingo. Gambling and drinking ain't much of a sin to them. As you say, the men don't like to work for others. They been hunning and fishing for themselves a long time, I reckon, and it's hard to knuckle down to a straw-boss.'

'We saw the Governor one day,' Evvie said. 'He was passing in a speedboat. The Congressman was with him. They'd been hunting geese. The whole boat was draped with geese. Strung on rawhide, I think.'

'Did he wave at you-all or anything, the Governor?'

'The boat passed by so quick, and he was picking his nose. My father said the geese belong to the Governor, every goose and everything else in the marshes. He said those people, the Governor and the big mucky-mucks from New York with the oil company, was passing close to the levee to let us smell the geese. My father's a funny man. He makes us laugh when he's not bilious. He needs sixty dollars pretty bad right now. It would get us a big house to go on our doorsteps.'

'Those birds are in your rice,' said Tobin. 'Look at them yanking up the shoots.'

'I don't care.'

The visitor left. Evvie wondered whether he were angry because she had mentioned the money, whether or not her father had already asked Tobin for the loan. He cast a lean blue shadow over the pale fuzz of the rice field. He was awkward and slouchy. His receding back dwindled off to a jouncing dot against the distant levee. Enormous clouds lumped against the east were dark and heavy with rain. In the creamy mud of the field where the sprouts grew soft as hair, the birds prowled about like happy vermin, pecking at the rice blades. Evvie jumped up and swung her whip in slow circles, then cracked it well. From the field below her, swarms of birds leaped upward like fragments of an explosion. Their wings made sounds. The flock passed overhead like a black net flung. She cracked the whip again. The scared flock broke into several ragged fragments.

On her way home she studied the crawfish and the shy frogs looking at her from the ditch-bottom. The water was still, except for one rippling smile where the surface was tickled by minnows. Everywhere she looked in the water,

rafts of cloudy frog eggs were moored to the weeds and the
bits of débris, and she could see the fierce dragonfly nymphs
feeding on the eggs.

When she reached the levee road it was dusk. The library
boat was tied to a rickety wharf. The librarian, a one-armed
woman with a happy brown face, who knew all the fishermen
in the bays and bayous, emerged from the boat and waved
to Evvie. Walking behind her toward shore was the Negro
Shoepick. He carried a few library books and a guitar decorated with mother-of-pearl. Behind his ear was a partly
smoked cigarette. The two stopped on the plankwalk, and
Shoepick handed the books to the librarian, and plucked his
guitar. The woman stood smiling as Shoepick sang:

> If Ah evva go to jail
> Bonka bonk bonk bonk
> If Ah evva go to jail
> Bonka bonk bonk bonk
> If Ah evva go to jail
> They'll be hawg-tracks
> By mah trail.
> Bonka bonk bonk bonk!
>
> If Ah evva make greens
> Bonka bonk bonk bonk
> If Ah evva make greens
> Bonka bonk bonk bonk
> If Ah evva make greens
> Ah'll seddle em down
> Wid soldier-beans.
> Bonka bonk bonk bonk!

Evvie, lingering, pretended to be interested in something
in the bushes, half-aware of the Negro's song, and still thinking
of the frogs and crawfish — that to a crawfish, human beings
went down the road walking backwards. The Negro singing
his song seemed to be angry, frowning deeply and singing the

words in a sort of groan, never smiling once. The words of the song went ahead of the notes of the instrument, jumping just ahead as though pursued by the plucked notes. The guitar was really used as a drum.

Speaking to the Negro, the librarian used the same tone that Evvie had noticed her use when speaking to children. She said, 'Now, don't you read the end of the book first to see how the story turns out. Read it carefully. Read them all carefully, and they'll do you good.' Shoepick was not interested in that. He took the books and bowed his head and walked off. The librarian called after him: 'Did you write your letter yet to Chicago?' He turned and shook his head, smiling. He turned up the levee road, passing close by Evvie.

'Good evenin,' he said.

'Good evening.'

In the night-time Evvie would sit in a corner of the kitchen to write a theme. She used the back of the washboard, resting it on her knees. The kitchen table could not be used for lessons, since it had to be cleared and moved into a corner for the twins to use as a bed. Ever since Commodo's foot had been bitten by a rat, the little boys refused to sleep on the floor.

Evvie's composition dealt with Louisiana products.

'Molasses, oil, sulphur, and salt,' she enumerated aloud.

'Lumber and strawberry,' said Mrs. Crochet, threading her needle by the lamp.

'Yes, and Easter lilies right here. Oranges, seafood.'

'Rice, cotton, perique tobacco and fur, darling. Oyster shells. Sure. They mash them up for chickens up north to eat, them shells. It gives lime.'

Topal said, 'A whole lot of tourists go to New Orleans. They look at the old buildings and smell the French Market and so on. All those old buildings are apartments. People take their dogs outside to walk them. You've got to be careful, because the dogs sign their names all over the sidewalks. Put that in.'

'Yes, Papa says you've got to play hop-scotch, like,' Evvie said.

Evvie liked geography. Unlike history, geography had a shape and a color that could be seen from the window. It was folded into hills and ravines, smoothed out in plains, or it fell from the clouds and ran over the world in wrinkles that were all named. The Delta winds and vapors belonged to geography; the big dunes of oyster shells; the clotheslines leaping like colored puppies; the bearded waterspouts; the naked willows heavy with birds; the rumbling truckloads of oil-pipe; the foggy sun bare as a skull. Geography made strangers strangers, such as the ones from Texas, or the passengers leaning on the rail of a white ship in the river.

'Mama, what's the most valuable lumber?'

'Cypress, I think.'

'Orangewood,' said Topal.

'Whoever heard of using orangewood!'

'For manicure sticks they do.'

Evvie said, 'Pine and the magnolia. Cottonwood, oak, ash, and elder and the poisonball tree. That's a good one! Myrtle and cedar, rosewood and sycamore. Jule found a piece of rosewood on the river floated down. And duckwood. That's composed of anything light for carving. That's an industry too — carving decoy ducks for hunters.'

'Cedar's the wood they took for Christes' cross on Calvary,' said Mrs. Crochet. 'It's bad luck to burn it in the stove, but it makes a lovely coffin. I want me a cedar coffin if possible, you all. The myrtle tree give berries. All the candle was made out them berries in olen time. Put that in the composition, darling . . . *She* never gunna think of that, Orelia Badeau. And listen, orangewood I remember is good for lodge hammers. Them lodge hammers. Uncle Placide's lovely lodge hammer that he used it at the lodge meeting, it was made from the same orange tree that Theodore Roosevelt tied his horse when he hunted ducks here that time. One of you all went and loss it when you was little. The Indians I got for chirren.'

'Topal lost it.'

'You lost it.'

'You lost it. And they pave the streets in town with blocks of pine. What else, Ma?'

'Don't bother me. My cocoa done turn ropy with you all, and here come your Paw, I guess. Stayin out tell happass eight with his gall bladder.'

Commodo came in the door, and as usual blew wind through his lips, 'Whew!' as if he were nearly exhausted. He said, 'When I pass by the window you was lookin happy. When I come inside, you look like you got a tick in your girdle. Straighten your nose. We got company outside.'

'God dog it, that stickin-plaster of a pole-vaulter again! Hide that turdle-meat!' Mrs. Crochet hissed, kicking a piece of discarded clothing under the stove. 'I'm a son of a bugger, if ——'

Dave Tobin walked in, smiling, carrying a jug half-full of sherry wine. Topal, sitting on the floor, jerked her bare feet under her skirt. The sherry wine was passed around at once, and drunk from variously shaped cups and glasses. 'Me, I think you all are got enough to drink aiready,' Mrs. Crochet complained.

'Listen, you all,' said Commodo after a while. 'I think our troubles is over in this house.'

All the faces turned toward him. He kept them waiting, humming a tune as he wiped his derby hat on his sleeve. Evvie stole a glance at Dave Tobin. His florid face shone after a shave, but behind one jawbone was an area of red stubble the razor had missed.

'Say what you gunna say,' Mrs. Crochet fussed. 'I got kids to scrape sometime tonight.'

Evvie saw that Tobin was taller than her father, looking around him bashfully, throwing his weight from hip to hip. To her, his loose body seemed capable of being folded up and laid away in a drawer.

Commodo said, 'I been tellin you all, time and time and again, we got no troubles a dollar won't cure, and that's a fack. We got us a doorsteps and all we need is a house. Shoepick's got a big house and won't pay taxes. The Drainage Board wunts to get that property soon as the river goes down and Emilien Perdu sells his caddle and comes out the marsh to hole the meetin.'

'Shoepick oughta be ashame to not pay his taxes and they gunna sell his place,' said Mrs. Crochet. She looked down at Paul, who was trying to put a prune-seed in the baby's ear, and screamed, 'Awright, Mister Paul Crochet, you wunna go to town and get your hair cut on a horse, eh?'

Commodo threw his derby hat across the room, stamped into the adjoining room, returned, and stood with his face purple. 'Can I get listened to or not when I got something important to say around this crazy-house?' he pleaded.

'Go ahead and talk,' said his wife.

'Guess how much a person can get that lovely property for?' Commodo asked. 'Keep still, Mr. Tobin. I give you three guesses. Three guesses.'

Gussie then backed up against his mother and pounded on her knee, and fixed his big eyes on Dave Tobin. 'I got no time for your gubernatorial palaver,' said Mrs. Crochet to her husband as she unbuttoned Gussie's romper seat.

'*Sixty dollar!*' Commodo yelled. He calmly gulped his wine. He walked into a corner and stood looking at them with his arms folded. 'Now, who do you think's gunna haul off and buy that property before the Drainage Board gets a chance?'

'Who?'

'ME!' Commodo dealt his chest a great dull blow.

'Goddle mighty!' Mrs. Crochet muttered, turning pale.

'Now will you go to work and listen to me?'

'Goddle mighty!'

Commodo skipped over to his wife. He danced before her. The air was full of his flopping fingers. 'We can raise any crop we wunt, Duck! Woopy! Again, Shoepick's got two hundred orange tree on that place. Barren trees, all barren plenny fruit, and then some young ones. In udda words ——'

'You got sixty dollar, you ole rangatang of a fool walking all over your shoestrings with your sherry-wine ideas?'

Commodo gritted his teeth. His eyes blazed. He walked suddenly to the middle of the floor, and ferociously flinging his pointed finger toward Dave Tobin, bellowed, 'This man's gunna *lend* me the money *next pay day!*'

Mrs. Crochet stared, fidgeting with a button on her dress, her face an angry mask, her eyes deep and dumbfounded. The children all were quiet.

Dave Tobin broke the silence. 'Sure,' he said quietly. 'By rights a fine property like that should never belong to niggers. It ought to belong to some nice, hard-working people like you. Shoot! Sixty dollars is no amount of money. And pay day's ten days off. I can stall off my landlady easy. Pay

me back when you're able, Mr. Crochet. Why — why, it
might change this whole family's life.'

That night before bed, Commodo and his wife sat on the
big ornamental front steps. A solid place to huddle and plan.
A handsome perch to sit close to the river's silken wash and
dream.

'It's gunna match this doorsteps good, that house,' Commodo said. 'Me, what I'm gunna haul off and do, I'm gunna
clean the ditches before we move in, even. That might be
my lass drainage work — my lass and my bess.'

'Clothilde pass here and tole me a boy down the road run
one of them Spanish daggers in his eye playin blind man
buff,' said Mrs. Crochet. 'They got them things growing all
over Venice where Arthur stays. I'm worried.'

'I'll get a honeysucker vine for the front gallery, too.'

'He's so careless, Arthur. I can't solve him, me.'

'You don't wunt a decent place to live in, it looks like to
me, Duck, from the way you don't even listen at me.'

'You stink of wine. I don't believe it, anyhow. I don't
hardly know that Tobin.'

'Never mind, you hear him say I can borrow the sixty
dollar.'

'Me, I been fooled too much. My whole life I been bluffed
and bluffed.'

Mrs. Crochet sighed, and waved the mosquitoes away from
her legs.

'There's time this year to plant a little crop of okra,' said
Commodo.

'Listen, I don't care one way or anudda, you hear? I'm
disgusted.'

'Aw, Duck.'

'Mark me up black and blue with your ole rough hands.'

'I wish you could stop worryin, Duck.'

'I worry about Arthur in the night when the sun goes down. I worry about Topal and all the neighbors is laughing behind her back and she gets meaner and meaner to me and everybody. That durdy gool of a Tayo Delacroix, him he drove the mule he name after Topal right pass the church Sunday when the people come out, a dirty white mule and got a big hind laig all swole up. I worry about Evvie, she axin me why do people get married, and Miss Nellie, her she keepsa pesterin me to tell the chile about sex.'

'That's easy like rollin off a log to do.'

'Why don't you try it, you?'

'The girls at school musta done tole her, Duck. They know all about sex, and insex, too, such as tamperin with their own cousins.'

'God knows what them little pip-chippies is telling her, they know so much these days.'

'The girls change life in high school these days, Duck.'

'I wonder where Arthur is tonight? He's so bole and careless.'

Commodo was no longer listening. He said: 'I'm gunna haul off and slash down Shoepick's camphor trees in front so you can see who's passin on the levee. Later on, we might get a pressure cooker. Woopy, Duck, you can put things up! Vegetavles and fruit in jars!'

'I been bluffed too much since this doorsteps come on the house.'

'Hush, I got it all figured up, me. That's why I made friends with Tobin and you called him a stickin-plaster. I knew I could borrow the money from him. Thang God this property comes to me jiss at the right time. Duck, you know something?'

I'm at the awkward age right now. Not ole enough for a pension and too ole to get a job.'

'It wouldn't be right to do such a thing to poor Shoepick,' said Mrs. Crochet. 'To take a man's property like that.'

'The Drainage Board don't think that way. I say if he wunts the property, leave him scratch the ground and pay taxes.'

'Misère! You ain gunna tangle me up in that business tell I see the sixty dollar firss. Show me the sixty dollar.'

'Ha, ha! My little Duck. You gunna see! Leave it to me.'

The dripping mist over the black river was solid as rind. Mrs. Crochet dug her chin into her palm and brooded. A hidden frog made a sound like the winding of a clock.

Evvie was standing in the doorway, a pale shape in pants, waiting to bid her parents good night. She asked, 'Mama, are we really going to get that big house?' She stooped and kissed her mother and father.

'Don't listen at him, darling,' said Mrs. Crochet. 'It's anudda one of his head-dreams. And don't go tellin everybody in school, because the Drainage Board might fine out we wunt the property. Never tell people your business. Jesus never tole nobody His business.'

5

THE GROUND ENJOYS TO BE HOED

THE CLIMBING moon grew smaller. The wind, stroking the crouched backs of the trees, was warm as fingers. Everywhere, field mice and reptiles and crawfish in polished armor were twitching out of the warmed soil to study the moon.

Mrs. Crochet was leading her daughters toward the canebrake far behind their home, where the secret patch of Easter lilies was hidden in the canes. They stole through the weeds softly, speaking only in whispers, stopping now and then to look behind.

'The canal bridge oughta be showing up,' said the mother.

'I don't know why we've got to do this at night,' Topal said.

'Because the land back here don't belong to us. Now hush before I slap you crooked.'

'Watch me jump that stump,' Evvie said. 'I take after my father, because my bones are soft.'

'Your bones are jelly, and all of you is jelly,' said Topal.

'Better you'd look at yourself with your round shoulders because you won't straighten up,' Mrs. Crochet told Topal.

'I've got nothing to straighten up for.'

'A man oughta keep his land clean,' said Mrs. Crochet. 'If I owned this piece, you'd see it clean as a baby's behind, winter like summer, and all kindsa kitchen food sprouting clear to the ditches, and gangs and gangs of white laycorn hens. Say like my poor Papa, "Milk and honey." '

'Keep your honey and give me some grocery ham,' Topal said.

'Easter lilies for money. Corn and chickens for the pot. Right now, in the front of April, I'd show you how to set out tomato plants growed in a tray underneath the stove, and lovely bell peppers. Them bell peppers is only the thing to stuff and bake on a Sunday when a person's got company with shrimp and crumbs. Take the cover of a coffee-can. Prog it fulla holes for grating the stale bread good. Scoop out your bell peppers and stuff in the pulp and shrimp. Sprinkle the crumbs on top. Put you a dob of butter on top, then haul off and slide them in the oven. Goddle mighty!'

Mingled with the circling chant of mosquitoes was the secret gurgling of ditches all around. A cheesy fragrance from the spangled barrens beyond the canal flowed over the brakes and the neighbors' harrowed fields. Mrs. Crochet was a dark streak of a woman scrawled in the moonlight, stubbornly bowed, but with her muzzle raised and her angry hands tearing aside the brambles that barred the way.

They reached the canal. Black humps of myrtle lined it. It was a valuable stream, meant to solve the Delta's biggest problem — getting rid of water. The diked river, higher than the land, took no water from these fields. The canal's course, in a land where waters commonly flow without design, was emphatically straight — planned on paper, dug by man, recorded forever on bonds with golden borders. The Crochet girls remembered the red-faced surveyors and their lanky one-eyed instruments that could find truthful directions from the stars. The canal's surface was a compact mass of moonlit hyacinth foliage bleached and withered by the recent frost. Everywhere, the disturbed mosquitoes sang.

They tiptoed over the canal bridge. Out in the marshes, beyond the second canal, a frog-hunter was coughing. A loose board on the bridge bumped loudly under someone's foot. Mrs. Crochet clicked her tongue impatiently. Sounds of frightened rustling came from the withered leaves below, followed by several labial splashes. Then again the fretful coughing from the marsh. Mrs. Crochet darted nimbly ahead and up the opposite bank. She stood with her skirts lifted high, listening. The faint coughing in the distance was repeated again and again, like a petulant cry.

Mrs. Crochet turned to Evvie. 'Go in. Wiggle. Hold the canes so they won't bounce back and crack me. Wiggle.'

'I know.'

The canes grew more rankly than any planted thing. Evvie walking ahead held them apart. She smelled honeydew. Topal was in the rear, cursing the mosquitoes. The canes engulfed them all. They were like hunted insects prowling under the bristles of some vast animal pelt.

'I don't like this a bit,' Topal grumbled. 'Listen, will you wait for me? Mama, make her go slow. Something's flying around hitting my face.'

'Wait for her.'

'I'm supposed to be a rabbit. A crawling rhinostrich always squinching through the canes like Evvie Crochet on nothing to eat. My hide is human.'

Evvie said: 'Mama, Papa says the landlord looks like a man smelled a flower with a bumble-bee in it. The purple nose.'

Topal stopped and smacked her thigh, and her hoarse laughter rang out, peal after peal.

'Listen, you!' Mrs. Crochet said through her teeth. 'You wunt us to get caught with the marsh fulla neighbors shining frogs? Bad enough the people can smell the lilies a mile, nilly. On damp nights, me I'm holding my breath somebody don't pass under these canes for rabbits or deers and get a whiff of this pretty smell and tell our landlord.'

They went on quietly as they could, wedging a path, grunting, muttering, heaving a sigh, wiping a face, glancing at the outer leaves far above that glittered like moistened dirks.

'It smells sad like Requiem Mass,' said Evvie.

'Holding my breath all winter long, like you see me here, scared somebody'll find out and tell Jewpray we planted lilies in his canes. Goddle mighty! We'd go right smack to jail. Somebody would.'

'Mama, who'd go to jail?'

'I be switch if I know, me. Somebody'd pay. Your father or another person would pay the law by the courthouse.'

'Father Pennygrass knows the lilies are back here. You confessed it that day, you said.'

'Oui, I done confessed it like it was a sin. I confessed it. I made up my mind.'

'Mama, I don't think it's a sin, even.'

'Not to God it ain't.'

'Father Pennygrass would take up for us. Shoot! If old Dupré had us arrested, Father Pennygrass would crawl him, Papa said. He'd crawl him.'

'Not to God it ain't no sin,' Mrs. Crochet said. 'Shucks! You think God's got time to humbug with little ole transgressments like that? I never hardly leave my front yard, me, to injure a neighbor, and the land in these canes is going to waste to the 'coons and rabbits, and ole Jewpray's wife, her she can pay a dollar for vanishing cream to nourish off the wrinkles at her age of life. She's knocking on fifty-two, the way I count, and look at her pounding the levee in purple. Tell that to God! She oughta wash the egg off his vest.'

'Papa should have confessed the sin, I think,' Evvie said.

'I don't know, me. It's over. I made up my mind.'

'He's the father of the family, and ought to carry the sin.'

'Ouch, damn it!' Topal cried.

Evvie said, 'Maybe the priest wouldn't have given Papa absolution if Papa had confessed it, because Papa's a big man. Maybe the priest felt sorry for a woman because his own mother is old.'

'Listen, you!' Mrs. Crochet said. 'Priess or no priess, nobody gunna feel sorry for me like I was fallin to pieces and ole. It's only justice, I guess the priess figured. Again, the land rather be worked. Anybody knows the ground rather be worked than be neglected to the canes and deers.'

'The ground likes to be worked and moved around,' Evvie said. 'The ground enjoys to be hoed.'

'Sure.'

'Sure.'

'Smell the lilies!' Mrs. Crochet exclaimed. 'They jiss as pretty as they smell. God dog it, that been a rock in my shoe all the time, that smell! I dunno why people ain't smelled them before, the busybodies. Topal, you got the tablecloth?'

'Yes, but I don't see many blossoms open. Mostly buds. I told you the flowers were not ready to be broke off.'

'Never mind, there's plenny if you look good.'

No frost or storm could touch the rows of Easter lilies hidden here. All around the plot of lilies was a solid wall of canes higher than a man could reach. In the moonlight the waist-high lily stalks were stately, bristling wet. The masses of buds and trumpet blossoms were dazzling white.

'Mon Dieu, if my Papa coulda saw this!' Mrs. Crochet said. 'If that ain't a pitcha! Don't touch them yet, you all. Mama gunna sit down and ress and look at them.'

'Less us all look at them!' Evvie said. 'Sit down, Topal!'

'For goodness' sake!' Topal said. 'This time of night? I could sleep till times get better.'

'It makes a pitcha for sure, and I'm proud,' said Mrs. Crochet. 'We oughta all be proud. Only the thing I ask Almighty God is for a big-big piece of ground some day to raise plenny lilies some day, out by the road where people can see them insteada hiding them like damn culprits and criminals and thief-sneaks always bird-dogging through the canes while others is dreaming in their bed.'

'I'm proud as anything,' said Evvie.

'You better be, damn it! Both of you all better be proud and remember this night when I'm layin in the cemetery when this whole Margin gunna be fulla lilies when the people get sense.'

Mrs. Crochet's fingers rummaged the soil. She clutched a handful of the soil. She rubbed the black mealy earth between her palms, sifted it through her fingers. She trailed her fingers through the loose ground, thinking. Her eyes were dark and fierce and glassy, her jaw hung loosely, as in the middle of some terrible word. Evvie smelled a pinch of the earth. The harsh black soil had been laid down here in the Delta by the river. The river had brought it from the states of the North, laid it here like a present for those who would come.

'Get your lazy behinds up off the ground!' Mrs. Crochet barked. 'Less start breaking flowers. Break only the ones that's open all the way, now!'

They went down the long rows gathering the lilies, snapping them from the tops of the stalks while they slapped the angry mosquitoes from their faces. Each formed a bag of her dress to hold the flowers. The great blossoms were chilled and crisp, spread open as widely as they could, in order to show their whiteness to the night, to cast out their cordial fragrance to tempt the fickle moths. The purpose of breaking the flowers was to give added strength and size to the bulbs in the ground. In Grass Margin there was no market for blossoms. Bulbs could be sold to city florists for forcing. Mrs. Crochet had been years building up this stand of lilies from ten bulbs given to her by a friend six years previously.

'All the little white babies in the canes!' Evvie said. 'Mama, they're just like little white babies looking at the moon!'

'They mess you up like babies,' Topal said. 'All this old pollen dropping all over my dress.'

'Mama, if we get that property of Shoepick's — *if* we get it — then you can raise big crops of lilies right out in the open.'

'I don't know anything about any property.'

When they finished, the tablecloth was piled full, and still thousands of unopened buds remained on the stalks. Mrs. Crochet gathered the corners of the tablecloth and slung the bundle on her back. 'Walk behind me, you all. If any drops, pick them up so we don't leave traces. What we gunna do, we gunna come back a few days from now and break off some more that's open.'

It was hard going through the thick canes. The bundle on her back was larger than Mrs. Crochet. Mosquitoes were biting her legs to the knees. The three crossed the bridge. The mother staggered over like a spider with its huge egg-sac on its back.

'Let us take the bundle now, Mama,' Evvie said. 'It's too heavy.'

'Who? Too heavy for who?'

'You worked all day.'

'Eh bien! How many time I didn't carry oranges when I was a girl and other kind of stuff in the night! In City Price we broke oranges by the moon regular. My sisters and Eunice Saucier and plenny other girl. I forget. Look like they had more moonlight in olen time. You talk about we used to work! Ask Papa. When he come dragassing up the road to see me, I was always busy, busy. How many time that boy didn't haul off and pack cucumber by the lantern and the schooner waiting by the wharf when me and him was sweet-heartin for the Chicago Produce Market! Nobody never saw me and my fella sitting on the wharf half of the night getting too familiar and mopping out one another's throat and so on, like the girls these days when they was work to do and big-big families to raise like people had in olen time. No indeedy! My mother had fourteen chirren.'

Topal said, 'Six of them died. That's the way it was.'

'And eight of them lived! Eight strappin chirren, taking the strank of the ones that died, like. You remind me of the ones that died. When I was a girl, they nailed up and buried your kind.'

Evvie thought, 'When tonight will be olden times I'll say, "I always helped my mother. She confessed about planting lilies in another person's canes. Just before I joined this Order, we got a lot of money. We carried the doorsteps to the new house, and we planted our bulbs along the levee. There were no more smell-melons by our bay-gall, and Papa sat on the porch with a palmetto fan all pink and gray, fussing about too many kinds of vegetables on the table." '

Topal followed her mother to the kitchen, where Commodo

was sitting on the floor with the radio ear-phones on his head.

'How you feel, Pa?' Topal asked him.

'Who? I feel good as new. Move out my light.'

They stepped out of the light and watched him. With a pair of rusty orange clippers he was cutting at the skin of his bare heel. His wife sat beside him. Commodo's undershirt was open. Coils of hairy fat hung around his middle. 'Me, I'm cutting aloose the careless flesh from off of the bottom of the back of my heels,' he explained. He snipped off a fragment of skin, rolled it between his fingers, dropped it on a piece of paper near-by.

'I'll show you some careless flesh,' said Mrs. Crochet, unlatching her own shoes.

Commodo said, 'Proud flesh bunched up behind the heel burns like ole hell walking the road.'

'I'll show you some corns. Take a look at this.' Mrs. Crochet's foot was finely veined, small and white, like a girl's. There were corns and a bunion.

'White like a quail-egg, the pore little ole foot,' said Commodo. He bent over and placed a kiss on the white instep. Mrs. Crochet slapped him.

'Look my feet how ugly,' said Topal.

'She wunts you to kiss hers too,' said the mother. 'I used to have pretty feet, me, whilst I was carrying my shoes down the road to the dance. Your Papa used to hide with them boys to tie knots in the weeds to trip us and see our legs rolling down the levee that time. Every Friday night.'

'She wants to talk about olden times today,' Topal said.

'Sure!' Commodo said. 'She's happy we gunna be owning our own home. Sassy toes!' He smiled at his wife.

Topal pulled up her dress and examined her legs to the thighs. She suddenly remembered her round shoulders and straightened them.

'Philip was in that gang of bad boys,' said Mrs. Crochet. 'He was a limb, the prettiess one, and the worsess one for bringing fiddler crabs to Benediction and all like that, him and Mitch Holt. That Philip! Look how ugly he is today, so ole and church-eyed and brocky-faced and discouraged. And jiss think, Tawny Ludrovich is got two boys in the Navy. Who else, Duck? Edwin Jeanfreau. Claudie Allen. Poor Claudie Allen that got drownded in the river with his load of oysters. He had on hipboots and couldn't swim when a ship upset his pirogue. That's one boy the river shouldna got. After he got drownded his grammaw would lean on the persimmon tree by the levee and call us every day when we pass from school. "Lil girl! Oh, lil girl! Any you all see Claudie Allen up the road?" Claudie had a boil on his bottom before he got drownded. His grammaw been tending to it. When we pass from school she would stand there with her box of sulphur salve, looking for Claudie and he was drownded. She turn childish.'

Commodo discarded another bit of heel-skin, and removed his ear-phones. 'This world, the next, then the fireworks,' he said.

Mrs. Crochet studied her bare foot. 'When a person dies, their feets lay kinda sideways, the same as sleeping, except if you got a paralytic stroke they straighten out tight like you been dancing. That's what I'm gunna die with, I think. Paralytic stroke, half of me at a time like poor Papa. But he wasn't scared a bit, taking Extry Munction. I heard him tell the priess, he says in French out of the good side of his mouth: "Father, my leff side done gone arready. Is it too late," he says, "to confess you the things my leff hand stole when I was young and the girls it squeezed?" Always a joke, him. He keppa axin if half his soul done took the road to Purgaterry. Wasn't that a way to die?'

'Your father was a fine, treacherous man,' said Commodo.

'It was funny to him. His leff side done arready gone. Him and Claudie Allen's up in heaven tonight, Duck.'

There was a knock on the back door. A voice outside called Evvie.

'It's Elna Jeanfreau, I think,' Evvie whispered to her father.

'God dog it to hell!' Commodo muttered. 'They wunt me to work tomorrow, I bet.' Commodo was at this time working on some ditching for Pierre Durot. The Durots and the Jeanfreaus were bitter enemies.

Commodo went to the back door and elbowed Evvie aside. 'Come in, Elna, honey,' he said. 'They ain got no etiquette aroun here.'

Elna was a tall young girl clad in overalls, bright-eyed and freckled. She said, 'Mr. Commodo, my father say could you please shovel him a ditch tomorrow before the rain in the kumquat grove because you know that ground good, he say.'

'Sweedart, not the way I feel now,' Commodo answered.

'He say he can get somebody else, but he like you to do the work.'

'Me, I been in bed with the doctor. He got me on a dite. I'm dizzy. I'm out of breath. I'm langrid. My pults are beatin fass.'

'Papa say we gunna butcher a nanny-goat tonight.'

'Well . . . I dunno if I can work, me, the way I feel langrid now, tell him. I'll leave him know in the morning.'

'He wunts to know tonight.'

'He's on a dite!' Mrs. Crochet called from the next room, where she was on her knees saying her night prayers. 'He can't eat goat no more.'

'That's a shame,' Elna said. 'We got lovely crabs too. We got oysters from a new reef. We got plenny-plenny curlyflower, and Papa say Killy's patchin the oven to bake a pudden tomorrow, he say.'

'Tell him I'll leave him know.'

When Elna passed under the front window, Mrs. Crochet, who was kneeling by the window saying her rosary, said loudly: 'They wait till they kill a goat to give him a job of work. Fix the oven! Choke the goat! Mister Commodo's coming to work tomorrow!'

'Say, you!' Commodo roared. 'Are you saying your prayers or castratin your neighbors which in there?'

Mrs. Crochet came into the kitchen holding the rosary. She said, 'Me, I'm getting sick of people battlin over you, fightin each other to feed you tell it's coming out of your ears.'

'Ain't you a fine-lookin wife to take charge of my big house if I get it?' Commodo asked.

'Go to hell!'

Commodo turned away. He said, 'Better you'd put away that holy rosary, or else back up to the crucifix and hold it over your nasty mouth.'

'Better you'd feed my mouth and bring me some pudden and curlyflower some time and the ress of your hungry chirren. Get outa my sight.'

'Who?'

'You! You selfish, overgrown marsh-boar. I wish I was a Protason so I could tell you what I'd like to tell you tonight. Get outa my sight before I kick you, some place!'

'Who? Kick who?' Commodo uttered a great laugh.

Mrs. Crochet aimed a vicious kick at her husband. 'I'll make you langrid!' she cried. Commodo danced lightly away, taking the pose of a confident boxer, and laughing derisively. She stamped after him, cursing in French, trying to scratch and kick at the same time. With a kind of joyful light in her eyes, she swung the rosary. It whistled through the air, and the beads struck her husband across the face.

'Mama, the rosary!' Evvie cried.

Commodo looked at his wife, his mouth hanging open. 'Awright,' he said. 'Hit me with the sacred rosary.'

Mrs. Crochet spun around, and bursting into tears, stamped out to the front porch and sat on the swing.

Commodo walked out of the house to the rickety little wharf. Topal was throwing the last of the Easter-lily blossoms into the river. The water was invisible, marked only by the long chain of blossoms borne off in pale clots.

'The turtle doves been billing and cooing?' Topal asked.

'Me, I can't stand this any more,' Commodo said.

'Take it easy, Pa. Look, I been throwing them slow, one by one.' She flung another flower. It curved through the starlight, struck the water, and was hurried away, a blurred spot retreating. 'You blame me for being glad I didn't get married?' Topal asked.

'Nobody never tole me you was glad, you.'

'Well, I am.' The vast dark stream traveled hurriedly, but with barely a sound. A brightly lit Coastguard cutter creeping upstream on the opposite side groped along the river's ragged sleeve, searching for bootleggers hauling liquor from a schooner outside. 'While we're talking, let me tell you something, Pa. I want to go to town and see if I can get in Woolworth's.'

'Maybe when they light candles by my feet.'

'Okay, then. I'll be twenty-one in seven more months.'

Topal went inside. Commodo followed presently. On the front porch he leaned his shoulder on the post near where his wife sat in the creaking swing. He stood rubbing one bare foot across the other, staring into dark space. 'Me, I dunno how to courage you when you nervous,' he said. There was no answer. Sounds came from the house next door — someone clubbing a sack of dried shrimp on the floor, a squealing phonograph, a chair dragged. The Coastguard cutter's waves were heard coming ashore.

A thin and nimble shape skipped down the levee embankment and stopped in lanky silhouette against the purple sky, then crossed the front yard stealthily. It was Arthur Crochet. He was carrying a paper bag full of squids. His mother was especially fond of squids. The porch swing creaked. Arthur advanced toward the swing.

'Ma.'

The porch swing was still.

'Ma.'

Commodo grumbled, 'What you sneakin around this house about?'

'Nothing.'

The bag of squids tumbled through the dark and fell on the porch with a soft plop. The figure in the yard moved across the grass and mounted the levee in quick leaps.

'Hipplecrite!' Commodo bellowed.

6

SEE THE BIG RIPE ORANGE

HAVING SENT part of the money earned in the rice field to the mail-order house for a name-pin made of gold wire, Evvie went to the post office every afternoon to wait for the mail truck. The poisonball tree before the post office had not been burned by frost; and now, sprouting thickly, it cast a pale shade where passersby could stop to lounge.

Tayo Delacroix, the local barber, who had been Topal's fiancé, lately had taken to noticing Evvie. He came every day at mail time and sprawled under the tree near where she sat until the truck arrived. To the same tree he tied the mule he had named after her sister.

'What gunna be written on the pin you sent for?' he asked, pecking nonchalantly at the grass with his pocket-knife, 'Evvie, or Evvie Crochet, which?' He had shifty black eyes that avoided hers. He was a distant marriage-relative of her mother's.

'Evvie,' she said. 'Just Evvie.'

The clotted patches of driftwood in the river glinted in the sun as they swiftly waltzed past, and Evvie's eyes followed them moodily. The barber, pretending not to care whether she answered or not, would go on asking pointless or impudent questions, pecking at the grass, looking always elsewhere when he spoke. Evvie hoped the name-pin would come today. It would be made of fourteen-carat gold, the catalogue had said — her name in gold. She thought it would be nice to wear such a pin, because ships wore their names on their breasts.

'Do Topal cry for me?' the barber asked, flipping his cigarette into the air. Evvie turned and glared at him.

'Don't get mad,' he said.

'Who's mad?'

'Do she?'

'No.'

'Did the ole house fall down yet?'

'No.'

'Don't invite too many people to the fish frys. It might fall on them.'

Evvie saw Dave Tobin shuffling up the road with a pair of pants from the pressing shop swinging on a hanger. Her thoughts brightened to see his ugly amiable face. Her mind saw the lovely doorsteps nailed on Shoepick's house, which Mr. Tobin's loan would buy for her people.

He stopped and flung himself down near her. He spoke in a low tone the barber could not hear. 'Up above where the road's paved, fiddler crabs and snakes are mashed on the concrete. It's thick with them, the road, cooking in the sun. They smell good. This morning riding the truck we rolled over a snake, a cottonmouth moccasin. The wheel slapped him up in the air, and he fell right in the driver's lap, old Bergeron. He was too scared to stop the truck or anything. But the snake was dead. Rolled over and dead. Wasn't that something?'

'I mean.'

'Listen, I never come back to see your folks because I'm on the night shift now.'

'Sure.'

'Tell Papa I ain't forgotten him. My pay day's next Wednesday. I'll bring him the money, tell him.'

'I'll tell him. Thank you. I've been thinking and thinking about that big house, Mr. Tobin. All of us have, I guess.'

'Aw, shucks!'

Tobin did not know what else to say. He sat holding the blue serge trousers on the hanger. The barber on the other side of the tree was examining him. Tobin always got his hair cut up the road in Lacroix. Tayo spat. He looked very mean and lonely.

Tobin took a rolled paper from his pocket. It was a panoramic photograph of a line of men standing beside one another. 'This was taken at Freeport Sulphur plant,' he said, showing the picture to Evvie. 'See if you know anybody there.'

Evvie pointed. 'This is you!' she said. 'The first one.'

'Keep looking all the way.'

Evvie studied the picture. Suddenly she cried out with delight. 'But the last one is you, too!' She couldn't believe her eyes. 'It must be a twin brother, I guess.'

Tobin laughingly told her about the trick. First he had stood first in the line on the left. Then, after the camera lens had snapped his picture and passed on, he had run around the camera and stood last in the line, where the camera had taken his picture again.

The barber pecked at the grass, his scowl deepening. 'Keep quiet, Topal!' he said to the mule.

Evvie looked at Tobin and smiled tentatively. She said, 'I heard you punching your punching-bag last night. It was late.'

'That was this morning,' Tobin said. 'Four-thirty, about. Yeah. But you were not awake so early. You're a early bird.

I reckon they can hear my punching-bag across the river nearly, and that's because the shed's got a tin roof, no doubt. I hope I don't disturb all the neighbors.'

'Topal woke me up coming to bed,' Evvie said. 'Sometimes she writes letters all night to her Pen Pals in different towns away from here. Don't tell her I told you. She told one of them her father is a retired commodore, and it's not true. Papa used to be captain of a little bitsy towboat. The Pen Pal names cost her one cent each. Some sort of club they have. She sent somebody another girl's picture for her own. She thinks she's ugly, Topal. Don't tell her.'

'She's not ugly. She looks kind of like you.'

Evvie gazed down the road, her eyes wide, her face lost in perplexity. 'I shouldn't have told you about those Pen Pals,' she said.

'Don't you worry I'll repeat it. Not a secret you trusted me with. Is your mother glad? Is she happy about that-there property of Shoepick's?'

'It's hard to make my mother glad,' Evvie said. 'She won't talk about the property. I don't think she believes it yet.'

'I like your mother,' Tobin said.

'Thank you.'

They were talking in tones lower and lower. The barber had moved closer to them, trying to hear. A two-wheeled dumpcart was approaching down the road, moving with a very slow jog, like a seesaw. The Negro driver was lying on the seat crossways, dozing. The cart was loaded high with freshly cut orange-tree branches.

'Mr. Stanjovich is thinning his orchard,' Evvie explained. 'He's cutting down lovely big trees, every other tree.'

'Why?'

'Orange trees around here are too close together, and they

grow into one another. In olden times when they were planted, there wasn't enough drained ground to plant them far apart, just a narrow strip along the levee. Look! One of those branches still has a lovely orange on it. See the big ripe orange!'

Slowly the old dumpcart swayed toward them. On top of the pile of branches near the rear, a single bright orange dangled, one that the fruit pickers had missed. Evvie, Tobin, and Tayo the barber all watched the dangling orange. When the dumpcart was passing by, one of the wheels struck a deep hole in the road. The whole load shifted, and the branch bearing the orange fell to the road.

Tobin said, 'Wait, I'll get you the orange,' and jumped to his feet. At the same time, the barber got up and sprang for the branch in the road.

Both men reached the fallen branch at the same time, and together stooped and took hold of it, then stood up. They looked into each other's eyes with their eyebrows lifted, surprised. Neither let go. The barber was almost as tall as Tobin, and heavier.

'Leave go,' he said.

'I want this orange is all,' Tobin said, smiling.

'Never mind, Mr. Tobin!' Evvie called.

Tobin, holding on, reached with the other hand to pluck off the fruit. 'I'll just take this for the little girl,' he said.

The barber jerked the branch toward himself. Tobin looked at him, his smiling face growing sober. 'Now listen . . .'

They stood facing each other. The barber spat sideways through a crack in his teeth, his lip lifting and closing like a camera shutter. Two boys, one white and one black, skipped out of the post office and came running. The white boy edged near, put his head on the side, and looked up into

Tobin's face with one eye closed against the sun. An oil man driving down the road stopped his automobile and turned off the key. The block of ice on his front bumper began to make a pool in the road.

Evvie did not know what to do. She glanced anxiously up and down the road. She felt as if she were waiting for a cannon-cracker to explode. The postmaster came out of his building and watched, shading his eyes. Other people gathered. Walking backwards slowly, Evvie withdrew from the circle of tight stillness engulfing them all, toward the house next door where the voices of children at play came:

> Heavy, heavy hangs over your head,
> What shall I do the redeemer,
> Fine or superfine?

Tobin began pulling the branch and the barber toward him, hand over hand. Tayo jerked. There was a thorn in the wood, and it gashed Tobin's thumb. He lost his temper and yanked the branch around sideways, swinging the barber off his feet. He broke off the fruit and tossed it to Evvie. It went between her hands and struck her chest, and rolled down the embankment. The barber, sitting in the shell road, reached into his hip pocket.

'Take it easy!' the man in the automobile called.

Tobin spun around. Tayo had something white in his hand. 'Texas bastard, come on!' he said. Evvie was running for home, her head between her shoulders and her dress popping in the wind. She took a curve in the levee yelling for her father, and like a streak she passed the gaily painted dumpcart, on which the Negro lay, still dozing . . .

Tobin smiled, opening and closing his fists, walking away from the barber. 'Hell's far. The little girl wanted the orange,' he said over his shoulder. 'What's the matter with this fellow, anyhow?'

Tayo followed Tobin, inching sideways toward him with his legs spread widely, the weapon held behind him. 'Come on,' Tayo said. 'Come on, you Texas Protason bastard, coming down here taking our jobs and monkeyin with our girls. Come on, you big mudda ——'

'Tayo!' shouted the postmaster through cupped hands. 'He'll kill him!'

Tayo leaned backward to swing. The white object cracked against the side of Tobin's face, and rolled over the road. It was a marble slab about an inch thick, cut in the shape of a heart, such as grateful petitioners place at the feet of saints' statues in church. The point of it was broken off and worn. On its face in gold letters was the word *Merci*. Tayo recovered the missile and placed it back into his pocket. He glanced at Tobin lying in the road with his hands stretched out and one leg flopping, then he walked toward the post office. Suddenly he broke into a wild gallop, looking backward as he passed the post office.

When Commodo and Evvie arrived, Tobin was sitting against the trunk of the tree holding a wet handkerchief to his ear, and a chunk of ice in his hand. His eyes were glazed. His ear was crushed and bloody. Commodo and the oil man brought Tobin to his boarding place in the car.

Tobin did not go to work that night. He lay on his bed in boarding place until dusk, with a pan of wet cloths beside him and a box of aspirin. At dusk, he dressed and went down the levee road. His left ear was swollen in the shape of a bluish bag. The Crochets were gathered on their front doorsteps. Tobin waved his hand, but did not stop.

'I make a bet he's gone, him, after that Tayo again,' said Commodo.

He went inside and put on his coat, then followed Tobin down the road.

'Remember, you got no insurance!' Mrs. Crochet called after him.

Paul hopped up and down. 'Oh, Gussaaaay!' he called. 'Come less us go see the fight! Big fight, Gussie!' Gussie came running.

Mrs. Crochet said: 'Here, here! Come back! Go back in the yard and fight that woodpile before I mauldrag the daylights outa somebody!'

Gussie began to cry, and to beat the side of the house with his cap. Paul threw himself to the ground and kicked. 'I wunna see the fight! I wunna see the big fight!'

'I bet I'm gunna pull somebody's eyes out and tie them together,' said Mrs. Crochet.

Evvie went to bed early, and she tossed in her sleep and dreamed. The flag had blown off its staff in front of the high school, and was slowly floating through the air high above her. She thought she was trying with great exertion to pursue and recover the flag, striving to shout for help, lugging her impeded feet through bogs full of an itchy and gummy substance. She reached a field planted to okra, the stalks rising taller than she. Hemmed in by long pointed okra pods that glittered like javelins and brushed their fiery, stinging hairs across her face and hands, she pressed through the thicket until she heard someone following. It was Tayo Delacroix, the barber, walking toward her with the flag in his arms. He was dark and shining, as though his body had been oiled, and he wore a hat that was a small, red-tiled roof. He began to chase her through the okra thicket, trying to throw the flag over her. As he drew near her, she tripped and sprawled. Then she awoke.

She heard her father talking to her mother. He was walking about the room. He came into the front room in search of something. Under his heavily thudding bare feet, the vases and the window-panes rattled. He went into the next room and settled into bed with one of his great yawns, which could have been heard out on the levee.

'Mr. Tobin, him he don't know these people around here,' Mrs. Crochet was saying. 'You know something? Some of these people is bad, yes. Making a fight over a orange. That Tayo been lookin for trouble all his life. Tell me what else.'

'I tell you tomorrow,' said Commodo, yawning again. 'Me, I been dragassin around sense early this evenin.'

'Tell me the ress, durn you.'

'Who you durnin? Who you durnin?'

'Go way. It's only in the night time you love me.'

'Who?'

'You dunno nothin about love, you.'

'Why I wunna talk about love when I got you?'

'Tell me the ress about the fight, Duck.'

'I done tole you Mr. Tobin's all right, if he don't get kilt before Wednesday's pay day. They dragged him to bed in Zhule's house, and Zhule fix him a cot, and he's restin. He won't wunna fight tell tomorrow no more, anyhow.'

'I hope he pulled off that Tayo's ears.'

'Tayo got a busted mouth. His mama come and get Tayo. She takes up for him, same as you with that sassy Arthur Crochet.'

'A tree shades its own ground. Tell me the ress, how it happened.'

' ... So Mr. Budrovich was sittin in the barber chair, him, talkin about that sheep milk. They use sheep milk in Europe where he come from to make cheese in Dalmatia. Tayo was jiss finish cutting his hair, and he was combing them. Firss thing you know, Tobin come and call Tayo outside, and they begin punching one anudda. Me, I separated them apart.'

'That was your juty.'

'They come bussin together finely again. I tole Nick Badeau I say, "Go see where's the Justice quick!" They was beatin one anudda around the road, and Mr. Tobin, him he knows how to box-fight good. But Tayo knocked him in the ditch, and he laid there a minute, then he got up and made for Tayo, and guess what Tayo done. He kicked him.'

'God bless!'

'He was crawlin around the road with his tongue way out, Tobin. Slow like wounded otter.'

'I don't wunna hear no more.'

'It ain much more to hear. Zhule put a ice bag on it, and then the doctor come. When I leff Zhule's, Tobin was ready to go after him again. He's gunna do it, too.'

'There goes your sixty dollar,' Mrs. Crochet said.

'Don't be so rancid. Tobin gunna lass tell Wednesday, Duck.'

7

I LET OUT ON PAPA'S PANTS

EVVIE WORKED for an afternoon in the orange grove of Mr. Willy Stanjovich, helping to pick the last of his orange crop. Working with her were several white and mulatto girls, all dressed in denim pants and bright blouses, climbing in and out of the sunny trees with their canvas bags on their shoulders. The mulatto girls all wore large hats to prevent the sun from darkening their complexion.

The girl in the tree next to Evvie called: 'Here come Tayo wid his barber-bag!' She was a plump mulatto about seventeen, with large flabby breasts hanging over the tree branch. Evvie leaned out to see Tayo the barber entering the grove from the levee, swinging his bag. His little fox terrier trotted around smelling the trees.

The other girl said, 'Him, he godda come evvy Monday to shave Mr. Willy's ole sick paw up in his baid. He chodge fo bits to shave sick man and five dollar for dead man. He walk a long way to shave him alive because pretty soon he gunna shave him dead. Oui! Dawn leave him see me, Evvie, because he gunna try and tease me lak all the time, dat crazy foo.'

'I don't see you trying to hide,' Evvie said.

Tayo's arrival caused a commotion. From all over the

orchard, plump dark faces peered through the leaves, white teeth flashed. An orange was playfully thrown at Tayo, then another. Presently a rain of fruit was bouncing through the ferns and spiderwort on the ground, amid a chorus of laughter. Evvie laughed, too. The wind was rocking her tree, an icy breeze from the river's surface, which was frigid from northern snows.

The barber swaggered to the tree next to hers, and looked up at the mulatto girl. 'Eh là bas, sweedart!' he called. 'You wunna clip them orange nice, you hear?'

'Go sid on a tack, you!'

'Why you never come let me shave under your arms yet, Vanilla?'

'You go way, you Mr. Tayo! I'm busy!'

Tayo made a great business of avoiding Evvie. She peeped and saw there were unhealed scratches on his face. The other girl pretended to be busy clipping oranges, but her dark heavy-lidded eyes were dull with lust. Her flame-colored blouse, her sleekly greased hair in the cordial smell of orange blossoms, gave her the look of a drowsy tropical bird. Evvie was angry with the barber. She watched him walk off without a glance at her — the supple working of his densely packed shoulder muscles, the light careless placing of his feet, the cocky joy of the dog bounding behind him. Evvie would have liked to write Tayo's name on a blackboard over and over, for the pleasure of rubbing it out.

On his way to the house, Tayo turned to smile at the oranges pelting the ground about him, and his gold teeth gave off wicked sparks. He turned again, shouting, 'You all come get a ride in my new barber chair some time! White like a bath-tub! It raise up and down wid a foot-pump! I give you a nice ride!'

'Me, I bring my minnie-cat and make her be bad on your chair!' one of the girls yelled. Screams of laughter rang through the swaying trees.

Later on, Evvie descended her ladder to dump her fruit and get a drink of tamarind water which the cook had made for the workers. Climbing down out of the sun, standing under the tightly interlocked branches, the girl was in a strange gloomy region. The light, reflected from patches of soil somewhat whitened by newly spread fertilizer, was an unearthly damp gray. The gnarled groined tree trunks, swollen almost to bursting with sap, marched in straight columns in all directions.

When she had taken a drink of tamarind water, she went around the house to the cistern. She was surprised to see Dave Tobin lingering there. He had come in unseen from the rear road. Evvie walked toward his khaki back, the freckled red neck and red hair, the surgical plaster bunched over his left ear. When he turned around, she saw a large bruise on his nose, and one side of his lips swollen.

'Good evening,' he said through his puffed lips.

'Good evening.'

He reached over and poured her a drink of water. 'We going to get some warm weather,' he said.

'I guess so.'

'Soon, anyhow.' He was turned away, looking through the leaves at the sky. He smelled of bitter medicine, no odor of sulphur now. Evvie thought of the barber in the house so close, and she was afraid.

'I come to buy a shipping of fruit for my mother, to send her by mail,' Tobin was saying. 'In spring she loves the fresh oranges, unwrapping them and putting them in a bowl like they do. So much better than our Valley stuff, the Creole fruit is. I lay they're fixing to bust the ground for cotton back home about now ... You all couldn't raise cotton here. I think it would bear all leaves, no good squares for cotton like at home. But you might plant some for the looks of the flowers, watch the flowers change their colors. My folks back home raise mostly cotton and cattle and melons.'

'Does your face hurt?' Evvie asked.

'Some.'

'Gee.'

'That fellow don't fight fair, Miss Crochet. It's not right the way he did me.' Tobin's face was creased in puzzled wrinkles.

'Listen, you didn't come here for oranges,' she said.

He turned his bruised smile upon her, and answered in a mild, half-guilty way. 'I come partly for that, anyhow. Honest.'

'You better go home, Mr. Tobin, and not be following that Tayo around.'

Tobin laughed. She observed that Tobin and Tayo the barber had the same kind of laughter.

Then Tayo was seen coming out of the house. Tobin walked toward the other man directly, carelessly dragging his squeaking sandals.

The barber's smile changed to a dark grimace. Willy Stanjovich emerged from the house. The Dalmatian blinked continually, twitched one side of his resin-colored mustache, and said, 'Now, now, boys, no start nodding on my place. Go outside on road, please.'

Tayo put his bag down, and shed his coat uncertainly. 'Son of a bitchin pole-vaulter,' he muttered.

Tobin slouched straight toward Tayo. The barber laid out the palms of his hands toward Stanjovich. 'You see him?' he said. 'The Texas bastard is following me around. He didn't get enough lass time. Keep him away from me. I tole you. Listen, you bastard, I dowunna hurt you.' Tobin drew closer. 'All right, you axed for it.'

Tobin caught hold of Tayo's swinging foot. 'You don't kick me this time, brother. You going to fight fair.' He swung his fist, and the barber staggered.

Evvie crouched behind a tree, her fingernails between her teeth, the other hand beating the tree trunk. She gave all her attention to the barber, who was sobbing as he danced behind his dark lifted fists. His head was drawn down between his shoulders. His eyes sparkled out of this shell like a hungry snapping-turtle's. The fruit pickers in their tinted blouses were scrambling out of their trees.

Sometimes the men wove about each other softly and slowly, and in the unnatural gray glare among the twisted trunks spotted with vivid green blotches of algae, they waded through the hairy ferns and waving dasheens as though under water — eye-sockets wild, laboring for breath, gasping, drowning. Then they would leap into swift action that could hardly be followed by the eye, and the silvery acrid dust of trampled fertilizer floated in wisps about their legs, and the thudding of their punches was a wonderful sound.

Tayo gave ground according to a plan. Most of Tobin's wild swings failed to land; but whenever one did the barber tottered backward with a low whinnying sound. Finally a loud smacking blow on the windpipe sent Tayo tripping and sprawling over a bright pointed mound of oranges beside the house. Fruit rolled out in all directions. Tayo wallowed in the oranges, stood up and slipped down, with Tobin on top of him punching away at his face.

Stanjovich was now sitting quietly on his doorstep watching

the action with a mildly critical eye, as though it were staged for his benefit. Tobin's face did not look much like a face. Evvie's stomach was sick, to see Tobin mechanically pounding on the barber.

Standing behind Evvie, the mulatto girl called Vanilla was shouting: 'Bite him, Tayo! Bite the bastard!'

'You shut up!' Evvie said.

The mulatto grabbed Evvie's arm and swung her round. 'Listen, God dog it, I rassle you right now, me!'

'Pick on somebody your size,' said Evvie with tears in her voice.

There was a sharp scream from one of the girls. Evvie turned and saw that Tayo was on his feet and running toward a chopping block by the rear of the house. Stuck in the block was a long oyster knife. Tayo jerked it out, and with the sobbing, whinnying sounds coming from between his teeth, he ran toward Tobin. Another shrill cry rang out somewhere. Tobin half-turned, quickly looking about for something on the ground. He put out his hand and ducked. Tayo was gouging his back with the knife. They grappled, and both fell. Tayo's hand holding the knife was pumping up and down, twisting and slashing. Stanjovich joined the fray. Evvie hid her eyes.

She watched them putting Tobin into the automobile. She ran and got him some water. He lay on the back seat. Both his eyes were swollen dark and pulpy, his nose and lips ran blood. A towel wrapped round his thigh was soaked. 'Thanks, folks. I'll be all right. I'll whip him yet. I'll do it yet. Thanks, Miss Crochet. Tell Papa I'll be seeing him.' She took the glass, and pulled the blanket closer about him. Her own eyes were inflamed with crying. Through the blur of tears she saw Tayo going down the road, dabbing at his arms and face with a handkerchief. His dog bounced jauntily

behind, followed by small boys jabbering in French. Somewhere a woodpecker was signaling to its mate on a dead tree:
Dut-ut-ut-ut-ut-ut!

Going home later, Evvie recalled the fight, the wonderful
sight of angry men striving to hurt each other's bodies, showing what men were really like, with their short hair and dark
secret pockets, and their wiry legs that knew which way to
jump without thinking. She thought of her strange dream
about Tayo the barber, and Dave Tobin's teasing. What did
Dave Tobin think or dream about here in Grass Margin, on a
peninsula far out in the sea? Tobin's people she imagined to
be gentle — tall and fair and humorous, moving among the
melons and their cattle on dry feet. She thought Tobin ought
to go back to the high climate and the neighborly people
he had sprung from. She felt herself identified with Tayo the
barber, with people like him, and she was miserable, because
it seemed proper.

She did not want to go home to break the news. She lingered on the road, but had to go at last. Reaching there she
walked through the house without a glance at the twins and
the baby playing on the floor, without looking at Topal and
her love-story magazine.

Her mother said, 'Look, darling, I done let out on Papa's
pants! Him, he don't like them. Ain't they nice now? The
doctor said they don't fit. How you like them?'

Commodo, twisting in front of the mirror, said, 'The backside look like a family of niggers moved out. Before hell, what
do you all take me for?'

'How much money did you make today?' Topal asked
Evvie.

'Not so much. We knocked off. They had another fight
in the grove, Tayo and Mr. Tobin again.'

Mrs. Crochet laughed sourly. 'That's the fine pole-vaulter was gunna lend your father the sixty dollar, and today's pay day and he never showed up here yet. That's a fine ticket, Mister Crochet. Your friend Tobin's a regular fighting-cock, the way it turns out now. You truss any stranger come along. I guess he was hunting the barber to pick on him again.'

'He hunted him to make him fight fair,' Evvie said.

'Don't get excited,' said Commodo. 'He gunna show up tonight. In udda words, that sixty dollar is practically in my pocket.'

'But he's hurt bad, I think,' said Evvie. 'Tayo stabbed him all over with an oyster knife.'

'Jesus, Mary, and Joseph!' Mrs. Crochet cried. 'Tayo! I hope and pray Arthur keeps away from that gang of gools Tayo goes with. They cut people up and steal ringbuoys from the lighthouse depot, and bootleg whiskey too.'

'Me, I'm taking a walk to see about this,' said Commodo.

'Listen, you better haul off and stay away from that!'

Commodo changed clothes in there, making a great racket with the warped drawers of a bureau upon which the roof had leaked. He came into the kitchen to wet his hair at the bucket. 'Where at's my hat?' he asked. He looked in the oven of the stove, but found it empty. This was the place he kept his hat to prevent ants from attacking it.

'How we know where's your hat?' his wife asked.

'You hid my hat. Where's it passed to, I ax you?' He turned around in circles. '*Where at's the damn hat?*'

Nobody answered.

Commodo wildly flung open the kitchen door. He stepped out and looked under the kitchen steps. They heard the crashing of various objects being yanked out and hurled over the yard. Presently he returned, crossed the room, leaned on the wall glumly. He looked steadily at Topal.

Topal said, 'I hope my tongue rots out with a eating cancer if I took your hat.'

'All right, damn it,' he said. 'I ain't worryin myself more sicker than I am about no money for a decent place to go on our big doorsteps before this one falls on us and a decent place to sit your behinds and screened windows. Nobody aroun here cares if we get Shoepick's place. I wash my hands in it. I wash my hands.'

'Don't forget under your arms,' Mrs. Crochet said. They all laughed. Commodo's face was turning purple.

Evvie said, 'Floors ought to be made like a parrot cage, so you could pull them out and dump them without sweeping.'

'You ought to be in a parrot cage yourself,' said Topal.

Commodo suddenly hurdled over the baby and dashed to the back door. 'Try to change the subjeck on me!' he yelled. 'I'll show you! I'm gunna go off without a hat, God dog it! I'll show you!' The back door slammed with a terrific bang. Everyone winced and glanced at the ceiling, expecting the kitchen to fall.

'Goddle mighty! Come back here!' Mrs. Crochet screamed. 'He's goin without a hat! Get him back!'

Commodo returned. Mrs. Crochet pointed to the miniature pantry in the corner. 'The firss time in twenny year he put his hat where it belonks, and he forgets about it.' Commodo opened the pantry door. This place was piled high with discarded shoes, all shapes and colors of worn-out shoes and boots and slippers. There was also a hatrack on which Commodo's derby was hanging. He grabbed it and walked out.

Later, Mrs. Crochet was pacing up and down the levee road, waiting for her husband, waving a grass mosquito-brush around her. In the evening the foggy willows were clotted like damp hair.

The twins were playing in the back yard, screeching and jumping about. Paul yelled: 'Looka me, Ma! I can move the house!' He had his hands on a corner of the old kitchen, shoving with all his strength. 'Looka me, Ma! It moves when I shove it!' Gussie ran over and joined his brother, and together they shoved.

Mrs. Crochet waved her arms frantically and screamed, 'Here, here! *My God stop it, you all!* YOU WUNNA SHOVE IT DOWN? Get away, before I hammer somebody to sleep! *Get away!*'

She clutched her pocketbook, and glanced anxiously at the darkening sky. She held her cheek in her hand and stared in the direction from which Commodo was supposed to come. A man riding a sled dragged by a horse passed by. '*Il est bon' heur!*' he said. 'Nice weather.' Mrs. Crochet said, 'Oui.' The runners of the sled squealed across the shells of the road. The man turned and looked back with a dark frown of concern.

Evvie came out of the house and walked toward the levee with feigned indifference, kicking at the grass and looking at the sky, and occasionally glancing furtively at her mother with her big serious eyes.

'What do *you* wunt?' Mrs. Crochet asked.

'Nothing.'

'Go make your lessons.'

'Mama, your grits are getting cold.'

'Me, I dowunna eat. I got no appletite.'

Evvie lingered, sitting on the side of the levee, pulling down her skirts, toying with a clump of bright flea-bane. She said, 'Papa hasn't been gone so very long, Ma. I guess maybe he's getting the money from Mr. Tobin and he hates to run off too quick.'

'I don't know nothin about no ole money. I come out for air.'

Evvie chewed a blade of grass and gazed across the yard at the front doorsteps, which always seemed to look prettiest at sundown. She said, 'I'd like us to get a big house before I go off to be a Little Sister of the Poor. Then I'd get to live in it a little while.' With her finger she drew lines in the air, blocking out the stout dimensions of a house above the doorsteps, and putting on an ample roof jutting out over the sides like a cool hat. 'I guess Papa will have to go to the courthouse to pay. I don't understand much about that.'

In a little while Commodo came walking alone down the winding road with his hands in his pockets, printed as a solitary black figure against the baleful green and crimson cracks in the gray sky.

'Ax him if he got the money,' Mrs. Crochet said softly to Evvie. She herself went and sat on a log. Commodo passed her by and walked down the levee slope toward the house.

'Papa, did you get the money?' Evvie called.

Commodo did not answer. He kicked an orange out of his path, and went on.

'Is that Tobin dead or dyin or what?' Mrs. Crochet called.

He turned his head and looked at her, then went on into the house. Mrs. Crochet did not follow him. She sat on a log beside the road for a long time. After the sun went down she walked into the house. Commodo was sitting on the back steps with his elbows on his knees. All the children were quiet, and the baby was quiet. Mrs. Crochet took from the stove the plate of grits they had saved for her. It had cooled and hardened. She carried it past her husband and out to the back yard. She scraped out the contents. Huey, the rooster, a very old fowl with thick scaly legs and only one tail feather, hurried across the yard with beating wings and wolfed the white lumps of grits in a few moments.

Evvie went to church with her parents. On the way, none of them said a word. Commodo had not spoken once since he had gone up the road to see about Dave Tobin. While they waited in church for the Way of the Cross to begin, Evvie could hear the boys gathered outside arguing about the fight in Stanjovich's orchard. The church was not yet fully lighted. Mrs. Crochet went up to a side altar, and kneeling, she dropped a nickel in the box and took a blessed candle and lit it. She said a prayer, asking God to try and keep her from having any more babies. Father Pendergast crossed before the altar, stopped and bent one knee, then passed. He glanced at Mrs. Crochet, and he frowned. She pretended not to see him. The priest had many times forbidden her to spend any money on blessed candles. 'You need your money,' he would tell her. 'Do you think Almighty God is a heel? He doesn't want your poor nickels. He wants you to eat well and be strong, and above all happy. Say an ordinary prayer in your pew. He'll answer it just as well.'

Mrs. Crochet scowled at the priest's receding back. She placed another nickel in the box, and lit another candle. Now she expressed another intention. 'Please Lord of Hosts, Keeper of the Reins and the Heart, Tree of Life, please, please hear my prayers and let us get the money some place before the river goes down and Perdu comes from the marshes to hole the meeting and pass the resolution to buy the property, and we can labor for You and raise our chirren right. Amen. And please dear Jesus take another intention, and I'll burn the candle next week for sure. Please dear Jesus make my husband's health get well. Amen. And please try and not make me conceive any more. Not even any misses for their mother to be their grave. Amen.'

On the other side of the church, the colored section, the Negro Shoepick's sister Juarelle was kneeling before a blessed candle she had lit, begging God to make Mr. Synoground in Chicago pay her brother something for his Chilblain Stomp, so that he could pay his back taxes and prevent the sale of their house before the river went down.

After the services when they were walking home, Evvie was thinking about Dave Tobin, and about the Shoepick property. She remembered the place, a large high house with the willows cleared away in front, giving a clear view of the broad river with the ships passing to and from New Orleans, and exposing the place to exciting eastern gales. It had a fine fence in front, the only fence in Grass Margin. And it had a tiny cracked doorbell which gave a frightened bleating sound whenever its tail was pulled.

The family continued plodding on in stony silence. Neither Commodo nor his wife had talked since leaving home. Evvie wished they would start talking.

'Papa, Delta means the Greek letter D,' she said. 'The Delta is really shaped like a D in Greek, isn't it?'

'I disremember.'

Other churchgoers straggled past. Automobiles sped by. Clouds of dust lit by glaring lights completely hid the people on the side path from one another. The flying shell grit was stifling.

Mrs. Crochet said, 'God dog it, look how that Bruce Holt drives that car! His parrents ought to be ashame to lend it to him to kill somebody. I say them automobiles is ruining the younger generation.'

'The younger generation is ruining the automobiles,' said Commodo.

Evvie thought of the fig trees in the front yard of the Shoe-pick place. They grew like plump green clouds huddled under larger white ones, and they threw grateful shade all summer long, and bore bucketfuls of tempting fruit.

Evvie braced herself inside, and asked boldly: 'Papa, are we going to get that money for the property, or not?'

'Leave him alone!' Mrs. Crochet barked. 'Don't beg him to tell us ef the Way of the Cross didn't soffen up his grouch.'

'I was just asking.'

'Don't you see he's got the moo-cows? He wuntsa keep it to himself, as if we're worried about the ole property. As if!'

Commodo said, 'A terrible thing done happened today. In udda words, they took Dave Tobin to the hospital in New Orleans. They don't expeck him to live, po fella.'

Mrs. Crochet vented the hard dry laughter that sounded like the croaking of castanets. 'Now where's your sixty dollar!' she crowed. 'Didn't I tell you I believe it when I see the money, you ole rangatang with your head-dreams?'

'Aw, go to hell.'

'Yah! Yah! Go head and curse right outa church in front of this chile that's gunna be a Sister, you heathen of a sour-stumick Indian! A hundred barren trees! Go clean out the ditches! Where's all your pretty head-dreams with the screened windows practically in your pocket, you stupid ass of a dinwiddie trussing any stranger come along with his buck teeth and his punching bag, trying to tangle me up in your crazy ——'

'Mama, the people,' Evvie said.

Mrs. Crochet swung round and waved her pocket-book in Evvie's white face. 'Listen, you wunt the how-they-call-it slapped outa you on this road?'

Evvie threw her arm over her face and cringed back into the weeds. She tripped and sat in the dusty grass.

Commodo hurried on ahead. When Evvie and the mother reached home, he was on the floor with the radio ear-phones on. Mrs. Crochet in the next room undressed angrily, flinging her girdle across the room and kicking her shoes into the air. In the kitchen she picked up a water glass, smelled it, poured a drink. 'Listen,' she announced. 'Tomorrow I'm going to work in the swimp factory.'

Evvie stood with her mouth open, plucking at her dress. Commodo took off his ear-phones. 'Can I please listen to my Strange As It Seems or not?' he asked patiently. 'It taken me twenny minutes to tune in.'

'No!' Mrs. Crochet screamed. 'No! Me, I'm sick and tired ——'

Commodo leaped to his feet and strode out the door. Presently he returned, and taking a lantern, lighted it and went out. They heard unusual sounds outside — noises in the back shed. Mrs. Crochet parted the curtains and peered anxiously through the window. A bucket was being filled at the cistern.

'What the hell and Saint John Burchman is the ole ranga-tang doin out there?' Mrs. Crochet asked.

Commodo came back into the house, yanked off his shirt and shoes, spitefully grabbed a towel, and stalked off.

'Papa, what are you doing?' Evvie asked.

Commodo turned. His eyes glared like gun muzzles. 'I'm gunna take a bath!' he bawled, looking at his wife venomously.

Mrs. Crochet was dumbfounded. She stammered, 'To-night?' But Commodo was gone.

'Temper,' said Mrs. Crochet. 'Him, he dunno what to do to spite me.'

Just then the baby inside began to cry. T. J.'s voice was as deep as a man's. Topal came from the front holding the baby, and placed him in her mother's arms. '*Shut up!*' Mrs. Crochet screamed. The baby yelled louder, beating on the mother's face. Mrs. Crochet turned distractedly, then hurried out to the back shed.

Commodo was naked. He grabbed the towel. Mrs. Crochet propped T. J. in the corner. 'Here's your chile,' she said. 'Take him. Mind him. Hush him up. Give him away. Throw him in the river.' She slammed the door so angrily that it bounced back open. Commodo crept from the tub to close it. T. J. kicked the floor and roared louder.

Commodo took his bath in a determined manner. He soaped his armpits spitefully, and worked up a fiercely seething lather on his chest hairs, ignoring the roaring baby.

Inside the house, Topal and Evvie were looking out of the window toward the back shed with troubled faces.

Commodo soaped his rag and reached high to squeeze it down his fat back. He slapped it over backward and up around under his arms, twisting convulsively, dodging, bending, grunting, and puffing while flakes of lather sailed all over the place. His noises were loud enough to be heard on the levee road. Very soon, the baby, watching his father's interesting movements and the huge squirming shadow on the wall, gradually stopped bawling and began to follow Commodo's movements with clear, staring eyes. With deep muttering growls, Commodo soaped his lower body ferociously. He bent over precariously in the little tub to scoop up water to rinse his legs. Standing up, he almost slipped, and regained his balance only by whirling his arms in the air.

'*Mmmmm!*' the baby said, frowning and stretching out a
hand.

Commodo muttered and spat and cursed. He got out of the
tub and squatted over it. He dipped the rag into the water
again and again to squeeze it over his body. 'Whew!' he blew,
partly through the nose, partly the mouth. '*Whew!*' The little
tub was cutting his flesh, and soap was in his eyes. He tried
to get up, but his feet slipped. He fell farther down into the
tub and remained wedged, kicking and swearing. In a rage,
with his burning eyes closed, he got out of the tub and groped.
Finding it, he raised it clear over his head and poured its contents over himself with a tremendous chugging, snorting, and
hissing. He groped for the towel.

'Ba-ba-ba-ba-ba!' cried the baby, slapping his hands
against the floor as he crawled toward his father.

While Dave Tobin lay between life and death, attended by a
surgeon employed by the sulphur company, the river was rising toward its seasonal peak. Soon, it would begin to drop.
Then, Emilien Perdu would return to hold the Drainage
Board meeting concerning Shoepick's property.

Mrs. Crochet tried to forget about property. Not Commodo. He watched the river swell, bringing great revolving
mats and islands of driftwood to pile up among the willows
of the shore. He waited on the levee early mornings for his
brother Dewey to pass the Margin piloting a ship. 'Dewey
gunna get a chance to lend me that money,' he cheerfully
told his wife. 'What you wunna bet I get that sixty dollar?'

'A bee went down Girlie Jeanfreau's bosom this mornin, and
she pulled off her dress in front of all the bean pickers,' Mrs.
Crochet answered.

One morning, Dewey Crochet went by, leaning on the

bridge rail of a rusty Greek tramp ship, waving to Commodo. Commodo, running along the levee, made frantic motions, beckoning with his finger, pointing to the house, then going through the movements of a man eating and drinking and hauling in a fish on a line. Dewey Crochet replied with a shrug. Then he tapped all of his pockets, and spread wide his empty hands. Commodo abruptly turned his back on the ship, and went into the house to forbid his children ever again to wave at Uncle Dewey passing on a ship.

8

WE GOT NO TROUBLES A DOLLAR
WON'T CURE

'PAPA, tell us a story, Papa!' Gussie begged one night.

The twins were straddled on their father's knees by the kitchen stove. Topal sat on a bench by the window minding the baby.

'Don't pester Papa when he's empty from being on a dite,' Commodo said. 'Be nice lil boys when Papa hungry.'

'Tell us about the mules!' Paul pleaded. 'Papa, the mules, the mules!'

Mrs. Crochet laughed by her dishpan. She looked at Commodo. His face was a dour, sagging cloud. He said, 'Papa done tole you about them mules.'

'Make him tell you again,' Mrs. Crochet said, 'how he loss his good job with the mules that time.'

'Heck, I'm tired hearing about the mules,' Topal grumbled.

'Mind that baby and don't listen,' said Mrs. Crochet.

'I'm tired minding the baby too. I'm like a prisoner and a slave around here.'

Commodo said, 'Everybody gotta cooperate around here tell I'm able to get Mama a nigger girl.'

'You got one right here now.'

'I got my eye on a good one up the road,' said Commodo. 'In udda words, it won't be long you gunna see Mama pounding the levee in dressmaker clothes. "Am I fat as the woman next door?" she's gunna be axin.'

'I'm young and I ought to be out,' said Topal. 'Soft-ball game at Port Sulphur. At Venice a dance. I saw a lugger pass in the river with a bass-drum on top.'

'Me, too, I oughta be out. But looka me minding these chirren for Mama, and so tired I could sleep tell times get better and I don't complain. Why? Because we got no troubles a dollar won't cure.'

'I'd like to know who's going to mind *my* babies and carry them to the clinic,' Topal said.

Commodo finished picking his teeth with a feather, and began his story, 'Well, when Papa was captain on the *Blessed Trinity*, Papa was without a license and always afraid for his job, because it was twenny-two dollar a week, and you and Paul and T. J. wasn't thinking about being born.'

'So they had a barge of mule. Big sugar mule, taking them down from New Orleans to Home Place for the levee contractor, fair current but a head wind in the river that day. A barge of mule and a head wind! The mule man in town say, "But they send me a barge too small for thirty head of mule!" He say, "Commodo." I say, "Sir." He say, "What you gunna do?" I say, "Load them up! Chase the mule aboard! In udda words, it's my business to take the mule down the river."'

Topal carried the sleeping baby inside, then she returned to her window-seat. The stars above the orange trees outside were spun into fine webs. Commodo's rocker croaked and croaked. 'We load them mule. It was tight fit. But the sides of the barge was not so strong, no, and me, I was scared all the way them mule would go overboard. But come to find out she took the swells nice all the way down apass Myrtle Grove.

So me, I tole the nigger Cake Lasalle, I say, "Wake me up ef
the wind change, Cake," and I laid down on the donkey breakfass and gone off to sleep, and that's where I done wrong. A
man can't never tell about a load of mule, you understand?'

'Yes, sir,' said Evvie, sitting on the floor with her face
lifted toward her father's. Gussie was now on the floor playing with a crawfish, and Paul was asleep in his father's lap.

'Your father paid heavy for that nap, him!' Mrs. Crochet
called from the next room.

'Me, I'm still payin, Duck!' Commodo called. He held
Paul close and rubbed his chin over the boy's hair, and
chuckled.

'Couldn't be trusted by the boss!' Mrs. Crochet replied.

'Hush up. I was tired, me, that morning. I was up the
night before to your poor Papa's wake.'

'Couldn't be trusted! Say like my poor Papa, "I wouldn't
truss you to watch a bucket of gull meat." Sleeping on a load
of mule. No wonder we got nothing today.'

'You gunna see what we'll have some day!'

'You been sayin that since the bayou had ice.'

'There they go again,' Topal said.

'You hush up, honey,' Commodo told his daughter.

'Are we got a home with the fussing and fighting since that
Tobin went to the hospital? I swear, I'm leaving here. You
watch.'

'I'm axin you to hush up, honey.'

'— and live in Lacroix and work in the shrimps and pass a
good time before I've got to settle down to something like
this in a boxwood shack with ferns growing in a chamberpot
and a pillow for a window-glass.'

'I'm beggin you to hush up,' said Commodo.

'Kick her out!' Mrs. Crochet called sleepily. 'Kick her out!'

'I'll go whenever you say! I can get in Woolworth's in town. Maybe I can get in other places.'

'Go tomorrow! Go tonight!'

'I'll go.'

'Go let Woolworth's mole your character, but don't come dragassin back in a week, you hear?'

Commodo grabbed his hair and roared, '*Jesus Christ, cut it out*, CUT IT OUT!'

There was a long dead silence. One of Gussie's crawfish on the floor flipped its tail. After a while, Commodo's rocker started gently to croak again. The terrible oath still pervaded the house. Topal sighed heavily, staring out of the window.

'Confess that!' Mrs. Crochet said in the next room. 'Confess it when you go to church, you hear?'

'Papa, the story,' said Evvie.

'Yes, I went to sleep!' said Commodo. 'I don't care who knows it. I was tired from poor grandpa's wake. My lips was chapped all the time, bleedin and peelin from the wind.'

'Something the matter with his blood,' Mrs. Crochet called.

'I used to couldn't smoke,' said Commodo. 'Ask Mama.'

'Or hardly kiss me in the winter time at all. Of course he never wants to kiss me much any more hardly, winter like summer.'

'Wait till I come to bed!'

'What else, Papa?' Evvie prompted.

'So one of them mule was a bad ole mule, been lookin at me up in the pilot house, studying up debment with the whites of his eyes. But he was always lookin at *me!* I say he didn't have no good qualities, no. I taken notice he was ole-ole, and faded green, like, and a slanty white scar on the rump from a fire or else a luckamotive, and they had all kindsa bob-wire godges on his hide from sneakin under fences, and sores on his lips from eatin rose bushes ... So while I was sleepin a big Morgan boat pass by, big stuck-up Morgan ship, and she made great big swells. Firss a couple small swells, then the three big one, Father, Son, and Holy Ghost. Son of a bugger! Me, I rolled off my donkey breakfass and hit the deck. Come to find out the barge was rockin and almost turn over from them swell. The damn Holy Ghost! That's the one crawled under the barge and lifted it high up as the sky nilly. Them mule was all slippin around. Firss thing you know a timber broke in the railing on the port side of the barge. Pretty good!'

'Confess that!' Mrs. Crochet called. 'Cursing the Holy Ghost.'

'He's cursing the swells in the river, huh, Papa?' Evvie said.

'Sure, sweedart. So that green mule, him he was a ringleader mule. He mix up with all the good mule, and watching me all the time with the whites of his eyes. All the mule start tremblin like a leaf, hoofs slippin around, and me and Cake hollin, "Whoa!" and all the firemen standing on the stern of that Morgan ship was laughing, them durdy buggers. That bad mule was shovin through the good mule, and lookin at me all the time. Then he went close to the water and look in the river. Then he look at me over his shoulder, and *tock!* — overbode he went. It taken him a long time to come up, yes. And he blown his nose and look up at me, and start swimmin for shore. *Tock!* Anudda mule overbode followin him! *Tock-tock!* Two more mule gone!

'Green was in the lead. Him, what he went and done, he laid down his ears for shore. *Tock! Tock-tock-tock!* All the ress of the mule dive in before we could jump on the barge and stop them. You talk about I was mad! It taken us all day and night to round up them mule on shore, and spend seven dollar renting ponies from the Filipinos at City Price and ropes. Some was in the rice and some in the canes and some bogged down way out in the floatin plairie, them mule.

'Now, they had a church at City Price. It was built on the ground in olen time. The green mule, him he keppa runnin around the church, and me behind him on a pony talkin sweet. I put my pride in my pocket. In udda words, *I* coaxed, *I* coaxed. Cake, him he come to help me catch the green mule. To head him off, Cake run around the back way and me the front. I meet Cake on his pony, I say, "Well, where at's the mule, Cake?" He say, "I swear, Cap, I believe he up on the roof!"'

'Will you jiss listen at that man!' Mrs. Crochet called.

'All the doors was closed, but Cake say, "Maybe he went in the church and close the door!"'

'Well, me, I rush in church, I say, "God dog it, whoa!" Come to find out he *was* in there! Well, it was colored Babdiss Church, but they had a confessional box, and that was a telephone booth floated down the river. Well, the green mule, he begin to stomp and back up tell he got his legs tangled up in the bell-rope, and the bell was ringing like I don't know what. Ba-long! Ba-long!'

Mrs. Crochet called from the next room, 'Every time he tells it he puts on more.'

'So the people thought the river buss the levee, and come running to fill the sandbags. Me, I walk up close with the bridle. That mule hauled off and backed up his behind right in the confessional box, beatin the floor and pullin the bell-rope untel the bell come aloose and fell down on his head. Then he jumped and buss through the crowd with the confessional box jammed tight over his backside and draggin the bell by the rope down the road, and ain't nobody seen him tell this day.'

'Shame on you, tellin false lies to the chirren!' Mrs. Crochet called.

'You don't know a mule, Duck!'

'Who don't, and Papa used them tell he died in his lovely rice to haul and plow? Who don't?'

Topal sighed and walked to the other window. Her red lips were curled thickly. She looked at her fingernails. She turned and walked out the back door. Evvie held her chin and looked at her father, her big eyes beginning to twinkle. She burst out laughing. She fell back on the floor, overcome with merriment.

Mrs. Crochet appeared, holding T. J. The baby was digging his fists into his eyes, winding up for a good cry. Mrs. Crochet reached over her head for the string of red peppers suspended from the ceiling. She broke off a pepper, and tore it in half. 'Fix the clinic milk, darling,' she told Evvie. 'Your father puts on more every time he tells that-there story. The plunder that man's got in his head! The plunder!' She flipped out one of her breasts and rubbed the hot pepper on her nipple, squeezing out as much pepper juice as she could.

'Let me see can I get Pittsburgh,' Commodo said. He carried Paul into the next room, and returned to sit by the radio with the ear-phones on his head, digging his knuckles into his ribs. 'Firss, something whistles around my livers like a little bitsy siren blowin. If I'm in church I can hear it plain. Then I get the pain. Gas is the curse of my life.'

Mrs. Crochet put T. J. to her peppered breast. The baby sucked a spell, scratching contentedly at his mother's neck. Suddenly he hammered the breast away from him and opened his mouth to roar. Quickly Mrs. Crochet rammed the nipple of the milk bottle down his throat. 'I don't see much sense in the radio, me,' she said. 'Aw, what they doin the poor lil fella! Poor lil man! Yes, he's a sweet boy!' T. J. slapped the bottle away, stiffened his spine in a backward curve, sucked in a lungful of air to roar. Quickly the mother's breast was stuffed back into his mouth. 'Poo! Nassy!' Mrs. Crochet said. 'Nassy-nassy!' When the baby pushed the breast away, the rubber nipple was rammed into his mouth. 'Mmmmm! Nice bot-tee! *Nice* bot-tee! *God damn it, that's all I've got*, you little...'

'Confess that,' said Commodo.

'Come, darling precious sweedart! *Nice* bot-tee! If that ain't what you can call a durdy trash, to spit out the clinic milk, and wuntsa suck something that ain't nothing tell he puts on hip-boots in the marsh. He won't drink bolly-water and he won't drink clinic milk.'

'When I get the program it's noise,' said Commodo. 'When the house is quiet I can't get the program. How long I been needin my own room for the radio and the funny papers, I done forgot. Please take T. J. in the shed while I catch this man talking about smoke-sausage for Evvie.'

'Oui, Evvie likes to listen about smoke-sausage she'll never smell. *Nice* bot-tee! Look, *Mama* likes the bot-tee! Mmmmmmmm!'

'I sold the middle buster to buy that drugstore milk,' Commodo said. 'I say let him cry. The poor lil fella got to learn how to not suck his mama, because pretty soon if we get that property we gunna be better off, and T. J. gunna have anudda lil sister, maybe. Take him in the shed before I get mad with the sirens blowing in me, Duck.'

'Now he's drinkin it! Look how nice. Wait till I tell Miss Nellie.'

'I jiss like to sit here connected up to Pittsburgh, Duck,' said Commodo. 'Jiss think! Connected to Pittsburgh!'

'Listening at smoke-sausage talk with your mouth watering is the only good the radio does for us. You think that Topal went off somewhere? Me, I'm so tired I could drop. Morning tell night, and no headway.'

Evvie said, 'I heard in school Mr. Tobin is getting along better.'

'I wish I had a orange,' Mrs. Crochet said. 'I could murder me a landlord on any dark road tonight. Jewpray, that ole skinflint, was here this morning, and I seen him lookin at the Valencia trees in front. Him, he was trying to see places where the chirren mighta broke off fruit on the trees. I felt like rubbin the rotten fruit in his face that been layin on the ground sense the lass blow of wind that the poor chirren's scared to touch them and catch a kick in the tail from me. How can he receive Communion Sunday after Sunday I don't know.'

'That's when you live in a rented house,' said Commodo. 'But don't say nothin to the ole worm-goat, Duck. You gunna see that man beggin me for a cup of okra seed some day.'

The back door opened. Topal came in. She looked at her mother gravely. 'Somebody wants you in the back shed,' she said.

Commodo said, 'I'm warnin you, me, that boy can't come inside that door, him, tell he begs my pardon, and the dogs is got to quit sleepin in this house.'

'Who said he wuntsa come in this house?' Mrs. Crochet stepped over Gussie's sleeping form and went out the back door. Evvie held the baby, and put her ear against the crack of the door to listen.

Commodo said, 'Me, I oughta go up to borrow a file for my shovel. I got elder roots to go through tomorrow. Topal, you wunna come with Papa up the road? I'm goin far as Mitch Holt's.'

'I got my feet to rench,' Topal said.

'This family don't click together much,' said Commodo. 'I been sittin here thinkin something's gotta be done. Them two outside is whisperin something, and I oughta go out and slap that boy crooked for callin his mama outside. I been sittin here thinkin we gettin in a rut, pullin every which way. But all that's gunna hafta stop when we get a property of our own. I been sittin here thinkin.'

Topal went to the front room to massage her bosom.

9

IT SWEETENS OUT A
PERSON'S BLOOD

'THE OLE rangatang is mad like a bull at you,' Mrs. Crochet whispered.

'Did he see all the plunder-wood I piled up on the river-bank?' Arthur asked.

'He musta. He used it half up arready hugging the stove. Who you got with you, darling?'

'Tony and Jake.'

Arthur wore a carbide bull's-eye lamp on his hat. He swung his head to and fro until the light's beam, glittering with dancing insects in the mist, showed two dark youths sitting under a tree in the orchard. Both boys were gnawing on great long sandwiches from the grocery store.

'That Tony,' said Mrs. Crochet.

'Ma, I kilt a buck on Yellow Cotton with Tony's Remington.'

'If them federal agents finds out! Bull's-eyeing deers againss the season! Goddle mighty, my head is splitting.'

'Look the horns, Ma. Feel how heavy.'

'He's on a dite again, but God knows the balance of us can use the meat.'

'They helped me, Tony and Jake Schulingkampf. I get the hind quarters. Listen, guess what I brought home especially for you, Ma. The livers.'

'Thank you, darling. Miss Nellie, her she keepsa ordering me and my lil Indians to eat livers. It sweetens out a person's blood.'

'My third deer, this fellow, and I'm not eighteen. But I guess it makes no difference to him inside. I'm still a baby. I still got to have the sugar-tit and go to church.'

'Try not to pester him, son, so much any more. Igno him when he's cross. Who's got a good father, it's Nee-nee Jean-freau. That man takes his boy out hunting and all like that. Me, I hope this gunna be the lass time you take the canes, Arthur.'

'When you see me taking the canes again, you'll see him driving me to it. I like to stay home, Ma, but I've got to come and go, come and go. I get nervous. Especially in this house, bumping into babies whenever you turn around, stepping over babies, and got no place to hardly sit down or bring a pal in. I get nervous.'

'Come drive me another stake by the boom, darling.' She handed him the sledgehammer from the shed and a stake of wood.

Arthur went to the big schooner-boom that leaned against the house to keep it from falling. The stake that held the boom in place had rotted. He broke off the rotted stake and began driving the new one. The sledgehammer made a circle in the light from the window.

'He's your father,' said Mrs. Crochet in a low voice. 'He knows you a good boy. You oughta mine him. Please, please, Arthur, mine him for my sake. Me, I'm worried about enough arready, Topal got no husband and twenty year old, and Ev-vie smelling herself, getting cranky sometimes, or walking around with her mind in the Ural or some place.'

Arthur drove the stake with gusto, his body following the

circling maul, with a virile grunt behind each blow. 'I'm telling you this boom is rotten itself, Ma. They need a new boom
or a new house one. Topal ought to be out working.'

'Her! If she ain't a rancid! She's sweet as sugar to Evvie
jiss to get Evvie in a good humor, then she turn aroun and
talk sarcastic. If that ain't what you can call opening the door
for the cat and then slamming it on his tail! Say like my poor
Papa, that's the Crochets all over.'

Arthur finished driving the stake. They crossed the yard
and stood by the shed. Arthur asked, 'Did you hear any more
news about that Shoepick house to go on our doorsteps?'

'That Tobin, him he's still in the hospital, and where else
we gunna get money? The river soon be goin down, and pretty
soon you gunna see Emilien Perdu sell his caddle and come out
the marsh and hole the meeting and pass the resolution for
buying that property. If we do get it, I want you to help work
my Easter lily. Those bulbs is bringing good money. I'll pay
you good. But be a good boy for Mama. Papa knows you a
good boy, only rough. And them dogs! Where's the dogs at?'

The beam of light shining from Arthur's head swung round
and revealed three gaunt and ghostly white hounds sitting far
back in the corner of the shed. As soon as the light fell upon
them, they wagged their tails. Two of them began to crawl,
then they all crawled back and forth, shuttling past each other,
scraping their bellies across the shed floor, beating their tails
loudly against the floor as they looked at Mrs. Crochet.

Arthur said, 'How's that for trained dogs, Ma? I told them,
God durn it, not to dare to move from this shed, and not to go
near the house! They do exactly like I told them. How can
that one inside be cruel to dogs like that? If they were she-
males always dropping pups, I wouldn't say.'

'Poo! They still smell! Arthur, why don't you put a wire

ring on their neck for the mange? Let me put rings on them
tomorrow. You see, that's what's makes Papa mad, them kind
of a things, bringing home the mange to stink up the place.'

'I'll get a mess of mange-grease from the drugstore.'

They walked to the side of the house. Mrs. Crochet looked
through the kitchen window anxiously. She scanned her
son's face, to see how he looked in full lamplight. 'Arthur,
why you don't shave?' she asked. 'You look terrible with
whiskers. It's like the hairs on salt meat.'

'I been trawling shrimp and no time to fool.'

'Like a greasy trapper in the marsh all winter you look.
That's what pesters your father.'

Tony and Jake were creeping away through the trees without a word. The mother and son stood by the kitchen window
looking in. Inside Commodo was shambling about the room
barefooted, like a big, shaggy, bothered animal, absently
peering here and there about the stove and table, scratching
his hip. They saw him find the baby's bottle. He glanced
about him, then put the nipple to his lips and sucked out the
few spoonfuls of milk that remained. Arthur began softly to
giggle. His mother glanced at his white teeth shining over the
sparse golden beard. Her eyes twinkled.

'Shhh!' she whispered.

'You think I ought to go in now, Ma?'

'Yes. Tell him you gunna bill a doghouse to keep the dogs
in. Go beg his pardon, darling, it ain't hard to do. Wipe your
feet.'

They went in. Mrs. Crochet stood by the dishpan and made
a loud noise with the plates. Arthur glanced at his father and
said, 'Hello, Papa.' Then, with a wide flourish and a business-
like face, he dumped the hind quarters of the deer on the
table. 'Whew!' The thudding impact almost put out the
kerosene light.

'I'll cook in five minute,' said Mrs. Crochet. 'Don't you all get impatient tell Mama finished here. I'll make smashed potatoes, too.'

Commodo paid no attention to his wife or to the quarters of venison. He was looking steadily at Arthur, his lips tightening.

Mrs. Crochet said: 'Now we gunna have meat three times in one week. Miss Nellie gunna be glad. We been trying to help her out, so she can put us in the green tabs. She say shoot for the green.'

Commodo looked steadily at Arthur. Presently he said, 'Who sent for you to come back here?' in a low metallic voice. He had not moved a muscle since Arthur's arrival.

Examining his hands, which were swollen from paddling over Yellow Cotton with the deer, Arthur murmured, 'I'm sorry the dogs rolled mud on your bed, Pa. I deserved a beating.'

'You make Papa lose his temper with them dogs,' said Commodo, 'and pickin up leavin home whenever the wind change.'

'They won't bother you again, Pa. Not them dogs out there.'

'A thing I wunt somebody to please tell me is this: why does them dogs come in here and roll mud only on *my* side of the bed all the time?'

'Don't worry. I got them trained now, Pa, to mind me. They're trained to keep away from the house now. Guarantee.'

'But watch them close, son,' Mrs. Crochet said. 'Tomorrow, what I'm gunna do, I'm gunna hang rings on their neck, and Arthur gunna bill a doghouse, Duck! A cute lil doghouse!'

'Always on *my* side of the bed they got to roll. All right, Arthur. I give you anudda chance.'

'Cigarette, Pa.'

'No thanks.'

'You welcome.'

'That's all right.'

Arthur said, 'Looks like I never can kill a really big deer. I mean a big one. Shucks. A deer one man can carry is no deer.'

Arthur walked around the house, looking for changes which might have taken place since his departure. There were none, except that the floors shook more when he crossed them. In the front room Topal sidled up to him and whispered, 'Gimme cigarette!'

'Tomorrow.'

'Arthur! Please! Gimme ——'

'Let go my pocket. I got none.'

'Please! I'll go to the toilet with it. Please.'

'Here.'

Arthur went into the kitchen, rolling up his sleeves, baring thick, sinewy forearms. The meat was broiling. The house felt fine. Mrs. Crochet stood with the big fork slapping the venison steaks over and over, salting them well. Blue smoke thickened the air. The pot of potatoes chuckled busily.

'How's things in the swimp fleet goin these days?' Commodo asked the boy. 'You all makin good money?'

'Heck. I've quit Pauly's boat, Pa. Not enough money in it.' Arthur was being very grown-up with his father. And he reached down and gave the twins each a nickel. 'Not enough money in shrimps these days. Old man Dupré's getting to own the fishermen body and soul.'

'Everything bumps against that fella turns to money.'

'Sure. Pauly owes him over a hundred dollars. When a fisherman is broke, Dupré advances oil and groceries for part of the catch. Pretty soon he owns the boat. He owns a big share in Pauly's boat. I'm going to find something else to do.' Arthur strutted back and forth. He did not notice his mother at all, and Mrs. Crochet enjoyed that. This was a man-to-man proposition. Arthur went out the back door, stood there in the lamplight, and called: 'Hey, Pa! Can I see you a minute?'

When Commodo joined him in the yard, Arthur said, 'Keep this under your hat. Old man Dupré ——'

Mrs. Crochet looked out the back door. 'Listen, you all!'

'What you wunt?' Commodo asked.

'Well! What you call this kind of business that Arthur can't talk in front of his mother and bruddas and sisters?'

Arthur led his father to the back shed, and spoke in low tones. 'Old man Dupré is messing around Shoepick's sister.'

'But no! Jewpray, our landlord? Juarelle?'

'I caught him, Pa.'

'The ole humpback codger, I'm a son of a bugger!'

'He came down to our boat one day. We were tied up at Venice. Dupré gave Pauly a dollar for us to go play dice. Then he tried to get Juarelle to go in our boat with him. He was begging her.' Arthur offered his father a cigarette, and held the light for Commodo, and man-to-man, continued, 'Keep it under your hat. They tell me Dupré's buying that little piece of land next to Shoepick's and planting young trees.'

'The ole mule-skunk, he wuntsa be hangin aroun near her!'

Arthur said in a lower tone, 'Pa, I got seventy-five dollars coming to me from Pauly. I'll give you what you need for Shoepick's property, you hear? Before Dupré pays the taxes to make Juarelle.'

Commodo gulped in the dark. 'Arthur — you ——'

'Shh! We'll surprise Mama when Pauly pays me, eh?'

'Arthur — God dog it to hell — I ——'

'Shh!'

'Son, you ain't been bootleggin out there?'

'Heck no! I been workin like a dog.'

At the supper table waiting for the meat to be served, Commodo drummed excitedly on the table and stared into space with eyes big with plans. He said, 'I hope you gunna be a help to me, Arthur, from now on. I say I don't mind you havin some fun.'

'Sure!' Mrs. Crochet cried. 'Nobody wuntsa hole you down, Arthur, aroun here.'

'Who!' Commodo bellowed. 'Hole who down! Listen to me, boy, I'm proud you wunna be a man. It's good for a young man to hunt work to make money and run aroun a lil bit. You can make money with me, too. Jiss wait! I ain sayin nothin yet. I got you practically fixed up arready. In udda words, when you get aroun twenny-one, I tell you what I'm gunna haul off and do, me. If God spares me, I'm gunna make a drainage expert outa you. That's the importantess line of work on this river. Me I never realized it when I used to be a layman. I'm gunna learn you some day all I know about drainage for nothin, and you better keep it in the family. I'll try you out with the shovel soon some day. If you make good with me, you can go get jobs for yourself, all I care. I mean it.'

Mrs. Crochet stood with her wrists limp and fingers dangling. She glared at Commodo. 'It ain enough we got one in the family,' she said.

'One what?' Commodo asked.

'Never mine. Here's your meat.'

'One what? In udda words, one what, we got in the family?'

'One ditch digger, God dog it.'

Arthur spoke: 'Papa means ——'

'I know what he means. He call it a drainage expert.'

Commodo pushed away his plate. He sat glumly worrying his peeling lips. He got up abruptly and went over to his wife. He took her arms and turned her around to look into her eyes. 'Remember that,' he said. 'I'll never forget it. A ditch digger. All right. A ditch digger. I'm on my back againss the wall, sick and hungry from the dites and the sirens and the gas, but I'm never gunna forget. A ditch digger.'

Mrs. Crochet jerked away and returned to her serving. 'I feel mosquitoes in this house,' she said. 'Arthur, go like a good boy and see if the front door's open. I feel ——'

Arthur raised his face quickly. The father and son glanced at each other. Arthur started off, but Commodo held up his hand, and walked to the front of the house. Mrs. Crochet looked at Arthur, raised the palms of her hands, and threw her eyes upward.

Commodo returned from the front. He was smiling sweetly.

'Come in here and take a glimp at something nice, you all,' he said. His words were soft as berries. He smacked his lips, rubbed his hands, and reached into a corner for the broom. Mrs. Crochet took the lamp, and the three went into the second room.

Arthur's three white hunting dogs were curled up on the bed, on Commodo's side. They all looked up and began to beat their tails.

'Don't touch my dogs!' Arthur yelled.

Commodo leapt and swung the broom. Every vase and window-pane rattled. Mrs. Crochet screamed, 'The house!

The house!' The broom smashed the globe of the big ornamental parlor lamp by the bed, and Commodo's rush upset
a chair and table. Paul and Gussie ran into the yard, while
Evvie in the kitchen screamed. The dogs scampered about
the room, uttering blood-curdling yowls. The quaking house
made sounds like the chattering of huge teeth. Arthur ran to
let the dogs out the back way, followed by his father. 'Damn
it, let my dogs go!' Arthur bellowed. He crouched by the door
to take the blows meant for the animals.

'Let me at um!' Commodo bawled. 'Ay-yi-yi! Let — get
— get — will you get outa my way, you durdy tramp!
Get ——'

The children in the yard were hopping about and screaming. Mrs. Crochet took hold of Commodo's hair from behind.
'Help! Help!' she screeched. 'Get the deputy! Get the deputy!' Topal had taken charge of the venison to prevent it's
being spilled and trampled. Holding the meat, she raised
her face toward the ceiling and bellowed for help. Arthur
succeeded in opening the door to release the dogs. With the
broomstick whacking his back, he crawled out himself and
ran off in the dark.

Commodo stood in the door panting, purple in the face,
shouting into the fog, 'No good rat, take that! Take that!
And don't come back!'

'Go to hell!' Arthur called from the yard.

'Curse your father that raised you, durdy tramp, durdy
rat and trash and bum. Stay away!'

Mrs. Crochet released his hair and ran out after Arthur.
In the house next door a window was lowered softly. The wide
silence of orchard and river and marsh returned.

The mother and son stood on the levee in the pallid mist;

and except for the night birds and the lewd bawling of a bull over the river, the night was as still as a chalky cavern. Arthur shivered in his shirtsleeves. The three white dogs were now scampering back and forth on the road in figure eight's and skidding curves, chasing one another in the foggy moonlight.

'Come in where you belonk, Arthur.'

'I want my clothes. I've got money.'

'I say he won't touch you. The house is mine too.'

'You want me to take the canes barefooted and no coat?'

'Misère. Don't go. Listen, I know he cooled off. Lass time you run off, you wasn't gone ten minute —— *Arthur!* Come back!'

'I want my clothes. I'm going to town and spend my money. I can stay with Tony tonight.'

'Mon Dieu. Wait.'

Arthur waited for his mother to come back. He was crying, and the tears rolled into the thin whiskers on his chin. In the urgently murmuring river an anchored ship's bilge-pump started throbbing, a strange piece of machinery from far away, where men were sleeping safe and warm. He wished he were on the ship.

When his mother came with his shoes and coat, he kissed her, and passed his hand over the chilled surface of her rough, woolly, earth-colored coat. 'Be a good boy for Mama, and say your prayers good. Ask the Sacred Heart to watch over us all, and don't smoke too much.'

'Don't worry, Ma. I'll go now and get some supper at Tony's.'

'Wait a minute!' she said, disengaging herself from his embrace. 'Damn it, wait a minute.'

She marched down the levee slope, across the yard, and into the house. When she returned she was staggering through the moonlight with a heavy sack on her back, and a package under her arm. She dropped the sack at Arthur's feet. 'Now!' she said. 'Now!'

'What's this?'

'Your meat you brought. Yours. You brought it home.'

Arthur opened the newspaper package, liberating on the foggy air the good strong odor of broiled meat. 'The balance of it's in the sack with your clothes,' his mother said, 'the raw legs. Take them to Tony's.'

Arthur sank down by the roadside and bit a chunk from one of the thick steaks. A car with blinding lights was coming, suffusing the whole night with pale glare. Arthur ducked behind a bush, pulling his mother down beside him. Both of them stooped over low to avoid being seen.

Now the car had stopped by a house down the road, and there came sounds of boys and girls talking and laughing. Arthur and his mother crawled farther down the levee slope into the thick dusty weeds. The dogs followed them, sniffing and flailing their tails. Arthur handed his mother one of the hot steaks. She sat holding it in her hand, with her head bowed to avoid the light of the near-by car. Arthur chewed loudly.

The Crochet house across the road was silent beside the tall ragged cypress, and the huge ornamental doorsteps glistened with dampness under the moon. The front door squeaked, the pitch of the sound raising at the end like a soft timid question. The door opened to a small crack. It chirped and opened farther. Topal emerged noiselessly. Her white bare feet, very long, prehensile and sly, trod daintily down the wet front steps. She crossed the front yard in a series of swift runs and pauses. On the levee she stood listening a moment, then sped across the headlight glare and squatted down beside her mother. Arthur handed her one of the steaks. Mrs. Crochet's steak was still untouched, hanging in her hand.

The door of the Crochet house squeaked again. Evvie stood in the doorway uncertainly. She looked back into the dim house. Carefully she closed the door. She walked over the front yard in a bewildered manner, looking right and left. She went up the levee's hump and stood squinting down the road into the glaring light. She heard a sound from the bushes. 'Ssss!' and the noise of a dog crunching a bone. She crossed the road and went down into the weeds with the others. Arthur passed her a piece of meat.

The lights of the automobile down the road were being played with. They went alternately bright and dim several times, then remained extinguished. One of the girls in the car screeched delightedly. All the Crochet children ate hungrily, sucking the bones, stamping their feet to dislodge the mosquitoes, licking their thumbs.

Mrs. Crochet at last lowered her face and tore off a chunk of the steak in her hand.

The door of the Crochet house opened very slightly, and one of Commodo's eyes appeared in the moonlit opening. It remained there for a little while.

10

CAN ANYBODY BUSS A TWENTY-DOLLAR BILL?

AFTER ARTHUR went to town and spent his seventy-five dollars, he worked for Tony Quarello's uncle down below the Margin, and lived there. Mr. Quarello raised cabbage and other truck, and also had charge of two of the Government lights placed on high steel towers along the river to aid navigators in steering. Mr. Quarello paid Arthur six and a half a week, which took care of his board and left him two and a half for himself.

Arthur would meet his mother every Wednesday night on her way to church, where she was making a novena. She would give him the news from home, and he would give her fifty cents.

'Me, I put this fo bits all the time away,' she said.

'I want you to spend it on your own self, Ma.'

'No indeedy. I hide it. I'm saving up. When I get enough, what we gunna haul off and do, we gunna go to the show on bank night, my whole family except you; and between the seven of us, I say we ought to win the money to almoss pay the taxes and get that Shoepick place. Again, I got my novena to the Sacred Heart, every Wednesday praying to the Sacred Heart for something to happen that we get that money before the river goes down and Emilien sells his caddle and come out the marsh to hole the meetin and pass the resolution. So we got two chances, us. If God don't see fit to condescend it, we got a chance to get it on bank night. Don't tell nobody, Evvie or Topal. I wunna surprize them.'

'But that's a funny ticket, Ma. Putting the Sacred Heart in competition with bank night. It's a screwy thing to do.'

'You lemme alone! You all lemme alone! I got my way to do somethin, instead of waitin for your father with his brain-dreams that he done bluffed me a thousan time. I got a feelin.'

'You've been to the fortune teller, it sounds like.'

'No. I got a feelin.'

Arthur liked to cut and trim the cabbages in the sun all day. He sat on his haunches. He and Tony walked on their haunches from cabbage to cabbage, and they often smoked cigars while at work. In the evening after the good big Dago supper they would stroll down to the poolroom and mingle with the men. Arthur was gaining weight rapidly, getting taller, and when dressed in the clothes he had bought in New Orleans he cut a trim figure.

One of Tony's duties was to cross the river in a pirogue every evening and light the range lights his uncle had charge of. After Arthur came to live with them, Tony began to shirk this job, absenting himself on various pretexts. Mr. Quarello would ask Arthur to please paddle over the river and light the lights. Soon, Arthur found himself doing this job every day.

He grew to detest this task. The old cypress pirogue, hollowed from a root by Tony's great-grandfather, was filled with ancient cracks and holes patched over with rusty tin. Its bottom, which had been dragged over reefs and clamshell bottoms for nearly a hundred years, was worn thin as grocery cheese. It leaked so badly that Arthur during a single crossing had to stop paddling many times and bail it, and between bailings to paddle frantically to recover progress lost through driftage downstream. In bad weather, during a rain, a blow or fog, with a big liner likely to appear at any moment throwing great high swells, it was grueling work and risky. A man overturning in the river wearing hip boots was practically doomed. Arthur was too proud to complain, but he kept his eyes open for another job with room and board, and perhaps more of a future.

With the help of Father Pendergast, he soon found a job as helper on one of Willy Stanjovich's trucks that hauled fruit and vegetables to the French Market farmers' market in New Orleans. Two or three times a week the truck went to town with a load of oranges gathered from small growers along the Margin, remaining in New Orleans a day or so, returning down the river road for another load, and going back to town at once. After Arthur, taking his turn at the wheel, became hardened to navigating roads as rough as the river at its worst without breaking too many springs or crushing more than his share of fruit, he was satisfied with this job. While on Grass Margin, the driver would usually turn the truck over to Arthur to go around loading fruit. Arthur would go down the road blowing the horn in a certain way, until soon his three dogs would come out of the riverbank willows to get the bones he brought them from the market, and to ride around Grass Margin with him.

Evvie met Arthur on his truck one evening. He was driving alone. He stopped the truck, leaned out and grinned. The three dogs looked at her through the slats and wagged their tails.

'Gee,' Evvie said.

'Hey, Sis! Want a ride?'

'It is all right?'

'Sure! Heck, come on, I'll ride you to Venice. Going to pick up our load of fruit. Got to get right back to town while prices are good! Very busy!'

People moved out of their way, and stood in the roadside weeds looking after them, blurred by their dust. Evvie's hair was glued to her face by the wind, the breath was knocked out of her continually by the dreadful jolting.

Arthur kept on talking. 'Heck, they keep us busy as a cat on a tin roof! Soon as we get to the market in town, Henri goes to sleep! I stay up all night!' he bellowed with pride. 'Display the fruit and meet the peddlers that come to buy! Plenty people around the market! Bright lights, radios playing, the new kind with loud-speakers, farmers from all over the state, hoboes and sailors and garbage pickers poking around the fruit we throw away! Plenty traffic! Restaurants for coffee and sandwiches all night! Hot tamales! Snowballs! We kid the girls all night! Heck, I get my kicks!'

'Did you hear anything about Mr. Tobin?' Evvie shouted.

'Naw! They tell me he's getting better!'

'Where is he? What hospital?'

'Mercy Hospital!'

When they returned with the load, Arthur stopped to let Evvie out at home. Mrs. Crochet ran out, followed by Topal with the baby, and the twins.

'Hey, Ma! Did a man come to see you about buying your lily blossoms?'

'Quit joking me, Arthur. Looka how he goes to New Orlean with dirty fingernails!'

'No kidding, Ma. I met a fellow in town works for a

florist, and he said his boss was going down the river hunting lily buds to ship to St. Louis. I told him to come see you.'

'As if anybody could haul lily buds on the roads we got! Leave him come. I'll sell any day, God knows.'

'I'm going to go see some florists for you, Ma. Maybe they could ship them by boat to town.'

Mrs. Crochet straightened Arthur's coat collar. 'Listen, darling. I heard some of those fella taking fruit to sell for the people steals some of the money. They sell the fruit for like a dollar a bushel and bring the people like eighty cents, the durdy gools.'

'Aw, sure, some of them do. Heck, some of them knock off two bits a bushel after they take out commission.'

'Goddle mighty! I hope you don't do such things, you and Henri.'

'Not me.'

'If he does it, that Henri, you gunna be blamed too.'

Arthur started his engine. 'Move, you all! I'm busy!'

'Me, I been worried since you got that job, the temptations and so forth in that durdy city and sleepin in a ole truck with a high school education and no pillow.' She suddenly turned to her children. 'Get inside, you all! Listen, darling,' she said in a confidential tone, 'two bits more, we gunna have enough for bank night at the show Friday.'

'Here's a quarter, Ma.'

'Friday night, darling. I don't wunt *him* to know it yet, or them other little bladder-mouths.'

'I'll be here with the truck that night, Ma. I could drive you to the show, you all.'

'That'll be lovely, darling. Whoa! What we gunna do about him inside, when you and him don't talk.'

'He can ride the truck. It's all the same to me.'

'Awright. Jiss don't say nothin. Me, I'm gunna see about it.'

In the night time before turning over to sleep, Evvie would lie watching the blurred image of the Blessed Mother. Topal would be in the kitchen smoking a cigarette as she read, or wrote to her Pen Pals. Commodo's snores, beginning with a thin metallic grating noise and rising to a deep thunderous sloshing like stones dumped into a bog of mud, filled the whole house. At this time Evvie was offering up fervent prayers for Dave Tobin's recovery, for her successful completion of high school next year, and for divine guidance in choosing her vocation as a Little Sister of the Poor. She loved the Virgin Mary, and while praying she clenched her hands, gathered her mind together intensely, pointing it toward the Virgin in heaven and resolutely holding it there until finished.

Once she wrote a note to Dave Tobin at the Mercy Hospital:

Dear Mr. Tobin:
  We all hope you are doing nicely and on the road to recovary, and we often speak of you. All is the same since you left. Mama's Easter lilies have green buds all over. They will be very pretty. That is all for now.
                          Your friend,
                          Evvie Crochet.

She kept the note in her drawer for a day, then tore it up. This gave her an idea, and she wrote another note to tear up:

My Beloved:
  I implaor you not to come see me again. I could not endure it. I must be strong for both of us. We will meet never-more in this life. I am practically on my way to the convent. In other words, do not be sad, but try to find happiness in your monisterry. Till we meet in heaven,
                          Your beloved,
                          Evvie.

On Friday evening returning from work, Commodo found the family dressed in their best clothes. He wondered what was in the wind. The children hovered around their parents, waiting for some hint of where they were going. Supper was eaten without much talk. Commodo leaned in the doorway watching his family eat. They had boiled carrots and luncheon meat. Commodo said, 'I had carrots too. Miss Tardeau, she cooks them nice, but she put hunks of butter all over them, and make me feel like it was wrong to eat, on account of my dite. Fred, him he brought home a bucket of goose gizzards from the ice house. Hunters leff them at the ice house a long time ago, and they never come back, and Mr. Wendt, he give them to Fred. But she put plenty butter on them. I felt like I was doing wrong.'

Afterwards Commodo met Evvie in the back yard. 'Where you all are going, all dressed up?' he asked.

Evvie shook her head. 'Mama wouldn't tell us.'

Commodo went in and sat on the front steps awhile, then returned to the kitchen. He made several trips like this, from front to rear of the house. Nobody in the family was saying a word, Occasionally one would stare at the other.

'What you looking at?' Topal asked Evvie.

'Nothing.'

'You little feen.'

Commodo said, 'Quit fussin with your bess clothes on.'

'Maybe you can tell us where we all going,' Topal said.

'Sure, that's easy! This is Friday night, eh? In udda words, I think you goin to the talkin pitchas. *You!* Not me!'

When they heard mention of the show, Paul and Gussie jumped down from the top of the armoire and began to dance and beat on one another. They ran to the front porch, where they screeched and hopped up and down wildly.

'Listen, Duck,' Mrs. Crochet said.

'Not for a thousan dollar!' Commodo roared. 'Aw no! Aw no! Not with them chirren and that baby there. I tole you lass time.'

Mrs. Crochet said no more. She went into the bedroom and lay on the bed.

'Heck,' said Topal. She threw her pus-colored cotton sweater across the room. Evvie followed her to the front porch. On the porch, Paul and Gussie were gleefully heaving each other around, yelling and singing. Commodo stood looking out of the back door. Presently he went in and walked back and forth in the bedroom, opening a drawer and closing it, straightening the rug with his toe.

'Jiss listen out front,' he said. 'And you expeck me to go to the show with chirren like that, you.'

His wife did not reply. She lay staring at the ceiling. Commodo went out, and soon returned, lingering about the room. On the front porch, Evvie craned her neck to peer back through the house.

Commodo said, 'When them twins get in the show like lass time, one's gotta make pee-pee, the udda one gotta climb on the seat and block off people in the back, if you call that a pleasure. Far as that baby, you know what gunna happen. He gunna wake up in the middle of the pitcha, and me, I gotta take him outside in the mosquitoes and get his lil go-go specked like a marsh-hen egg with the mosquito bites.'

Mrs. Crochet said nothing.

'I guess you wunna stay and see the show twice, eh?' he asked.

No reply came from the bed.

'Langrid like I am, don't you dare to talk to me about seein the show over twice and come home after ten o'clock.'

'Who said anything about a show I like to know?' Mrs. Crochet asked.

Commodo kicked a chair out of his way. He went to the bed and pointed his finger at his wife. 'Me, I'm tellin you for the lass time,' he bellowed, 'I'm not — gunna — stay — twice! And Topal got to mine the baby. And you oughta take the tinkle-pot for Gussie or something. And furthermo, I got one single livin dime to my name, so don't ——'

'If I wunda go to the show,' Mrs. Crochet said, 'I got the money saved up right down in that syringe over there. But I don't feel like goin to no show after all your gubernatorial palaver. I got the headache.'

'Take you a asparin,' said Commodo. 'The air gunna do you good.'

'Me, I hate to leave this house, because it ain't pretty enough to make me glad to come back to it again.'

The Crochets plodded down the dusty road. Commodo carried T. J. on his shoulder. In the little houses along the Margin as they passed by, curtains were parted and faces peered out at them; or groups gathered on doorsteps returned their greetings with gaping surprise.

'Talkin pitchas!' Paul shouted at a small boy sitting with some people on a doorstep.

Mrs. Crochet kept casting furtive looks behind her. Very soon, the big truck with Arthur driving it came bumping down the road in a storm of dust, and stopped.

'Mama, it's Arthur!' Evvie cried. 'Now we can get a lift!'

'Oh hello, darling!' Mrs. Crochet exclaimed. 'I'm a son of a bugger! What you doin down this way?'

'Jump in! Jump in! I'm in a big hurry!'

The three dogs in the back of the truck, when they saw

Commodo, tucked their tails under them and crept into a corner. Mrs. Crochet got in and motioned Commodo to sit beside her. But Commodo hung his head and toyed with a pebble with his toe. Arthur said, 'Tell him there's some sacks in the back he can sit on.'

'Messyou Crochet,' the wife said, 'would you please go in the back with the Indians as a favor for me and give me that little sprinklin-can to hole and save us poundin the levee for two mile and catch the show before bank night gunna be over?'

Commodo gave his wife the baby. Both the girls got in the front seat, Evvie sitting on Topal's lap. The boys climbed in the back, danced about joyfully, pitched themselves on a pile of burlap sacks. 'Stay sittin down!' Commodo grumbled. 'Stay sittin down before you crack your necks off with the road-holes deep as China!' He climbed in himself, muttering at the cringing dogs. The truck started, and Commodo's great backside struck the pile of sacks and bounced. The truck roared and bumped down the twisting road, swinging from side to side atop the high levee, leaping almost clear of the surface whenever a deep hole was struck. Commodo, wallowing and tossing on the sacks, grabbed his derby hat and yelled: 'Tell him to go slow! Tell him slow down!' From the cab of the suddenly slowing truck came Arthur's voice bawling: 'Tell him the road's better a little further down!'

In the dark movie show, Evvie sat with her head tilted back. The name of the film was *Torrid Jeopardy*. The story concerned a young woman about seventeen years old called Joycine Withers. The setting was an African jungle. Joycine's father had been poisoned by a treacherous servant, and she had taken over his business of collecting ivory, going about the rainy jungle dressed in immaculate riding breeches on an elephant. Evvie sat away from her parents, up near the front.

Everything was going fine with the Crochets. The baby was asleep in Mrs. Crochet's lap. Topal sat on one side of her; on the other, Commodo's head nodded peacefully. In the row ahead, the twins sat in fairly well-behaved silence. Mrs. Crochet paid little attention to the picture. She did not like Joycine's pointed breasts, and her trick of gazing right at her, Mrs. Crochet, with half-closed eyes. Mrs. Crochet was conscious of her well-mannered family. Gussie squirmed now and then, but his mother behind him would merely take hold of the short hairs on his neck gently as though she were picking a flower, jerk them upward and whisper, 'Listen, Worms!'

The fight over the stolen ivory was in progress. The feature picture neared its ending. Mrs. Crochet's lips moved: 'Please, Almighty God let one of us win a prize if it is Thy holy will. Please let one of us win a prize if it is Thy holy will.' T. J.'s ticket, which Mrs. Crochet had insisted on buying although none was needed, was rumpled in the sleeping baby's fist.

Old man Marigny, the crab fisherman, came and sat next to Evvie Crochet. His moist flickering face approached hers closely, and remained there while he discussed some newly discovered points about the merits of cow's lips and ears for bait, as compared with birds. Until she was compelled to turn her head deliberately the other way.

In the seat behind her was an alligator hunter of great prowess named Tee Jule — son of Jule the storekeeper. Tee Jule leaned over and whispered to Evvie, 'Hallo. Hallo. Dis is Tee Zhule.'

'Hello.'

He sat on the front edge of his seat with his warm face a few inches from Evvie's ear. The air was heavy as wool, buzzing with talk under the rasping of the voices on the screen.

This was in the earliest days of talking pictures. Tee Jule was following the action on the screen with comments close to Evvie's ear, 'O-o!' or 'Mmmmff!' or 'Eh, bien!' The old crab fisherman next to her gave off various strong odors. His principal smell was that of an old ash tray, but another, almost as strong, but absolutely new and original with the man, drifted about him which Evvie sat striving to identify. Was it scorched horse hoofs? Mildewed Christmas tree ornaments? Decayed linoleum? Air from an automobile tire? She did not know.

In front of her was a strange young man. His arm hung over the back of his seat. He was swinging his hand. Often it would graze her knee. Or his hand wandered disconsolately about the back of the seat, searching, searching. One fingernail drummed on the wood, or it plucked at a broken place to produce a twanging noise. The young man was not interested in *Torrid Jeopardy*, but sat looking idly one way and another; and at intervals he would suddenly turn and stare at Evvie in the flickering light, as if he thought he had been spoken to; or he would look around for another girl to stare at. Then he would resume the disconsolate drumming and twanging. Evvie's eyes traveling down the side of his silhouetted face traced the bumps of large pimples which her mother would have given anything to squeeze.

Before the picture ended another man came groping down the aisle, stopped and examined Evvie, and sat beside her. It was Tayo the barber.

'Hey,' he said.

'Hey.'

Now she was hemmed in by men of different ages. Tayo fixed himself in his seat, his arm resting against Evvie, his legs sprawled. Evvie drew away, but such a movement placed her against the old crab fisherman. Tayo's arm, that she had once seen flashing its hooked punches at Dave Tobin, was live and hard and strange. She felt a hot drowning sensation, during which the Marigny odors of fermentation or brackish decay washed over her; the nibbling of the young man's claw in the front seat mingled with the soft, gleeful muttering behind her. She swallowed, wrung her fingers, tapped the floor with her heel, while staring upward without seeing the blazing images floating back and forth across the screen.

'Rotten pitcha,' she heard Tayo say. He leaned the hot weight of his burly shoulder farther against her. 'You like it?'

'Yes.'

'Where at did you come in?'

'Yes.'

His fingers were prowling over the back of her hand, barely touching the fine hairs, cold as little shadows creeping past a sun. Tayo whispered, 'Me, I wouldn't wunna hole a job like that fella, carrying a woman's bundles and lookin at a elephant's behind all day.'

Evvie did not answer.

'If that punk dies in the hospital,' he said, 'that pole-vaultin friend of yours, I got a self-defense I can prove. You gunna be widness, you. Sure.'

Evvie jerked her leg away from his.

'I betcha fertilizer from a elephant would make tomatoes big as punkins,' he said.

Through her dazed torpor, Evvie heard a baby yelling somewhere. It was the husky bass voice of little T. J.

Mrs. Crochet fumbled in her lap for the bottle of clinic milk. The baby had awakened in a fright. He was roaring. Heads were turning in front to look back. Commodo, snoring lightly, slept with his chin on his breast. Mrs. Crochet in her hurry dropped the baby's bottle. It started to roll over the floor toward the front of the theatre.

'Catch it!' she whispered to Gussie sitting in front of her gaping at the picture. 'Catch it, durn you!' She rapped the side of his head with her knuckles.

'OUCH!' Gussie howled. 'Say, you!' Every head in front of them turned.

'Go get that bottle, you little ...'

Gussie slumped down in his seat and bawled. 'Get it, Paul,' said Topal. Paul slid to the floor and reached for the bottle, but his hand knocked it out of his grasp. He flattened himself and began to crawl under the seats. Someone's foot touched the bottle, and it went on its way. As Paul squirmed past their legs, people clicked their tongues, or looked down and reached in the darkness to feel. The bottle turned and rolled across the center aisle, fetching up against the foot of a man down near the front, who picked it up, left his seat and walked toward the rear holding the bottle and looking for the location of the baby's bass voice.

'Thank you, thank you,' said Mrs. Crochet, reaching for the bottle.

Commodo was still sleeping. Mrs. Crochet settled herself to wait for the picture's end. Joycine Withers had seen her ivory hunters, led by the wealthy ne'er-do-well trying to recover his self-respect, vanquish the rival tribesmen in combat. The ending dragged interminably. Mrs. Crochet murmured another prayer for good luck in the prize drawing, and began carefully preparing herself for disappointment.

Suddenly she thought of Paul under the seats. She craned her neck. 'Listen, I wonder where at's Paul,' she said to Topal.

'I got no idea.'

'Jesus, Mary and Joseph! Supposin he's stomped or somethin up under them seats some place?'

'I got no idea. *Try to think where you would go if you were a little boy under the seats.*'

Mrs. Crochet nudged Commodo vigorously. He raised his face. He looked around. He smiled, reached for his derby hat, started to leave the seat.

'Duck! Paul's up under them seats some place! Go see!'

'What seats? Who?'

'*Paul!* God dog, *Paul!* Go see up under the seats. Do somethin!'

'What the hell and St. John Burchman ——'

'Under the *seats* up front! Go look for Paul! You understand me, you dinwiddie?'

Commodo, pushed from his seat, disturbed the row of people to get out. His figure wandering bewildered up the aisle, brightly blurred round the edges, was huge in front of the screen.

'I remember with a pang the day I called you a weakling,' said Joycine Withers to the ne'er-do-well. 'You were so sweet about it all, you dear!'

Up toward the first row, a minor commotion attracted Commodo's attention. A woman was standing, looking down and feeling round with her foot. 'For God's sake,' she said. 'For God's sake.' People near her were peering down in the dark.

Commodo began pushing himself into the row. 'Pauly, honey!' he whispered loudly. 'Pauly!'

'I'm comin!' said a small voice under the seats. 'I — can't — find it!' He was crying.

'You come by Papa, you! Crawling all around the theatre?

Mama got the bottle and T. J. sleepin, and you, you keepa crawlin.' He reached down and took hold of Paul, and carried him back to his seat. He sat beside his wife. 'Remember this, you hear?' he said through his clenched teeth.

'A accident, Duck.'

'Neglection.'

His wife pressed his hand and whispered, 'Jiss a lil while longer, Duck. Looka. Mr. Willy going up front with the box of numbers. You got your ticket? Pauly, you got your ticket?'

'Yes mam.'

Commodo leaned over Paul. 'Shh! Hush now, sweedart. Listen, we all gunna be up in the rhinestones if we win a prize, sweedart. Shhh! Listen, ole Mama, she gunna be walkin aroun sayin, "Can anybody buss a twenny-dollar bill?" '

'Me, I ain't hatchin on no rhinestones, I guarantee,' said Mrs. Crochet. 'Why you wunna tell the chile that for?' Then she settled back and whispered a final prayer.

The lights went on. There was loud noise everywhere. The place was jammed to the entrance. Commodo said, 'Me, I thought they was gunna show that nudiss colony.'

'They done arready showed it, you durdy thing,' said his wife, slapping his leg. 'It was in the news.'

'Modi! I wunda see the nudiss colony.'

Mr. Willy Stanjovich, who owned the theatre, was on the stage clapping his hands for order, looking around the audience, twitching one side of his long mustache. 'Hey, jiss minute!' he yelled. 'Jiss minute! Now we vunt nice lilly gel to pick noombers. Who's gun pick noombers for us?'

A small girl left the audience and went up to the stage, pulling up her stocking. The box of numbers was shaken.

The little girl turned her head and reached in. In her seat Mrs. Crochet closed her eyes and winced for the coming blow. Stanjovich took the folded paper from the girl. 'Hey pipples!' he screamed. 'Hey pipples! Vatch looky noomber, and remember ve give away eighty dollar nex Friday and be sure to come. Now vatch looky noomber for forty five dollar!' The slip of paper was unfolded. Stanjovich called the numbers: 'Sickus! Two! Four! Seven!'

Far in the rear there was a screech. A woman very red and palpitating jumped up, waving a ticket. It was Miss Nellie, the health nurse. As she fluttered up the aisle, Mrs. Crochet waved at her and nodded vigorously. She returned the greeting. 'The first thing I ever won in my life!'

'I coulda tole you that,' said Commodo, as Miss Nellie passed on. 'Jiss looka them mission bells ringin on each side of her.'

Mrs. Crochet sat quietly and erect, looking straight ahead. Commodo laid his big brown hand softly across her leg and drummed his fingers lightly. She jounced the baby, eyed the stage, sighed.

'Where's Evvie at?' Mrs. Crochet asked. 'We gotta be goin. Topal, honey, you take the baby little while.'

Commodo sat watching Miss Nellie receiving the first prize. Deep staccato mutters and growls issued from his tightened lips. The strange woman next to him turned and glared, and shrank away from him.

The Crochets went up the aisle. They waited near the entrance for Evvie, and for the awarding of the remaining prizes. The second prize was drawn by a Filipino fur buyer. A strange oil man from Texas took the five dollar award. The Crochets went out with the first of the crowd.

Evvie Crochet felt Tayo the barber moving along behind

her. Before turning to go his way, he squeezed her thin arm and whispered, 'Come here tomorrow night, and I treat you. I wait for you.'

Outside, automobile lights were flashing on, horns blowing, oyster fishermen and oil scouts from the big marshes pushing through to get to their boats in the river. Evvie was conscious of the place along her arm where Tayo's tough warmth had rested, as though he had printed there a permanent mark, very bright and hateful. She turned and saw Tayo encounter another girl and take her arm.

Gussie kicked at the clamshells on the ground and grumbled, 'Shucks, Ma, the good guys was niggers in that pitcha.'

11

MAKE OUT WE PLAYING A GAME

MRS. CROCHET wanted her family to stand where they would be seen coming from the movies — particularly by her assorted cousins from up and down the river — even though when they saw the Crochet family, people leaned toward each other and whispered about Topal's broken engagement. Commodo smiled broadly and lifted his hat in exaggerated fashion whenever someone they knew looked in their direction.

Suddenly he spied Mr. Dupré, their landlord, coming out of the show. 'God bless! Look ole Poison Ivory,' he told his wife. 'We got to hide quick!' And he herded the family through the crowd toward a big truckload of crabs that stood in a pool formed by its own drippings near the highway.

The Crochets gathered behind the truck. Mrs. Crochet held the twins pressed against her legs; Topal had the baby; and with his derby hat Commodo fanned the mosquitoes away from T. J. Evvie stooped to look out from under the truck. She saw Mr. Dupré in the crowd talking to another man. He wore a gray business suit. He had shrimpy pink face, a clipped gray mustache, silvery eyebrows joined into one long eyebrow shading his sharp eyes that moved restlessly, noting every face that emerged from the theatre. As usual he was chewing something, the nature of which nobody knew. It was something very small, because he kept working it to the front of his mouth with his tongue and grinding or cracking it with his front teeth.

He wore his well-known Panama hat, which was rumored to have cost twenty dollars, with its blue band spotted with large white dots. Both his hands rested on his silver-knobbed walking cane, which had come from Nova Scotia with an early ancestor.

Evvie asked, 'Mama, why don't we want Mr. Dupré to see us?'

'Because we owe him rent, and because it ain his business we come to bank night, and because we don't like him aroun us.'

Commodo said, 'In udda words, ef ole Poison Ivory sees us, he gunna say to himself, "Mighty funny they can go to the show when they owe me rent."'

'Nobody's going to stop me from going to the show,' Topal said.

The twins were getting sleepy. They began to whine and slap at the mosquitoes on their legs. Mrs. Crochet said, 'Evvie darling, do some trick for your bruddas to keep them quite. Watch Evvie, now, she gunna do some tricks.'

Evvie sat on the grass. She gravely took hold of her right foot and brought it behind her neck. Then she did the same with the other foot. 'Ha, ha!' Mrs. Crochet laughed softly. 'Looka Evvie doin tricks!' The boys were not amused. Gussie stamped his feet and whimpered, burying his face in his mother's skirt. 'I wunna go home! I'm tired!' Mrs. Crochet caught hold of her hair and groaned, 'You talk about I could throw my neck under some automobile.'

'Heck, I'm going,' said Topal. 'What kind of business is this?'

Commodo said, 'Stay where you are, sweedart, Injoy your-self, you all. Looka all the people! It's a nice thing to watch all the people and they can't see you. Less make out we playin a game. Don't get excited. Ole Jewpray gunna haul off and take the shellroad soon.'

Evvie could see just over the top of the levee, and through the blades of grass, watched two lights burning fretfully far across the wide river. When a tiny blade of grass moved, it obscured the distant light momentarily. She thought of Joycine Withers and her ne'er-do-well. Watching the lights over the river, she made a rhyme:

> One if by land and two if by sea,
> They showed Joycine Withers and her lover to me,
> Everybody but the big bad Jeopard, you see,
> I wonder where can he be?

Then she turned to her mother and said, 'Here come Arthur's dogs. Mama, look how skinny they look at night!'

Arthur's three white dogs, now very dirty, were wandering among the people, looking up at the faces, smelling the legs. Commodo whispered, 'Don't move, nobody! If them dogs sees us, they gunna give us away. Don't get excited.'

The crowd was thinning out. All of the cars except Dupré's were gone. Dupré stood watching the women straggling from the show, and nervously nibbling on the substance in his mouth. 'Keep still!' Commodo warned. 'He gunna dragass in a minute.' Paul and Gussie, tormented by the mosquitoes, were both crying softly and stamping their feet.

'For God's sake!' Topal said. 'Hiding like criminals!'

'He's not gunna leave tell all the women is gone,' said Mrs. Crochet.

'That's Orelia's cousin from town over there,' Evvie said.

'A pip-chippy,' Mrs. Crochet said. 'Shakin her body to

pass a ole man, and got nothing back there to shake. Them and their crazy dites and suntans.'

One of Arthur's dogs spied the Crochet family hiding behind the truck.

The dog loped happily over toward the crab truck, but when he saw Commodo's legs, he changed his mind. He dropped his tail and went off to one side. He sat in the road. He looked at the row of legs under the truck, his head now on one side, then on the other, his tail knocking on the ground. Once he growled and barked, swinging his tail vigorously.

Old Dupré saw the dog. He looked fixedly at the truck. While his companion went on talking, he leaned over sideways, the bright eyes under his shaggy brows fixed on the weeds that partly screened the truck.

'Poison Ivory, he sees us,' said Mrs. Crochet.

'Well let's go, then,' said Topal.

'Keep still!' Commodo ordered. 'He can't prove who it is, him.'

Now the other two dogs came and sat near the first. The three of them lay fully outstretched, with their chins on the ground, muzzles pointed directly at the Crochets. When a movement took place behind the truck, one or more of the dogs would raise his head, whine and thrash his tail.

'Possay!' Mrs. Crochet whispered loudly.

Topal was shaking with suppressed mirth.

'He gunna go now,' said Commodo. 'His wife is home sick.'

Dupré bade his friend goodnight, and went to his automobile. He got in behind the wheel, but did not start the engine. They saw him light a cigar, his keen eyes glance at the crab truck through the cupped glare of the match. The last of the little knots of people broke up and left. The front of the movie show was strung with brilliant lights, each surrounded by silently wheeling moths, and illuminating a wide area of perfectly bare ground surfaced with white shells as far out as the levee. This wide bright space now contained only the trio of dogs, and Dupré's car, with occasional wisps of cigar smoke drifting out of it. In the period of silence that ensued, the trickle from the crab hampers in the truck sounded very loud. Mrs. Crochet kept the faces of the twins pressed against her to muffle their crying.

'I say he's looking right at us,' she whispered.

'I know it! God dog it, keep still!'

Topal whispered, 'This won't be really funny until the driver comes and takes the truck away.'

Nobody answered her. Commodo stooped and fanned his hat around the legs of the whimpering twins. Evvie peeped out from under the truck, her head fallen sideways on her shoulder dreamily. The space beyond the weeds was like a great stage cleared for some perilous action that would bring all the dispersed people hurrying back to the spot. She saw one of Arthur's dogs get up and begin to wander about uneasily, whining softly now and then, glancing over his shoulder, searching the ground with his nose, until he came near Dupré's car. He lifted his nose, pointing it toward the car. He turned away, growling, the hair along his spine slanting upward. Again he turned and faced the car, and began to bark. A loud sound came from the car, the stamp of a foot against the floorboards. The dog dropped his tail and, joined by the two others, scampered over to the crab truck, crawled under it and gathered where Evvie was sitting. Evvie reached out to stroke the head of one of them. The others crawled near to be caressed.

'Stop pettin them ky-yoodles!' Commodo whispered.

Mrs. Crochet said, 'Leave her ago, you! Them's my son's dogs.'

Commodo stamped his foot. One by one the dogs slunk off. Topal snickered, 'Find your own truck to hide behind.'

Just then all the lights of the movie show snapped out.

Nobody budged. The stars gradually drew into view, soaring high as vapory stairs. Evvie heard her brothers' muffled whimpering against her mother's legs. No sound at all came from Dupré's car over near the building. There was the long wait while the sky whitened with the coming of the lesser stars, and hunched forms of trees and bushes seemed to steal out of the dark and sit crouched around the truck. Mrs. Crochet felt her way closer to her husband, who took over and pressed against him both the twins. Topal went nearer her father. Evvie walked on her knees through the grass until she sat close by Paul and Topal; then she felt the hitherto unknown sensation of her sister's hand resting on her shoulder.

In a little while, Evvie felt Topal's hand tap her shoulder and withdraw, and she got to her feet and followed the family stealing off through the weeds. Topal was again venting her sly mirthless giggle. But to Evvie this was a taste of good danger or magic, scaling the levee toward the stairways in the sky. There were warning whispers everywhere ahead of her. When she gained the peak of the high road, the talk ahead grew less guarded.

Her father was saying, 'Take care with the baby, darling, there's an oil drum here. Watch that rope. Come, Mama.' His voice was rising, and now Dupré in the car might have heard if he cared to. 'Nobody gunna stop us from walking the road! Leave anybody try and stop us! Anybody!'

'Or goin to the pitcha show!' Mrs. Crochet said loudly.

'We gunna go to the pitcha show all we wunt!' Commodo shouted as they turned into the levee highway.

'We gunna haul off and go tomorrow again!'

'And take our chirren, too!' Commodo bellowed.

After they had gone a distance up the highway they heard Dupré's engine start faintly. They all stopped and looked back.

'Sacré nom! He comin this way!'

'Don't get excited,' Commodo said.

The lights of the automobile swept round and up into the highway. The Crochets moved over to the path beside the road. It was very exciting to Evvie. The lights of the approaching car threw her shadow far ahead, like a giant's, and the shadow kept growing shorter and shorter. Her father was a brave man. Nobody on earth could stop them from going to the show, because her father had shouted it for all the world to hear, even the nameless powers of darkness. The car was upon them. Something would happen now.

Dupré's car stopped abreast of the Crochets.

Dupré did not say anything, only put on his brake and took the motor out of gear. Then he reached over and opened the rear door, and the front one, and waited. He waited for them to get in, looking straight ahead, biting on the gnawed substance in his mouth, and saying nothing. The Crochets hesitated, neither getting in the car nor going on their way. Without looking at the Crochets, Dupré gave a sudden nervous jerk at his Panama hat brim and stepped on the accelerator until the engine roared like a nettled beast. The Crochets were startled. They got into the car hurriedly, Topal and Evvie in front, and the others in the rear.

The car started off. Nobody said a word. Dupré drove carefully, with set jaws, as though all the power of the machine resided in his head, controlled and restrained. He snaked the car between the yawning holes of the road, and he grudgingly gave it more power when a smooth stretch drew near. They passed a shrimp cannery whose windows spilled yellow light and rich-smelling clouds of steam, swung around the sharp loop where the cemetery nestled with its cluster of pale tombs, and went on up past the long row of tight-lipped and darkened cottages of the Margin.

In his own good time, Dupré spoke. His voice was clear and abrasive, but his words were frugal. 'I want to see you, Crochet.'

'Me, too, I wunda see you, Jewpray,' Commodo answered, and nudged his wife. 'It's nice weather, eh?'

Another long silence fell while the car wound on between the trees, now and then overtaking some people walking home from the show, whom Dupré slowed down to examine in every case, with his tiny eyes that looked at everything and saw nothing that was not negotiable. Their headlights showed plainly the green trees, misty towering willows on the river side of the levee, and the squat fecund oranges on the other. Evvie felt sorry for Mr. Dupré, because few people liked him, or visited his wife. It was rumored he had locks on his doors. Everything he touched turned into money. Most of the fishermen were indebted to him, and trappers leasing his marsh lands paid him one-third of their catch. He smelled strongly of *vert de vert* roots, the Creole herb of olden times which his wife put in his clothes as a scent. Boys were always playing pranks on the Duprés. Just the other day, Evvie had heard that some kids had put pelican eggs under Mrs. Dupré's setting goose. Evvie tried to see what he was chewing on. She had never before been so close to the man who owned the windows she looked through, the rain in the cistern, the holes in the roof, the shadow of the big cypress tree pointing at the front doorsteps.

162   THE GREAT BIG DOORSTEP

'I've got some ditching,' Dupré said. 'I want it done next week.'

'You sho come to the right man for drainage work, Jew-pray.'

'I want all the ditches cleaned on Shoepick's property.'

'Eh?'

'Nigger Shoepick's. About a week's work.'

'You went to work and bought that property?' Mrs. Crochet asked in a tight voice.

'No.'

Commodo said, 'Hush up, Duck, it ain't none of our business why he wuntsa drain a nigger's land. We know how to close our ears against the gossip goin aroun this river.'

'I was jiss wonderin, because they say the drainage board gunna buy the place when the river goes down and Emilien Perdu sells his caddle and come out the marsh and hole the meetin and ——'

'I don't know,' said Dupré. 'I don't know. You can do the work for the rent you owe me. We'll call it square. Week's ditching for two months' rent. I like your little family. Do me a good job and we'll call it square.'

'All my jobs is good jobs.'

Dupré said, 'I see the kids next door made a battleship out of Shoepick's father's fine old pirogue. Lazy, shiftless, irresponsible and slovenly as Shoepick is, that's how upright and ambitious the old father was that he buried in that front yard. He's the one showed me how to grow grapefruit and kumquats on the same tree. While Shoepick picks a guitar in his packing shed, the alligator grass is taking charge of the whole place. I say people don't need to be in want down here. It's their own fault. Every place down here oughta to be clean and prosperous. I spit on them. Heh! Heh! Heh!'

Topal said, 'There's plenty of alligator grass on your land back of our house. And snakes. All color snakes and stuff.'

'Don't you wunna hire somebody to cut it?' Commodo asked. 'Listen, Jewpray, I fix the back shed too. You wunt me to haul off and fix the place up? The whole place ain't got no good qualities hardly at all right now.'

'The back steps is rotten as the devil,' said Mrs. Crochet.

'Hold on,' Dupré said.

'Two windows won't close because the house leans over and the walls is slanty.'

Dupré quickly opened the doors to let them out in front of their house. They got out and ranged themselves alongside the car on either side. 'Three window glasses are gone,' Topal said.

'Hold on.' Like a man trapped, Dupré looked around at the Crochets surrounding him.

Commodo said, 'The roof leaks in four places, and we gotta move the furniture when it rains. It's like playin checkers with the furniture all night.'

Dupré said, 'You're not renting the land; you're renting the house. It's all right for five dollars a month, with a big chicken yard you don't use, except for one rooster.'

'One day I was sleepin with a piece of saltmeat fat on my foot where I run in a nail. A rat come out the hole in the kitchen floor and bit me. I got the scar.'

'Oui, and the holes of the toilet got splinters. When you sit down, they hurt you. That ain't fair. No door on the toilet. We got to use a sack.'

'The cistern got no cover,' said Commodo. 'Mosquitoes gets in and lays eggs and they turn into wiggle-tails.'

'Miss Nellie, her she says it ain't good to drink wiggle-tails.'

'A big lake is under the house,' said Topal.

'Whenever it rains,' Mrs. Crochet said. 'That's why everything miljews in my house, and crawfish lives under the house, and the salt won't run, and ——'

'Hold on!' Dupré said. 'My own things mildew. Everything mildews in this climate.' He shrank farther away from the family ranged around the car. He put his car in gear. They all watched the car drive off. Dupré called to Commodo, 'I'll see you at Shoepick's Wednesday!'

'You better run off! You better!' Commodo called after the car. He pulled up his pants and spat. 'God dog it, you better! You ole son-of-a ——'

'Don't curse him, Duck,' Mrs. Crochet said. 'His wife is sick.'

The next day, while passing on the levee road, Commodo saw that the grove of young orange trees adjoining Shoepick's property was being plowed. This was the young orchard Dupré was rumored to have bought as a pretext for spending part of his time near Shoepick's sister.

Lingering, Commodo discovered Dupré himself, sitting on the bank of the ditch that separated the two properties. Dupré was supposed to be supervising the busy plowman, but his head was turned to watch Juarelle next door. Juarelle was dancing on a sack of dried shrimps to remove the shells. Her hands were raised high, holding on to the limb of a grapefruit tree, and the warm sheen of her arms played among the leaves. Every time she stamped the sack with one foot and lifted the other, the yellow clusters of grapefruit on the limb nodded in rhythm with the jouncing of her breasts, and her hip was thrown out sideways in a proudly heaving curve. Commodo, stopping to watch the gleaming slice of live soil curling off the plow between the plowman's marching legs, stole another and another look at Juarelle's dancing body. But this was a lewd and tempting sight, and presently Commodo, as he had been taught to do, pulled his thoughts away and directed them toward something else — anything else. He began quickly to mutter words at random. 'Daylight saving time, make the world safe for democracy, tall oaks from little acorns grow, the pause that refreshes.'

But old Dupré he could not forget. Dupré was a nasty old man, with his expensive Panama hat and silver cane. Commodo thought about the gleaming slice of beautiful soil curling off the plow, and he had an idea.

That night he ordered from a seed house in town half a pound of Johnson grass seed. He told nobody about his plan. The seeds arrived two days later. The following morning Commodo rose before day. He went up to the young orange grove next to Shoepick's and sowed the seed among the clods, where the wind would sift it deep and rains would melt the clods to cover it well. Johnson grass, used elsewhere for grazing, in the Delta's mild climate and rich soil was a dreadful pest whose roots could be exterminated only at a prohibitive expense.

'Now, take that, Messyou Dupré!' Commodo grumbled. 'Now your land ain worth a settin of buzzard aigs. Now go head and mow that grass five time a year and pile it aroun your little trees. And me, what I'm gunna do, I'm gunna go over every night and get some to feed my mules when I'm gunna live in Shoepick's house some day. Woopy!'

Just then Commodo saw Juarelle come out of the house next door, and hang on the line one of her salmon-colored undergarments. He turned his head as he saw the rising sun turn her legs into rounded shadows swelling large at the top. Mounting the side of the levee, he whispered resolutely, 'When a steam vessel and a sailing vessel are proceeding in such directions as to involve risk of collision, the steam vessel shall keep out of the way of the sailing vessel.'

12

HE'S SUBNORMAL AS HE CAN BE

EVVIE WAS awakened by a northbound flock of geese clamoring high over the house. The morning smelled of fog. Sluggish coils of mist rolled past the window. Dust from the road, mixed with fog, drifted into the house and left a gritty coating on the furniture and floors, and beads of moisture rolled down the mirrors, heavy as tears. Outside, the pet racoon rubbed his damp paws over and over his muzzle while he squinted up at a stealthy cuckoo jumping soundlessly from branch to branch through the grove.

'To have the inside of your shoes durdy when you go to put them on from that shellroad duss!' Mrs. Crochet said.

She passed the hairbrush over and over her round head and down through the wavy black mass of hair. 'Topal, go negs door and see what time it is. Everybody better stay outa my road today, what I mean. Me, I'm gunna light a fire to cook what? That same ole worry every morning.'

Evvie slyly took her three bean-bags out of the bureau drawer and hid them, so that her mother would not cook the contents.

'Gussie! Come from unneat the bureau before I kish you with the heel of my shoe,' Mrs. Crochet fussed. 'What do I wunt? What did I come in here for? Pauly, you and Gussie go out and see if we got a rabbit in the trap, and blow both of your noses. Evvie, you, when you finish your prayers, take the levee and get Mama a dime hunka green shoulder by Zhule, not too fat or you take it right smack back. Who put bread-cruss on my new girdle? I'm gunna give this place a good cleaning, you all.'

'My God,' said Topal.

'You don't like it?'

'I'd let the place rot after last night, the bird-dogging around and hiding behind a load of crabs, and what he said to us.'

'I got plenny time to be embarrassed! I can give up and lay down, me!'

'Kerosene and excelsior I'd use on it before paying rent on this pile of mildewed splinters.'

'Pfyuh! Pfyuh! He-he-he!' Commodo laughed from the bed. 'Miljewed splinners is pretty good!' He tickled the lower lip of the baby straddling his belly. 'Ah-goo! Ah-goo! Say, "Hurry up and tend to me, somebody!"'

T. J. beat the air with his fists and laughed.

Mrs. Crochet said, 'Don't nunna you all mention Shoepick's property to me again close up to me. I say enough is enough. I bet any money he's gunna pay them taxes, and he ain gunna pay them for poor Shoepick's sake. Enough is enough about that-there nigger place, with a man buried in the front yard for lagniappe. My son's a working man. He can take care of me when I'm ole and done renching diapers.'

'Listen at somethin importan, you all!' Commodo cried. 'I got a baby sittin on this stummick waitin. He turn rancid in the night. Who's gunna come tend to him? Looka him laugh! Yes! Looka him laughing, Mama! Yes! Say, "Hurry up, Mama! Bad ole Mama! I'm like a chicken-neck! Nobody wunts me! Yes! And my crazy ole Papa, him he got a job to hole!"'

'Put him in his box and leave him scratch tell I get the breakfass down,' said Mrs. Crochet.

'Did you hear him say it's people's fault when they're in want?' Topal asked. 'He looked right at Papa and he threw the hint.'

Commodo sprang up with the baby in his lap, and pointed at the ceiling. 'Learn a lesson!' he bellowed. 'All of you all learn a lesson from that! I say he hates us all! All the way down to this innocent lil baby, he hates us because we got nothing. He's *gotta* hate us, because we pester his conscience!'

'Do you have to turn lavender?' Mrs. Crochet said.

'No, but everything bumps against Jewpray turns into money. I remember he had six caddles one time. He sent them in the marsh by the sea, and a miracle happened, because he forgot about them. A long time afterwids it come a high river, and Jewpray thought about the caddles. When he went down there, come to find out they had fifty head of caddles waitin in the water with their hoofs rotten and nobody to tend to them. So everything bumps into him turns into money.'

Mrs. Crochet said, 'Evvie! Are you gone by Zhule's, or standing in there listening to your paw's cotton bull stories?'

Evvie sidled out the front door as quietly as smoke.

Going down the road, she felt a weight growing inside her, a painful and yet pleasant urge to go and see Tayo Delacroix, to pass by his barber shop. Fog hid the dripping willows. Far overhead the geese were screaming on their way north to breed. The velvety droplets of mist rolled past her eyes. She opened her eyes widely. There appeared to be worms crawling up in the fog, or swelling heads of cauliflower, swollen edges and swirling cores rolling over and over. She reached one zone of absolute, blinding whiteness. There was no sky, no trees, no pointed roofs, and she stopped and gave up, feeling herself on the edge of one bit of earth. Or she was standing in the swaying belly of a huge beast.

She heard the crunching of rubber tires approaching, and a whistled song. Someone was coming to rescue her.

The bicycle stopped. The rider was a boy named Bruce Holt, a friend of Arthur's. Bruce was in college in New Orleans studying engineering, a sophomore. He was home for the Easter holidays.

'Jump on the back, if you're going my way,' he said. 'Where are you going so early?'

'Jule's. It's not early.'

Bruce had never noticed her existence before. She guessed he was being friendly because in the fog there was hardly anything else to do. Bruce had grown taller and self-assured. He had a smooth and serious face, soft and hairless as hers.

'Hold my belt tight,' he said. 'I'm in a super-hurry.'

'I'm holding the seat tight.'

'You're going to fall. Figure the center of gravity, see? Never mind, skip it. Here we go.'

Evvie grabbed his shoulders to keep from falling. They were skinny and warm. 'I told you,' Bruce said.

He climbed the pedals like one on a slippery mountain, and went on whistling. It was the Chilblain Stomp, very well rendered. Evvie had a secret name for Bruce, Smarty Pants. The back of his leather jacket had pictures on it. There was a Popeye, some flying pennants, a hand holding out a rolled-up document that looked like a diploma. The diploma was labeled, Hold That Tiger, You Lug.

When they reached a smooth piece of road, Bruce went

very fast, then let go the handlebars and elaborately placed both hands on his hips. Smarty Pants again. His shirt was white broadcloth, tucked into silky corduroy pants, and his handkerchief peeped from his hip pocket like an impudent tail. During their high school days, Bruce and Arthur had decided they would go to college together and study medicine. Once, from a respectful distance, Evvie had seen them perform an autopsy on an old dead cat, named Audrey. Audrey's hardened arteries had been swapped by Evvie to old man Marigny for coffee coupons. The embroidering outfit she got for the coupons was given to another girl in exchange for a kitten.

'Gee, you can ride!' she said. She liked him to be Smarty Pants.

'The sprocket's haywire.'

'I mean you can ride!'

'Heck. Sometimes I think it's great to be young, before you have to face this messed-up world. Listen, you saw that fight in Stanjovich's orchard. I'm going to ask you something technical now. If you don't know, don't be afraid to say so. Is Mr. Tobin a scientific fighter, or a slugger.'

'Well . . . he's both.'

'Hmmm. You mean an all-around fighter. It burns me up, missing that fight, and nothing but a bunch of women there. A good fight gone to waste. These women and children — no use asking them what happened.'

'I didn't enjoy being there.'

'You wouldn't. That's how women are — encouraging the men to fight over them, then hiding behind a tree to cry.'

'Who encouraged them?'

'I heard they fought over you. In a common brawl.'

'They fought over an orange. That's the way men are. Here's where I get off, and thanks very much.'

Bruce stopped the bike. He cleared his throat, tightened his lips, examined Evvie to the toes and wagged a vexed forefinger near her face. 'If you want some friendly advice,' he said, 'you'd better stay away from that guy Tayo and spend more time procuring knowledge, the way things are in this country today. It's none of my business. You were seen in the show with him the other night, see? Monking, I'm afraid. Where was your brother? Does Arthur know about this fight in the orchard, and the way the Puritans are talking around here, probably? And Dave Tobin. Old enough to be your father! Another thing, do you realize Tayo Delacroix is subnormal?' Bruce's voice rocketed to a great height, then slipped and fell into ragged pieces. He narrowed one eye, drew closer, lowered his voice. 'His people married relatives too close to them! What does he know about the difference between truth and logic? What does he realize about procuring knowledge and all like that? I shouldn't have to tell you he's super-dangerous to a trusting young girl. Listen, if you don't demand your mother to give you the facts of life, you're going to wake up one day and find yourself laid.'

Evvie noticed a faint mustache of coffee on Bruce's upper lip. She said, 'I don't really like Tayo, but a person gets bored here. I know what you mean. I don't like him that way.'

'That's better! You don't have to like your relatives just because they're relatives, either, like the people around here, so clannish. I'm going to tell you something, if you can take it. Listen, a real individual can hate his own mother. I could hate my own mother if I wanted to.'

Evvie blinked and swallowed. 'Are you studying to be an individual?'

'Who? I am an individual. I think you are, too.'

'Sure.'

'You might not know it, see? It's the way you look at things. You probably feel dissatisfied with your family.'

'Sure.'

'You feel like you want to do something different from your family, and the old-fashioned ways burn you up.' His lip with the coffee stain clamped down on the last word, and his eyes bored deeply into Evvie's. 'And everything you learn in school is a buncha static.'

'I went on a cucumber diet once,' Evvie said.

Bruce frowned, compressing his lips until his chin was wrinkled like a peach-stone.

'Nobody knew about it at home,' Evvie said.

'That's where you did wrong. You should have told them all. Your stomach is supposed to be your personal property. Nobody's supposed to stop you from expressing yourself.'

'It was to reduce the waist-line. I did it on the sly. I didn't care.'

'You should have had nuts and soybean bread. Damn it all, a fellow can't do that sort of thing in college.' Bruce's face suddenly became perfectly vacant. He looked into space, far down the foggy road.

Evvie considered Bruce as being terribly educated. She had an instinctive desire to have him know this. 'Bruce, what is a Jeopard?' she asked. But Bruce was still looking down abstractedly into the foggy distance. He pulled one cheek around to the front of his face and gnawed little fragments from the inside of the cheek while his eyes opened wider and wider. His lips were puckered over near the opposite ear.

Evvie said, 'Hey, Bruce, watch that girl coming. I bet she turns around and looks at us after she passes by.'

The approaching Negro girl was swinging a little basket in

wide circles, skipping, muttering to herself, fussing at some imaginary person. When she noticed Evvie and Bruce, she quit doing those things. Passing them, she lowered her head, flung her big white eyeballs sideways at them, lifted her upper lip and greeted them with a barely audible sound through her nose: 'Eng-yenh.' She went on for a few yards, then turned her head to look back.

'You see,' Evvie said. 'Now watch her do it again.'

The little Negress walked on, and presently turned again. After walking a safe distance, she boldly turned around completely, walking backwards, staring at them, frowning and mumbling. Suddenly she forgot them and went on skipping, muttering, swinging her basket. The fog dissolved her.

Bruce had apparently noticed nothing of his. With his lips open and his eyes wide, he was still gazing into space. Evvie, falling herself into an abstraction as deep as Bruce's, left him standing in the road and dreamily wandered off toward the store.

Waiting her turn at the counter, she lounged in a dream. Bruce had made her think of the city. She had heard New Orleans commented on many times by girls in school, by the kids of truck drivers who hauled fruit and produce to the French Market. New Orleans was a place where river water was sold like beans or coal-oil, where people all had locks on their doors. From now on in her mind Bruce would belong to all the soft images she had gathered of the place — walking with his careless leather jacket under street lamps wet like grapes, past all the sharp corners through busy crowds, somehow without colliding. In Evvie's picture of the city there were old women waiting with empty baskets; telephones ringing in vacant rooms; ferocious throngs yelling at the ballpark; fat lazy sparrows crossing the river on the ferry boat;

thousands of shower baths hissing; thousands of knuckles cracking; ropes of smoke hauled across the sky; boys sitting in trees for a week; plump fingers cupped under peanut vending machines; happy girls swinging their hats.

She saw Bruce walking past the Cathedral by the Square. There had been a wedding. The limousines had rolled away. An old yellow priest clucked and shooed at the children in their colored clothes, then he locked the tall doors. The drumming of heels faded. The old Cathedral stood black in the dusk with its thorny steeples. A small Negro girl came out of the shadows, crossed the street to the Cathedral entrance, then two more Negro children. The three stooped, forming themselves into black balls as they crept about the sidewalk, very busy and frightened, their brushing hands scooping the wedding rice from the pavement. A man, half turned, watched them from across the street. This was the truck driver Evvie had once heard telling her father about the incident.

During the day in school, Evvie's mind constantly dwelt on Tayo the barber. By the time she alighted from the school bus that afternoon, she had decided to take a casual walk down past the barber shop, just to prove she was an individual.

Tayo's shop was outside the levee, built on stilts high above the reach of flood water. Over it was a sign:

THEOPHILE
DELA ✠

Evvie looked into the shop as she went by. Tayo was busy with a customer. He had on a white coat. Evvie walked a ways down the road. She went down to the river edge, and for a while sat on a tuft of willow roots. The fog was cold, the water's surface chilled by the melting ice of the north. The staggering river's breath was heavy with the odor of its own strange liquors. It made her feel sad. She did not know what was the matter with her today. She took her books and climbed back to the top of the levee.

As she passed the barber shop, Tayo came out. He leaned his shoulder against the door-frame, smoking a cigarette, and fixed her with his stuffed-moose gaze. He spoke and she answered. After she had gone by, he called to her, 'Evvie, where you goin?'

'Home.'

'I wunt you to mail me a letter when you pass the pos office.'

'All right.'

He motioned her to follow him into the shop. He acted as though he had been expecting her, as if he knew she would not refuse to go into the shop because she did not know how to refuse. There was hair on the floor of the shop. Some of it was in patches, each of a different shade, and some in a heap mixed up into no color, or into the color of raw veal. From the big porcelain chair, a man might look at the river and see the white fruit liners pass, with a red and a green eye at night, and in the day a roaring white mustache.

Tayo said, 'You like my shop. Sit in the chair. Feel my new chair. Simulated leather. And I mean guaranteed simulated. Feel it.'

'I can see it.'

She wanted to leave now. She went to the door and did a few steps of a tap dance. Through the window she saw scores of black-hooded laughing gulls wheeling and grabbing the air with their wings over the foggy wharf, making a great commotion with their boisterous laughter. A boat was tied up out there.

Tayo said, 'Come see what they doin!' Evvie went to the window with him, and looked along his brown wrist to the long claw-like nail on the end. The boat was named *And How*, a lugger rigged for trawling. A group of boys on deck were squatting round a small heap of dead fish. A smiling Negro stood watching them with his legs crossed in the shape of a figure four. The boys had a can of lye. With driftwood sticks they were cramming lumps of lye down the gullets of the dead fish.

'Me, I showed them that trick,' Tayo said. 'Watch something.' Tayo cupped his hands and yelled, 'Eh, la bas! That's enough! Fling it! Go head!'

The boys heard Tayo. They all looked toward the barber shop and smiled. Then one of them picked up by the tail the fish that was stuffed with lye and flung it far up into the mist. All of the gulls cried madly, and swooped. They fought over the fish in the water. One large gull, gaining possession of the fish, flew off, gulping the fish greedily. Suddenly this gull shook its head violently and fluttered down to the water, looking around with an angry expression, then hopping and twisting. The other gulls and the boys were all laughing uproariously, and Tayo standing alongside Evvie laughed, 'Kyanh-kyanh-kyank-uh-hoo! Uh-hoo-hoo-hoo! Ain't that crazy? Uh-hoo-hoo-hoo!'

Tayo moved closer to Evvie. 'We gunna do that to the blagbirds around here soon. Uh-hoo!' He laughed softly, close to the side of her face. 'They pull up the corn, the blagbirds.' Evvie, her nostrils white, moved, and started to tap dance. She wanted to dance her way to the door. 'Listen, don't go,' Tayo said. 'Kiss me goo-bye, eh? Don't you wunt me to kish you goo-bye?' Evvie was in a corner, and Tayo held out his arms to bar the way like a man cornering a fowl in a chicken-yard. 'I got somethin nice for you.' He crossed the shop and closed the door that opened on the road. They were alone. Tayo stood with his back to the door, smiling with his gold teeth that had dewberry seeds between them.

'Where's the letter?' Evvie asked. She knew how to keep from crying. You looked ahead and imagined it was all over, and everything was all right again. Tayo knew her father was a brave man. 'I'll tell my father.'

'Me, I tell him you all the time comin by my shop when I'm busy and so forth. You ain no lil gull no more. I say I done had two fights account of you. I put somebody in the hospital for you. The people knows it, your paw too. I ain gunna hurt you. Me, I fight anybody tries to hurt you, sweedart. Try the new chair.'

'No indeedy.'

'You done right to come by my shop, sweedart. I been waitin for you. Whatsa matter with me? Do I smell like swimps and sulphur? Sit down there. Do I need a shave and do I roll cigarette with brown paper? Whatsa matter with my chair, by God? Anybody knows that leather is real simulated. I paid enough. Am I got something the matter with me?'

'I don't know.'

'I never talked this much in my life. Then I'll meet you in the willows or the canes at night whenever you say, and nobody gunna know. There you are! You can go now, and some night I blow the whistle by your house like this.' He cupped his hands into a hollow ball with a hole, and filled his chest with air. Watching her closely, he blew a long dove-

note. 'That's what you can call fun, yes, at night. Mon Dieu!
The little boy around here, they don't know nothing, sweedart.
Get you in trouble, you understand? Me? No chance!'

'All right, I'll go.' She backed toward the door. Tayo
smiled and took her hand. She stood looking into his eyes.
Her hair was bothering her forehead. She stuck out her chin
and lip and blew upward. 'You said ——'

'You and your sister gunna laugh at me tonight,' Tayo said,
in a new tone. He saw her frightened. He smiled. 'Promise
when I blow the dove you gunna say, "Mama, I gotta go out
to the toilet!" Promise.'

'For what?'

'Uh-hoo! Uh-hoo-hoo! Uh-hoo-hoo-hoo-hoo-hoo-hoo!'

'I wouldn't need to go to all that trouble to kiss you if I
wanted to.'

Tayo cleared his throat, tightened his lips, examined Evvie
to the toes, and wagged a vexed forefinger near her face.
'Me, I give you some advice,' he said. 'When I blow the
whistle in the night, you come out. You let me take care you,
sweedart. Then you gunna keep out of trouble, yes, because
listen, the first man come along — boom! you gunna fall down.
Because why? Because you good-hearted, ain't you?'

'Yes.'

'You donno how to say no. Somebody treat you nice, you
dunno how to say no. That's why you better let me take care
you, stay out of trouble. You know why I wunna get you,
me? For spite. Your sister turn me down. Me! I wunna
show her I can get somebody else right in the same house,
by God. Ain't that swell?'

'Sure.'

'So you gunna be my pal. Please. We gunna have fun.
And me I take care of you nice. No trouble if you be my pal.

Now you gunna lemme kish you, sweedart. I never talk so much in my life. Kiss me.'

Evvie pushed him away, sped to the window and climbed. 'Christ! Hey!' Tayo yelled.

Evvie dropped through the air about ten feet and landed in the thick weeds below. She recovered her schoolbooks and ran to the levee. Tayo was leaning out of the window, holding his lower lip between his fingers. Turning homeward, Evvie heard the laughter of the boys and the gulls out in the river.

The next afternoon, Evvie went on the road at mail time, hoping that Bruce Holt would come along. She wanted to have a lover to carry around in her mind. In a little while she saw Bruce's mother's car coming. Bruce was at the wheel. Passing her on the road, Bruce saluted her briefly with his horn, and increased his speed. His dust enveloped her completely. She stood coughing and rubbing her eyes. She looked after the car and smiled. 'It-shay!' she muttered.

She thought about Bruce that day. She remembered him in the grammar school class pageant on graduation day, dressed like Napoleon, carefully balancing his pompous hat on his head while he transferred Louisiana to the United States with a stroke of the pen, and with the other hand kept scratching his ribs and hips. It seemed that on the way to the graduation, Bruce had found the nest of an orchard oriole. Handling the nest, he had unknowingly spread bird-mites all over his Napoleon coat, and the mites began to reach his skin just as he was on the stage ready to sign the great document.

In the evening she wrote him a letter, but it was silly. She tore it up. She toyed with her pencil and tablet. She wanted to write a letter to a man. She thought of Dave Tobin.

Dear Mr. Tobin:

We all hope you are getting better. Please write some time and tell us how you are. It was a fine thing for you to fight over me, and everybody says you really conquared that Tayo. He is a sub-normle beast.

Well, there is no news from here. Mama's lilies are full of buds. I guess they will be thrown away. Oh, well.

I am so bored. But I guess you are too. Ha. Ha.

I do get my kicks and thrills some times. Yesterday the post master came from town in the mail plane that runs to Pilot Town. It landed in the river near the P.O., and when the post master got out, the Pilot offered me a ride. We went high up in the air thousands of feet, I forget how many it was. We saw the whole Mississippi Delta, the crooked river shining, the marshes all colors of green and brown and the Passes dumping in the Gulf like silver threads. The Delta is shaped like a Human Hand, the fingers are the Passes branching out in the Gulf. How beautiful and thrilling! In other words, we saw like a heron or goose. The Pilot sent me a big box of candy, that is bon-bons. I don't like him so much.

At this point Topal came through the room. Evvie grabbed the letter and put it under the tablet. Later she hid it in the little box in which she kept her snapshots, postcards, and other keepsakes. She did not want the letter to be seen, because the airplane incident was made up.

13

LISTEN HIM RUN FROM A OWL

THE WINDS of April scourged the trees all day, and on windy nights Evvie found a perverse pleasure in lying awake in the dark, feeling alone when everybody else was asleep except Topal in the kitchen. The wind worried a loose piece of tin on the roof, a sound like cold cymbals. Oranges on the trees would bump against the side of the house. Bump. Bump-bump. When the wind grew angry its gusts sounded like a scythe scattering mown foliage, while bits of clamshell grit from the road pelted the house. One sound stood out of the general chorus of noises, the laughter of a loon, and she could picture him alone on the black river riding the pointed troughs of the waves, shaking the water from his head. The bird's laughter sent an icy thrill through Evvie's flesh. She liked it.

Just then her mother in the next room sat up in bed and cried out. Mrs. Crochet was having one of her nightmares. 'Catch him! Catch him!' she cried.

Commodo jumped up and began wildly to feel around him. 'Where? Where?' he asked.

'Arthur's falling overboard!' Mrs. Crochet cried in the voice that seemed to come from under water. 'Quick! Catch him!' And she got out of the bed.

Commodo groped after her, climbing out of bed. 'Where?' he asked. 'Look out! Where?' The two were walking across the room together. Then Commodo bumped into a chair. He awoke and began to curse. 'Say, you!' he grumbled, shaking his wife. 'Wake up! Before hell, why you wunna eat crabs before bed, you?'

When they returned to bed, Mrs. Crochet was weeping, and Evvie heard her father's sleepy voice trying to comfort her. 'My son,' she cried. 'I had a terrible dream about my son! Listen to that storm. Goddle mighty, where is he, I wonder, on that road some place in this storm.'

'Go to sleep, Duck. This ain no storm, jiss a little sheep lightnin an a poop of wind.'

Mrs. Crochet left her bed again and lit two blessed candles to protect the house against blowing down. Then she went out into the yard.

'Duck!' Commodo called. 'Where you goin?' She did not answer.

Mrs. Crochet felt her way around the yard to the schooner boom that held the kitchen up. She passed her hands over it, and felt around the bottom, where the rotted part was located. The stake in the ground was not doing any good. The boom was moving every time a hard gust blew. Mrs. Crochet went to the shed and found a stick of wood, which she placed as a wedge between the boom and the stake. Then she went in and moved Gussie and Paul from their bed on the kitchen table and put them on the floor in her bedroom. As soon as this was done, the wind died away. It was very quiet outside, so that Evvie could plainly hear the cistern in the back yard leaking on the drainboard, a slow lonely tapping, several taps and a pause, like a blind man's cane.

Tayo Delacroix, passing on his way home after visiting his

woman up the road, every night would blow the dove call for
Evvie to come out. Evvie was pleased. She wanted the
strong and savage fool to come around calling her; and, safe
inside among her people, she liked to be frightened by the
call.

One night she heard the call from the road, then later it
sounded again and again off to the side of the house among the
orange trees. The bell of a passing ship struck three times,
half past nine. Again the dove note came, this time farther
toward the rear, deep among the trees, luring her attention all
the time farther back from the house.

Evvie went to the kitchen, but checked herself near the door
as she noticed that Topal was standing before a propped-up
mirror. Topal had been acting very curiously for the past
two days, going about singing songs, and even smiling frequently. This was because a young carpenter from New Orleans working on a building near-by had talked to her frequently on the levee, and had asked her to go to the show with
him in his car.

Evvie craned her neck to see what Topal was doing. Both
of Topal's hands were moving in greased circles around and
around her bared breasts. Confused, Evvie turned to leave;
but Topal heard her and turned.

'You dirty little spy!' she whispered.

'I wasn't spying, Tope.'

'What do you want — out of bed?'

'I'm — I'm going to the toilet.'

'You're a liar by the clock. You're spying.'

Topal, stripped to the waist, drew herself up to her full
height. Her naked chest swelled and sank furiously. It was
griddled with secret bones peculiar to see, and the stunted
knobs of breasts glowed after her diligent kneading. 'Go

ahead and laugh!' she whispered hoarsely. 'Let's see you laugh once.'

'I'm not laughing.'

Topal reached savagely behind her and clutched the bottle she was using. 'Tell Mama, you hear?' she whispered, shoving the bottle under Evvie's nose. 'You see it? It's T. J.'s cod-liver oil from the clinic. Now go tell her!' She was backing Evvie around the room, waving the bottle under Evvie's nose.

'What did I ever tell on you?' Evvie asked.

'Everything! You tell everybody everything!'

'Not anything like this I never would.'

'Well, get going.'

Topal realized she was half nude. She jerked up her dress, wiped her tears, went to the window and stood with her head bowed, her spine sagging in its accustomed curve. The dove note sounded in the yard, very softly. Evvie made a movement to approach her sister, but she did not know what to do or say. And she did not want to go outside.

'Go where you're going,' Topal said.

Evvie closed the door behind her and stood there. It was very dark. The call sounded again. Tayo was in or behind a tree across the yard. Evvie heard Topal's hand on the door-knob inside. She hurried away toward the outhouse. Topal opened the door, looked out, and closed it. Evvie crossing the yard was conscious of her name, which often came to her when she was doing a foolish or embarrassing thing. Evvie Crochet. It tasted very stupid, the name. And, even though the darkness usually seemed to erase her name and make her feel anonymous and free, the darkness did not do so now. She heard Tayo's signal from the tree near-by. 'Pssst!' She went closer to the tree.

'*Evvie!*' came the whisper from the tree.

Evvie raised her hands and felt for the lowest limb. She swung back and forth playfully. She heard movements in the tree above her.

'Evvie!'

'Don't call me that!' she whispered.

'I'm coming down, me!'

'I'll go inside!' She took a firmer hold on the limb, and did the trick called skinning the cat. She was afraid of her power to make a grown man come and see her in the night. This power seemed now to be something very big, not belonging to her. It frightened and fascinated her. Tayo's footprints would be in the yard tomorrow.

Just then Evvie heard the slow heavy bumping of bare feet in the house, her father crossing the kitchen. She heard him talk to Topal. The back door opened. Commodo's oval body that looked like it was made of puffy bread filled the yellow space.

Evvie sprang up into the tree. Tayo's hand touched her shoulder. 'Uh-hoo-hoo!' he laughed softly. He had been out in the marshes to kill a deer for his woman. His pants were dripping water, and they gave off vapors that smelled of rotting vegetation. The kitchen door across the yard closed, and her father gave a great bellowing yawn as he sat on the steps to await her return from the outhouse.

'Don't be a-scared,' Tayo whispered. 'I never whistle so much in my life. Hold my hand.'

'Papa'll beat the living heck out of you,' Evvie whispered.

Tayo's faint giggle sounded between his teeth. 'Listen, you wunna see ef your papa's a brave man?'

'Shh!'

Tayo held his nose and produced a loud sound exactly like

the chill and tremulous cry of a screech-owl. Evvie felt the
prickles crawl to the roots of her hair.

'Do it again.'

She heard her father hurriedly leave his seat. He stood
hesitantly by the lighted window. 'Possay!' he shouted at
the tree. 'Possay!' Evvie felt Tayo's body shaking with mirth.
He held his nose and sounded the long eerie note again.
Commodo hurried away toward the front of the house. He
climbed over the levee.

'Listen him run from a owl!' Tayo said. 'He ain't so brave,
but that's awright. I like him. I ain gunna hurt him, because he married my third-cudden.' His reaching fingers
grazed one of Evvie's ears. She pushed the hand away, parry-
ing the searching fingers. 'He ain no good, and never will be
no good, but I like him, and I like you. I ain gunna hurt you.
We gunna show Miss Topal she ain't the only pebble on the
beach. I'll show her. Come up by me, sweedart.'

'Why is Papa no good?' Evvie asked, pushing at the invisible hand. It was a duel in the dark, with Tayo trying to
reach around Evvie's guard. 'Tell me why my father's no
good.'

'He's a Crochet.'

'Yes.'

'A Crochet.'

'Quit saying the name! Tell me what else about him?'

'He's a greedy-gut and a lummix!'

'Sure. Sure.'

'Shoot, me I could tell you all kind of things. He loves mud.
He walk on his pants in the back.'

'Tell me,' Evvie said. She moved closer to Tayo.

'Say you, I ain no back-biter. He's my fourth-cudden. You
gunna go back and tell your maw.'

'No! No!' Tayo's arm was about her waist. 'Tell me more.'

'He's lazy. Yall cistern been leakin five year. The fossit. He won't fix it.'

'And do we have to carry water from next door?'

'Sure. A washer. Jiss a washer for a nickel for the fossit. He never will be no good, and the rain gunna fall in your bed always.'

The invisible hand was sinking into her ribs. Tayo put his lips against her cheek. She turned her head, but allowed him to hold her against him. 'What else. Tell me about Mama.'

'Your maw awright, but *her* maw was a nasty ole woman.'

'Sure.'

Tayo began to giggle. 'She tied her babies while she was hoeing cucumbers to the fig tree all day so they couldn't crawl in the sun and get burnt and look like mulattoes. They got the bone-fever from the dampness and the shade, they say.'

Evvie fell into deep thought, figuring this out. She saw her mother as a baby with a rope tied around her middle, crawling around in the thick damp shade of a fig tree. Tayo's hand was revolving in circles round Evvie's shoulder blade.

The kitchen door across the yard opened. Mrs. Crochet stood there, silhouetted in her nightgown, and called: 'Evvie!'

'Yessam!' Evvie replied automatically.

Tayo jerked his hands away from Evvie, and started to climb down the tree, making a loud racket as he squirmed wildly through impeding limbs.

'Where are you at, for God sake?' Mrs. Crochet shouted.

'Up in the tree!' Evvie answered. 'I'm coming!'

On the ground, Tayo whispered, 'Here, this is for you. Don't show it to nobody.' He pressed into her hand a small cardboard box. The contents rattled. 'That's for you when

I come back anudda night.' Then he swished off through the grass.

'Say, you! What are you doin out there?' Evvie's mother called.

'I was trying to catch the owl up in that tree,' Evvie said.

'Get!' Mrs. Crochet swung her hand. The wind from it grazed Evvie's face. 'Get — back — to bed — you ...' Evvie leapt up the steps and ran through the house to the front room.

In bed, she heard her mother fussing. 'If chasin after owls at night ain't a screw loose ... Me, I don't understand what's gettin the matter with her lately.'

'She's got the adolescents. Leave the chile go, Duck,' Commodo said sleepily. 'We gotta buy her that book with the facts of life.'

Topal was awake alongside Evvie on the pallet. She said, 'You hear that? You better watch your step with them owls.'

In the darkness Evvie slipped Tayo's gift under the mattress. She supposed it contained candies, but examining it next morning she saw that it was some stuff for feminine hygiene. She was very angry at Tayo, and resolved never to look at him again. 'He ought to use it on himself!' she thought. But she rubbed some of the stuff in each of her armpits, to see how it felt to be fastidious and banish the worries of her sex. She hid the box in the back shed, for use on special occasions in future. Henceforth, seeing Tayo on the road in the daytime, she would straighten her golden hair and look the other way. And he never blew his whistle at night again.

14

WE GOT TO USE THAT MOON

THERE WAS a good moon during the dry spell, and for two days the mosquitoes were thinned out by the gruff Lenten winds. The Crochets received Communion, and walked home among their dark neighbors all gladdened by the Palm Sunday sermon. Bruce Holt walked home with the Crochets. All of them carried palm leaves or sprigs of arbor vitae or sweet bay which Father Pendergast had blessed in honor of Christ entering Jerusalem among waving palms.

Bruce walked alongside of Evvie, who could think of little to talk about, because her parents were there. And she was ashamed of her father's tennis shoes which had slits cut over the little toes. Old man Dupré's car passed them, driving faster than Evvie had ever seen it go, and the back curtain was pulled down. But Evvie glimpsed Juarelle sitting in the back seat as the car went by.

Mrs. Crochet was speaking to Bruce about his college life in Tulane University. 'You ain't gettin in bad company I hope in town, Bruce.'

'No mam.'

'A fine young scholar like you's gunna make your parrents proud. Avoid bad company, son. And I like you to go to the French Market sometime and see Arthur and talk to him, you hear?'

'Yes mam. Our class went there the other day to study the construction. They sure knew how to build in olden times.'

'Go see him where him and Henri sells the fruit. Me, I'm always nervous he might be in bad company — like right now when we all receiving Communion this morning and he's in town doin I-don't-know-what and oughta be here receiving with you like you all used to do together. I wish he was in college by you, and turn out to be a fine young scholar too.'

'Yes mam.'

Bruce picked up a clamshell and threw at a green chameleon twitching up a post.

'I guess you like school,' said Mrs. Crochet.

'Pretty well, yes mam.'

'And you got nice lessons?'

'Aw, we make experiments and problems and we listen to the lectures and stuff.'

Commodo was walking ahead of the others. A man came by in the river, floating downstream in a pirogue. The man was bailing out the pirogue with a tin can.

'Eh, Placide!' Commodo roared. 'What you say, bruddin-law? Why don't you bore a hole in the bottom to leave the water out?'

The man in the river waved his hand and grinned. All of the people on the levee road laughed. Commodo made a hollow cylinder out of one of his hands and smacked it with the palm of the other hand, and howled with laughter, as he always did after repeating some joke he had heard on the radio.

'The ole buck showin off embarrassing me,' said Mrs. Crochet.

'I'm surprized myself when I say somethin funny,' said Commodo. 'It jiss pops outa me. I hafta laugh myself. Pffyah-hyanh-hyanh-hyanh!'

'Did you ever seen a hurricane?' Mrs. Crochet asked.

'Who? I was raised with hurricanes, and I went to school with them. HYANH–HYANH–HYANH–HYANH!'

'You gunna think one slapped you crooked in a minute, embarrassing your family and Evvie and her little friend.'

Evvie smiled at Bruce, and the boy grinned. Bruce was not Smarty Pants now. He was a shy young scholar, with no opportunity to show off. Evvie decided that she was in love with him.

'Juarelle's pretty,' she said.

'Pretty for Grass Margin,' said Bruce. 'But her brother's ugly enough. I kind of respect Shoepick. He looks like a mean nigger, but he's all right. He took me to his house last night and sang some of his songs. He showed me how to stuff a bird.'

'I feel sorry for him,' Evvie said. 'They stole his song.'

'I helped him to write a letter about that to the man in Chicago. We worked a long time, and did a good job, if I say it myself. But then Shoepick tore it up. He wasn't satisfied. His floor was full of letters torn up that he wrote.'

Later that day Evvie met Bruce on the road. Bruce was playing with a snapping turtle he had found crossing the levee. Evvie stopped and stood by. Bruce did not notice her. She watched him teasing the reptile with a large stick, poking at the turtle's nose. He seemed to be teasing her instead of the turtle, poking the stick into her face. The turtle's vicious head flashed out of the shell. Evvie gasped. The ferocious jaws snapped the stick, sinking deeply into the wood. Bruce raised the stick and swung it back and forth, the turtle clinging to its end. Bruce went up the road without a word to Evvie, swinging the turtle in wide arcs, leaving Evvie standing where she was. He looked to her like a small kid, years younger than she. He dropped the turtle when he tired of it. Walking among the willows outside the levee, Evvie followed Bruce, recovered the turtle, which was still clinging to the stick, and took it home for dinner.

She stayed in love with Bruce for days.

In the nighttime Mrs. Crochet said, 'Thang God for a good moon.' Her voice was fretful. The moon was needed for their secret work in the lily patch. She had been making many visits by night to the patch, digging here and there around the bulbs to see how much they had grown. Just when rain was needed, there had been none. 'Diapers on the clouds in April!' she fussed, 'and no fog when you wunt it. Fog in the canes every morning would be a blessin to give my lilies a drink. Jiss a drop for each. Fog in the canes! My God.'

'Still you believe strong in lilies,' said Commodo.

'I believe in lilies.'

'I say I'll take okra and oranges to make a livin if we get that property.'

'Okra's a rancid line of work. You and your okra, the Crochets. I feel my wristes on fire jiss thinkin about pickin okra. Far as oranges, they got too many oranges in the world. Miss Nellie say California fulla oranges raised by fotten tractors, and the owners don't hardly live on their land. Them rich people go to their groves once a year to humbug aroun wearing them cowboy pants in a automobile. Florida's fulla oranges. Again, they starting in Texas to plant our kind of crop, and sending their men over here to hunt the oil unneat our marshes. Me, I don't understand such a crazy, tangled-up, fishin-cackle way to run the world. Come, Evvie, we gotta use that moon. Less go mulch bulbs.'

'Mama, why do you always take your empty pocketbook to the field?'

'It ain empty!' Commodo laughed. 'It'll take her all night to name you what's in it, excep money, excep money.'

They all laughed at Mrs. Crochet.

Evvie and her mother crept through the back weeds and canes. The lily stalks in the patch bore thousands of white buds which the drought and the cool weather had retarded from opening.

Evvie liked to work under the moon when the mosquitoes were few. For mulching, they used dried cane leaves gathered from the ground in the adjoining cane thicket. They crawled about on hands and knees, and with their fingers scooped the heaps of shriveled leaves and carried them to the lily rows to spread thickly around the bases of the stalks.

'They gunna seddle down their own self,' Mrs. Crochet said. 'They gunna make a tight mulch the sun can't get through. In a drought, that ole sun drinks up moisture like a drunker.'

'Shh! Somebody's on the road!'

'*This mulch gunna keep cool the greedy roots!*' Mrs. Crochet whispered, '*and dampen the bulbs to make them swell up!*' She patted the mat of dried leaves over the earth that still held the sun's warmth. 'Pack em, honey! God dog it to hell, me, I wunna see them bulbs fatten lovely, drink up all the water they can steal, swell up lovely and big and yellow like gold! Don't you listen to him about that ole okra, the damn Crochets. I wooden have my girls pickin okra when it don't do no good to wear a stockin on your arm, the terrible stingers they got that I don't know why Almighty God gives them to a plant at all and wunts people to eat it.'

The earth where they gathered the leaves was cold, damp,

pungent as a ginger cake under the thick mat, black and glistening in the moonlight streaking through. As Evvie crawled over it, and her quick arms reached, and her fingers scurried outward to claw, the ground awoke before her. A frog plinked, squirmed out, snapped open and away. A scared beetle trickled down the pokeberry leaves. A skink or a tiny cricket fled. On all fours with her face hanging over the ground, she felt like a scrawny beast herself, cousin to the creatures that haunt the earth's pores and drink its secret vapors. Her mother was a larger, older animal sharpened by the years, with eyes growing more clear and careful as her bosom dried, and a wry heart humble to God alone.

'Mud's not dirt,' Evvie said.

'Only when people is around,' Mrs. Crochet said. 'Trees and bushes is clean. I know the lilies is proud, but then its funny our dirty hands is gotta help them stay alive tonight.'

'Sure.' Evvie smelled her dusty wrists. 'Mud is mud. Dirt is dirt. There's all kinds of different dirt, Mama.'

'For real dirt, you gotta look around a person's house. Kitchen dirt's different than the parlor. A automobile is no place for cobwebs to hang. Smears from people grabbin a white door is hard to come aloose, yes. That gray seddlement that congregates in the pipe of a icebox is the nastiess. Throw it in the yard, and a pig would take the road, and it ain got no name. Look how company brings dirt on their feet, and takes some away on their sleeves. A person can always smell a ole baseball in a drawer, the whole drawer smells, and that's the tangled-up smells a boy brings home. That T. J. gunna do it some day, the lil rascal. My God. The smells of a boy.'

Evvie said, 'The stuff in the bottom of a man's pocket is funny dirt. And the funny ball of fuzz that rolls ahead of the broom when you sweep. I wonder what it's made out of? It keeps getting bigger and bigger, and it's hard to corner with a broom.'

They worked until their backs were tired. They left the patch and squirmed through the canebrake. On the high road across the canal they saw the yellow light in their kitchen by the distant levee, and they heard a baby squalling.

'Jiss looka them,' said Mrs. Crochet. 'Still sittin up, and it muss be after nine o'clock. That house falls to pieces when I go by my lilies.'

Evvie said, 'Mama, you know what I feel like eating?'

'Don't start that, girl.'

'Boiled corn.'

'My God.'

'Just boiled corn, but plenty. Four ears.'

'My God.'

'Long ones, hot from the pot. Hold it over the pot till the water drips off. That steam is sweet. Those soft milky grains busting in your mouth, I'd play those ears like a harmonica. I'd go all the way across on three rows of grains, then back on three. And would I suck the end of that cob where the grains get smaller and disappear!'

'Veal round for me right now,' the mother said. 'Tender veal round, thick as the little finger. Fresh soda crackers, and roll them with a bottle fine. Buss your eggs and use only the yolks, beat them with a spoon of cream's the way to do it. Dip your meat in that, then roll it in your crumbs and leave it stand till the crumbs soaks up the egg and it won't come off in the fryin-pan, but make a crispy cruss to keep in the juice. Fry it light brown and drip off every lass drop of grease caffle. Watch out you don't buss that cruss. That's what I could use right this minute, me, with potatoes raw sliced thin

and salted and baked dry tell they swell up like a bubble.
Them potatoes is good for Papa's sour stummick, on accounta
no grease. Less us shut up.'

'Mama, I didn't know you could cook butcher meat so
nice.'

'Who? Listen, don't get me started about when Papa was
on the *Blessed Trinity*, because I'll make you cry with the
dishes.'

As soon as they reached the back kitchen steps, Paul and
Gussie came running, eyes popped, each trying to get ahead
of the other.

'Mama! Guess who's here!' Paul cried. 'He's got ——'

'Muncle Dewey! Muncle Dewey!' Gussie interrupted.

'He's got — say, you! Lemme tell her ——'

The boys were trying to shove each other out of the doorway.

'Well, lemme come in, before I mauldrag somebody, actin
like Indians in front of Uncle Dewey. Hello, Dewey! I'm a
son-of-a-bugger! You made up your mind at lass to come see
us.'

Commodo's brother Dewey was walking up and down the
kitchen with T. J. in his arms. T. J. was sucking the man's
necktie. Dewey Crochet was very large, and well dressed.
He was one of the best pilots at the Station down near the
mouth of the river.

'Hell, for tree months I come close to shore and blow the
whistle every time I pass on a ship, and nobody comes out on
the levee until you need me,' he said. 'I didn't know if you
was livin or dead which.'

'Oui, we livin skeletons. Excep your brudda here that the
neighbors is feedin him tell he's ready to buss.'

Paul and Gussie dashed to the front room and came running

back to show what Uncle Dewey had brought for Commodo
— a few used neckties of fine quality, a fine, slightly-worn
pearl-gray Stetson hat, and a pair of button shoes.

'For three months I run my ships nilly up againss the willows and blow the whistle forty-leven times, and nobody comes
out. They don't care about Uncle Dewey untel they wunt
something, do they, do they?' he asked, rubbing his nose
against the baby's nose.

Commodo said, 'Go look under your pillow, Duck.'

'My God, when is Jewpray gunna fix your house,' Dewey
asked. 'When I come in and walked on the floor, the whole
place shaked. No studdin for the walls, only one by twelve
planks, and the top sills is made outa two by twelves, that
heavy stuff come off the levee revetment years ago. It's top-
heavy.'

'Go look under your pillow,' Commodo told his wife.

Evvie followed her mother into the bedroom. Under the
pillow was a folded paper. Mrs. Crochet took it into the
kitchen. It was a check signed by Dewey Crochet.

'Sixty dollar! Sixty dollar!' she screamed. 'Our property!
Oh, Duck, our property! Our house to go on the doorsteps!'

'Woopy!' Commodo yelled, and grabbed his wife. They
danced about. Mrs. Crochet clutched Dewey's arm, kissed
him, and the three embraced and danced. The children
smiled and ran to and fro, and little T. J. began to bawl.

'Commodo tole me about that nice property,' said Dewey.
'How come you didn't notify me before that you needed
money? He been runnin aroun here like he swallowed a lime
kiln, and never think of axin his brudda for the money that's
got a studdy job!' Dewey's face was red with embarrassment.
Everybody was standing around with red faces, smiling.

When the excitement subsided, Mrs. Crochet slipped away

and went to the beautiful front steps, and stayed there awhile
to get control of her tears of joy, to say a prayer of thanksgiving
for the fulfillment of her novena, to think of reasons why this
miracle could not possibly be true. When she returned to the
kitchen, she went gloomily about, with the old fierce light in
her eyes, saying nothing. But presently she went to the oven
of the wood stove and took out Commodo's old derby hat.
'Thang God the rangatang can throw this ole trash away now!'
she said gruffly. 'Listen, you all, who wunts to go heave this
trash in the river?'

'The one that chunks that hat in the river goes after it,' said
Commodo.

'Dewey, honey, you go throw it away,' said Mrs. Crochet.
'You gave it to him, and you can throw it away.'

Dewey said, 'No, leave him go, sweedart. If he likes the
derby, leave him have it. Me, I paid seven dollars for that
derby in 1916. It turned green on me because it blew overboard on me, and the Third Engineer in that ship went to
work and dried it by the boilers. It turned green.'

'The ole thing draws ants, and still he fancies it,' said Mrs.
Crochet. 'I never had a livin ant in my house before that
hat come here.'

'Leave him wear it,' said Dewey, 'and he can use the Stetson
I brung tonight to go to church and all like that with the
fambly. I say that derby never drawed no ants when I had it.
It's mighty funny.'

'Let's cook,' said Topal, sensing an approaching argument.

'Any place he puts it, the ants come, Dewey,' said Mrs. Crochet, 'excep in the oven.'

'Me, I never seen a hat draw ants,' Dewey said.

'Put it on the floor a while, you gunna see the ants come.'

'It needs a new sweatband,' Dewey said. 'It never drawed

no ants for me. Red ants likes sweat. I guess the Stetson I brung tonight gunna draw ants too, and the shoes and stuff I brung.'

'Mais non! That Stetson's lovely, Dewey! Gray's his color, because his eyes is blue. Listen, them ties and shoes and stuff is lovely. The idea! Thanks, Dewey. Thanks.'

'I could find somebody glad to get them things at the pilot station.'

'Now hush up, Dewey Crochet!' Mrs. Crochet kicked at the seat of Dewey's pants. 'Listen, it might not be the derby that draws ants. It might be him. Something the matter with the rangatang's blood.'

A complete silence fell, and it was awkward. Topal went to the front room and took a cigarette and match from Dewey's coat pocket. She went to the front steps and lit the cigarette. She took hurried puffs, waving the smoke away with her hand. The young carpenter who had asked her for a date had gone back to New Orleans, and she had resumed the habit of smoking she had learned from Tayo Delacroix, and given up trying to hold her body straight.

Mrs. Crochet inside carefully folded the ties and took them to the bedroom. Dewey Crochet walked back and forth, jouncing the baby. Evvie sat in a corner with a worried look on her face. She wished her uncle and Commodo would begin drinking and talking.

Mrs. Crochet came back and said, 'Hunt a chair, Dewey! Did they tell you our Arthur's driving a truck now? You ought to see him drive that truck once. So proud!'

'Red ants likes sweat,' Dewey said. 'That wasn't a bad hat. It never drawed no ants at the pilot station. The pilot station is the cleaness place in the State of Louisiana.'

Mrs. Crochet glanced darkly at her brother-in-law. 'Before

hell, my floors is mopped every livin day,' she said. She stooped and rubbed her hand on the floor, and showed it to Dewey. 'Fine a scrap of duss on my floor or trash! Fine any!'

'1916 to 1919 I had that derby, and not a solitary inseck. It's mighty funny, that's all I know. We particular as ole hell about bugs down at the station. I never saw a roach there. I never saw a thousan-laig. I never saw a bedbug. Not even a fly. Not a fly!'

'Hush up with the ants!' Commodo called from the next room. 'Everybody got ants, the rich like the poor and Protason like Catlick or Jew. I never seen a ant take the road when he seen a pilot comin.'

'Ants lives on trash and garbage,' Mrs. Crochet said.

Dewey Crochet walked nervously back and forth, bouncing the baby faster and faster while T. J. beat his fists and began to crow with delight. 'The bess way to fight insecks is soap and water. Soap is cheap, but elbow grease is hard to find in any fambly. It ain today I learned how to be clean.'

'Trash draws ants,' Mrs. Crochet said, 'and it's gotta stink pretty bad, too.' She slammed a pot on the stove, lifted the pot, put it down, moved it back and forth. Then she began to walk the floor in opposite directions with Dewey. 'Bring trash in a clean house and what happens? You gunna have ants and thousan-laigs following the trash.'

'Trash coss seven dollars sometimes,' Dewey said, 'and keep some people from poundin the road naked.'

Commodo bounced out of the bedroom and flung his finger into the air above his head. 'Ef we naked,' he howled, 'we honess! I got corns, me, on my hands, not on my behind, thang God!'

'Who?' Dewey shouted. 'You gunna tell me I don't work? I been on that river sense I was that high. By Jove. I don't

ax no health nurse how to live, and shoot poor innocent birds
to get coupons for a curtain-rod.'

'Your backside gunna be glad when you dead,' Commodo
said.

Evvie in the corner put her head on the side and frowned
deeply, studying over her father's last remark.

'Okay,' Dewey said. 'Give me back my trash. I give them
to somebody got no insecks and got some gratitude. I give
them to Red Bienvenue like I been giving him my pants and
coats because he's got gratitude. My clothes fit him because
he works his fat off in the field to keep his well-raised chirren
plump.'

The twins sitting on the floor gravely watched big Uncle
Dewey. They were fond of him. For years he had been sending the family bundles of old funny papers, some of them
printed in strange languages, dropped on the levee by the
pilot of the daily mail plane.

Commodo said, 'Some talks about hard work that they
never did nothin stringent in their born days' life.'

'You mighty right!' Dewey answered. 'You oughta know.
Again, some people got no responsibility excep making jokes
and lookin at their tongue all day in the bottom of a ditch and
everything that throws a reflection. If you know what responsibility is, after you get a start in life you got it easy. I
like to know how I come to be a pilot?'

'Who? Anybody can be a pilot if they got influence. Me, I
spit on influence! The hell with it!'

'Duck, your daughters!' Mrs. Crochet said.

'They jiss like politicians, the pilots,' Commodo went on.
'They are politicians, think they God Almighty and the people
that paddles a pirogue across their river is trash. What do they
do excep eat and sleep and come close to shore with the ships

to sink an honess man's boat, and hardly ever lay a hand on the wheel?'

'Is that so?' Dewey retorted. 'You go learn the bottom of that river and tell me where the big muds is. I like to see you.'

'Eh bien! Hyanh-hyanh-hyanh! Me, I can teach you things about that river!'

'I like to see you in a head wind and high river steer a oil tanker with a empty bow!'

'Before hell, I got a pitcha of that river bottom in my mind, like you see me here. That pitcha unrolls like toilet paper in my head when I move up that river.'

'I wunna see you swing a big tanker in a head wind with a empty bow around Cowshit Point like I hadda do the other day, with a monkey-face Jap skipper peepin at you down below.'

'I coulda had a easy job today,' Commodo said, 'I coulda been a politician with the road paved in front of my house and drudge-boats named after my babies. Me, I wooden use influence! I spit on influence. I'm a sick man, but I don't need influence.'

'You and your sickness holes hands on the road and laughs at the ress of us. Who made you sick? Who made you wouldn't eat nothin but fried meat when we was kids. Blame the fried meat. Blame the poor fried meat that your windows won't open and frogs is breedin under your house today.'

'To hell with influence,' Commodo said. 'I married the girl I loved, and that's why I'm workin hard like you see me. I wooden marry no politician's third cousin. The hell with influence!'

Dewey shook his fist in Commodo's face. 'Don't you start traducin my angel that's lookin down from heaven on you tonight!' he screamed.

'I never traduced her! I said she was a politician's third cousin, and you married her. I can't help it that she hauled off and died.'

Mrs. Crochet stepped between the brothers with her fingers in her ears. '*I done heard enough!*' she screeched. 'Now the both of you all quit fussin like chirren over what's past and gone.'

'I'll mauldrag him!' Dewey Crochet said.

'Shut up, now!' Mrs. Crochet commanded. 'Philomene was a lovely girl and a perfect lady, and too good for any dinwiddie around here.'

Dewey handed the baby to Mrs. Crochet. 'I'm gunna shove off,' he said coldly. 'I come to see your little fambly and have some peace and company for a change. I'll see you when you wunt something from me again, you hear? I'm goin up the road. Listen, I like to have that skull.'

'I thought you leff that skull for Arthur,' Mrs. Crochet said.

Commodo stepped up. 'Leave him have his ole skull. Arthur don't wunt the ole skull.' He reached over his head and opened a screened hanging-safe that dangled from the ceiling. In more prosperous families, such a container was used as a place to store surplus or left-over food. Commodo brought out a human skull and handed it to his brother. This was an Indian skull discovered in a Mayan ruin. A ship passenger had presented it to Dewey some years previously. Dewey had brought it to Arthur when Arthur was supposed some day to go to medical college.

'Here, take your ole skull,' said Commodo, his face racked by emotion. 'We took it with a good heart, that skull. It was a token of you, Dewey. Me, I'll never forget this night. Things is never gunna be the same, mock my words, Messyou Dewey Crochet.'

'Can I have a piece of paper or a paper bag, please?' Dewey asked with chill formality.

'Dewey, you dinwiddie, why you wunna act so rancid?' Mrs. Crochet asked. 'Gimme that skull, god dog it! Now sit down! You all ack like chirren, both of you all.' She placed the skull on the window-sill. Paul and Gussie shrank away, sliding their backs along the wall. Topal always used the skull to frighten them into obedience when the mother was away.

Uncle Dewey went solemnly to the front room. He returned with a floursack on his back. The sack was bulging. 'Here some stuff I brung, if you all wunt it,' he said. 'If you don't wunt it, throw it in the river because it might draw ants, or give it away to somebody got some gratitude. I'm goin up the road to see Mateo. I be welcome in Mateo's house.'

Dewey lingered. He folded his arms by the window, looking out into the darkness with his keen pilot's eyes.

Mrs. Crochet kicked off her shoes, rolled up her sleeves and reached into the sack. 'You sit right smack in that chair, Dewey Crochet!' she ordered. 'Listen, don't start me fussin at you! The idea! Topal, darlin, light the stove. Evvie, get Mama some water next door. Oh Duck! Looka! A big redfish! Jiss looka the size of this redfish that ole rascal brung us!'

'I seen a redfish before.'

Dewey said, 'Smell it if it ain't poison maybe.'

Topal hopped over to the stove and raked the ashes. Evvie grabbed the water bucket. Excitement possessed the twins. They ran back and forth through the house. Gussie tripped on a rug and Paul fell over him. The baby in Commodo's arms began to bellow hoarsely.

'Sweet peppers!' Mrs. Crochet shouted. 'Now I know what he wunts me to cook. A court boullon, eh Dewey? Look at the lovely bell peppers out of season which I dunno where the ole rascal ever got them this time of year! They come off a ship from Florida, huh, Dewey. You begged them off a cook on a ship, huh? Huh, Dewey?'

'I dunno,' Dewey said.

'Poor Evvie was wishing for boiled corn. Jiss ole boiled corn.'

Dewey glumly unbottoned his shoes for comfort, and let down one of the straps of his suspenders.

15

YOU IN LOVE WITH A
SOFT-BALL TEAM

THE LEAVES under the moon lapped over one another and shone like the scales of a fish, and a rug of black shadow was spread under each tree. As she reached the corner of the house with her bucket, Evvie saw a pale form detach itself from the side of the house and steal off toward the levee — one of the neighbors who had been crouched under the window to hear what Dewey Crochet was saying, and Commodo, during the big argument. Evvie paused, startled for the moment, then she went quickly through the trees toward the house next door.

She began to sing. Everything was swell! Everything was exciting! She could smile to herself at the woman standing under the window to eavesdrop. She crossed the ditch separating the properties. The people next door were in bed. She took a bucket of water from their cistern. Evvie's bucket had a hole in it. The water trickled out. Evvie lugged it through the dark as fast as she could, her body leaning far sideways, her knees knocking, her legs repeatedly pricked by briers. She did not mind. Her thoughts sang excitedly while she grunted. 'Good white water to make red gravy. Hot fish, white as snow. There went an owl. When the blood-blister grows out to the end of my fingernail, I'll tell Bruce good-bye during a

storm on the levee, and go off to the convent.' Then she sang
aloud: 'Oh, the monkey wrapped his tail around the flagpole!'
But her great haste caused her to knock the bucket against an
unseen stump and spill most of the water. She went back to
the cistern for another, giggling. She lugged it as far as the
sloping ditchbank. Here the earth had been wet by previous
drippings. Her heel slipped. She fell on her backside with a
bump, and rolled down into the dry ditch with the water on
top of her. She picked herself up and went back to the cistern.

Everything was lovely. The big quarrel was over. Uncle
Dewey had brought everything necessary for a good court
boullon — sweet peppers, garlic, thyme, bay leaves, parsley,
onions, canned tomatoes, twelve allspice in a paper, two lem-
ons, and a small flask of sherry wine. And knowing there was
never any bread left over in this house, he had fetched a chunk
of stale bread from the kitchen at Pilot Town, and the butter
to fry it in.

Topal mashed the allspice in a saucer, and its aroma filled
the kitchen. Commodo, with a glass of Dago wine under his
belt, was deftly slicing the pale pink, transparent flesh of the
big redfish, while Mrs. Crochet was mincing the onions.

'Cut me up three cloves of that garlic fine,' Mrs. Crochet
told Evvie. 'Tope, you quick cut up the parsley and thyme
and a lil piece of bay leaf and three bell peppers. Somebody
open up two cans tomatoes.'

'Don't get excited,' said Commodo. 'Take a blow. Drink
wine!'

'Oh, the monkey wrapped his tail around the flagpole!'

'Thang God, everything I need! That Dewey! He knows
jiss what to bring. Never mind, sweedart, I make a court
boullon you gunna smack your lips. Here, Dewy, stop eatin

my seasonin and open these tomatoes. That man can eat allspice raw!'

'Don't get excited!' Commodo bellowed. 'Drink wine. Nonc Dewey brung two gallon the bess Dago red, an he got it off a Dago ship from Europe, so it's boun to be good. I wunt everybody to drink wine. Less us drink a toass! To Shoe-pick's property and a terrible crop of okra! Poor Mr. Tobin, I wisht he was here. The doctor got me on a dite, Dewey, but you gunna see me buss it tonight when my crazy ole brudda come to see me and my ole lady flings a court boullon supper with sherry wine in it. Woopy!'

Dewey drained his glass and refilled it. He filled Mrs. Crochet's, and gave some to the girls and boys. He gave a sip to the baby. T. J. was sitting on the floor playing with the skull. 'Looka my lil ole deckhand, he wunts to be a doctor!' Dewey laughed. 'He's strong like a deckhand.'

'Are you going to see the soft-ball game at Port Sulphur tomorrow, Uncle Dewey?' Evvie asked.

'That's one reason why I come up here.'

'But what you call that new game they all playin?' Mrs. Crochet asked. When it was explained to her, she said, 'Me I dowunna see no women playin no ball game, and you better not go lose your money, Messyou Dewey Crochet!'

'Leave him go, Duck,' Commodo said. 'That's only the pleasure he's got is gamblin money.'

'I guess gamblin gunna be my downfall yet.'

'A fine man like you, it's a livin shame to pitch your money away on soff-ball and dice,' Mrs. Crochet said. 'Voilà! Now I'm gunna make my roux! Evvie, cher, regarde vous, if you wunna see how Mama gunna do it.' Mrs. Crochet put two tablespoons of olive oil in her heated pot. Evvie came and stood near. She put in two tablespoons of flour, and stirred

while it browned. Into this she dumped the minced onions
and stirred until they turned pale brown. Next the two large
cans of tomatoes were added. 'Bien!' she exclaimed. 'Now
you see, I'm gunna put in all the ress of the seasonin and
leave that cook awhile. Then I put in five glasses water, and
when that's gunna boil, put in the slices fish and squeeze in
two lemon. After that cooks, put in half a glass sherry in a
tumbler-glass. Mmmmmm! Mes enfants, mes enfants, ça
c'est délicieux!'

After the fish was added, Mrs. Crochet allowed Evvie to fry
the toast. Evvie sliced the stale bread thin. She was proud.
She put a big spoon of butter into the frying-pan, and fried the
slices crisp. Over these slices of toast the court boullon was
to be poured in serving. There were two slices for each
helping.

Mrs. Crochet drank more wine. Her eyes were beautiful.
She waved her forefinger in Dewey's face. 'Dewey, sweedart,
you jiss gotta talk to that brudda of yours and make him turn
a new leaf over.'

'I'll buss his jaw for him!' Dewey said. 'What he been
doin?'

Mrs. Crochet turned away. Tears came into her eyes.

Topal said, 'Heck, Ma, cut it out.'

'Mon enfant Arthur,' said Mrs. Crochet, wiping her eyes.
'Il est sleeping in a orange truck with a high school education
in la ville tonight, all on account of your fine brudda runned
him in the canes.'

'Tell him the ress!' Commodo barked. 'Tell him about the
dogs rollin mud on my bed!'

'Now, now,' Dewey said. 'That ain't my business, you all's
private fights. I say leave every man keep his own fambly
tame.'

'My son Arthur.'

'That's a thing I better not mix up in,' Dewey said. 'I got enough, me, losing a lovely wife, dragging along the road all by myself, hunting somebody to please cook me a helpin of fish. I'm a lone wolf.'

'Mon enfant Arthur belonks in this kitchen tonight.'

'Soon as she starts talking French with the wine, you know what's going to happen,' said Topal. 'I hate to see Dago wine come in this house.'

Mrs. Crochet turned on Topal. 'Watch me put little notches on somebody's scalp with this bread-knife.'

'Here's to Shoepick's property again!' said Dewey. 'And a break in life! I'll send you all a nice persimmon tree to go by the toilet. I love that fruit like I love my mother.'

'I rather no property without my boy alongside of us helping us to get ahead.'

The smell of frying bread mixed with the tantalizing vapors from the big pot flowed through the house to the front porch, where Paul and Gussie, tired with romping, lay half asleep. The boys got up and sought the kitchen.

'Mama, I'm hungry,' said Gussie.

'Me, too, Mama.'

'Get out my road!' Mrs. Crochet warned, carrying the pot. 'Evvie, you and Paul and Gussie sit on the floor. Bring the fried bread, Evvie, cher. Pour more wine, Duck. Bouvez d'vin et vivez joyeux! Sit down, Dewey. Sit any place.'

'Woopy!' Commodo shouted. 'It's a livin miracle how that woman can fling together the grub so quick! My stummick is in my nostril.'

Gussie and Paul ate from pie plates, Evvie from a pan. The slices of fish floating in the gravy were white as clouds, sweet and flaky. The fried bread, after soaking up the seasoned gravy, became smooth, rich, mixing and melting with the firm sweet flakes of fish in one's mouth.

'Watch out for bones, you chirren!' Commodo warned. 'Don't get excited! Eat slow! When you eat fish, eat like Papa. Feel aroun with your tongue. Keepa feelin and stabbin aroun with your tongue for bones. Take a blow, Evvie. No hurry. Watch for bones. Looka Papa.' He was chewing a mouthful of fish. Now and then he would stop chewing briefly while a bone encountered by his busy tongue would be cornered and chivvied to the front of his mouth for ejection. Evvie ate until her whole body was tingling, droning with a pleasant lassitude. She walked into the front room in a sort of daze, one hand on her stomach and her eyes bulged.

Later in bed, the night flowed past her like a heavy torpid stream bearing all sorts of oddly shaped and colored impressions. There was the bright yellow head of a prothonotary warbler which had appeared in the window that morning. The crisp squeaking of Mr. Tobin's sandals and the red winking of the sandals themselves. The song that Shoepick made floated past slowly, and the tune caught on a thorn or a talon in her mind and remained there trailing in the warm eddies of sleep. The song was there, the truculent laughter of drums among the wailing reeds. Fully awake, Evvie whistled it between her teeth. . . . Her mother in the next room was snoring with Dewey's check under her pillow. The long soughing snores came gently, but the sound was an angry one. In the kitchen she heard Uncle Dewey's rich bumbling pilot voice, which itself presently became the warm soothing stream tugging her off to sleep.

Pouring wine, Commodo shoved the glass into Dewey's

face. 'Drink, or else I'm gunna slap the hell outa you,' he said. 'You understand me? Listen, we got only one life to live. Raise up the glass and down the hatch!'

'When I think of my poor Philomene,' said Dewey, shaking his head.

'Raise up the glass and listen what I'm gunna say!'

'That woman was a prince,' said Dewey. 'A prince.'

'Listen, you bastit.'

'Looka them beautiful chirren,' Dewey said, pointing to Paul and Gussie asleep on the kitchen table in the corner. 'Them innocent faces. I coulda had some like that. I coulda kept them plump with the money I fling away. Women and dice! What do I care? What have I got to live for?' Dewey put down his glass and grabbed Commodo by the arms, and shook him like a rat, bellowing, 'I didn't deserve her! I didn't deserve her!'

'Listen, you bastit.'

'Why did I lose her?' A crafty look came into Dewey's eyes. 'I lost her because I didn't deserve her,' he whispered close to his brother's face. 'I always knew I'd lose her. I knew it!'

'Listen, you bastit.'

'Them lovely chirren. Them sweedarts. Them Creole belles!' Dewey struck his forehead. 'Me, I'm gunna see them chirren on the dark bridge, goin up the river in a storm, with a hundred lives in my hands. Little precious sweedarts of a darlin Creole belles. Listen, will you give me premission to do that? Can I jiss close my eyes and see your precious chirren in the dark and the rain all alone? Will you lemme do that? Will you?'

'I love you, you bastit!' Commodo said. 'You hear that? I love you!'

Dewey clasped Commodo's hand. With the other hand he took hold of Commodo's head, bent it forward, rubbed it, slapped it from side to side. 'I can still whip you like I did that day. You remember? I wiped the marsh up with you. You remember? When you kill that alligator, what did we fine in his belly? A mink that come outa one of my traps. His toes was in my trap. And you claimed the mink jiss because you killed the gator. You remember how I wiped the marsh up with you, you ole bugger? You better be caffle I don't do it again, you don't treat them little sweedarts and Creole belles right.'

'Listen, you scrunchin my hand.'

'You ain't gunna mine me seein a pitcha of your precious little sweedarts on a dark night?'

'Ouch! Did I ever mine what you did, you bastit? Answer me! Didn't I tole you this house and everything I got is yours? Answer me! Ouch! Listen, you ——'

'Who wunts your house, furnished with coffee coupons? By Jove! All these cups and saucers, and your fine big parlor lamp that been out of style forty year. Coffee coupons!'

'Answer me, you bastit. Did you heard me say I love you?'

'I love the little Creole belles and precious sweedarts.'

'Shut up!' Commodo bawled. 'Listen, you see this house? It belonks to you. Everything! We been bruddas and we gunna stay bruddas againss the world. Am I right or am I wrong?'

'You right!'

Commodo stuck out his hand. They shook hands. They drank again. Dewey sat down. His head slowly sank forward. He muttered. Commodo poured the last of the Dago wine into his own glass and gulped. He went over and slapped Dewey a whack on the head. 'Listen, you! I love you! I love you! You see this house? Take what you wunt. Take my clothes! Take the bed I sleep on! Take my chirren! You wunna carry them in your head on a dark night? I give you somethin better! I let you take them in your arms right now! Listen, you wunt them twins? Take em! Take everything!'

'Aw, the hell with your house,' Dewey said. 'I gotta walk aroun tiptoe, scared it gunna fall down. Listen, you better go pay Shoepick's taxes before old man Jewpray pays them for his sweet little Juarelle. Go head! Don't bother me! The hell with your house!'

Commodo stood swaying. 'Awright,' he said. 'Curse my house.'

'Is it yours? Is this your house? Is it?'

'Curse my house.'

'The hell with ole Jewpray. The hell with him and his houses!'

'You cursed my house. Don't change the subjeck. The only house I got so far. You cursed it.'

'Shut up!'

'You come here makin a slave outa my wife to cook for you, and you curse my house.'

Dewey backed Commodo into a corner and shook him. 'Listen, I done give you a check to buy anudda property and raise your darlin little fambly and say a prayer for the only friend you got, because me, I'm sick of livin.'

'You cursed my house.'

'What have I got to live for? What have I got sense I loss my lovely Philomene excep soff-ball and the radio, I'd like to know? I done heard her voice in the dark all alone on the bridge at night. She tole me she's waitin for me *on the udda side of the bar!* Shhhh!' Dewey staggered backward. His hip brushed the skull off the window-sill. It struck the floor, rolled to the middle of the room and lay rocking. 'She's waitin for me tonight! Now you see why I drown myself in soff-ball and gamblin?' Swaying like a man on a ship, Dewey stooped and took hold of the skull. He reached out to put it back, and it fell again. Picking it up, he sat on the kitchen bench with the skull dangling in his hand. 'Soff-ball helps me forget Philomene,' he said. 'Life is a tess. You all think I love soff-ball? *I hate it!* When you see me clapping and rooting and betting money, I'm eatin my heart out for poor Philomene.'

'You cursed my house. Go way!'

'Life is a tess.'

'You cursed my house. You support the soff-ball team from Crippleduck Bayou, a dollar worth of this and a dollar worth that. Captain Dewey gunna buy us new caps! Captain Dewey gunna buy us this and that! Then you come cursin your own brudda's house.'

'Life is a tess,' said Dewey, waving the skull, his thumb in one of its eyes, forefinger in the other — his big gloomy face rolling. 'Life is a tess of your manhood, the guts and bollicks. Looka me! The public sees me laughing, wearing nice clothes and rootin for my soff-ball team. They think I love it. *I hate it!*'

Commodo reared back, leering, his fat forefinger wandering in the air. 'You a hipplecrite! You in love with a soff-ball team, you ole rooster! Ole rooster! That's where your money goes. Everybody knows that. Woopy! You got a harem! Woopy!'

'Sure. There goes Dewey Crochet! Ha, ha! Looka how happy Dewey Crochet is! Good ole Dewey! Looka how happy!' Dewey rose to his feet. 'It's a lie! I'm livin a lie!'

'You hit me with that skull and I'm gunna haul off and buss the hell outa you, you ole rooster.'

Dewey looked at the skull in his hand. He swayed, staggered, fetched up against the wall. He regarded the skull sadly. 'I tole the man that was studying Indians in Yucatan I had a nephew was gunna be a doctor. My godchild. The man gimme this fine skull. Now Arthur's driving a truck, bird-dogging the chippies aroun the French Market. Workin for a ole Slavonian!'

'Slavonians is nice people,' Commodo said, raising his heavy head and trying to focus his eyes on his brother.

'They use newspaper.'

'Arthur's no good, and never will be no good.'

'Now he's drivin a truck, my godchild,' Dewey said.

'Ain't you got your skull back?'

'Life is a tess.'

'Shut up,' Commodo said. He sat with his head in his hands. 'I got somethin importan to decide tonight that's been layin on my mind for twenny year. Is my wife a hex because I'm no good, or am I no good because my wife is a hex?'

Dewey took down the door between the kitchen and second room. While he was carrying it, the door slipped and fell with a tremendous crash, and the room rocked. He picked up the door, and stood it against the wall. When visiting his brother, he always used this door as a bed. He went outside to look for the pair of wooden trestles.

He walked about the orchard in wide circles, falling into a ditch once, and then running into a young tree full of thorns. He made his way back to the yard. He tripped over a chicken coop and sprawled.

'Yes, I got bollicks for brains!' he shouted. 'That's right!'

He waved his fist in the air and yelled, 'That's better than brains for bollicks! I'm a river pilot! The hell with the public!'

A voice said, 'Uncle Dewey, what's the matter?'

It was Topal.

'Help me fine my horses, sweedart. Help you ole lonely uncle, darlin. My horses to sleep on.'

Topal found the two trestles, and carried them into the kitchen. With great exertion she raised the door and placed it on the trestles. Her father was in bed. She went out to help her uncle.

He placed a hand on her shoulder and got to his feet. He staggered off balance. There was a squealing sound under him. He had become entangled in the pet racoon's chain. The coon was thrashing about, squealing, snapping at Dewey's legs. Topal crouched in the dark, feeling around for the animal. She slapped at the animal, and the coon backed away and was quiet, pulling at his end of the chain, which was wrapped round Dewey's legs.

Dewey lay on the ground. 'Never mind,' he said, 'I sleep right here. I'm a ole animal myself. We all animals.'

'Turn over. Let me untangle you so you can come inside.'

'No! I dowunna. A man's a animal and life is a tess.'

Topal sat on the ground beside him. 'Don't take it so serious,' she said. She slapped his drooping face gently. His beard was harsh as a file. 'I thought a pilot could hold his liquor good.'

'Ha, ha! You little devil. You a devil. Where you been since supper?'

'Sittin on the wharf out there smoking your cigarettes and listening to the family dirt.'

'Don't be downhearted, my lil Creole belle.'

'Who's Creole? I'm Cajun and proud of it.'

'Don't be downhearted. Listen, Tayo Delacroix not good enough for you. Tell Uncle Dewey why you wunted to marry him?'

'I dunno. I guess he's got the strongest back around here.'

'By Jove. Listen, I'm gunna introduce you to a nice young pilot.'

'You've been saying that since I was a young girl. Bring him on, Uncle Dewey, any time. He don't have to be young. Any old pilot will do.'

'Life is a tess.'

Topal finally untangled the chain, and got Dewey inside. He went to sleep on the door on trestles. Topal awoke early to see if Dewey was all right. She went into the yard to gather some things which had dropped from his pockets. The eastern sky had an ashen glow. The ragged shoulders of the cypress tree in front of the house were swaying among the tangled clouds. A single heavy sliver of rain broke along her arm. She heard the rain strike a little distance north, sweep hoarsely over the land and river, and gradually fade off. None fell on Mrs. Crochet's lilies.

16

NOBODY EVER SAW A NUN
ON HORSEBACK

AFTER UNCLE DEWEY went up to Port Sulphur to see his soft-ball team play, the Crochets set about thinking of what should be done about cashing the sixty-dollar check.

Evvie had a bright suggestion. 'Oh, Mr. Dupré'll cash it! Mama, he cashes checks for so much on the dollar, and it's cheap as anything for white people. That's true.'

Topal looked up over her magazine, and her lip curled. She clapped her hands and exclaimed in the tone of a very young child: 'And he won't take out for the rent we owe, Mama!'

'Well, can't we tell him we *need* all of the money?'

'Oh, sure, dumbbell! Maybe he'd lend us some more, too.'

'A man that's got locks on his doors like Jewpray muss have locks on his heart,' Mrs. Crochet said.

Commodo was lying on the floor under the bed with his head sticking out. He said, 'They got plenny ways a person can cash a check. Leave that to me. Don't get excited. Somebody bring Papa a match.'

Mrs. Crochet said, 'Me, I like to know why you always got to be layin under the bed. That's uncoot.'

'It's cool, Duck, and out of everybody's road. Watch a dog or a animal hunt him a place to ress. My ole Grampaw Seesaw Crochet learnt us that. He used to lay there to carve decoy ducks. That was a man with sense up in his head, ole Seesaw.'

'And fish-scales in his prayer-book. Me, I wish you seesaw yourself outside when the chirren waitin to straighten up.'

'Leave them make the bed,' Commodo said. 'I ain in nobody's road. This is one place I can ress, because I can lay catty-corner. I wunt a great big bed some day I can lay catty-corner in, you all.'

'Firss of all I wunt a house with a honeysucker vine,' Mrs. Crochet said. She sang as she bustled about. She fussed with her children in a pleased manner. Warm green sunlight off the orange trees flooded the cool rooms. Almost tenderly Topal smoothed down T. J.'s hair as she fed him from his bottle. Evvie juggled her bean-bags.

Commodo yawned and said, 'I'm cravin a coconut to seddle my stummick. That was plenny Dago wine lass night. A coconut grated up. Them funny noises in my stummick! It sound jiss like a siren far away.'

'Better you'd dragass down the road with your brudda's check to cash,' said the wife, 'instead tellin cotton bull stories.'

'Duck, bring me Dewey's check. I wunna see how it looks in the daytime.'

Mrs. Crochet came from the kitchen holding a bar of dripping soap. She stood looking around her with a dazed expression. 'Goddle mighty!' she muttered, grabbing her cheek.

'What's a matter now,' her husband asked. 'Did you hide the check like I tole you lass night?'

'Keep quite, and lemme think!'

Topal said, 'She did a swell job of hiding. She can't find it herself.' She went to the bureau and yanked at a drawer.

'Don't start lookin at me,' Commodo told his wife.

Evvie slipped out of the house. She went to the side yard and squatted by a pile of black ashes where her mother had burned some refuse papers. She peered closely, examining the ashes. The pet racoon advanced the length of his chain, and stood up pawing the air and sniffing at her back. She did not see anything resembling the remains of Uncle Dewey's check, but she continued to poke delicately at the fragile sheaves of charred paper that fell apart at the merest touch.

From the house she heard Topal loudly announce the finding of the check where Mrs. Crochet had hidden it in the douche-bag, so she forgot about the disturbance inside, and resumed her play.

She lay on her stomach, her face close to the pile, where the crushed papers had opened from the heat to bloom out in the form of a crisp black flower with petals curled. Deeper down there were flakes of silvery ash, and these were stirred by her breathing. When she blew harder, the ashen flakes whirled high, and they danced like luminous midges in the sun. The bright midges settled, or some melted in the air. Their dust, she remembered from high school, might fall somewhere and bring a crumb of potash to a tree. Because all was well inside the house, and even Topal was laughing, Evvie felt free to be amused by the ashes, and to be excited over the wonderful knowledge that not even fire could destroy anything, but only change it, separating the gases from the ash.

It was a happy day. Her father's laughter was good, and her mother's fussing. Evvie was intensely in love with Bruce Holt again. She wanted to let him know that she knew that not even fire could destroy anything. She waited on the road at mail time. Bruce did not come. She did not mind. She walked up the road to meet her father with his bright shovel.

During the next two days, from the bushes, the sky, the talk of passers-by — even from school, Evvie tried to procure knowledge as Bruce had warned her to do. She sat on the riverbank to wave at Uncle Dewey as he passed on a ship, and tried her best to realize the great winding world of liquid soil existing there, the shelled and finny creatures peopling its depths, the hills and chasms of mud standing on its bottom, the ten-foot waves rolling upstream like heaving bosoms, the great bucking and plunging logs of drift, carried on by the current, forging against the gigantic swells.

Things at the house were going fine. Uncle Dewey's check had been given to Jule the storekeeper to cash. Jule had sent it to the bank in town for collection. They would receive the cash pretty soon, now. Then, Commodo would go up to the courthouse at Pointe à la Hache to see about getting the property. Paul and Gussie played at writing checks on bits of newspaper with school crayons, buying from each other great tracts of land full of nice mud puddles.

Evvie and Topal were friends for a whole day. Together they listened to the noon broadcast on the radio, adjusting the receivers so that each could hold one to her ear. The broadcaster had got hold of a young man from the country who was a wheelwright in search of a job. And Topal discussed with Evvie the virtues of the Shoepick house, and they decided which rooms they would like to have.

But Mrs. Crochet was bothered by the lack of rain for her lily bulbs. Quantities of water from the high river came through the leaky levee and purled mockingly through the ditches, to be gulped by the back canals. Mrs. Crochet trudged to the lily patch at night, and took Evvie along. Working briskly under the moon, they succeeded in covering with cane leaves the bases of all the remaining rows of lily stalks.

'That cover gunna hole the dampness what's there,' said the mother, 'and suck up a little more out the ground. Less go home.' ·

On the high road, mist smudged the huddled myrtles, and the moon was clean. A ship whispered hoarsely down the distant river, her glowing decks towering high over the glistening roofs ashore. An automobile swooshed by, bouncing over the holes, and its suction yanked at their clothing.

Mrs. Crochet said, 'You know whilst some moon is leff what I oughta do, me? I oughta drag up the road and take a glimp at Shoepick's house, because I never saw the back part of that-there land for years.'

'Oh, can I go too, Mama?'

'Brush your dress.'

Evvie turned several cartwheels on the shellroad.

'Stop that!' Mrs. Crochet ordered. 'Is that the way a girl gunna be a Little Sister of the Poor should behave?'

Evvie now wanted more than ever before to become a nun, because she was madly in love with Bruce Holt. She felt there would be no point in entering the convent unless she had a lover to renounce.

She went to her mother and took the older woman's arm sedately. 'Mama, if I couldn't be a Sister, I'd like to be an acrobat traveling around helping to support my family, high off the ground with searchlights on me, and my shoulders powdered white . . . Wouldn't it be funny if a nun would start doing cartwheels? Or riding a bicycle or a horse? Father Pennygrass swims in a bathing suit and he's a priest, but he's different. Nobody ever saw a nun on horseback.'

Mrs. Crochet said, 'When I was a girl I went to New Or-

leans for the Carnival, and on Moddy Graw Day we seen a
masker dressed up like a nun. She was walking with a clown
that had a great-big pasteboard head. That was a sacrilege.'

'Joan of Arc rode a horse,' Evvie said. 'She was lovely with
her sword, all shining. She looked like a boy riding the horse
with long legs, and tin pants on. Gee. Look how white the
road is, so white and lonesome, it makes me think of Ichabod
Crane. I bet herons are peeping at us from the bulrushes.'

'Them herons! I could get along without them nosey
things that eats our frogs. To me that's one rancid bird, unless
he's pot-roasted young.'

'Mama, sing something.'

'I got no more voice from hollin at you-all. Say you, what's
eatin you tonight? My God.'

When they neared the little backwoods blind tiger fre-
quented by Negro and mulatto farmers and trappers, they
saw the shanty dimly lit. Several dark figures were curved
over the counter, one thick sagging fellow with his face buried
in the crook of his arm. There was music, and some were
dancing. Wump. Wump.

Each man danced alone, in a sluggish, bumping movement,
swinging only the legs from the knees down, thumping the
floor with his soft boots or waterlogged shoes, producing a
deep, stubborn, protesting sound. Wump. *Wump!* The
heavy dragging feet were angry, or they were trying to ease
themselves by stamping the ooze from their surfaces. There
was no heated talk or repartee in the place, no play of wit or
laughter; and except for the dull shine of hip boots, there was
no light, no color, no hint of gaiety, audacity or vigor. A
torpid current of warm air flowed out through the doorway
with the smell of heavy sweet wine. As Evvie and her mother

went past, the music died, and among the men there was no cry of approbation, no movement of any kind. After they had left the place behind and were alone with their own brittle footfalls, another record in the saloon started to play.

'Listen, Mama, that's the song Shoepick made!' Evvie cried. 'I feel like dancing, but I wonder why it sounds so sad.'

'Maybe while he was making it, he knew they was gunna beat him out the money.'

Evvie began to snap her fingers. 'Elna's brother plays it on the harmonica, Ma.'

'If that nigger music ain't the contrariess! Listen that picaloo!'

'And the big sad trambone slipping around, huh, Ma?'

'My mother used to hate that willow-tree music. Stop wigglin! I like to know where you learn such things.'

Evvie pranced over the shells in time with the distant music, hardly able to keep her limbs in order. The notes sounded impudently casual, and yet quick. Each phrase ended with the finality of a cracking lash, rousing every tendon of the body to flow along with the beats that were at once wild and restrained.

As they neared Shoepick's property, Mrs. Crochet said, 'Me, I'm startin to remember back. Me and Papa passed here when Topal was a baby. Sure. They didn't had a road back here. A little coulee. We was in a pirogue. Papa was after grosbec. Every tree had a ness with young grosbec. We seen through the trees, the chickens in front. Shoepick's paw raised them. White laycorns. Right here he had pigs. I forget. Now this is the big bawg where always it's wet and nothing will grow. A big sink or a bawg, like, that makes the property not valuable because it uses up two arpents of land and breeds snakes and stuff.'

They turned in on the lane that connected the back road with the levee highway. Evvie was trying to recall the savage tune they had heard, but her mind had closed around it, leaving a clear blank place, like an oath written in water.

'This is where a person ought to put pigs. These big japonicas would shade them nice. Looka that field for corn! Come, darlin, I jiss wunna get a glimp of the back of his house, if it needs fixin. They got no ants, I bet. Never had none. Oui. God dog it, I sure remember the lovely chickens. Laycorns for aigs.'

'Mama, I won't mind having a back room.'

Mrs. Crochet turned on Evvie angrily. 'Who said we gunna get this house? Did I say that?'

'Papa ——'

'He's a dinwiddie. Don't you never let him tangle you up tell he shows you the cash. The laycorns was here, I believe, and they had plenny martin houses againss the hawks. They used to steal his hens. I remember so plain, they said one day a hawk how they call the *aile rond*, he come in their chicken yard, and the roosters took after the hawk. The hawk wounded a rooster and leff him lay, then he grabs a hen and gone. You think that hawk would eat rooster meat? No indeedy! That's what we gotta watch if we have chickens, them hawks.'

'Mama, I'll watch those rascals, and we can have martin houses.'

'And a person's gotta watch the rats. And watch them drunkers poundin the road in the night stealin hens to make chicken macaroni. They liff em off the roost easy with a stick. Day time too. I arready seen em use fishin-cackle, bait the hook with a worm and cass is over the fence and wind up the reel slow, and Messyou Chicken come and fight for the bait. Ain't that a way to steal a hen?'

Black shadows of the leaves were printed on the road edge. The mother and girl walked through the shadows, where the sand received their heels in silence and their shrinking forms could not be seen on the road. They were walking the lane dividing Shoepick's place from the strip which Dupré had bought.

'Mama, how come Mr. Dupré bought this place next door, and don't even live there, raising fruit?' Evvie said.

'Don't be inquisitive.'

They neared the old packing shed where Shoepick was known to spend the greater part of his time making songs, reading books or studying them, nobody knew which. Under the moon the building was bright with age.

'He's in there!' Evvie whispered.

'What we care? Can't a person walk the lane?'

'Mama, Elna says he studies lessons back here late at night. I guess he's learning to write the letter to the man stole his song.'

'It's nasty to steal songs, if Shoepick made it, which I wouldn't be surprized he did.'

Evvie tried to start the song off in her mind. The notes themselves eluded her. She could recall it dark and sad, but fast and sassy. She could recall how it made her feel — not gay, but restless and full of energy. They lingered by the little packing room, and through the window saw Shoepick sitting by a lamp, his pointed, shaven head bent over a book. There were other books on the table. Sweat was pouring down Shoepick's face, as though he had washed it without a towel.

'Tch-tch! The poor nigger!' Mrs. Crochet whispered. 'Studyin like a boy been punished. Look him read.'

The man's thick, hanging lips flopped loosely as he pronounced the words. When he met a word whose name he could not tell himself, he would bob his head, and the skin of his wet forehead would gather into wrinkles. Once he stopped reading to think. Raising his piercing, insolent eyes upward, he grasped his chin and his great loose lower lip into his hand and squeezed and twisted them. Evvie had the notion that his head hurt him. It was too small to think the way he wanted it to, and Shoepick was puzzled, and discouraged, and angry.

They went on. The shelled lane was cloven straight through the trees toward the river, where the moist willows silvered by the moon waved like tall plumage on a fan. Orange trees loaded with foamy blossoms leaned over the lane on Shoepick's side.

'A lovely stable, and no horses, only a mule to make garden,' Mrs. Crochet said. 'Juarelle raise vegetavles with the hoe. I wonder if they got tools and stuff? Shoepick's paw buried in the front yard, but our great big doorsteps would cover the grave up. A good ole man, they say, for not believing in God or wunting nothin to do with a priess or gravyyard. Papa said he was studdy as a jug. Less sneak in and see the cistern. That's the most importan thing.'

'But Mama!'

'Come. Who gunna see us?'

They jumped the ditch. A twig broke under Evvie's foot, and her forehead struck an orange on a limb. The rear window was lit, and they heard the desolate bumping of a flatiron on an ironing board . . . 'Juarelle, she working tonight,' said Mrs. Crochet. 'She wash for ole Poison Ivory's wife.'

They reached the cistern, a tall cylinder on a brick foundation. Mrs. Crochet began to thump it softly, moving her knuckle from the bottom upward, to determine how much water it now contained. She passed her hands caressingly over its cold cypress staves. 'Plenny water!' she whispered. 'Bit cistern for washin and takin baths!' In a crouched position she stole around the cistern, feeling up under the ends of the staves for possible leaks. She glanced at the gutter that led from the roof.

'Mama, here's where T. J. could play,' Evvie whispered. 'And look the long clothesline! The shed has two windows!'

Mrs. Crochet was trying from her hidden position to examine the condition of the back porch, the weatherboarding covering the rear of the house. In the moonlight the place looked all right, only in need of paint.

'Mama, the shed is close to the kitchen. Papa could build a plankwalk for bad weather. Papa's going to enjoy moving mud around with a wheelbarrow.'

'I guess you got the sixty dollar cash, eh? You worse than your paw, crossing the bridge before the horse is out of the stable. I dunno what I could do to you and that rangatang.'

Once again in the lane, approaching the little packing room, they heard a guitar being plucked. As they passed by, Shoepick was seen with his instrument across his lap. One black hand lay across the guitar strings limply. The thumb of the other hand was in the Negro's mouth. He was falling asleep. His head fell sideways, and the thumb slipped from his mouth. This awoke him. The thumb went back into his mouth, and the jaws began working up and down. His eyes closed peacefully. A hiss of laughter escaped through Evvie's nose. She walked away with her hand over her mouth. Mrs. Crochet giggled softly. Evvie started to run, holding in the laughter with her hand. Her mother hurried behind her. Both were laughing softly. One of Mrs. Crochet's shoes came off, sailed through the air and bounced over the road. She recovered it, then ran on following Evvie with the shoe in her hand. They both turned into the main road, holding each other about the waist, staggering with laughter. The setting moon was big. After they stopped laughing, they did not say anything on the way home.

17

HURRY UP AND TELL HER THE FACTS OF LIFE

GOOD FRIDAY was a day of fasting in the Delta. Most of the Grass Margin people took only bread and coffee without milk. The bell in the church did not ring all day. Before services an altar boy stood outside the church swinging a big wooden rattle over his head to call the people. It was a bright glassy day, and it was hushed and softened by race-memories of the Crucifixion, and sadly festive.

Evvie Crochet watched the red ponies grazing on the high levee, burning upon the sky. The horses, she thought, did not know it was Good Friday; but they must have known they were having a day off, because even their tails were quiet.

Commodo was saying his rosary by the front window, facing the front yard and the levee. Kneeling on a small oyster culler's bench, he was reduced to the stature of his younger daughter. His upturned soles, freed from the bondage of rubber boots, were plump and rosy, scrawled all over with witty creases; his jowls glowed and quivered to the jerking of his whispering lips; and his eyes were raised piously to watch a humming-bird outside capering for its mate.

The male bird, bedecked in shining green and gold with a blood-red throat, would dart like a bullet straight toward the female resting on a branch, then stop suddenly before her in mid-air, weaving a series of fine vehement notes spun out at so high a pitch as to be almost inaudible, then fly backwards a distance, to repeat the performance. A large blue-jay came and perched near the female humming-bird, cocked one eye at something high in the tree, and opened his murderous black beak in a raucous scream. The male humming-bird, with a cry pitched as high as the sound of a cork turned in a vial, streaked across the sunlight and fell upon the retreating jay. Then he returned and resumed his nuptial capers. Now he was swinging repeatedly through the air up and down in a large U-shaped design, with a loud humming of the wings upon each descent. In his prayers, Commodo kept time with the flashing rise and fall of the bird:

> *Haily* Mary
> *Full* of grace
> The *Lord* is with thee...

When he finished his prayers, he lost interest in the court-ship outside. He tiptoed across the room to his wife, leaned out near her with his eyebrows raised, and whispered, '*Who gunna dye* the *East-aigs* for Paul and Gussie I brung?'

Mrs. Crochet whispered from the side of her mouth, '*Topal.*'

Soft footsteps were heard approaching in the adjoining room, and Commodo began talking at random in a loud voice, 'Sure, I bet any money Zhule brings us that money tomorrow ... Evvie, sweedart, please make noise when you come in a room. You got a habit of driftin aroun soff like a pirogue, and people all the time callin you a sneaky.'

Evvie's face went blank with concern. 'How, soft?' she asked. 'I naturally walk that way, and again I'm afraid the house might shake too much if I run or walk too heavy. I can't help it.'

'In udda words, if you barefoot, cough in your trote or sniff up your nose or something for politeness, because this family gunna be up there soon in the rhinestones, darlin, and you gotta be a little lady.'

Topal called from the next room, 'You all better hurry up and tell her the facts of life!' Then Topal laughed derisively.

Evvie looked at her mother. Mrs. Crochet looked at Commodo, dropped her eyes and turned her head. Topal was still laughing in the next room, and they heard the stamping of her feet.

Commodo thought of the innocent little humming-birds courting outside. He snapped his finger at Evvie and said, 'Go quick, sweedart, and take a look out that window!' Then he edged toward the door of the adjoining room, and with a cunning smile at his wife, slipped out of the room. Evvie went to the front porch, slyly looking out of the corners of her eyes. She saw nothing out there but a touring car in trouble on the road — a big, ancient Pierce Arrow sport model full of Negroes dressed up for Good Friday.

But she saw that one of the Negroes, a skinny yellow one wearing a lavender silk polo shirt, was out on the road. He was blowing into the valve of an inner tube, and nine dejected Negroes in the car watched him intently.

Evvie glanced over her shoulder into her house in a puzzled way. She studied the scene on the highway again.

The yellow Negro's hair was all shaven except for one perpendicular tuft in front that made him seem to be running through the wind with an expression at once bold and frightened; and the big red inner tube framed his face. When he inhaled and blew a breath, his eyebrows wrenched themselves into a ferocious scowl; his bulging, angry eyes glittered directly at Evvie; his neck swelled to a greater girth than his head; and his cheeks popped out enormously and turned pale.

His whole body trembled violently for several moments and grew taller and taller. Then, still watching Evvie, he removed his mouth from the valve and spilled out the air, while his body collapsed and sagged.

With a perturbed look on her face, Evvie watched the Negro do this several times.

Inhale; raise the eyebrows.

Scowl; swell up; tremble.

Expel; collapse.

Again. Inhale . . .

She went into the house wearing a bewildered look. Approaching her father in the kitchen, she looked at the floor. Commodo gave her cheek a tender pinch, and smiled knowingly into her eyes. 'That's your firss little lesson, sweedart, and Papa wunt you to go think about it and be a good little girl,' he whispered. Evvie raised her upper lip enough to show two front teeth briefly, then softly walked out the back door, to sit pondering beside the guava tree.

Mrs. Crochet, glancing at Paul and Gussie rolling around the floor, went into the kitchen and whispered to Topal, 'You gotta dye the East-aigs for the chirren's ness. The ress of us is goin up the road to hunt greens for our Good Friday dinner. You go by Zhule and get a nickel of East-aig dye. In the armoir you gunna fine a dudden aigs Papa brung. Boil em and dye em nice.'

Evvie, her parents, and the twins worked a long time on the big levee behind Grass Margin that ran parallel to the one along the river, to keep out the sea. They were gathering wild greens to be cooked for dinner. Greens were scarce, because cattle were pastured there. Evvie idled, watching her family stooped under the great white clouds. With hands on knees they hobbled about slowly, curved downward and intent, serious dark faces swinging from side to side, as though hunting something which had fallen from the sky. In the vast, burning blue space, the shouted talk of her parents was dimmed and made pure and clear, and the distant yelps of the twins were remote and sad. Gussie and Paul were looking for bits of clover to use for their Easter nests in which the Rabbit would lay the eggs.

'God dog, I been huntin greens, me, on a Good Friday all my life,' Mrs. Crochet called, 'and they never brung me much good luck to this day!'

Evvie jumped up and called, 'Mama, Father Pennygrass said a working man's family don't need to fast or abstain. You get excused for being poor!'

Commodo stood erect and stabbed at the clouds with his forefinger, and with his face turning red, bellowed: 'For belonging to the clergery, that Pennygrass is the broad-mindess man on this river!'

Topal found the dozen eggs and boiled them. She was excited over dyeing the eggs. She put on her shoes, and with a lot of folded burlap sacks, made a cushion in the wheelbarrow for T. J. She put him in the wheelbarrow, and rolling it down the road, went to Jule's for the egg-dye. T. J. fell asleep on the way. There was a little empty shed alongside the grocery store. Topal left the sleeping baby under this shed.

There was nobody in the store. An old otter sleeping on the counter opened one eye and closed it. Topal passed her hand down over the otter's body to the end of the tail. An automobile stopped outside, and a man walked into the store. Topal stood erect.

'Nickel of aspirin,' the man said.

'I don't work here.'

'No aspirin!' Jule called from the next room.

The man went to the front door and turned. 'Miss, excuse me, do you know any girls hunting work?'

'No, sir. What factory?'

'Belle Plume, up above Port Sulphur. Studdy work in the shrimps. Crab-picking later on, and maybe we'll pack figs and all like that in summer. Nice clean cabins for the girls. Your folks live here? We want nice family girls, white ones, not too young and wild. Cheap board, big cisterns. Your family here?'

'Yes, sir.'

'Look, I'm going down to Venice. I'll pass on this road going back at half past eleven. If you decide, wait on the road with your things.'

'They need me home.'

'Well . . .'

'Try the gray house below. There's a mast-pole laying in front. They've got five girls.'

Topal dyed the eggs. She rolled up her sleeves and swept the kitchen clean. She washed the oilcloth tablecover with its worn designs of a goat, a fish and a rooster repeated over and over. She carefully arranged the rows of teacups for the dye, the tissue-paper pictures to be transferred to the eggs, the greased cloth for polishing.

The house was very clean and silent. T. J. was asleep in the front room. Topal in her tuneless voice kept humming a popular song she had heard on the radio. After dyeing each egg, she polished it and placed it on the window-sill in the sun. When she had finished, she backed off and studied the row of colors. She reached out to rearrange the eggs, backed off, switching her dark head from side to side.

She hid the eggs in the armoir, slipping them between the folds of a quilt. The baby was now awake and playing, crowing in his deep voice, beating on the sides of the pasteboard oatmeal carton that confined him.

In the bottom of her father's coat pocket she found a few pinches of dry tobacco crumbs. She tore an oblong piece of paper from Evvie's school tablet and rolled a cigarette. Then she put on the ear-phones of Commodo's radio, and sat with her back against the wall, studying her bare feet, sucking on her cigarette, relishing the peace. On the radio came the voice of a minister preaching. Topal turned the dial to another voice, that of a woman sobbing in the aviation serial, *Ruby Beacons*. This voice was soon interrupted by a knock on the door. It was Bob LaRoque.

'Your father is working, him?'

'He's hunting greens for dinner.'

'I like to see him about ditching tomorrow. Tell him come by and see me, honey. I got more ditching. And give him this.' Bob handed Topal an envelope. 'Zhule just now give me that to bring your paw. And tell Mama here some nice chicken bones for the dogs.'

Topal took the paper bag. She opened it and looked inside. It was filled with chicken bones from which the meat had been eaten.

'Them is nice soff bones,' Bob explained, 'and come offa young spring chicken. A dog can grine them up good, and won't choke like on hen bones. Tell Papa we got a big spring chicken on ice for him tomorrow, saving it tell he come to work.'

Topal raised the envelope to the sun. It contained Uncle

Dewey's check. She could distinguish the color, and the thick black signature. She walked away and left LaRoque standing on the steps. She tore open the envelope and removed Uncle Dewey's sixty-dollar check. On its back were stamped the letters N. S. F.

Topal rubbed face-powder on her white shoes. She had changed to her best dress. She made a bundle of old clothes wrapped in newspaper. In another package she put some copies of *Truth Stories* and *Love Dramas*, and her packet of letters from the members of the Pen Pals Club. She found a pencil and took Evvie's school binder to the table and wrote:

> Dear Papa:
>   I have a good job. Am leaving. Goodbye and good luck. No hard feelings. This place is not big enough for us all. Let Evvie watch the baby now. Since I was a little girl I have been waiting for us to get a break. Here's Uncle Dewey's check, No Such Funds. That's the way it will always be. Don't kid yourself. I will only grow into an old hag here, fighting and fussing and no place to be alone any time. The kids keep getting bigger and bigger, and no place to be alone.
>   Your loving daughter,
>   Topal Crochet.

For a long time she stood behind a tree near the levee, until the shrimp factory man came in his car from Venice. There were three girls in the car.

'So they let you come,' the man said.

'I guess so.'

Topal got in the car, and it started off. 'Wait!' she said. 'Can you wait just a minute? I forgot something.'

'O.K.'

Topal was afraid a wind might come up and blow the house down on the baby. She ran inside and took him from his oatmeal carton, and carried him to the side yard, where the racoon was tied to the guava tree. She snapped the chain off the animal. The freed coon whizzed across the yard, turned and skidded several feet, bounded up a tree. Topal set T. J. on the ground. She passed the chain around the middle of his body. Immediately the baby tried to pull the chain off, and looked up at her with big worried gray eyes. Little by little his lower lip began to protrude. Topal turned to gather some clamshells, which she put into a tin can near-by. The corners of T. J.'s mouth started to droop. Topal rattled the can and handed it to the baby, then sped away.

T. J.'s mouth came apart and he let out a hoarse yell. The tin can dropped from his grasp. He started to crawl after Topal's retreating figure. The tin can, rolling off, rattled loudly. He stopped crawling and looked around at the can. It was rocking back and forth, the contents jangling. The baby returned to a sitting position and, still yelling, slapped at the can angrily. It rolled toward him. He grabbed it and raised it to hurl it from him. Clamshells spilled in his lap. He picked one up and tried to stuff it into his mouth. 'Mmmmm!' he said, grabbing handfuls of the shells, and trying to pour them into the can. The racoon came out of hiding and approached the baby, sniffing.

Arriving at the Belle Plume cannery, Topal and her companions were shown to the cabins they would occupy, and told to be ready for work after lunch. The wooden cabins occupied by female employees stood against the sky on the naked prairie near the cannery. A walkway, one plank wide, led from the highway across the soggy ground far back to the isolated cabins, which stood near a canal, where the shrimp luggers that fished in the Gulf were tied up. All around, out and out to infinity, the soil was boggy and gray, studded with scrubby tufts of salt grass, pocked all over with deep cloven hoof-holes all filled with water. In this boundless space there was one tree visible, several hundred yards away — a dead, bleached cypress with bare branches near the top twisted in the shape of the upraised hand of a sinking swimmer, dripping long strands of Spanish moss. These branches bore clusters of dark, melancholy cormorants. Swarms of fiddler crabs crawled everywhere, over the mud and across the plankwalk, and all around the piling which raised the cabins above the reach of storm tides.

In the cannery, the girls all stood by the work-tables picking and squeezing the shrimps from their shells. The girls had newspapers wrapped around their legs against the mosquitoes — black headlines, rotogravure sections, comic supplements. Clouds of fishy steam dimmed the lights, swaying among the girls, rolling over the ceiling. Mosquitoes wandered leisurely about in the steam, and the workers were continually flapping their shoulders against their cheeks and ears to mash them.

As the afternoon wore on, the task she performed seemed more and more pointless to Topal. She had no friends among the girls. The whole business felt unreal. There seemed to be no reason why she was here picking shrimps. The incessant talk and laughter sharpened her sense of isolation. It seemed designed to exclude her.

Once someone chirped brightly, 'Eh bien! We gunna get tomorrow a big-big-*big* batch of swimps, Booboo said.'

This remark caused a general satisfaction which Topal could not understand. It only made her realize that there would be a tomorrow here — more shrimp-picking — more tomorrows. The dwindling heap of freezing shrimps would be replaced over and over by other heaps cheerfully dumped before her

like a mountain high and frozen. The man who did the dumping seemed to think he was doing her a great favor . . .

Supper at the boarding house was shrimp jambalaya.

Leaving the boarding house, Topal caught a glimpse of the
little post office across the canal. She had a desire to go and
ask for mail . . .

The three Venice girls went on to the village by the levee,
and afterwards returned with some boy friends in a car il-
luminated all over with red and green lights, with a lighted
Kewpie doll on the radiator, and all kinds of bright nickel
accessories fastened on here and there. They asked Topal to
go along. Having no good clothes, she refused. She watched
the girls skip away over the plankwalk. These people had a
way of traveling safely over plankwalks without even glancing
down. Occupants of the other cabins, singly or in groups,
were leaving for the village, until soon, all of the cabins were
deserted except Topal's.

Hers was the last cabin in the row, the farthest out on the
prairie, in perspective the smallest. A tall trellis was in front.
The cabin seemed to be leaning out with a hand raised, as if
to say, 'Me, too!' Then, from the porch of the cabin could be
seen the big wet marsh with its ponds full of salt water, in this
region always inching toward the river, trying to reach the
river, to worry the big stream, to divert it before it reached its
logical mouths.

Topal entered her cabin. This cabin had one great room.
Its total space was almost as great as that of the Crochets'
home on Grass Margin. It had never been occupied before.
There were two beds, two chairs, two dressers. The rest was
empty space, full of echoes and neatly done in gray paint that
shone beneath the big bright electric light.

She crossed the floor as quietly as a thief, but it creaked loudly as she traversed its great distance. The lonely walls were high and bare. There was no sound. She touched her newspaper bundles. The packages gave out loud crackling noises. She walked back and forth, looking for nothing, trying to avoid the places that creaked and startled her. She went to the front porch and huddled there awhile. Far away, a neglected calf bawled and bawled. Smoke rose in the dusk from the distant village homes.

She went inside. She caught sight of her face in the mirror. The surprisingly familiar image, with its remembered defects emphasized by the bright light, seemed stupid and forlorn. Topal suddenly felt a crushing sense of the pointless stupidity of having left home with such a face. She went to the window. With her hands she formed a hood around her face, and pressed it against the cold pane. But nothing was visible in the black prairie but the little red cattle fires, where sparse herds gathered and let the smoke roll over them to drive away the mosquitoes.

She turned back toward the hollow room.

She thought of the brave note she had left her father.

With sudden diligence she opened her bundles and put her stuff away, and by this act momentarily felt herself a permanent part of the room. She whistled a song. It was only about seven o'clock. She opened her bundle of Pen Pals correspondence. Now these letters were not connected with loneliness as they had been before. They were connected with home, the place where they had been received. There was no point in receiving such letters unless you were safe in your home. She could see them now full of the shameless childish confidences of strangers. Also, they sharply reminded her of the great size of the land, the terrifying strangeness of its far places. She lay on the bed, and presently began to weep.

She felt better. Wasn't her home right down the road? Sure. She was still in the Delta, smelling the familiar odor of fermenting marshes, hearing the river. The ship whose whistle she heard would pass Grass Margin in a little while. The dread far places were a long way off, and they could not come near. The good wide spaces would keep them where they were. Her brother frequently would be passing on the road! Arthur was a fine kid. In her mind she named his ways — his pert whistling, his yellow head bobbing over the tops of the weeds on some willful secret errand. Arthur would approve of her flight from home . . .

She would take a bath. She had a job, now, and yet her home *was* right down the road, and the bus went down every living morning. She had a whole dollar in her purse, too, that would take her home whenever she chose to go. She went to the central cabin, an old building where the bathroom and toilets were. This place, which was in nobody's charge, was scattered with assorted trash, empty lotion bottles, candy wrappers, heaps of newspaper unwrapped from the legs of the girls. On a window were three jacks, shaped like the magnified snowflakes seen in school primers. The bathtub was ringed with dark body-oils and draped with sodden towels. On the walls, names and epithets were penciled, along with derisive comments of former workers. On the inside of the door, in letters written with a lipstick, Topal read:

> BREAKFAST SHRIMP
> DINNER SHRIMP
> LUNCH SHRIMP
> GOODBY

She returned to her cabin, groping across the twisting plankwalk. As she opened the door, the electric light went dim and slowly died, as if a mechanism in the door had put it out. She felt her way to the bed and quickly crawled between the covers, remaining there all night, sleeping and waking. Cattle came in the night one by one to scratch their sides against a corner of her cabin. At first she did not know what the noise was, the heavy rubbing sound of hair and bones and hollow ribs across the wood, and the dull fumbling clatter of horns . . .

In the morning she was relieved, almost gay, because she was going back home. The bus soon would come. She left the cabin with her things, tripping lightly over the plankwalk, kicking half-playfully at the dense masses of fiddler crabs that swarmed over the planks, looking over her shoulder like one whose cunning has balked a pursuer. She had told no one of her intention to leave. When she reached the high road she felt a great surge of freedom. With her shoulders thrown back, she faced the cold river wind. She smiled at a man passing in a car. She looked boldly at another who was rinsing a trammel-net on the locks of the canal.

A boy passed by. 'Hey!' she greeted him. Then she had a sudden whim. 'Say, kid, which way is New Orleans?' she asked.

The boy jerked his dirty chin in the direction of the city. He had a basket of fish on his shoulder.

'When's the bus go up?'

'This evening.'

'Okay. I'm going home. Been working in this hole a long time, saving my money. I'm going to town to buy a car. Listen, you can't buy a car around here, eh?'

'Nome.'

She went toward the bus stop, carelessly swinging her bun-

dle. On the way she encountered a man in a black suit carrying an armful of placards he was distributing to advertise
malaria medicine. The man, perceiving her buoyant state,
grabbed his pipe from his mouth, made room for her on the
path, and said through his nose, 'Good munning good munning nize munning.'

'Good morning! Would you kindly tell me when the bus
goes up to New Orleans?'

'Sefternoon, around — uh — you can find out ——'

'I guess I've got to go there to take the airplane for California?'

'Hey? Kellyfornia? Oh. Sure. Kellyfornia. Yes. Sefternoon. If uh — say, I'm going gupp to town myself. My car
is over by the Custgod Lending, but ——'

'Uh ——'

'Uh ——'

'No, uh — I've got plenty trunks. Great big old trunks.
Heh-heh-heh! Thanks.'

'Heh-heh-heh! Dess awright.' The man dug into a canvas
bag. 'Here. I give you semple our madacine, for malaria,
cremps, nuz-blid, hadache efter you ride hoze-beck, and certain troubles.'

Topal thanked him and hurried off. The bus for Grass
Margin was coming.

The spinning prairie was green. The rushes climbed over
the high red horizon. Here, as if to ease one's bludgeoned en-
trails for the dreadful gravel ahead, the road was paved a little
way, and the bus rattled, but did not bounce high. Topal occupied a rear seat, looking out of the window at the enormous
turning disk of the earth. Everywhere, roused larks were
slanting off; kingfishers along the road dived out of the wires;

loggerhead shrikes eyed the passing coach fiercely. Topal watched them, and watched the scattered grackles sown over the sky; and she wondered why birds stay^d in a place affording so few perches to land on, when they might fly down to Grass Margin and live in the friendly trees . . .

She furtively opened the packet of Pen Pals correspondence, and began to tear up the letters. The first was a thick one from a lonely railroad telegrapher high in the mountains of Arizona. Through her fingers hanging out of the window the fragments leaped and scattered, then on the road suddenly turned and chased behind the speeding bus.

Topal crept through the orchard. She flattened herself against a tree, and peered through its fork. Among the stout hale trees, the Crochet house was grayed by sun, and all wrinkled. The rear room, leaning far over in the remembered shape of a problem in long division, seemed to have settled farther sideways during the night. Now Topal could hear voices, the despised sound of her parents wrangling in the front room.

The back door opened. Her sister Evvie came out, lugging a heavy bucket, her body toppling sideways like the house in which she lived. But she was singing, and her thin tanned legs flashed through the sun to the ditch. Returning, she threw the bucket away over her shoulder and turned a cartwheel. Then, muttering to herself, Evvie limped off, imitating a person with one leg shorter than the other.

The voices inside were heard again. Darting from tree to tree in a wide curve, Topal reached a hiding place near the levee. She listened.

Mrs. Crochet was yelling: 'Don't tell me! Don't tell me!'

'Shut up!' Commodo cried.

'Strong like I am, I can't wash or cook or sew for somebody needs help? I can't mind babies yet for some oil man's wife or something? Where my pride is got me to so far? Miss Nellie say she can fine me a job! Somebody see where's Gussie if he fell down the closet! I can work! I'm a woman still got brains and plenny strank! I ain ole!'

'I done heard enough!' Topal heard her father bellow. 'You ain goin out and work while I'm livin and strong! Now shut up!'

'You a sick man with your cricks and sirens!'

'I ain't!'

'You are!'

'Am I sick this mornin?' Commodo bawled. 'God dog it to hell, the condition of this family is my fault. I been sittin here thinkin. I oughta be dead! *I'm a failure!* I could haul off and run from here to the Ural to hide my face! I truss everybody! I trusted that pole-vaulter! I trusted that skink of a Dewey Crochet that he snake-in-the-grassed me with a bum check and the firss time he comes close to the levee I'll give him a load of buckshot! I runned my son away from home! I runned my daughter away from home! It oughta be me leavin home! I'm a failure!'

'I like to know where would we be if it wasn't for you! I'm the one, far as Topal, that runned her off. God knows I did!'

Topal behind the tree smiled and blushed. She straightened her skirt. She adjusted the cords around her bundle.

'Get outa my road!' Commodo shouted. 'I'm a failure.'

'You ain't! Shut up your mouth and see can you open this window!'

'Get outa my road!'

'You go back to bed where you belonk and you ain't slepp all night! Open this window and get to bed!'

'Get outa my road before I beat down your ears!'

Topal heard sounds of scraping feet and a chair bumped into. The voices died off in the rear of the house into faint grumbles.

Topal drew closer to the house. On the front porch Evvie was down on her hands and knees, with her skinny pointed rump hoisted high, reading a funny paper. Topal stepped out into the open yard and approached the big ornamental front steps. She swung along as casually as though returning home from an errand. She came up behind Evvie, who turned and blinked, her lips falling apart. Topal, returning Evvie's stare, made big eyes and shoved her face to within a few inches of Evvie's.

'Gee,' Evvie said. 'Where . . .'

Topal knelt beside Evvie. She started reading the funny paper. She jostled Evvie. She slid the comic sheet closer to herself, and shouldered Evvie away. Evvie leaned sideways against Topal's heavier body, and tried to see over Topal's shoulder. Topal turned and shoved her sister with both hands. Evvie came back and grabbed at the paper. A corner of it tore off in her hands.

They got to their feet and struggled savagely for possession of the paper, uttering not a word, but making loud bumping and scraping sounds, and breathing hard. Once Topal fell off balance, and her hip struck the house with a great bump. There was a crash in the front room as the statue of the Blessed Virgin smashed upon the floor, followed by a scream inside and the patter of hurrying feet.

Evvie dashed away, jumped from the porch, and leaped off through the trees. When she reached a big tree to hide behind, she peeped at the house. Commodo and Mrs. Crochet were standing in the front doorway, craning their necks, peering at Topal, who was on all fours reading the funny paper. Presently Evvie saw her father take his wife by the arm, and the two disappear inside.

Evvie started to throw bits of dried orange peel at a fiddler crab. The crab jumped off sideways, then stopped and raised his little claws belligerently at Evvie, and pointed his popped eyes at her. Evvie removed one of her shoes and hurled it at the fiddler, pouting.

18

YOU BEEN NEEDING
GOOZE-GREASE ALL DAY

IN THE morning the house seemed forlorn. Paul and Gussie and the baby were cross. Commodo stayed in bed, harassed by one of his minor ailments, with a wry look on his face, as though he smelled a bad odor.

'A thing I wunt you all to remember,' he grumbled, 'is to give my body to Tulane University when I pass away for them to study and fine out what was the matter I died. I been layin here thinking, and I can't understand why a man in this helty climate is gotta be pestered, pestered, pestered, livin on this fine alluviable soil too. I make a bet I got a unknown disease.'

Mrs. Crochet was at the sewing machine, a very old contraption with a broken treadle. She said, 'Doctor Wall, him he done tole you what's the matter. It come from the kitchen, what you got, and the bar-room partly. Whoa!' she called to Topal, who was sitting on the floor spinning the driving wheel of the machine for her — grabbing it hand over hand, as one furiously hauling in a rope. Topal stopped the wheel. She looked at her hands and sighed.

'Can't Evvie come turn it for you now?' Topal asked. 'I'm getting a water-blister by my thumb.'

'No. Jiss a little more tell I fix the hem. The dress is yourn, and you gotta spin the wheel. Me, I'm glad the style is switchin back to long dresses, because very few girls in the world is got pretty laigs. Evvie got to go to church like she tole Father Pennygrass to help those ladies to fix the altar, because tomorrow's Easter and Jesus rose from the dead. Look how pretty this mornin outside. Me, I wish I had a thousan dirty clothes to wash and hang out. Finish your coffee, Evvie, and don't be dreamin! All them udda girls gunna be there decorating the altar, darling. You oughta be glad.'

'Heck, I guess I'm just tired,' Evvie said in the kitchen.

'The coffee gunna strong you soon, darling. Come home after and get you a doze gooze-grease if you feel bad. Look Elna waitin by the shed.'

Evvie went through the back yard to join Elna Jeanfreau. Clouds were blotting out all traces of the sun, now. The dark ground was strewn with oranges in various stages of rot. Evvie stepped daintily over the sound ones, to avoid hurting any of the fruit belonging to the landlord. The cloudy orchard grew darker. Gussie and Paul were wrangling as they hopped about the trees, trying to capture and chain the pet racoon.

Evvie and her friend wandered down the high back road toward the church. From here they could see all of Grass Margin, and see on the other side the big reedy marshes disappearing into the bays of the sea. This road did not wriggle in the shape of the river as the front road did. Its white straightness obeyed the straightness of the canal by its side, and the eye could find a pointed ending in the hazes far ahead. It was surfaced with oyster shells powdered by the weather and the passing wheels, and on either side it was shored by clotted myrtles. The myrtles were full of vireos hunting insects.

Elna said, 'Today is nux vomica day. Less us not go to the church. Everybody got together along the Margin to poison the blagbirds with poison corn today.'

'I know it. I'd like you to hush up about that.'

'Everybody keeping the chickens in. Everybody put poison corn in the field. Nux vomica for the blagbirds.'

'It gets me sick.'

'Look!' said Elna, waving her arm. 'The blagbirds go like this. Zzzzzzzzzz! Round an round, and firss thing you know — tock! down they go to the ground, and they don't know what's a matter. Papa put good corn in orchard three days, and this mornin he trew corn soaked in poison.'

'The blackbirds don't do us anything.'

'Well! What your family's got? Nothing! No orange, no corn sprouts in you all's field so far, only smell-melon and beggar lice.'

Evvie said, 'I'm looking for a place to stretch on the ground. Let's find a place, Elna. Will you stay with me?'

Elna examined Evvie suspiciously. She hopped ahead and walked backwards before Evvie, looking at Evvie's averted face. 'What's a matter with you today, girl, and what are you honing for?' Then she skipped off. 'I'm goin see all the dead blagbirds in Sister Gravity's pea-field. Ole Sister Gravity always got the most blagbirds, because she's a ole blag witch!'

'I'd like to lay on the ground and put my feet against something strong, like a tree, and shove with my feet, and shove, and shove.'

There had been rain during the night. Elna dragged her feet through the slush. Now and then a huge crawfish brought out by the rain backed across the road with menacing claws raised. Elna amused herself kicking them off the road. In the robust wind, masses of tilting and rolling blackbirds swept over the old and the young groves. Some of the trees had orange hulls strewn under them, where the blackbirds had devoured the fruit. The girls reached a clearing in the myrtles near the grammar school. It was the place on the canal bank where the school trash was dumped. Evvie found a large stack of corrected school papers, and she brushed off the wet ones on top, and sat to rest. 'I sure feel lazy and sleepy,' she said.

Elna watched Evvie narrowly. 'Do you hurt any place? Your face is pink.'

'My back's heavy, like,' Evvie said.

'You gettin to be a lady, Evvie. I know what's a matter, poor chile. I bet a nickel. Don't you feel all give-inny? Shoot! You got the curse. Let me see something . . .'

'No!'

'Heck. That ain nothin. Every girl gets the curse. It come every month like the grocery bill. Everybody gunna treat you better when they fine out, and you don't need to go to school. Me, I got a lovely calendar I'm gunna give you home. It's got reindeers on it, and a man walking on tennis rackets in the snow.'

'Thanks.'

'Better you'd go home now. Tell your mama you got a toodache and lay down. From now on, you got plenny layin down to do. Are you goin home or to church which?'

'Elna, don't go!' Evvie begged.

But Elna was moving off. Evvie followed, but she could not walk freely to keep up. 'Oh, Elna, look!' Evvie said. 'I'll give you a stick of gum!'

'Listen, what do you expeck *me* to do for you?' Elna asked. 'I say you oughta stood home, any damn how. Quit following!'

Evvie buried her face in her sleeve. She whimpered and

stamped her foot. Elna walked off. Evvie followed. Elna stopped short. Evvie paused close to her. Elna took off her cap and threw it to the ground. It was a dirty orange-and-purple silk cap of the sort worn by soft-ball players.

'Everything I do, you gotta do!' Elna cried. 'I say you better sneak home through the canes and lay down. You wunt me to tell on you? I'll tell your mother.'

'No! No!' Evvie stamped her foot. She hung her head and sobbed, breaking down completely.

'All right, all right, all *right!* Hush up, cry-baby. I'll stay a little while. And *hush up* out on the road!'

When they returned to the clearing in the trees, Elna said, 'Gimme the stick of gum. Me, I'm sorry for you now, because this is a terrible thing, the seriousess time of life. You got to be caffle now. You know something? You better never let a boy do you anything no more in the canes. Not even one boy, unless you got a witness, you hear? I feel sorry for you. If it ain one thing it's anudda,' Elna sighed and stared gloomily at the canal. 'I bet you never did get a chance to go on the choo-choo with a boy yet, huh?'

Evvie looked at her friend with eyes full of misery.

'Well,' Elna shook her head sadly, 'it's too late now. You done had your chance. We live to learn, say like my mama. Now you got to fine you a husband.'

Evvie said, 'I don't want anybody blowing down my throat and swelling me up. So please hush.'

'Now listen, don't start crying again, because I'll leave. You're a nit-wit and a — a Evvie Crochet! Nothin but a Evvie Crochet, so goo-bye.'

'Elna! Please!'

'Well *shut up!* Listen, Evvie, I'll stay if you bend your bones! Shh! Shh! Go head. Bend your bones.'

Evvie dried her eyes. She took hold of one of her index fingers and gritted her teeth. Sniffling and sobbing, she bent the finger back until it touched the wrist.

'The udda hand!' Elna cried delightedly. 'The udda one!'

Evvie bent the opposite index finger back against her wrist. Elna watched closely, holding her own finger and bending it back as far as it would go.

'Now your laig, Evvie! Put your laig behind your neck!'

'No.'

'Then hug yourself like you did that day in physics!'

Evvie brought her arms around her body. Her continual sobbing made it difficult; but she finally got her arms wound around herself until her fingertips crawled toward each in the rear and met over the spine. Elna laughed, kicking her feet in merriment.

Something fell out of the sky. There was a loud beating sound in the myrtles, and a curious dim croaking. Evvie, looking into the myrtles, gasped and grabbed Elna's arm.

'Ouch!' Elna cried. 'It's only a poisoned blagbird fell, damn it, you hurt my *arm*, Evvie Crochet!'

'I'm sorry, Elna. I didn't mean to.'

'Well, quit *holding* me! And stop that damn *crying*. Come on, Evvie. Shhh! Shhh! It's all right, see, only a blagbird.'

The bird hung with the claws of one foot caught in the myrtle bark, its wings spread like fingers; its eyes opening and closing, staying closed longer and longer until they opened no more; its tongue suspended between the black beak. Elna got up.

'Elna, not yet!' Evvie begged. 'Don't go, please.'

'Me, I'm going Sister Gravity's and see how many. But listen, I'll stay a long-long time if you tell that story. You know, that story.'

'The king's guards were all fair, six and a half feet tall. The queen's guards were dark, and they were six and a half feet tall.'

'No, start where Raoul tries ——'

'Raoul came to the tavern on Valentine's Day, and some of the king's guards were there singing songs. When Raoul was joking with the barmaid, one of the king's guards named Geoffrey said, "I'll wager a guinea a king's guard can drink a queen's guard under the table." '

There was a long silence. Elna, lying on her back looking at the sky, was picking at a toenail.

'Well, go head, Evvie. Raoul went ——'

'I want to wash,' Evvie said.

'Huh?'

'Wash.'

'Heck.'

'You can go now. Thank you.'

Evvie was backing toward the canal.

Elna moved over and lay in the dry place where Evvie had been. 'I dowunna,' she said.

'I'll tell the story some other time. I'll see you at church tomorrow.'

'I dowunna go now.'

'You stay on the road, then. Watch out for ——'

'Like fun I will. Who was your slave when you was rich?'

Evvie crept behind a low myrtle to undress. She was laughing, shaking all over, biting her lip to hold it in, because there were strange terrifying floods of laughter waiting to pour through her and rush out and sweep her away beyond reach of anything. She lowered herself into the warm canal. She pushed the floating hyacinth bulbs away from around her, forming a clear brown place. The soft muck on the bottom was freezing cold. Evvie held on to the myrtle limb while the huge waves of laughter inside her ebbed away. With her free hand she rinsed her face. Elna did not come to look at her. She could see through the leaves the swarthy blur of Elna's impish face, the red bangs on the forehead brushed sideways by puffs of wind. For a while she stood motionless except for an occasional paroxysm of ebbing laughter, soaking herself in the tepid, barely flowing stream, and the silence came back. She could hear faint sounds now — a waterbird clopping like a man beating a pipe on the palm of his hand, and the slight persistent ticking of a bug near-by trundling a seedpod through the dead leaves.

An automobile stopped on the road. Evvie could hear her brother Arthur's deep voice talking to Elna, teasing her; then she heard Bruce's Holt's voice. She climbed from the water and dressed behind her tree. When Evvie appeared, the boys stopped discussing whatever it was they had been teasing Elna about.

Bruce Holt lounged behind the wheel of the car with his lifted knees on the wheel. Arthur Crochet beside him very nonchalantly flicked the ash from his cigarette. Bruce beat on the horn button, making the horn sound like a hen coming off the nest. He said, 'I borrow the car when my old lady goes across the river. Don't the car belong to the whole family? The old man's in the prairie, and the old lady's gone over the river to Uncle Mocco's boat works.'

An automobile bowled past like a glittering ball rolling.

'I don't want to go riding,' Evvie said.

'She's sick,' Elna explained. 'And don't none of you all ax what's the matter.'

'I'm not any more,' Evvie said. She folded her hands

primly. When she had first greeted her brother, the tides of laughter inside her had almost started beating out. Now they were forgotten, or they lay quietly against the thin shore of her mind.

'We're not begging anybody to go riding,' Arthur said.

'You said it,' Bruce agreed. Here in the company of Arthur, Bruce's manner was supercilious. And there was a shrill hardness in his voice. Here on the straight, high-speed road, far from the meandering old levee highway, the voice came to Evvie as a sound from the city, the brisk, clicking, polished place where he seemed now to belong. It brought back the brief images she had gathered of New Orleans — sharp street corners and bold gongs and the low frantic rustling of glittering shoes.

'I wouldn't go on a date with my own kid sister, anyhow,' Arthur said. Bruce laughed loudly. Arthur reached behind where his three dogs lay on the rear seat. He grabbed one of them by the muzzle and shook it from side to side affectionately. 'Hey, Evvie, tell old man Crochet I'm taking the dogs Monday to a fellow in town,' he said. The dogs were a dirty gray. One of them laid his tail along under his belly, shivered violently; and his yellow eyes, clear and wide and alert with apprehension, never left his master's face.

Arthur reached into his pocket for a letter he had picked up at the post office, and handed it to Evvie. 'Give this to Topal,' he said. The letter was addressed to Topal from Dave Tobin in the Mercy Hospital, New Orleans. Evvie noticed the stamp was upside down.

'Less go get a batch of Milky Ways,' Bruce said.

Elna said, 'Milky Ways nothin. I wunt a rood-beer. I bet yall got a false key, runnin your papa's car with a false key.'

'Shoot, who needs a key?' Arthur asked.

'Turn the static off and less go,' Bruce said. 'You kids coming along?'

'She'll go,' said Evvie, tossing her chin toward Elna. She disliked Bruce, acting smart for Arthur's benefit. She regretted being in love with him. She still wanted to tell him, before he returned to town, that not even a fire could completely destroy anything.

Arthur jumped out. Elna climbed in beside Bruce. She sat between the two boys giggling, taking off her soft-ball cap, squinting one eye into the rear-view mirror, patting her red hair. She moved close to Bruce and put her arm on his shoulder.

Evvie watched them go — the cracked-voiced boys who had outgrown their coats, the girl with her bangs cut crooked, the sad bony dogs. Heavy swells of laughter were rolling through her again, but again she stopped them by biting on her lip. . . . After a while she examined Dave Tobin's letter, wondering why Tobin was writing to her sister, putting his stamp upside down.

She walked homeward. The bold wind flaying her skirts out ahead enabled her to walk with hardly an effort. A man was at work in a near-by field. He raised his hand and called, 'Eh là bas! Whazh you papa?' Evvie raised her hand without replying. People were always asking about her father. She slacked her pace to see the farmer piling a large quantity of dead blackbirds into a mound. Over his head a flock of crazed or frightened birds whirled madly. The sky was a tattered gray.

The flock would dip groundward near the dead ones, rise and remain still, flapping; then it would scatter in a great sweep along the wind. One bird fell tumbling over and over from the flock, hopped about on the ground, and lay still.

The whole flock dove and gathered. They walked very primly around the stricken member. The farmer danced on his eager old legs across the field, took up the bird and carried it to the mound. He looked at Evvie and smiled. He poured oil from a can over the black pile of dead birds, and struck a match. From the black pyre a blossom of smoke rose suddenly. It curled, swung, was caught by the wind and rolled swiftly toward the highway.

Evvie screamed and ran, holding her head low. She heard the farmer's laughter. Once the flock of birds dipped down to examine her, and a bird fell near. The whole sky was filled with crying birds. Evvie sat in the road with her arms around her head, beating her feet. The overwhelming swells of laughter swept through her, a scalding cascade whose surge she could not stop. She made a ball of part of her skirt and sank her teeth into it, and pounded the road with her heels. The farmer's braying laughter drew nearer. The man was running toward her. Evvie got up and ran in the opposite direction. The farmer stopped and roared: 'Hoowah-hyow-hyow-hyow-hyow! Make hase! Hyow-hyow-hyow! Make hase! Make hase!'

'All right,' Evvie whispered, fleeing with fists clenched and blurred revolving steps barely touching the road. 'All right!'

When she reached the place where the Crochets' path joined the big road, she hesitated, afraid to go to the house. She lingered in the wind, panting heavily. Presently she crawled under the bridge that spanned the canal, where there was no wind. There was a pirogue pulled ashore under there. It was full of Spanish moss. There was a paddle, a jug half full of drinking water in the pirogue, and some crudely carved, unpainted decoy ducks. In a paper bag were the remains of a lunch — two slices of bread spread thickly with lard and sprinkled with red pepper. Evvie bathed her eyes with the jug water.

She eased her body into the deep sweet bed of moss in the pirogue, and soon caught her breath. It was warm under there, and the light was dim. She stretched her limbs. She rested there until the afternoon. The carpenter bees hummed loudly around the bridge. They had bored their deep round holes far into the cypress wood. Right near Evvie's head a bee had cut a round tunnel into a timber, kicking out grains of aromatic cypress dust, and his diligent buzzing down in the tunnel twanged all through the bridge. When an automobile sped past on the road above, the earth and the bridge were considerably jarred, and Evvie lying in the springy moss liked the feeling of her relaxed body bouncing gently with the earth. She could also hear the faint thunderous roaring of shrimp-trawler engines back in the bay.

Arriving home in the afternoon, Evvie found Topal busy in the back shed, dyeing Easter eggs. A pot was boiling on a charcoal furnace. There was a little basket of dyed eggs, and another containing eggs not yet colored.

'Tope, what you doing?'

'Digging clams with a rubber spade.'

'Whose eggs?'

'Papa went and showed the eggs next door, and they come wanting me to dye theirs too. Move! I've got to finish before your kid brothers come home and see what I'm doing.'

The back shed was scrubbed white. Flour-sack curtains were on the windows. There was a small empty packing case with a piece of bright goods tacked in ruffles around the open side, and above this a little mirror with a tin frame. The mirror made one of Evvie's eyeballs look as big as a walnut. Clothes hanging on the walls were covered by a flour-sack draw curtain. In a corner was the tiny telephone table which Arthur had built in manual training class. On it was an ornamental china lamp about six inches high, with a real wick and burner, which Topal had won at the movies on Ladies' True Blue China night. Evvie looked around with a serious face, eyes wide and thoughtful. On the bottom of the packing case dresser in a place the ruffled goods did not cover, she read the words printed in black: 'Approved By Good Housekeeping.' She started out, then turned.

'Are you going to live back here, Tope?'

'Till I get a better home. Any more questions, skink? Sure, take a good look, and God dog it, don't ever come here with dirty feet, none of you all, I'm telling you.'

'Where did you get the sleeping cot?'

'Next door. It was given to me. So I don't need to go in that house ever any more if I don't want to, except to eat. And if you all don't let me alone, I'm going to start bringing my grub out here to eat, like I did today. I met Arthur today, and he had dinner with me here, and he's bringing a flounder for me and him's supper. And where's my letter, missy, and why didn't you bring it right home?'

Evvie handed Topal the letter. Topal snatched it, and went to the window to read it. Evvie went out. Reaching the window, she looked in. Topal inside was reading Tobin's letter with her back against the window. Evvie stood there and read Tobin's letter through the triangular opening of Topal's arm:

Dear Miss Crochet:
    I was so surprized to get your two letters, as you didn't pay any attention to me when I lived in Grass Margin. Yes indeed I am getting well fast, but will have a limp in the left leg where

the oyster knife went deep, and I have a cauliflower ear. As if I'm not ugly enough already! But I will attend to that barber when I get out.

No I'm not bored, the hospital is busy and lots going on always. However, that does not mean I would not feel honored to see you when next you come to old N.O. And yes indeed, I would appreciate some good Delta oranges. What you said about the box of bon-bons made my mouth water. Did the mail-plane pilot ever come back? It was right nice of him to take you up in his plane, and for a quiet little homebody you sure explained your thrills fine. I felt like I was along. No such luck!!!.

Will wait for early reply. Write some more adventures you have. It's lonesome some times here.

Yours (?)

David Tobin

PS. — Don't let the airplane pilot string you along. Tell your papa will be able to lend him the $60 soon as I get back working.

Suddenly Topal felt the presence looking in the window. She spun around, flung the curtains wide. Evvie moved off toward the front of the house. At the cistern she looked back. Topal, looking at her, leaned on the sill and smiled. There was a cunning look in her eyes. Evvie grinned at her sister.

In the house, Evvie found her little keepsake box. The letter she had written to Tobin was gone. Other unmailed letters containing accounts of imaginary escapades were missing.

'Who's that sniffing in the front room?' Mrs. Crochet called from the second room. 'Who done caught a cole in the head on a big Easter Sadday?'

Evvie walked into the second room. Her mother was putting cloths dipped in river water to her father's side. Commodo lay on the bed, groaning, while he smoked a cigarette and stroked the head of T. J. who slept beside him.

'Me, I'm gunna fix you some gooze-grease,' Mrs. Crochet

said to Evvie without looking at her, 'and head that cold off. You been needin apple-cations of gooze-grease all day. Did you all fix the altar nice for Pennygrass?'

'Yes mam,' Evvie said. 'Lilies mixed with roses.'

'I hope Jesus gunna take a glimp at this Margin some day and give a hand to those that needs it. The prayers that goes up in the sky in this place! Keep still, you ole rangatang.'

'I don't know, me, why you gotta be doin this,' Commodo muttered. 'River water towels never did me good.'

'God punished you for eatin a whole chicken at LaRoque's on a fass day and white beans and fawn livers ——'

'Did I abstain from work, or did I dig for three hour? Pennygrass knows a workin man can't fass.'

'Shut up and lemme finish, with not a dinner dish washed today yet.'

'Mama, I'll wash them,' Evvie said, turning to leave.

'Come back here!' Mrs. Crochet cried. 'What's that mud all over your behind? Good Goddle mighty, will you jiss looka the condition of that chile!'

'Mama, I've been playing Go In And Out The Window with Elna, and ——'

Mrs. Crochet swung the wet cloth at Evvie's dodging head. 'I'll Go In And Out The Window you!'

Evvie's skinny legs carried her leaping through the house and out the back door. Topal was in the yard pounding dried shrimp in a sack. As Evvie sped past her she sang:

> Go in and out the window
> As we have done today...
> Stand back and face your lover
> La, la, la, la, la-la-la...

Evvie sat under the tree watching Topal. Topal had pretty hair, bluish-black, fine and glossy, full of curved lights in the sun. The dark areas under her eyes made her look attractive. But her dress color was faded by washing, worn off by rubbing against things, erased by fog and sun. Topal had nice legs, thin, but shaped for work and dancing. They almost offset her round-shouldered posture and lack of a proper bosom. Evvie wanted her own legs to fill out some, because with bony limbs she would never look like a real woman. She watched Topal take the shells beaten off the shrimp over to the pet racoon and sprinkle them before the animal. Suddenly with a friendly smile Topal looked around into Evvie's appraising eyes.

'I guess he's going to be my boy friend now,' she said.

'That's nice. I don't object.'

'He's a passable fellow, young enough for me. One day I'll ride to town on Arthur's truck and see him at the hospital. I'll stay at Aunt Lucille's on Tchoupitoulas Street.'

'Gee. That's nice. I'm glad.'

Evvie's sweet words irritated Topal. 'It won't do you any good to object,' she said.

'I don't care, Tope.'

'It won't do you any good to care.'

'Well, I didn't say it would.'

'It won't do you any good to say it would.'

Evvie walked away, muttering.

Topal ran after her, and grabbed her wrist from behind.

'What were you starting to say?'

'Nothing.'

'What were you starting to say?'

'Nothing. Ouch! I was going to say what you do is your own business.'

Topal turned Evvie's arm loose and gave her a shove toward the house. Evvie made her body rigid, leaning back against the shove. She went as far as the kitchen steps, then walked back toward her sister. She picked up a stick of wood lying there, and faced Topal. 'Don't think I'm still a baby, you hear?'

Topal moved close, jerked the stick away from Evvie and threw it away. She said, 'Listen, punk,' and grabbed Evvie. She bent the younger girl's body in half, and began to spank her.

'That doesn't make me a baby,' said Evvie, giggling, relaxing. 'Go ahead and spank. You can't make me a baby any more. Oh, look who's coming! Turn loose, Tope! It's Mr. Dupré!'

19

YOU WAS BANKING ON
A SUPPOSITORY

OLD DUPRÉ the landlord was walking in off the levee road. He was smiling! With his walking cane, he reminded Evvie of a mock turtle in a picture book. Topal in her soiled dress dashed into the back shed. Behind the landlord was a tall stout nun, a sister from one of the orphan asylums in New Orleans, who had come to get oranges for the poor. Evvie scooped up the colander full of dried shrimp to hide them in the house, and ran in to tell her mother, 'Mama, here comes old Poison Ivory with the sister for fruit!'

Mrs. Crochet wiped her hands and turned around and around distractedly. 'Goddle mighty, me and my house is rotten with the dirt! Don't make noise, nobody! Shhh!' She tiptoed to the window and peeped out. 'The same fruit sister that come lass year, Duck!' Suddenly she swung around and slapped the side of Evvie's head. 'I could *kill* you!' she hissed. 'Durdy like a pig and the sister is comin. Go get on something clean!'

Evvie sulked off, frowning over her shoulder. 'I got no clean dress, well.'

'Put on Arthur's overhalls! *Do* something when you see the sister here! Look at her! Looka the durdy little spink, stand-ing ——'

'His overalls are too long!' Evvie whispered.

'Roll them up, you little ——'

'Heck, I don't see why we've always got to be hiding from people!' Evvie said, rummaging in the armoir.

'Evvie, sweedart,' Commodo said, 'don't you wunna become a sister?' He left his bed with the spread wrapped around him like a ravelled toga, and shuffled to the window to peer out beside his wife at the figures moving among the trees. 'Don't you wunt them to take you to town nex year to become a sister on the new bus? Hurry up and run out and tell them Papa's working and Mama's negs door or somethin.'

'No!' Mrs. Crochet said. 'Tell them we gone across the river.'

'Suppose they come in, Duck? Suppose Jewpray come walking in to get a piece of cord or somethin?'

'He won't. Shhh! Don't wake the little sprinklin can in that bed up. Look ole Poison Ivory, like he owns the world, and still got egg on his vess.'

'Duck, he's a ole Midas,' said Commodo. 'He's a ole Midas and a ole Simon Legree.'

'Sure. So proud he's carryin the sister aroun. One hand robbin the poor and chasin after a poor nigger girl, and the other hand givin windfall fruit to the orphans. Oh Duck, look the little orphans! Ain't they white? Look how white! Don't the sisters dress them sweet?'

Four little white orphans had come from the truck on the levee and joined the party in the orchard. They wore blue dresses, all the same color, nicely starched and ironed; black shoes and stockings, straw hats with elastic running around their fat white throats. Each carried a little basket for the oranges she at once began to gather from the ground.

Evvie came out of the house and edged her way along the

wall. Arthur's overalls were much too large, and Evvie had gathered the excess waist material into a lump in the rear. She saw Mr. Dupré walking about with the sister and the truck driver. With his silver-headed walking cane, in fastidious little flipping movements, he was rolling off to one side the good oranges for the little orphans to pick up. One of the orphans kept looking at Evvie while she picked up fruit. She was about Evvie's age, and walked with the stiff erect carriage of the chapel rank, and had dark eyes, very friendly, brimming with friendly light. Her face was shining from soap and water. Her hair was gathered into two strands plaited so tightly that the skin of her temples was pulled back, making her eyes slightly narrow, like Chinese eyes. She kept looking at Evvie, and when picking up an orange, still holding her spine rigid, she would suddenly bend her knees and sink, then, with the orange in her hand, bounce back into a standing position.

The tall sister walked about quietly. There was heard only the faint brisk rattle of the big wooden rosary swinging from her belt. The sister reached out her heavy, work-roughened hand and touched Evvie on the head.

'That's Evvie,' Mr. Dupré said in a tone he would have used to point out a banana peel in their path. But when the sister smiled and hugged Evvie to her, Dupré smiled too, and said, 'This is Sister Margaret, Evvie.'

'Make yourself at home, Sister,' Evvie said.

Evvie passed on, because Sister Margaret did not seem to have remembered collecting fruit there before, and telling Evvie she might some day become a nun if she were a good girl. Evvie heard Mr. Dupré telling the sister, 'She's the father's favorite. I told you about him last year. The fat one, digs ditches, big as a house and the children hungry.'

'Oh, yes, the poor man!' Sister Margaret said. 'And you promised to reduce their rent, Mr. Dupré.'

'I did. I reduced it.'

'God will bless you surely.'

'Not that they appreciate it.'

'Ah, sure they do appreciate it! Now you go long and be a lenient landlord. They'll pray for you, because they're obliged to. You leave that rent alone, and be a lenient landlord to God's poor.'

'I'm easy enough. Ask anybody.'

'A good, kind landlord to the poor, and be on the safe side. Give them the benefit of the doubt, God's poor ones struggling to keep alive and greet our Savior with good fresh corns on their hands and knees. Are they Catholic?'

'Yes, Sister.'

'God bless us, I'm thinking I've seen the little one before. Let's give her a Saint Joseph.'

Sister Margaret called Evvie and gave her a little brass case. Evvie pulled the cover off. There was a pleasant popping sound, and there tumbled out into her hand a small lead likeness of Saint Joseph. 'Have your pastor bless it,' said the sister. 'Do you know who it is?'

'Saint Joseph, Sister. The father of Jesus.'

'The *foster*-father of Jesus! Do you remember anything about him?'

'The flight into Egypt, Sister. He walked by the donkey and the Blessed Mother rode with the Infant Jesus, and Saint Joseph was ——'

'Ah, I see you bow your head when you say "Jesus"!'

Sister Margaret did not mention anything about Evvie becoming a nun. Evvie did not mind. She had no real lover to renounce for the religious life. Sister Margaret strolled toward the rear, with her hand on Evvie's shoulder. 'Sure a wonderful country,' she murmured. 'Green as an old woman's home. The wild geese we saw this morning! It must have been a thousand! What's that I smell?'

'The people next door skin muskrats and throw the meat in the field, Sister.'

'Phew! You don't say! What for? And hasn't the trapping season been over a long time?'

'Yes, Sister. But they trap anyway. Some of the animals they catch have little young ones in them.'

'An outrage! And you smell this all the time, then?'

'When the wind is west, Sister. You get so you don't notice it much.'

'I notice it. Are these people Catholic?'

'Yes, Sister.'

'Phew!'

The horrid smell was suddenly gone. The orange blossoms' perfume chased the other away. Sister Margaret and Evvie stood on the ditchbank. The nun's hand was deep in her mysterious pocket, which was stuffed with tempting gifts — peppermint candies, penny balloons, holy pictures — for the little children the nun met in her work of collecting fruit for the orphan asylum.

'A wonderful place!' Sister Margaret said. 'Look the sweet little fence around the chicken-yard next door. Made of a net, isn't it?'

'Yes, Sister, a seine. An old seine.'

'Sure it's sweet. People could live such a holy life here. A fair country, barring the mosquitoes, filled with good things all around. Where are your parents, Evvie?'

'Across the river, Sister.'

'I think I remember them now. They're good people. Your

father's a lovely, upright man. Obey him always. If he's lax about church, remind him. A gentle reminder. From the little ones, sure it often helps.'

Sister Margaret fell silent again, and she pressed Evvie against her ample body. In the stillness Evvie heard a long rumble like faint thunder. It was coming from inside the nun's stomach. At first Evvie wanted to laugh, but there was no one to laugh with. She cleared her throat vigorously to cover up the sound. 'Sure I'd fight with me senses in this place,' the nun mused. 'No doubt the body is forever roused from its proper chastisements and meditations and lured sideways to the things that flatter the flesh . . .'

'Yes, Sister!'

The nun looked down at Evvie, her eyes twinkling. Again the deep rumble sounded inside her body, and Evvie cleared her throat energetically. Sister Margaret's face was raised, and Evvie saw the whiskers in her nose. Nuns were no different from other women. She stole a glance behind the white fluted bonnet, and saw the nun's hidden hair. It was jet black, thick and live, cut in short locks, not a streak of gray. Nuns hid their hair because nothing lovely was supposed to be seen, and hair was a lovely thing.

The little orphans were about finished gathering the good fruit. The one with the eyes pulled sideways by her plaits stood behind a tree, peeping at Evvie shyly. Sister Margaret's heavy hand patted the bones of Evvie's shoulder. Evvie rested her cheek against the harsh black serge. It hurt her skin. She did not want to wear clothes like this.

'Is that someone crying?' the sister asked.

'My little brother, Sister.'

'It sounds like a grown boy crying . . . Well, don't you want to go see about him?'

Evvie backed away from the nun, holding on to the overall material bunched up behind her. 'I guess so,' she said, then turned and ran for the house.

Topal, hiding in the back shed, whispered, 'Are they gone?'

Inside, Mrs. Crochet had T. J. on her knees attending to him. The twins were playing quietly. Commodo lay on the bed holding his side.

'Did you ax the sister if you can go to town next year and get in the convent?' Mrs. Crochet asked.

'No mam, I forgot.'

Mrs. Crochet put her hands on her hips and glared.

'I didn't think about it,' Evvie said.

'Well, I'm a son-of-a-bugger! Jiss listen at that! The dinwiddie forgot.'

'Now don't start fussin,' said Commodo. 'I ax you nice.'

'She forgot.'

'I didn't think to ask.'

'Looka her! Looka her standin there like a spink, telling me ——'

'I changed my mind,' Evvie said.

'Will you jiss listen at that!'

'Well, Mama, you said ——'

'I said it was nex to my heart to let you be a sister. I said ——'

'Will you please, please go in the yard and fight,' Commodo said.

Evvie said, 'Sometimes you would say ——'

'Shut up your mouth! What did you say lass year when the sister tole you ——'

'I said — the sister said ——'

'Shut up! Answer me! What ——'

'Mama, I said ——'

'Didn't you say right in this room ——'

Commodo knocked over the pan of water. 'Merciful Jesus H. *Christ* Almighty Limited!' he screamed at the top of his voice.

Mrs. Crochet ducked her head as from the lightning, and crossed herself.

In the dead silence she went softly to the window with the baby, and looked out. The nun, the landlord, and the orphans in the act of bearing their baskets to the truck on the road, had all stopped dead, and were looking back at the Crochet house. Sister Margaret said something to Mr. Dupré, who shrugged and went on. The nun, shading her eyes, gazed intently at the house. Then she motioned the four orphans to go ahead, and followed them with her hooded face bowed, her veil flapping in the wind.

Evvie tiptoed from the room. Mrs. Crochet went to the bed, put the baby down and took up the wet cloth. 'Turn over, you blasphemish Indian,' she told her husband.

'You talk and you talk and you talk,' Commodo said.

'Misère. Misère. The trashy Crochets.'

'Take a blow.'

'Why don't Almighty God sink this house in the river and send down the brimstones and scatter the bones of the ingrateful chirren and sick people and the ingrateful sons and daughters ——'

'Talk — talk — talk! Rub me, Duck. We jiss as good as anybody else. Take a blow.'

'That gawkward little spink is the cause of it all. A Sister of the Poor in my front yard listenin.'

'Evvie's good as a piece of bread.'

'I'll tend to her. I'll fix her clock, me.'

'You got no right. Not a sacred thing like that. God got

to seddle things like that. He call the ones that he call, and he don't call the ones he don't call. You can see what she got in her heart, you?'

'*She wanted to be a sister!*' Mrs. Crochet screamed. 'And me, how many time I didn't pray and pray for her?'

'Chit-chit-chit! The chile change her mine. In udda words, A, you was bankin on a suppository, and B, you got nothin to do with it. Rub me down lower.'

'Awright, Messyou Crochet! Jiss anudda belly to feed! You see where you layin? You layin on your back, eh? Who gunna feed them if you stay there, and me, I keepa having more chirren every couple year almoss, and can't pass one of my chirren over to the service of God that He's giving me more and more! Where's the colorin pepper in this house tonight to make a gravy? White gravy on my table tonight to disgrace my mother that was such a particular cook's memory! Tomorrow black coffee on your two dollar when you can work. I wunt somebody to tell me what we gunna do, me.'

'Press hard by the end of my ribs,' Commodo said.

Mrs. Crochet ran into the next room. She grabbed Evvie by the shoulders and yelled, 'Get you a husband, you hear? Start right now, tomorrow! Keep open your eyes, before you get humpback and rancid.'

'All right,' Evvie said. 'All right, Mama.'

'And if a man speak to you on the road, turn your head the udda way and listen good.'

In the late evening, Commodo felt better. He went out to squat on the levee and take a look at the Old Man. The little *Blessed Trinity*, which he had once commanded, was due to pass by towing the weekly barges of oyster shells up the river.

Commodo sat on his heels under the soft Easter Saturday sky, looking out over the river. The Old Man was slick and rosy, flowing without any driftwood. The water soon would begin to drop, now, and Emilien Perdu get his cattle from the marshes and return to hold the meeting of the drainage board. Commodo frowned and sighed.

Suddenly he turned and cupped his hands. He yelled at the house: 'Duck! Ohhhhh Duck!'

He heard Evvie on the front steps cry, 'Mama! Papa wants you out front!'

From the back shed came Topal's voice: 'Mama! Papa wants you out front!'

'Tell her to hurry up!' Commodo bellowed.

'Tell her to hurry up!' Evvie called.

'Mama! Hurry up!' Topal cried from the shed.

Mrs. Crochet, running around the side of the house — carrying T. J. and followed by the twins, both crying and begging her to wait for them — was panting from exertion. 'Where he's at?' she shouted. 'What's a matter?'

'On the levee, Mama!' Evvie called.

'What's a matter? What's a matter?' Mrs. Crochet shouted. The baby was crying, and Paul and Gussie fought each other to get ahead.

'Duck! Here on the levee!' Commodo yelled. 'Come quick and see something!'

'Can't you wait!' Mrs. Crochet stopped at the foot of the embankment and looked in both directions to see if anyone were coming on the road, then began to climb the levee side. One of her stockings had fallen and fouled her shoe.

'Carry that baby for Mama!' Commodo ordered.

Topal took the baby and climbed swiftly ahead of her mother. Evvie helped the twins up the levee's slope.

'What happened? What happened?' Mrs. Crochet panted.

'Oh, Mama, come see!' Evvie called.

'Now shut up your mouth, you all!' Commodo bawled. 'Leave her come see herself!'

Mrs. Crochet struggled up and stood alongside her husband. Commodo pointed to the big full moon rising between the budding willows. 'Ain't that a pitcha?' he asked his wife.

The whole family was lined up on top the levee. Evvie and the twins all held hands.

'Is this what you get me off the clothesline for, you old rangatang?' Mrs. Crochet asked, slapping Commodo's head, then taking hold of his arm. 'I thought a tanker rammed the levee, me.'

'You gunna tell me that ain't a pitcha?' Commodo asked.

'I thought a tanker rammed the levee or something.'

'You can see the moon jumpin up. Look it move up through the willas.'

'Papa, what makes the moon go up?' Paul asked.

'I disremember at this particular moment.'

'The earth turns around the moon,' Evvie said.

'The earth turns on its axis,' Topal said.

'The moon turns around the earth.'

Commodo said, 'It's only certain time of year you all gunna see a moon like that moon jiss at this time of day. It was only two-three time in my life I seen it, me. That same kind of color, and got reflections in a slick river. The Ole Man's slick, Duck.'

'Slick like cocoa, but it's making up for a blow, the sky. Look over there. God watch over a man in a pirogue in Grand Bay tonight. Look the moon, sweedart! Big-big moon! Yes! Big-big moon, Papa!'

'Leave him down to roll with his bruddas in the grass, Topal,' Commodo said.

'Watch him he don't roll in the water. Them boys is gettin so rough.'

'Leave him roll!' Commodo laughed. 'Leave the lil ole sucker roll.'

The family laughed at T. J. rolling in the grass, kicking his heels, climbing over his brothers, who were careful not to hurt him. T. J. laughed until he was seized by hiccoughs.

'The people in them houses over the river is all tired out,' Mrs. Crochet said.

'Uzelain Petitfuls is ironing her Easter dress, I bet,' Evvie said.

The Crochets all sat in the cold stiff grass. The Negro Shoepick was passing on the road, walking far behind his sister, and softly singing one of his songs:

> Emmy Emma Lena, brang mah overhalls
> Gitcha hard soap peelin and de wawta blue
> Cuzza drudge-boat snortin tell de haid man falls
> Cuzhya hafta hurry ovah wid mah overhalls
> Yow! Chickle-a-bonk-bonk
> Chickle-a-bonk-bonk.

'There's a man don't care what's gunna happen, and the river startin to go down,' Mrs. Crochet said.

'He knows how to try his bess and not to worry,' Commodo retorted. 'He's got no troubles a dollar won't cure, and he know his luck gunna change.'

'Mama! Look the shootin star!' Paul cried.

Mrs. Crochet raised her face and murmured, 'Say like my papa, "God's throwin away his cigarette to go to bed." He sure ain't botherin about us.'

'Papa, over this way is the Head of the Passes,' Evvie said.

'Don't you remember the time we went on the boat?' Commodo asked.

'I remember the whistle on the boat,' Evvie replied, 'and a man gave me popcorn.'

'She was only knockin on three years old that time,' Mrs. Crochet said. 'Me, I wonder where Arthur is this evenin.'

Evvie could not remember much. She could vaguely hear an echo of the swells of strange laughter that had passed through her earlier in the day. The moon, with the print of willow buds on it, seen in a new way now, made her feel that her childhood was all used up. She sighed. Her mother heard it. She touched Evvie's knee, frowned, and said harshly, 'You been needin gooze-grease all day.' Evvie could remember nothing more about the boat trip down the river. Her mind kept working, but it did not seem to move, only to point to one thing, like the kitchen clock that would tick on when the hands were stuck together at five minutes to eleven.

'Less go in,' Commodo said. 'The mosquitoes is comin.'

The baby crawled over and started beating on Topal's thigh.

'I wonder where Arthur is?' Mrs. Crochet said.

'This is the cocktail hour, you all,' Topal said.

Evvie sat on the grass for a while after the others had gone. Now the sun had been entirely replaced by the heavy moon.

'I'm the youngest woman in Grass Margin,' she thought.

She said it with her lips.

THE FLESH IS WEAK

EVVIE, TOPAL, and Arthur had supper in the back shed.
Arthur brought the fish he had promised, and Topal did the
broiling. Topal was proud, preparing a meal in her own
private quarters.

Arthur said, 'Tope, I'll sleep tonight back here. I'll get
my blankets from the truck. After while I'm going to Bruce's
house and wait for him to come from confession. We've got a
date, me and him, after he comes from church.'

Evvie wondered what kind of sins Bruce Holt had on his
soul. She liked to think of him in confession, humbled before
the priest, afraid to tell his sins. Evvie felt restless. The west
wind blew through the cracks in the shed, bringing odors that
told of a seasonal change, of the sun growing warm to cook
the winter's rotted grasses.

'Tope, can I sleep back here too?' Evvie asked.

'I'm running a hotel.'

'Just tonight, Tope.'

When Evvie asked her mother's permission, Mrs. Crochet
said, 'Ain't you got a house to sleep in? The idea!'

'Leave the chile go,' said Commodo. He was taking his
nightly exercise to chase away the gas, casting a great blubbery
shadow on the wall as he flexed his knees and rolled his fat

torso from side to side. 'Don't look so church-eyed at the chile. Leave her go.'

'Me, I dowunna see that ole shed. I wish that Topal hadda stayed in Belle Plume by her swimps, her.'

Evvie said, 'It makes me feel like we're playing housey, Ma, with all the little bitsy things and furniture back there, and the little bitsy lamp. I like it.'

Evvie moved her pallet from the front room to the back shed. She liked the renovated shed, because it was roomy. Also, being a woman now, she felt she ought to seek new surroundings, or change the old. Having become a woman, she did not intend to do nothing about it. Her life ought to change — to go off sideways in another direction.

Mrs. Crochet went to the window and watched Evvie drag the quilts through the shed doorway. 'They all wuntin to leave us,' she said.

Commodo bent forward, grunting, trying to touch the floor. 'Leave them have their fun, Duck. It's only temporary tell we get us a bigger house to go on our doorsteps.'

'Far as a bigger house, don't make me laugh. They making up anudda family back there, like. Leavin our house. We can't hear what they sayin back there. What are they doin? Anudda family. Goddle mighty, I'm nervous tonight. When Arthur sells his dogs, he's comin back to live with us. I know people catches diseases in that city from using them telephones. Strangers breathe in them and leave germs for innocent people. I ain't got no comfort worryin about him at night. Lass night I keppa thinkin about that nickel show burned down in town near the market where Arthur peddles. Innocent chirren, ole men, sweedarts roasted with their arms aroun one anudda because they ain't got enough doors to get out. Roasted alive! What do you care? You ain got no nerves in your body.'

'Now, Duck! Now, Duck! Don't get excited.'

'You got your ball of twine?'

'I got my ball of twine.'

'You goin up tomorrow mornin to lay down your lines for Shoepick's ditchin?'

'Oui. And I got my stakes arready cut. That's gunna be a wonderful job of ditchin, Duck.'

'You be caffle. Don't you try to domineer that Poison Ivory.'

There were loud sounds of talking and laughing in the back shed. 'Listen at them how jolly back there,' Mrs. Crochet said. 'Makin their own family back there. My family's bussin up.'

'Now, Duck.' Commodo slapped his hands against his abdomen and danced about, shaking the room.

Mrs. Crochet went to the back door and called, 'Evvie, you go on to confession!'

In the back shed, Topal went to the tiny telephone table and sat under the toy lamp to write a long letter to Dave Tobin. Arthur lay sleepily on Topal's cot. He had worked hard that day.

Evvie went to church for confession. She had not confessed or received Communion on Holy Thursday. On the back road the night was roofed by a living purple sky pierced by stars like holes in a vast tent. When the west wind died, the smell of warm fermenting bogs left, and light mists prowled the road off the canal. Soon these shapes turned to a solid fog. Evvie's tennis shoes made no sound. The soft fog followed alongside her like a presence, and it turned black, and Evvie, hearing voices ahead, hurried to get closer and use them as a guide.

'A pressure cooker!' a man's voice shouted as she drew closer. 'A pressure cooker! What you gon do wid a pressure cooker?' It was the voice of the Negro Shoepick.

'Put things up!' replied a woman whom Evvie recognized as Juarelle. 'Tunnips an carrots! Tomorrow mornin Ah'm puttin up mah vegetables!'

'Who give you de pressure cooker? Ole man Dupré, huh?'

'No! No! Ole lady Dupré! It's a ole pressure cooker, Shoepick! She done had it six years!'

'She wudden home, de ole lady, when you went by her house today! Ole man Dupré give it to you! Ah doan lak my sister takin presents fum a man, white or black!'

'She leff it there for me! He gimme it! She leff it!'

Evvie stayed close behind the couple. All the way down the road, Juraelle and Shoepick wrangled, and their contending voices guided Evvie through the fog. The whole community was talking about old man Dupré chasing Juarelle. Shoepick wanted Juarelle to stay away from the Dupré house.

'Ah got to hunt work an woshin some place to make us a livin!' Juarelle shouted. 'Dem people laks me. Dey feels sorry for me, because you doan work!'

'Ah does work!'

'De rivah's goin down! De rivah's goin down!'

'Ah works lak a mule, stompin de floor an pickin de guitar, an we gon have plenny money when Ah sells a song!'

The argument went on and on. Juarelle was terrified because they were going to lose their home. She would not believe Shoepick might earn enough to buy several homes. And she did not want to go to New Orleans and live with Plush Boardman. The road was long, and Evvie allowed herself to be drawn along by the hot crackling words ahead, remaining close to the strange phrases, yet no longer reaching for their sense, because she was on her way to confession, and it was time to begin examining her conscience for sins committed since her last confession.

She had stayed in bed one morning until eight o'clock for no reason, thus committing the sin of sloth. Father Pendergast always said it was far less sinful to neglect one's early chores for a fishing trip, or even an idle ramble, than to lie wallowing in bed. And Evvie remembered another deadly sin committed — anger. Anger on the road. Bruce Holt had choked her with the dust of his car, and she had given way to rage against him. Also on that occasion she had said It-shay. This was no grievous sin, but anger was. Evvie fixed it firmly in line in her mind, the red act of anger, right behind the pleasant flabby sin of sloth. She had been guilty of gluttony, too, the night Uncle Dewey had brought the fish. She could not remember how many times she had told lies by word or silence. In confession she would merely say, 'Father, I have been guilty of faslehood about three times a day,' and if her estimation were too high, she supposed God might save the difference for later use, or apply it as a sort of credit to cover forgotten sins. The sin of envy she dealt with in similar fashion, since she envied practically everybody. When she came to the sin of pride she was puzzled. She had never been able to determine when pride is a sin, and when a virtue. She habitually confused pride with humility. She knew that humility was something you felt in order to stop being proud. Most of the time she seemed to have no occasion to be humble. Often, as when the moon was rising out of the river, or when she was hearing beautiful music in church, she would strive to make herself feel small, unimportant, humble; but then she would find herself really feeling proud. At other times, on such happy occasions as when Uncle Dewey's check had been referred to, and her mother had said, 'We oughta all feel proud,' Evvie would find that her joy made her feel humble.

Shoepick and his sister had turned off the road into a lane

still wrangling. The church was just ahead, however. Evvie
could see the blue light of the windows printed on the fog.
She went over and over her sins, marshaling them in a line
in her mind and fixing them there firmly. Father Pendergast
seemed somehow pleased when a person brought him a great
long chain of assorted vices. Once when she was eight years
old after confessing a mortal sin, Evvie had said ' — but right
afterwards I helped Ma-mama do her work, Father.' And
the priest had cautioned her, 'That's fine, but don't tell me
your virtues. Only the big sins. Dig them out and bring them
here.'

In church there was a crowd. Most of the people were
gathered near either side of the confession box in which
Father Pendergast sat listening to the sins. Some people,
particularly those who had not confessed since the previous
Easter, had worried looks on their dark, submissive faces.
Evvie went to a pew and said a prayer, then joined one of the
groups waiting to confess. Once Father Pendergast left his
box, and talked to the people. 'Please don't stand so close
to the box. We have plenty of time. Move back.'

The group reformed itself into an orderly line. And now
Evvie found herself first in the line, near the confession box.
In the dim light the dark faces turned and stared right or left
vacantly, the eyes were lowered to study the clasped hands,
or they were raised and fixed upon the ceiling decorations,
while a heavy sigh was blown through the nostrils. A tall,
bony, square-faced man whose denim jacket hung loosely
on his hollow breast tiptoed into the church like a scared
marauder, with a shotgun, which he stood in a corner. He
bobbed downward and made a small hurried sign of the
cross over his face, and walked toward the jagged line of
penitents. The line suddenly grew shorter, closing against

him. The woman standing behind Evvie pressed tightly against her. Evvie drew away, until she stood but a few feet from the confessional, where two kneeling legs protruded, and the white rubber soles of a pair of basketball shoes. The waiting line edged forward again Evvie had to move closer to the confessional.

She heard the wicket slide open, and words were spoken inside, the dark murmur of a prayer. Some of the words were low, but the boy's voice at times would crack into a high pitch, and when this happened the words were audible to Evvie.

'Meat on Friday. Inattentive at Mass.'

It was wrong to listen. Evvie tried to step back. The old woman behind her stood firmly, unable to draw back. This woman was probably trying to hear what Bruce Holt was confessing. Evvie fixed her attention elsewhere. She prayed. The church was quiet, and it seemed to grow more and more silent, as though the building itself were now trying to hear.

'Yes, Father. Just thoughts. Lewd thoughts. Girl friends in school.'

'Natural. Fight them. Will power.'

'Thoughts follow me. Every day.'

'Games. Exercise. Books. Grace of God. The flesh is weak.'

'Lewd thoughts.'

'Nice Catholic girl friends. Dancing. Swimming.'

'Lewd thoughts.'

Evvie gave up her place in the line. She did not want to embarrass Bruce by being seen by him when he left the confessional. And, losing her place in line, now she would be kept there too late for her mother's peace of mind. She left the church and went out into the fog, which a fresh wind was sweeping away.

She went to the river road, dragging her feet pensively.

Suddenly she walked faster, then skipped, and presently broke into a run.

Her parents were talking on the front steps. Mrs. Crochet was laughing at one of Commodo's jokes. They did not want anyone else around, having come outside to share the bottle of beer they drank every Saturday night.

'Drink the lass little bit, Duck,' she heard her father say.

'Oil for the ole incubator,' her mother said.

Evvie went to the back shed. She walked the ditchbank that ran back there. Skilled in stealth, she walked quietly without trying to be quiet. Topal was still writing at the little telephone table. The door was open. Evvie stole into the shed. Near the door was a large hole in the wall. Evvie looked around, at Arthur prone on the cot, and at her sister's back hunched over the toy lamp. She reached far down into the hole and took out the box of feminine hygiene stuff which Tayo had given her. She left the shed unheard. The night had cleared. Evvie went to the wharf of the next door neighbor and waited, sitting on the grass. She smeared some of the preparation from the box under her arms, and melted some in her hands and passed it over her legs.

When Bruce Holt came up the road, he stopped in the starlight.

'I'm always meeting you in crazy places, like you're lost,' he said. 'Did they chase you out? Is Arthur home?'

'He's sleeping. He's tired out.'

'We're supposed to have a date.' Bruce hesitated. He returned and squatted on the grass near and behind Evvie.

'Why don't you go wake him up?' Evvie asked. 'It's a pretty night. You better not dance right after confession.'

Bruce looked at her. Evvie was watching the deep black river, hugging her knees, the side of her face pillowed on her knees, as she had seen Garbo do.

Bruce said, 'You talk like one of these puritans around here. The date's not that heavy.'

Evvie had removed her shoes. She was lying on her back making movements in the air similar to pedaling a bicycle. After doing this a few times, she stretched her legs on the grass, and began to raise and lower her upper body to touch her toes with her fingers. A faint trace of the perfumed antiseptic of the feminine hygiene preparation floated around her. It was fastidious.

Bruce jumped to his feet and jerked at his belt. 'Well ... we've got this date, and you're waiting for Tayo Delacroix or somebody ... Take it easy, now.'

'Oh, him! Even if I was, he couldn't come this early on Saturday. He's so busy.'

Bruce clasped his hands behind him and walked up and down the levee. 'I don't expect any thanks, but try to remember what I told you about Tayo that day. Far as I'm concerned, you do what you please.'

'A person has to be an individual.'

'You don't understand, Evvie. Heck, I can't tell you everything.' Evvie fell really in love with him now, for saying her name. She would never hate it again. 'I guess it goes to show what the world's coming to,' Bruce went on. 'A fellow sees it every day on the campus — these females! Do you think they bother about the mental caliber of their dates? Humph! Barber, bus boy, car hop, usher ... just a mad whirl to go places. Then I come down here and find the same thing. I'm not talking about you personally. Why, it's all over the country. Why in New Orleans they're wearing pants to play miniature golf, when the country's on the verge of a terrible panic, and high-school kids wanting to know what a jeopard is. Don't tell me the automobile's not responsible. There's hardly a sweet, simple female left anywhere.'

'Elna Jeanfreau is simple,' Evvie said. She had never been so excited before. She wanted to climb a tree. She did not know where her replies were coming from. She stretched herself on the grass and waited for Bruce's stern gloomy voice.

'Ask Arthur that,' Bruce said. 'I've talked to him about that nit-wit until I'm tired. He thinks she's the berries, and that's that, and we'd just as well let them alone until the affair burns itself out. I suppose you know what I mean.'

'I guess we'd better.' Evvie wriggled closer, held her chin, and looked up at Bruce across the great distance. 'I guess you meet lots of interesting females in the sororities, Bruce.'

'Now wait a minute! Please don't burn me up. You never met such super-subnormal morons in your life. I had a pal . . . I *thought* I had a pal. Well, she thought she was stringing me along — one day pretending to be interested in Orion the Mighty Hunter, and the next day rolling muggles between classes, and then throwing a regional novel at the biology professor, and a policeman taking her home. A uniformed policeman. I saw it. I stood behind a tree ——'

'Bruce, did you ever think that not even a fire can destroy anything — a letter, like, or a poem on paper? Part of it goes up in gas, and ——'

'Elementary physics. I said to myself behind the tree, "Well, old boy, you learned about women from her." So ——'

'I imagine it must be that way with love. Nothing can destroy it.'

'You mean if it's founded on the spiritual or the mental. I agree.'

There was a long, sad silence. The trees were like mourners in the South Seas, swaying together. Evvie was frightened by the great progress she had made.

'Well, you know what I mean, anyhow,' Bruce said. 'I

was glad to get away and come back here for a while. I didn't know it would change here so much, with this oil and sulphur business bringing in so many strangers. It used to be that a fellow could think in Grass Margin, and sort of commune with Nature, and sort of plan for the future, and when you were not busy with real important things, you could always find a nice simple girl to talk to, willing to learn something and procure some sensible knowledge, and she wouldn't think you were nuts if you talked about fungi or what have you.'

Evvie lay on her back, held her legs rigid, and began to raise and lower them.

'But the girls around here,' Bruce went on, 'are just the same as you'll find in any wild metropolis, with the movies, and Plush Boardman's band, and the whispering that goes on in those school busses. Sure — I keep up with these things! This is the place I was born. We used to walk to school in the dew when I was a kid.'

Evvie was blissfully gathering tufts from a pile of dead grass with her toes, clenching the stuff in her toes and making a heap. Her clutching toes encountered a big tuft with a clump of roots and soil on it. Taking aim over her shoulder, she flipped it backward through the air. She heard it strike Bruce. He threw it back at her. She sat up and returned it to him. It landed in his face. He spat out the bits of soil and crawled toward her. Evvie rolled away, eluding him neatly. She sprang to her feet, grabbed one of his legs, and yanked him over the grass. Bruce caught her wrist in a painfully strong grip. She ducked in a swift fluid movement, snapped round in a spin like a pivoting cotillion dancer, and leapt away free. She flung a handful of the grass at him and turned to run. Bruce stuck out his foot, and Evvie fell heavily. When he held her shoulders down and his strange odorless breath beat upon her, Evvie kicked at the stars while impending tears itched her eyes. His hands were hurting her writhing shoulders, and a piece of wood was rubbing her bony spine.

'Ouch, I'm on a nest of red ants!' she whispered. 'Let me ——'

When Bruce released her, she raised her dress and rubbed her hand over her thighs. Bruce quickly passed his hands down over her legs, but there were no ants on her. Evvie giggled and fled. She ran out on the wharf with Bruce behind her. Near the end of the landing, she turned her back to the river and faced Bruce. She started walking slowly backward. Bruce stopped. He withdrew, walking backward. Evvie followed. When Bruce would walk toward her, she would back up, giggling. They went backward and forward like this several times, until Bruce did not stop when Evvie's heels neared the end. There was a plank lying there, about two thirds of it on the wharf and the remainder projecting over the black water. As Bruce came toward her, Evvie walked on the plank. She stood on its end, jumping up and down and giggling. Bruce stooped and raised his end of the plank, and Evvie went into the river. Bruce dived after her, and stayed near until she swam ashore.

They waded ashore a long distance down the stream, far from the Crochet house, and they made a fire of driftwood, and stood by the curiously colored flames to dry their clothes. Across the river was another fire, where the bootleggers from Dutch Scenery were gathered, carousing after having brought in a big load of Scotch whiskey that day and transferred it to the trucks on the highway.

'This is what I call adventure,' Bruce said. 'Give me the simple rugged type of fun.'

'The fire stops you from seeing the stars,' Evvie said, 'but you know they're there, huh? I always wanted to know about the stars, but nobody around here can tell you anything. They'd laugh.'

'Why can't we see them on your porch or your wharf tomorrow night? I know a thing or two about them.'

'Gee. I'm game. Hey, Bruce, I think I'll major in biology if I get to go to college. I'm afraid I'll be in school an extra term next year, but keep it to yourself. I guess I'm going to flunk in history and physics both. The only thing I remember is that a fire can't really destroy anything, and the year of the battle of Hastings. It's the number of my aunt's house in town. But I've been thinking a lot about biology lately, specially today. Our new principal's mastering in biology. He's a nice fellow. And then you like biology too, don't you?'

'Don't consider me,' Bruce said. 'I'll be gone Monday, and glad of it, in a way. Is he young?'

'Not so very. A blond with a funny mustache, and he's married.'

'Evvie, I wasn't talking about you when I razzed the girls these days. Don't get me wrong. In fact ——'

'I guess I'm just like the rest, Bruce, but I'm young yet.'

'I wouldn't mind being your age again. The time I've wasted on dissipation and women! You've picked out a pretty good thing, biology. I might have time to help you when I get back. Why don't you drop in and see my mother? If you're talking about the berries, that's the thing the old lady is nothing but. And can she lend you the books! Biology or anything else.'

'I will. I'll write and tell you how we get along.'

'That's what you say now. Sure. You'll write.'

'Honest I will. Listen, Bruce, I guess you're going to be the one to tell Arthur, huh?'

'Huh?'

'About our being friends. He'd tease me.'

'I don't see where it's any of his business, Evvie. I'm not telling any of them. They don't tell us anything. Oh, I suppose I'll drop him a hint to sort of keep an eye on you while I'm gone.'

'I always did hate the sight of Monday. I hate it!'

'You're telling me?'

One of Evvie's hands was in shadow. Bruce's hand was next to that one. He moved his little finger sideways until it brushed Evvie's hand. Evvie dropped her face and turned her head. Bruce's hand covered hers. It was cold and sandy. A piece of driftwood on the side of the gray coals wagged its flame. It would not go out.

21

I'LL SHAME HIM TO THE
NEIGHBORS

ON EASTER morning it seldom rained or thundered. Dawn would rouse and scatter the dark cows on the rear levee that barred away the tidal marsh. Shadowy forms of ships stole past the Margin with their soft hollow breathing, making no echoes. But after the ships had passed, their great curled waves grumbled against the shore, the dogs came out to bark, and women awoke to examine the sky.

T. J. Crochet was quietly crawling around the bottom of the big pasteboard oatmeal carton. In the golden light of the front room, with his sleek flat head stretched out and his tongue delicately touching here and there the inner sides of the carton, he resembled the inquisitive cub of a cougar left alone to discover the taste of his den. He tried repeatedly to climb the sides of the box. A ragged shard of pasteboard projecting from the upper edge of the box attracted him. Finally after great patience he clawed and raised himself to his feet. Tottering jerkily, he sucked on the fragment of paper. Presently the side of the carton sagged outward, and the whole carton toppled and fell. T. J.'s head struck the floor.

'He done woke up,' said Commodo in the kitchen.

Commodo was sharpening his shovel by the stove.

'Me, I'm gunna try to have patience and raise a better

family from now on,' Mrs. Crochet said. To her, Easter was the starting of a new year. After the gray weeks of Lent, things and people seemed to begin all over again.

'Patience is the admiraless thing you got,' said Commodo. 'Take a look at me, and don't lose courage. Dave Tobin might come back tomorrow, or maybe some day before the river goes down and Emilien Perdu sells his caddle and comes out the marsh to hole the meetin and pass the resolution. If he don't, I got plans, me, playin aroun in my head. Some-times my head is spinnin aroun with plans like a piano stool, and maybe you think it ain goin no place, but while I'm turnin, I'm goin up or down like a piano stool, Duck. This mornin I'm goin up. The bess plan I got is a big-big plan, and that plan is to let what's gunna happen happen. Somethin's gunna happen to change our luck.'

'That's the way a person feels in the mornin.'

'So don't get excited.'

'Duck, you know what I wunna get you when I sell my lily bulbs negs fall? A brief case. One of them brief cases.'

'That's fine.'

Mrs. Crochet went in to attend to T. J. She leaned out of a window and called toward the back shed, 'Evvie, sweedart, go put two breads on the baker clock for Mama!'

Evvie came out of the shed and skipped to the front porch. The sun was up, and every polished leaf was still. She had been to church, and, after making a good confession and re-ceiving Communion, had walked home with Bruce. There had been others along, but that was all right. She reached up to the cardboard dial that told the bakery truck driver how many loaves were wanted, and moved the hand to the figure 2. Just then, the bright red bakery truck appeared on the road, and stopped. Evvie ran in to get the two nickels.

There was a new driver on the truck. He was a business-like fellow, and he did not seem a bit happy over the privilege of driving the bright red truck. He handed Evvie the two loaves. Then he passed out a ball of white cake wrapped in waxed paper. 'Tell your maw here's a free Coconut Island from the new driver,' he said. 'Tell her I'll carry them every day, and applecake, Honey Targets, Cinnamon Dreams fresh and all kinda rolls every morning. Is Mr. Crosette your father? Croselle — Cro ——'

'Crochet.'

'Tell him Mr. Dupré said he wants him to start that ditching as soon as possible. He asked me to tell your father.'

Gussie was standing near. Evvie said, 'Tell Papa Mr. Dupré wants him to start ditching at Shoepick's.'

Gussie ran into the house. The motor of the bakery truck ran on smoothly. The driver took the two nickels from Evvie. He smiled and said, 'Two tokens.'

'Huh?'

'Tokens, honey.'

'I don't ——'

'Didn't you ever see the sales tax tokens with the three-corner hole in the middle for the state to take care of the poor?'

'Sure, but we — the other driver never collected them. I know Ma-mama hasn't got any.'

'I'm sorry but I can't leave two loaves, tell her. It means my job.' The driver took back one of the loaves and gave Evvie four pennies and nine tokens change. 'You can have the Coconut Island.'

'Thanks.'

As the truck moved off Commodo came rushing out with his file and shovel. 'Where did he go?' he asked. 'What? Huh?'

Evvie handed her father the Coconut Island. 'That's free,' she said, 'but we can't get two loaves without tokens.'

'What the hell and Saint John Burchman is —— Where is Jewpray?'

'He wasn't here. He told the bakery driver he wants you to start that work.'

'I wunda show him with his own eyes I was sharpenin my shovel!' Commodo roared in an ear-splitting bellow at the retreating bakery truck. He looked at the Coconut Island in his hand, then stuffed it into his back pocket. He turned again and yelled at the cloud of dust down the road, 'I'm gunna haul 'off and do the ditchin on a big Easter Sunday! I'll shame him! I'll shame him to the neighbors!'

'That's all right, darling,' Mrs. Crochet told Evvie inside. 'We can use rice for dinner. That's charity, them tokens. Get me some water for me to scrape that T. J.'

On her way to get the water Evvie saw her father sitting on the chopping-block behind the back shed. He had a ferocious scowl on his face, and he was eating the Coconut Island. Evvie danced off through the orchard, swinging the bucket.

After breakfast Commodo said, 'Now Papa gunna go up the road and sacrifice his Easter mornin for pride, layin out a ole ditch. But we ain't gunna lose courage, eh Duck? Say like Miss Nellie, "Shun defeat." '

'Poor Miss Nellie.'

Commodo lingered around his wife, joking and passing his silly, sugary compliments, all cut in the same pattern like cookies.

'Me, I ain gunna shave no more if nobody gunna notice it,' he said.

'Go up the road, you dinwiddie, and I wish you take this little sprinklin can with you, so I can make headway.'

'Evvie, you wunna come with Papa?' Commodo asked. 'Come be my sweedart and take a walk.'

Evvie ran to the levee and waited for her father. She threw herself on the grassy slope and clutched the cold sweet grass with both hands. 'I'm holding on,' she thought. 'I'm holding tight to the world and it can't throw me off!'

It was a little after sunrise. They walked up the road between the chilly trees growing on either side that seemed to Evvie to draw apart to allow her to pass. There was not a shred of fog. The levee road veered one way, then another, without reason. The river was smooth, vast, brimming, tinted with streaks of colored light. T. J. sitting on his father's shoulder was sucking on a piece of hardtack dipped in condensed milk, jouncing himself up and down. He would roar and bounce and gurgle, while he beat on Commodo's green derby hat. 'Eh, là bas!' Commodo chided, 'Papa gunna spank, you rune his hat! If it ain't the ants and the miljew, it's you after my hat. Evvie, look the waterspout, honey!'

Evvie was skipping ahead, picking up clamshells and skating them through the openings in the willows and over the water. She was passing Bruce Holt's house, with the neat wharf in front, and a motor-boat suspended on chains from piling. All around the tall stern house were flower beds colored like fire and ice and milk and flesh. No one was around.

Evvie saw the waterspout across the river hanging from the clouds, a dark searching tongue swinging about, licking the horizon's jagged crust. And she could see far ahead the fig trees on the Shoepick property leaning out over the road. A cantering horse with a ragged rider passed them, the rags trailing in the wind, the hoofs sounding to her like 'Property-property-property.' In a little while there was a deep thudding jolt in the earth far behind the Margin. Evvie stood still, looking around, waiting for her father to overtake her.

'Papa, I feel the dynamite all through me,' she said. 'The birds stop what they're doing and listen. They're shooting for oil, huh?'

'They makin a tess.'

'Sure, they measure the earth trembles with a seismograph. We saw one in physics class one day. The oil company man brought the truck. It measures the trembles and marks them down.'

'That's fine.'

Commodo was busy thinking about his job. He was hoping nobody would be home at Shoepick's.

'I'm going to study up more on that,' Evvie said. 'That dynamite was like an earthquake. Papa, it *is* an earthquake, a quake in the earth.'

'I don't feel it all through me.'

'You stand too heavy, maybe.'

She walked along with him, spreading her steps to equal his, her arm around his ribs that were padded with fat. His tummy bounced and quivered.

'Papa, you know what I call Mr. Tobin? I call him Capital T in my mind.'

'That's fine.'

'Papa, Aggie was sleeping with her feet by the window, and she got the soles of her feet sunburned and blistered. Just the soles.'

Commodo said, 'Take this little pess, and don't talk so much. You musta been vaccinated with a phonograph needle this mornin. Hyah-hyah-hyah-hyah!' Evvie took the baby.

They cut across Dupré's new strip and came on Shoepick's property behind the packing room, where the new connecting ditch was to be laid off. 'Be quite, now,' Commodo said.

'I don't wunt them to see me. A white man ditchin for a nigger! Ain't that somethin?' They could hear Shoepick plucking his guitar in the packing room, a faint searching bar of music repeated over and over. Plush Boardman was in there with Shoepick. After playing the dance in Lacroix the previous night, Plush had taken too much to drink. He was sleeping it off.

Commodo could not get himself down to work. He looked toward the big residence anxiously. He jabbed at the Virginia creeper vines, and moodily slashed the yellow blossoms from a bush of acacia with his shovel. He could not become excited over visualizing a new ditch cleaving the tangled growths.

'Less go out front a minute,' he muttered to Evvie. 'Be quite, and don't let that little pess cry. Come.'

As they walked toward the big residence by the levee, Commodo bent over a pan of water put out for chickens and stuck out his tongue to look at the reflection and see if it was ripe, because the Coconut Island seemed to be still hanging in his stomach intact. Evvie wanted to get away with the heavy baby. Commodo crawled under Shoepick's house, then poked out his head and said, 'I'm takin a glimp at the joises of the floor. Watch out jiss a minute if somebody comes.'

Evvie stood pouting. Since finding a lover, she had resolved to quit sneaking around all the time. T. J. was bouncing himself up and down, sucking his bread, and might gurgle or roar at any moment. Suddenly between the leaves she noticed an automobile standing on the levee. She stooped to tell her father. Commodo put his finger over his lips and winked at her. There were footsteps in the house above him. He motioned her to come under the house. Evvie worked her way under with the baby. T. J. stopped sucking the bread and looked around with a worried expression.

'I say I only wanted to kiss your hand!' said a voice through the flooring. It was old man Dupré, talking loudly for deaf ears.

'This is your second little lesson, darling,' Commodo whispered to Evvie. Evvie was frightened and excited. She wanted to get away and still have the exciting words follow her.

'You ain't paid the taxes yet!' they heard in Juarelle's voice. 'I ain no charity piece!' There was the scraping of feet. 'You mussin my skirt! Today's Easter!'

'You better go, sweedart,' Commodo whispered to Evvie.

Walking down the road, Evvie was perplexed by many things. One thing bothering her was the fact that she would have to keep a secret from Bruce. She was ashamed that her family wanted Shoepick's property, and ashamed of her father crawling under people's houses. Also, she felt that there was something wrong with the movies from which she had learned about passion. She was really very ignorant, and her father wanted her to remain partly so. The baby cried all the way home, as if he resented being taken away when things were getting interesting. But Evvie did not pass Bruce's house with the squalling child. She cut through an orchard and took the back road home. A big dog passed her, loping down the road with a little dead chicken tied to his neck, fastened there to break him of the habit of eating young poultry. Life seemed very hard and uncertain. But the skies were clear, and promised to remain so, and to bring out plenty of stars in the night for Bruce and her to talk about. She tossed the heavy baby over her head. T. J. stiffened back his spine, curled his viciously kicking toes, and roared louder.

Juarelle and Dupré had gone upstairs. Dupré had promised to pay the taxes on the property within a few days. Commodo walked back toward his shovel and twine. As he passed the kitchen, he noticed that Dupré's expensive Panama hat was on a chair near the door, and leaning on the wall was the silver-knobbed cane which one of Dupré's ancestors had brought from Nova Scotia when the British chased the Cajuns out. On the stove was the pressure cooker given to Juarelle by Mrs. Dupré, with a low flame burning under it. Walking on, Commodo scowled at the ground pensively. He picked up his twine and a stake to begin work, then he had an idea to break up the love-making in Shoepick's house. His eyes shone.

He went to the house again, taking the roundabout way to avoid being seen from Shoepick's packing room studio, and crept up the steps into the kitchen. The old pressure cooker's gauge pointed to fifteen pounds pressure. Commodo had in his hand a tiny pebble, and a match ... He inserted the pebble in the hole of the safety valve, and when it dropped down and lay on the valve-seat, he stuck the match into the hole to keep the pebble there. Then he turned the valve of the oil-stove until the flame burned high, stole out of the kitchen, and went back to his work.

'Me, I keep on workin,' he muttered. 'It ain none of my business. So I'm jiss — drivin — the stake — in the — groun — and tiein the twine, and goin about my business, not meddlin with nobody — sacrificin my Easter Mornin layin off — a ditch — for a nigger ——'

When the explosion sounded in the house, and Commodo heard the cover of the pressure cooker hit the ceiling and bounce across the floor, he winced, closed his eyes, and made a wry nose. There was a scream in one of the upper rooms of the dwelling, and Shoepick's studio door opened, and Shoepick leaped far out into the yard in a curve like a high-jumper, scrambled to his feet, and sprinted toward the house screaming, 'Juarelle! Juarelle!' The wind blowing from the river brought Commodo the thick rank smell of highly concentrated cooked turnips. Plush Boardman came out of the studio, and he walked about in circles, blinking at the trees while his fingers fumbled at passing his belt through the belt-straps.

Commodo grabbed his ball of twine and shovel, and ran. He did not go in the direction of the house. There were old pumpkins and shells of pumpkins among the weeds. The shells of the dried pumpkins gave him no trouble; but as his feet clove neatly through the ripe pumpkins that lay everywhere, they doused him with pulp and seeds, and the stuff tasted bitter. When he slowed his pace to a walk, he found himself on somebody's land he had never seen before. 'It's enough to give a person the connery trambosis,' he grumbled. 'Who the livin hell is raisin these-here horse-beans? Don't get excited.'

He cleaned off his face, and dug a seed out of his ear. He heard an automobile go by on the road, and made his way to the highway. In a little while a truck came along, and he hopped a ride for about a mile down the road. Once the truck passed a figure walking down. It was old man Dupré. He was coatless, and had neither his hat nor cane. The truck driver slowed down, but Dupré did not raise his face to look. When the truck driver reached his destination, Commodo decided to walk on the levee the remainder of the way home, so he turned and took a path leading to the river through a grove of oranges.

Approaching the river, he heard sounds on the levee, fragments of music and excited voices. 'Before hell, I believe it's a parade or something,' he muttered, and hurried out to the levee.

A short distance away, moving slowly down the winding levee, was a sort of procession. In front was the Negro Shoepick, wearing old man Dupré's Panama hat, and holding the silver-knobbed cane. He was walking on the sharp clamshells barefooted. Behind him was Plush Boardman. Following Plush Boardman was a gang of his disreputable young Negro admirers. Boardman's face was streaming with sweat, and he was staggering slightly from liquor. His trumpet was raised toward the sky, and he was playing, mixing the music with fits of coughing and laughter. Many in the gang that followed him were drunk. Some threw back their bodies and stepped high. Others were singing the slow words of the song:

> Cha-cha-cha, prow-wow-lin Harlem
> Wid de chilblain eatin mah toes!
> Cha-cha-cha, prow-wow-lin Harlem
> *Bad* ole chilblain eatin mah toes!
> Ah wants a grabble-train baby
> To haul me where the gumbo grows!

Once Shoepick stopped, and removed the Panama hat, grumbled, and started toward the side of the road. Boardman pushed him on to the middle of the highway, and kicked him twice in the seat. Dust flew out of his ragged pants. He put on the hat and walked on.

In the front of every house near-by, people were standing, looking up the road. This was the colored section of Grass Margin. Some of the people waiting for the procession to pass were clutching each other and dancing with their hats over one eye, or leaning back screaming with laughter, while among the elders there was general silence, and an occasional mournful shake of a head.

'That's what you can call riff-raffs with no shame in their head on a Easter,' Commodo said to a tall yellow woman wearing dark glasses and standing next to him. 'What you call that business that they tryin to do, anyhow?'

The yellow woman looked at Commodo. She drew away from him. 'Don ax me, wite man, Ah jiss got outa baid an come ouch yer lak you come ouch yer to see. Ah don know no moden you know epsep what Ah see wid mah eyes. Willy, you come on back in out dat road an duss off dem stockins.' She looked at a Negro woman standing alongside of her, and they both laughed. 'Axin me what dey tryin to do an Ah jiss come ouch yer mahseff!'

Commodo muttered and walked off. He looked back at the procession once, then turned toward home. Something had happened to cause uproarious laughter behind him, but he did not turn to see what it was. A little black boy ran past him going in his direction, and stopped before an old woman lean-ing on a cane made from an umbrella rod. The boy raised his face to the old woman, and scratching the back of his long melon head, yelled, 'Grammaw, you know, he foun him wid his sista, an he tuk his hat an cane, an Plush made him putt on de hat and wawk de road! Shoepick! Loogit him leadin de parade, Grammaw! Dey gunna pass heah! Shoepick! Mr. Dupré gone home on de back road!'

Drawing near the old woman, Commodo shook his head. 'What you gunna see in a minute, you gunna see some trouble if them riff-raffs goes by the white people's houses down there! It's a outrage!'

'Assa.'

Turning away, Commodo hurried home. Evvie was on the levee playing quietly with T. J.

'Listen, sweedart, you didn't tole anybody about us crawlin under that house, huh?'

'I never tell anybody anything any more,' Evvie replied.

Commodo went inside and told his wife about the incident. Mrs. Crochet was horrified. She recovered her composure and sat watching him with her angry eyes, trying to decide whether the occurrence bode good or ill.

'So now we got us some freeboard and some leeway to get a hole of that-there property,' Commodo said. 'Woopy! In udda words, the taxes ain gunna be paid yet. We might still get it, Duck!'

'We gunna get it when that mule out on the levee gets the hecups,' Mrs. Crochet replied. 'Me, the only thing I wish that Arthur was home. If them drunk niggers comes by the white people's houses mistreatin a big white man's hat and cane-stick, look out! Some people gunna get cut or shot. You oughta go talk to that Shoepick and quite him down.'

'Leave em go, Duck,' Commodo said. 'Nobody gunna get hurt if the niggers stay by themself. This business is all amongst the niggers. Time the white people finds out what they doin, it's gunna be all over.'

The procession up the road avoided the white section of Grass Margin, turning back at the last of the Negro houses where the rice fields began and no dwellings stood, and re-turning to Shoepick's house. And the full story did not get around the Margin until next day.

Shoepick gave his sister a good beating in front of the crowd of Negroes. Then, reeling drunk, and swearing never to re-turn, he left with Plush Boardman in Plush's car for New Orleans, carrying in a mealsack his guitar, his clothes, and a half-finished letter to Mr. Synoground in Chicago.

'You come on wid me,' Plush said. 'Yo sister better come too. Dis ain gunna be no place fo you. Ah kin make room fo yo guitar in mah bann, or git you anudda job.'

'Ah nevva wunna see her again,' said Shoepick.

'Ah'm stayin by Papa's bones,' Juarelle said.

'Sho!' Plush Boardman shouted in her ear. 'Das okay! Das fine! We gon sen you de money pretty soon to pay yo taxes an keep yo house! Pretty soon! Everthing gon be fine!'

Juarelle stood among the people who shouted and waved at the automobile pulling away, with Shoepick lying in the rear in a drunken stupor. Afterwards many of Juarelle's friends gathered round to console her and offer any help she might need. Juarelle went back to the big house and sat on the porch with her hands folded, watching the group on the levee break up and straggle homeward.

'Now whenevva Ah goes down de road,' she said to herself, 'dey all gunna say I went wid a wite man de same lak mah Mama.'

Next morning she put Mr. Dupré's hat and cane in the little shed on his property next door. Old Dupré never went near Juarelle again. Nobody told Mrs. Dupré about the incident, because she was a very sick woman. In a day or so, people on the Margin generally forgot the incident — all but Commodo Crochet. 'The whole thing turn out jiss like I planned. Wait when I tell Dewey Crochet about it, the durdy trash!' he said to his wife.

On his way to New Orleans with a big load of oranges for the early Monday market, Arthur stopped his truck by the house and blew the horn. His mother ran out to the road, clutching her empty pocketbook.

'Hey, Ma!' he exclaimed, 'I'm driving the whole way to town and selling this load by myself! Henri's drunk and can't come!'

'That Henri!'

'I'll bring your four bits Tuesday, Ma. Do you want me to get groceries with it — some nice boiled ham?'

'No, I'll take the cash money. And you be caffle of them drunkers that's on the road on a Sunday. You takin the dogs to sell?'

'Yes mam. Then I'm staying in the shed with Topal after. Listen, I saw Allie. He might get me a good job at the Sulphur. They putting on men.'

'Don't bank on it, son. Keep open your ears for betterment, but don't bank on nothin. Only avoid bad company like a good boy. Them durdy gools under that French Market! I know em! They'd steal the horseshoe off of a person's toilet seat for junk.'

'Aw. Lemme get off the gravel before the rain!'

'Don't get in trouble up the road with them sassy niggers. They all drunk and huntin trouble after what happened today. They carry razor blades. Eat your dinner nice every day and supper. Your chess is so bony, I find.' The truck moved off, with Arthur's hand flapping at her from the window. 'GET YOU A T-BONE STEAK TONIGHT!'

Evvie on the porch watched the sky, reading the slow signs hanging up there or coming over the horizon to drift past one another. Clouds had obscured the pale sunset. Overhead, a great cloud sprawled, hanging motionless and black and chill; and the restless martins curved across its turgid skin. Evvie wondered whether Bruce would come, and at what time; and whether the kitchen clock was correct. She wanted to see Bruce's long legs coming from behind the trees, yet she was afraid that at any moment she might. There would surely be no stars for Bruce to talk about, and she would not be able to find anything to say. Evvie had decided to tell him the family secrets — about the patch of Easter lilies hidden back in the landlord's canes, and about Shoepick's property, because it would not be romantic to keep things from Bruce that were so

important to her. But how would she approach these sub-
jects? And what would Bruce think of her family?

She looked at the roadside trees from behind which his legs
would appear. What would she do when he walked in? Her
father was snoring loudly inside. The twins on the front steps
were filthy, and their wild mops of untrimmed hair made their
faces look tiny, starved, pointed, cunning, evil. The pockets
of her own sweater sagged. For the third time, she shed the
sweater and took it inside. If Smarty Pants did not like her
dress, he could go sit on a tack. 'I've been bluffed too many
times, anyhow,' she thought. And she called Gussie to play
beanbag with her.

When the wind blew hard and brought the first scattered
taps of rain, Evvie was alone on the end of the porch. The
long sparse threads of slanting rain pelted her shoulder bones,
and for a while she did not move to avoid them. The smell
of damp dust and washed orange blossoms, the banging of distant shutters, the fretful cry of a cow, the twitching runnels of
sandy water on the big front steps — all made her glad, because now Bruce would not come. His mother was careful of
his health. But maybe he had left home before the rain....
It was getting dark. The rain was making it swiftly darker.
She would count fifty. She looked at her shoes — Topal's
old blue high-heeled shoes. After counting fifty, she would
take them off and go paddling in the yard. After counting to
twenty, she went slower and slower. Inside she heard the great
commotion of her brothers scurrying to place the pots and
pans under the roof-leaks; then one of the running children
tripped and fell with a pan, and a loud argument started. Her
father awoke and bellowed at the kids.

Bruce Holt came running down the road. Hunched forward
against the white downpour, he turned in at the Crochet

house. When he saw Evvie on the porch, he quit running. He walked calmly through the roaring rain, turning his dripping face this way and that to examine the trees.

'God dog it to hell!' Mrs. Crochet screamed inside, 'I bet I'm gunna break somebody in half like a snap-bean!'

Evvie turned and climbed in the window.

'Bruce Holt's outside, Papa,' she told her father. 'You better see what he wants. He's coming in, Pa. He's on the steps now.'

'Well, well, well!' Commodo said, walking out with his shovel and file. 'What you gunna say, bruddin-law? Come in out the rain!' Evvie followed her father out.

'It's not raining hard,' Bruce answered. 'It's going to stop. Is Arthur home?'

'He ain under my roof no more, that sassy ——'

'He's gone to town, Papa!' Evvie said. She was standing behind her father. She began to try out the steps of her tap dance.

Bruce looked at the sky. 'Well . . .' He was searching his mind for something agreeable to say to Commodo Crochet. He said, 'Every time I see you, you're busy, Mr. Crochet.'

Commodo stuck out his chest and laughed. 'We gotta keep the ole kittle boilin, eh? Hyah-hyah-hyah-hyah!' He whacked Bruce's shoulder, then sat on the porch swing and made a serious business of filing his shovel. 'Hunt you a seat, son. This rain's gunna lass long, the way it looks.'

'They've been needing rain bad,' Bruce said. 'I guess it'll rain too much as usual.'

Evvie was glad the rain pounded so heavily on the tin roof, because its noise drowned the sound of water dropping into the pots and pans inside. T. J. was bawling in the kitchen, and again Mrs. Crochet yelled at one of the children to be-

have. Evvie sat far from her father and Bruce, on the opposite end of the porch, juggling her beanbags. She had not addressed a word to Bruce, and he had not once looked at her.

'It can't rain too much for me, like you see me here,' Commodo said.

'Nup. I guess not.'

'If it wasn't for rain, I wooden have a job to hole down.
You'd see me tugboatin on the river or some kinda ordinary
work like the others. Hyah-hyah-hyah!'

'Ha, ha! Cigarette, Mr. Crochet?'

Commodo started off talking about drainage. He touched
on all the types of soil found on Grass Margin, the drainage
needs of each type. He discussed every orange grove from
Fort Jackson to Venice. Around nine o'clock, Mrs. Crochet
came out. She discussed Arthur, then Bruce, then Arthur
and Bruce together. Then she drifted into the subject of bad
boys in Grass Margin, those of this generation and those of the
last — what had or would become of them. She knew more
about bad boys than Commodo knew about drainage. Evvie
was glad. She by herself would never have been able to keep
Bruce near this long. The rain continued to roar down.
Bruce was not saying a word. She could feel him looking
toward her in the dark. The purring of the rain and the drone
of her mother's slow bountiful words was putting Evvie to
sleep. She brushed a mosquito from her nose with a groggy
hand. The next thing she knew, she was on her feet and being
led by her father. At the door she said, 'Good night, Bruce.'

'Good night, Evvie.'

Then she turned and staggered through the darkness to the
porch swing. The high-heeled shoes made her walk like a
chicken with paper stuck to its legs. She held out her hand.
'Good-bye, Bruce.'

'Good-bye, Evvie.'

Inside, she fell asleep while removing the shoes and stockings, and curled up there on the floor. The wind shook the house all over.

Next morning she told her mother she had work to do before school time. She took twenty of the twenty-five cents she had been saving for a lipstick, and caught the bus, which went up an hour before the school bus. This was the bus which Bruce would ride to New Orleans, she thought.

Bruce got on at his stop. He had on a handsome summer suit, white shoes, a tan silk shirt with a large open collar. The volume of his baggage delayed the bus. Another passenger got on with him and took the empty place beside Evvie. Bruce sat in a vacant seat directly behind her. He touched her shoulder. 'Hey.'

'Hey.'

She tried to turn completely around to face him, but it could not be done without kneeling on the seat.

'That was some rain,' Bruce said.

'You're telling me?'

They both looked out at the fields and orchards rushing past, the sad green panorama bouncing as the softly cushioned bus leaped in and out of the great holes in the road. Puddles of still water dotted the fields, and the birds flew away, always away. The man next to Evvie was near-sighted, an old man bending down to peer at her twisted lap.

'I guess you had to swim home,' Evvie said.

'You're telling me?'

Nothing further was said until the bus reached the high school stop — after a quick, bouncing journey through the melancholy gloom of the primeval swamp along the Fort

Jackson reservation. The driver alighted to help Evvie down, but she was not thrilled by such attention now. She turned to Bruce. 'I'll let you know . . .'

'Don't forget.' His eyes followed her. As the bus drove off, they waved. Bruce's white teeth flashed.

Evvie was happy. The bus turned the curve and was gone. She would write to Bruce at once. She must tell him the family secrets that bothered her. It would take her a week to write the letter.

But she never had to write the letter. After the Crochets had a change of luck, and got possession of Shoepick's property, there was not very much need to.

22

A MAN IN THE RIVER WANTS

LILY BUDS!

A SHIP loaded with bananas from Honduras was held up at the Quarantine Station down below the Margin. A fireman was ill. For some days the ship was in quarantine. It was quiet warm weather, and to ventilate his cargo against ripening, the captain ran his ship diligently back and forth within sight of the doctors ashore. Some of the people up the river thought about the poor sick fireman; others thought about the cargo, and their eyes gleamed with the hope that the cargo would ripen before the ship's release, and be thrown overboard. Ripe bananas were of little value to the importers who shipped green fruit out of New Orleans.

One morning Mrs. Crochet was on the foggy riverbank getting stove faggots from among the driftwood, and she heard the donkey engines clanking aboard an approaching ship, and slingfuls of fruit splashing into the water. She clambered hurriedly through the tangle of driftwood. It was not yet daylight, and the moon was partly obscured by drifting fog. Now she could hear farther down the river the sound of many voices, and the noise of boats being dragged over the piles of driftwood. Before she reached the levee, swells from the ship growled against the shore.

Mrs. Crochet ran into the house calling, 'Topal! Topal!

The bananas! The bananas! Get a dress! Get a dress on quick!'

Topal sat up on her cot in the back shed, all naked and rosy, scratching her head and looking around. Evvie popped out of bed, then staggered across the floor. Commodo was up now, and yelling from the kitchen door. J. T. was yelling in the front room of the house.

'What's the matter?' Evvie asked, bumping into Topal's soft hot body. Topal gave her a sisterly shove, and she fetched up against the wall.

'Hurry up!' Mrs. Crochet cried from the kitchen. 'Take the river quick or you'll get leff, with the people gobblin up the bananas for the lass two hours. Duck, make em hurry! You know how they gunna be hungry for bananas today when the road's gunna be fulla peelin, peelin everywhere.'

Topal snaked into her dress. The cloth was ripe, and she handled it as though it were rare stuff of gossamer. Out among the matted willows she untied the family skiff, and sat in it. From the levee came Evvie's voice: 'Mama! Make her wait!'

Evvie sat in the stern. Topal rowed upstream through the sluggish clabbery water near shore. Evvie sat pouting.

'Skink!' Topal said.

'You, you mean.'

'Sit still in the middle. Listen, are you awake, or not? I can't pull with you sitting on the side dreaming like you lost your mother.' She skimmed the water with her oar, to splash Evvie in the stern.

Evvie was happy. The night before, she had mailed a letter to Bruce Holt, her first in reply to his first. They were sweethearts now. He was sending her a book about the fundamentals of biology. In her letter she had told him about birds. She had begun to study them, and to identify them from an old book. She had told him about a great lovely golden-winged woodpecker that had awakened her in the morning by drumming on the tin roof. The bird now following their boat from willow to willow and singing, 'Cheap pity, cheap pity, cheap pity' was a Carolina wren. She would tell Bruce.

She looked at her sister. The arches of the feet gripped the bench; the thighs brought down the knees firmly; the legs stiffened; the arms flexed back to end the strokes well. Through the moonlit fog the trees and bushes ashore had a lovely sheen. Poor Topal. Although she had received a fat letter from Dave Tobin the day before — written, not in the hospital, but in a cheap hotel — she was not happy. She would never be happy in old clothes. Evvie decided to tell this to Bruce. She was finding many things to tell him. But there were many more things not to tell. Very soon, however, she would have to tell him about the Easter lilies hidden in the canes — perhaps also smaller things about herself, which the mist now helped her forget. The water slid under the boat like soundless oil.

'The flicker is the state bird of Alabama,' she said to Topal.

From the trees along shore, heavy drops of dew were pelting the water with a faint musical trinkle. Evvie strained her eyes to see out in the great calm river, where jubilant voices told of people finding the discarded fruit. She could see nothing but the slow lift and fall of the coils of pearly mist. Ahead, a puff of wind wrought the mist into a shape that loomed slowly tall and spectral with a forlorn and ragged arm pointed shoreward. Then it settled over with its legs in the air. Now it stooped to recover its detached head; then it came apart in fragments that merged again into the form of a fat tumbling beast with a snout.

'Bail,' Topal said.

Evvie took the can and bailed. The river was sneaking into the boat through unseen cracks. She was putting it back where it belonged. She must remember this, too.

As daylight began to rise, Evvie saw that the willows along shore were beginning to leaf out. In the mist they resembled faint green clouds reflected in the milky water. The mist was like a gauze drawn across the red waste of morning. Evvie sat quietly, and she watched a mosquito sucking blood from her arm, the pulsating abdomen of the insect growing larger as it sucked, until it was thick and oval-shaped, full of her blood. Then, its wings singing loudly with the great weight they carried, it flew under the bench upon which she sat. She was not sure she knew how to spell abdomen.

'Say you!' Topal shouted. 'Are you going to sit in the middle so I can pull?' She was heading out toward the middle of the river. People could be seen out there, their upper bodies balled into round knobby specks. A pirogue would creep toward a dark spot in the water, then it would stop, and a tiny arm would reach out for the floating plunder. From far off, people were small and harmless, with no eyes to examine you, and their jests or curses were dimmed into faint yelps. The shore drew away slowly. Grass Margin was only a line of pointed roofs and smoking chimneys. It was pretty, the place where she lived. Seen from far out on the river, the Margin looked as if it had no human schemes or bothers — the roofs built sharp to cut the rain in half, dabs of paint brushed on by hands that liked a splash of color, the good puffs of smoke that a person's mind could follow down the chimney to a boiling pot. The river was a place where you could not stay still. It moved all at once — the whole vast brimming surface of it winding thousands of miles up the valley, moving all at once, always the same way.

'Now please stay still that you won't turn us over!'

The words came to Evvie like a stone in the dark. She came out of her dream and saw that the fruit floated down into infinity in a long slow chain containing occasional gaps where people upstream had taken their toll.

'If it's not your time to die, there's no use worrying about turning over,' Evvie said.

'Oh yeah?' Topal said. 'Suppose it's *your* time to die?'

'There's a bunch coming!' Evvie cried.

'Help me!' Topal commanded. 'Grab it!'

Evvie grasped the other end, and they lifted the bananas in. Evvie peeled one of the bananas and bit into it. It was freezing cold. It hurt her teeth, but the smooth gulps were sweet in her throat.

'Stop it!' Topal said. 'Here's another one! Quick! These are little spotted ones like Papa likes.'

Evvie sang, suddenly, at the top of her voice:

> Your beau's a Dago,
> Who told you so?
> He sells bananas
> Around Faranta's show!
> Chippie on the wire
> Chippie on the fence
> Chippie get a haircut
> Fifteen cents!

'I'm getting scared now,' Evvie said. 'We're all alone out here now, except way up the river.'

'Look behind you.'

Another skiff was coming.

'Two men in it,' Topal said. 'I mean *two* men. It's painted purple.'

'I saw it before in Dutch Scenery, Tope. Some oyster fellow. Look, he pushes instead of pulling, with the bow in front of him. That's a Tocko fellow they call Heavy. He rents himself out, and his boat. The other one's a stranger.'

'Now you're not afraid. You see men.'

'You're talking about your own self.'

'I could use one,' Topal said. 'One with big hands and feet. Big wide hands for grabbing and chunking. Big strong back you can slap and punch and it don't hurt him, and a big insurance policy. You wouldn't have a worry in the world.'

'Papa has what you say, and Mama has worries.'

'She makes me sick! You've got to let them think they've got charge of everything. Mama wants to have one leg in the britches.'

Evvie wanted to tell Topal about Bruce. 'Do you still like Mr. Tobin, Tope?'

'He's all right, but he always wants people to please walk on him.'

Now the other skiff was coming toward them. The man called Heavy waved at them. He pushed his skiff to drift near theirs. The other man, sitting in the stern, was dressed up, his polished shoes propped up out of the water in the bottom. Evvie had never seen him before.

As they drew near, he called: 'You people live here?'

'We live on shore,' Topal responded.

The man said to the boatman, 'See? They bend over backwards to be polite down here. Excuse me for living, Madam. I'm a florist from Nawlins. I sell flowers, you know.'

'We taut it was soft-shell minnie-cats,' said Heavy, the boatman. He made a round hole of his lips, and raised his watery eyes toward the sky.

'Let's skip the wise cracks. Does anybody raise flowers around here, Miss?'

Evvie blurted, 'Ma-mama ——' and Topal stamped Evvie's toes with her heel.

'It's Easter lilies I want, Creole lilies,' the florist said to Evvie, who looked off sideways. The sun's red light appeared and struck the stranger. He was an oldish man with a very red face, sunburned, covered with a fine silvery stubble, and his nose was peeling little scales. A bag of skin hanging over his throat seemed as if it once had contained another chin. His eyes looked angry.

'My mother has some growing around,' Topal said.

'Some. Have you got any idea how many, about?'

'No.'

The florist laughed sourly. Although rather thin, he was holding with his legs a tight globular paunch, or a haunch. Evvie was not sure which it was. He was holding it with his hands too, as the boat rocked. Again the sour laughter came out of his perfectly sober face. 'Thirty years in the business,' he said. The man was worried. Of that Evvie, with her experience with worried people, was sure. 'I never got up at four o'clock to hunt flowers before in the fog. Nobody can tell you anything. In Lacroix they said over the river. Over the river they say on the other side. Since yesterday morning I've been trying to find that family.'

'Was it Bumgardner?' the boatman asked.

'I've told you I don't know the name, brother. This Cajun or mulatto or Indian boy drives a truck to the French Market. He told another florist's driver, and that driver told my driver. We couldn't locate him in the French Market day before yesterday. It's supposed to be a big family somewhere below Lacroix with a big patch of Creole lilies in bud.'

Evvie looked at Topal, who frowned and made big eyes.

'I think Mama can sell you a good many,' Topal said.

'Hell, they all been saying that! A good many! I'm not looking for a couple of bouquets for a Mother's Day grave!'

'Set still in boat, please,' said the boatman.

'I want six or seven thousand fine buds, no humbug!' As he smoked on his cigarette, the smoke came out of only one nostril. Evvie thought that perhaps this was part of his trouble. 'I'll go see her, I guess. If it wasn't for this wedding and a big customer, I'd walk back right now. Old Axel Peniston's daughter. Her father hits the market four days before the wedding. Now he wants the whole damn house and cathedral plastered with these Creole lilies. No consideration for the florist. First they change the bridesmaids dresses and got to have flowers to go with deep apricot dresses, and I've been all over this country, and I never saw a deep apricot in my life. Now it's seven thousand lilies quick. I'd rather twenty funerals. No bother, no fuss, just send them what's on hand.'

'Kill the smell, why we use flowers for down here,' said the boatman. 'Bet a florist make good money on funeral. Pipple feel too bad to look and see how much the flowers is worth.'

'Listen, you're nuts! What do you know about it? They look damn hard, don't worry! That's what people think, the funeral business is all velvet! You're not talking to a damn undertaker now! Furthermore, do you know our whole funeral business is threatened? Do you know my funeral business is practically at a standstill?'

'Don't wave the arms. Hard to push the boat.'

'Practically at a standstill! Somebody started up this cursed "Please omit flowers" business again! The lousy ... twenty per cent of the obituary notices last month specified that. Why, he ought to be *boiled in oil*, whoever ... We invest heavily in beauty and service ... I'd love to start up a movement to omit shrouds, once, and see how they'd like that! Where are we going now?'

'You want to see these ladies' Mama, hey?'

As they approached the shore of the Margin, the florist waved away the mosquitoes. He took from his pocket a bottle of mosquito lotion, and glumly dabbed at his face and hands. The skiff bearing the two men came along just behind Evvie and Topal. When the boat touched shore, Evvie hopped and wriggled through the driftwood tangle, and sped over the levee. 'Mama! Mama!'

Commodo was on the big front steps amusing T. J.

'What the racket and noise and commotion about?'

'Where's Mama? A man in the river wants lily buds! He wants to pay for them! He'll treat us right!'

'Quite down, sweedart. What man?'

'A florist from town! There's a big wedding! They need them for the church and house! Seven thousand! He's been looking for us, Pa! Arthur told ——'

'Quite down. Mama's not home. Leave it to me. How you say he'll treat us right, darling?'

'I heard him say so.'

'He never seen us before, and still he's gunna treat us right?'

'But Papa, I heard him! He treats everybody right.'

Commodo sat on the front steps in his undershirt, waiting for the florist to come from the levee. Paul and Gussie, carrying in a bunch of bananas, were wrangling.

'Papa, he makes me take the heavy end!' Paul complained.

'Seddle your own fights, you all!' Commodo said. 'I ain no ruferee or a empire aroun here. Let the man pass!'

The florist walked up to Commodo, and Commodo stood up to greet him. 'My name is Beaumont Crochet,' said the florist. 'Maybe you've heard about the Crochet Nurseries.'

'Well I'll be damn!' Commodo blushed, then smiled shyly and lowered his head sideways.

'That's me, all right,' said the florist. 'What's left of me. These mosquitoes ——'

'But ——'

'Oh, you wouldn't see me going around personally like this if it wasn't important. I've got ——'

'*But my name's Crochet too!* T. J. Crochet, Senior!' Commodo's eyes shone with merriment. He grinned, and pulled in his face until he had three chins.

The florist took his hand out of Commodo's. He backed off slightly, and looked at the little house leaning askew behind the great handsome front steps. 'Quite a coincidence,' he said. 'I tell you. I've been looking around to buy ——'

'These is my chirren.' Commodo put on the green derby. He took T. J. in his arms and followed the florist. 'Parle français? My wife's gone to church. This fella's T. J. Crochet, Junior. I guess your family was Cajuns way back from Bayou Tête Noir, I bet. It seem like Grampaw Seesaw used to say ——'

'Oh, the woods are full of Crochets. Condiment Crochets and disinfectant Crochets and hay and grain Crochets ——'

'We're the drainage Crochets,' Commodo said.

'I tell you. I'm down here hunting for ——'

'It seem like Grampaw Seesaw ——'

Topal said, 'Papa, he came on business. Can't you see you're wasting his time?'

Commodo turned and stared at Topal. 'Who? Ain I got valuable time too? I'm a son-of-a-bugger. I got people waitin ——'

'He wants to buy Mama's lilies.'

'That's it, Mr. Crochet. I'm looking for a large quantity. Six or seven thousand buds, in fact. How many do you have? Where is your garden?'

'I dunno. They belonk to Mrs. Crochet.'

'But how many, Mr. Crochet?'

'I dunno, me. Plenny people up the road got a few.' Commodo went up and sat on the porch swing. The florist followed
him, and leaned morosely against a near-by post.

'Anybody would get irritable,' the florist said, 'after what
I've been through, running around since yesterday trying to
fill this order, trying to talk Jugoslavian and Filipino, and people looking like you owed them something when you ask a
question, and my business needs me back in town.' He stooped
and touched T. J.'s wet chin. 'A fine big boy you got there,
old timer. No, Mr. Crochet, I'll tell you. I been under a
strain. Got bad kidneys. Mouth tastes like it's full of ground
oakum, going off my diet like this.'

'No wonder, when you all drink that nasty city water.'

'I've got some kids myself. I wish they were country-
raised. One son dove in shallow water the other day. My
youngest daughter smokes cigars and paints pictures in the
abattoir. She went to Washington and got locked in the Cor-
coran Gallery. When they came in the morning, she had to
be taken to the hospital in hysterics. We've all got our troubles.
Couldn't we take a look at your lilies, Mr. Crochet?'

'I ain makin no promises,' Commodo answered.

Commodo, carrying T. J. under his arm like a package, led
the way through the dense canebrake. The florist following
him had his face all greased with mosquito lotion. There was
a gash in his seersucker pants just over the watch pocket,
through which dangled the pocket with the watch in it.

'Look out for jewberry vines,' said Commodo.

'Son of a so-and-so.'

'I tole you.'

'These gnat-bees, or whatever they are ——'

They came out into the open, where the long rows of un-opened lily buds hung shining with dew. Commodo put T. J. on the ground, and flicked the dried leaf fragments from his derby hat. The florist stood stupefied, blinking, his mouth hanging open. 'Uh ——' As he took out his eyeglasses, his hand trembled. 'This is — I never —— Where did this seed come from?'

'I dunno.'

Topal and Evvie were in the canebrake, peering out at the two men. The florist walked off a ways to recover his com-posure, to measure the plot with his eyes. He stooped and looked at the mealy soil, reached out and dipped his fingers in it, as carefully as if he were using a fingerbowl. He went to one of the lily stalks that was about three feet high, and counted its sixteen buds. 'Didn't you ever have any diseases at all here? Do you spray them, or ——'

'I disremember.'

The florist went back to where Commodo sat alongside the baby, nonchalantly trying to yank a wild hair from his nose. The florist said, 'I think I've found what we want right here. Of course ——'

'She raise them for the bulbs.'

'Never mind that. I might want the bulbs too. I might give you an advance on the bulbs today and take delivery in the fall. The bulblets you could keep for seed. Every year I might — hell, we might make a deal. I could advance your fertilizer, and even —— Listen, did any other florist see these? Wasn't that guy Haufhaus down here last week?'

'Don't ax me.'

'What time does she get out of church? Where's a tele-phone?'

'Up the river eleven miles. I better go in. You done seen the lilies. I better go.' Commodo rose to his feet.

Evvie and Topal stood among the canes, their round eyes shining. The baby was getting cross, whining, crawling toward the ditch. Commodo put out his foot and stepped on the baby's dress. He held his foot there while the baby tried to crawl off.

The florist said, 'Now suppose we get a rough estimate on your buds. Later we'll send for some stuff for a nice breakfast. To tell the truth, I guess I can use ten thousand or more, and pay you right here.' He took out a bloated wallet. He allowed a yellow-backed bill to flutter to the ground, then slowly retrieving it, said, 'Just imagine it! A Crochet way down here, in the same business as I am. Wait until I tell that to my brother! If we went into this thing together later on, I'd want to build a little insulated curing house right back here. Japan's been shipping this country improved bulbs, you know, and Chicago's getting particular. Come on, we'd better get a rough estimate before we talk turkey, huh? I'm a son-of-a-so-and-so! A Crochet raising Creole lilies in the Delta! Hold on a minute! There was a — when I was a kid around Decatur Street there was a fur buyer, used to wear a vest made out of otter fur, and ——'

'Mink fur. That was Grampaw Seesaw.'

'Well, what do you know about that! I guess he's long gone, now. His people were distantly related to distant relatives of mine! Ho-ho-ho-ho! So our folks were all Cajuns together romping all over Mammy Nature back on Bayou Tête Noir!'

'I was tryin to tell you that! Hyah-hyah-hyah-hyah!'

Evvie had bitten her fingernails until the quick was raw. The canes were thick as hair; and as they swayed in the wind, she kept moving her face from side to side to follow an opening through which to see her father and the florist. Thus far, she and Topal had heard nothing said by the two men standing among the lilies. Now gradually the voices came louder, and the men were using their hands to add shape to their words, or to nail them to their palms.

They saw Commodo grab his derby hat and swing it in a sweeping green curve: 'Two buds for a cent is robbery!' he howled. 'You ack like a hi-jacker and a Alkapony!'

The florist walked off, then returned. 'Do you know what my transportation is? my advertising? this "please omit flowers" business? and ——'

'If hothouse flowers worths a dollar a dozen, field-growed flowers worths one cent apiece wholesale. And I'm gunna tell you, my wife, her she dowunna sell them, no! I'm gunna get in trouble for this!'

'Wholesale!' yelled the florist. 'What do you mean? You're a farmer, not a wholesaler! It'll cost me a nickel apiece to get these buds to Nawlins and on the altar! Some are popping open right now! Here's one open! Here's one open! I can't use open flowers!'

T. J. was crawling along the ditchbank, tasting various substances that lay in his path, ignored by his father. Commodo jammed on his hat and turned his back on the florist, yelling, 'Awright! Try to find your lilies some place else! Go hunt! Jiss go hunt once! Maybe I look schewpid, but I know! I'll fling them away in the river! I done flung away plenny because anudda fella wunted them cheap!' He picked up the baby and started for the canebrake.

'Hey! Where are you going?' the florist shouted.

'I'm goin in and take a ress!'

'Hey! T. J.! T. J.!'

Commodo stopped and turned. 'My wife home now and lookin for me!' he called. 'You better come talk to her. She gunna be rippin mad, too!'

'T. J.!' The florist ran toward the place where Commodo had disappeared in the canes. 'T. J.!'

Commodo stuck his head out of the thick canes.

The florist, holding his wallet, said, 'I'll have to reduce the advance on the bulbs to a hundred dollars, then.'

Evvie peering between the canes clapped her hands softly when she heard the amount of money named, and nudged Topal.

'A hundred-dollar advance on the bulbs to be delivered in the fall,' Beaumont Crochet repeated.

'And a cent apiece for the buds?' Commodo asked.

'Okay! I'll gamble. Fifteen thousand buds at a cent apiece, and a hundred dollars advance on the bulbs. I'll gamble.'

The florist was peeling yellow-backed money into Commodo's trembling hands. Evvie bounced up and down on her toes, while in her mind she was holding a decimal point suspended, not sure where to place it among the three cyphers. Fifteen thousand. Three naughts. Two points to the left. 'A hundred and fifty dollars, eh?' she asked Topal.

'Sure, dumbbell.'

Commodo, folding the money, collected his wits and followed the florist. They passed through the canes near Topal and Evvie. Commodo, walking behind the florist, put his hand behind him and waved it vigorously at the girls. As he walked, the seat of his pants crinkled into humorous faces, too.

'Where can I get a boat right away?' the florist was saying. 'Got to haul these to the paved highway in a boat, or else these roads'll bruise them to hell.'

'You can rent one some place ——'

'Hell, I'll buy one. Let's hurry!'

'Don't get excited, Beaumont!'

'And I need two men. Where's a phone? Get me two young men with pep!'

'Okay, bruddin-law. Take a blow.'

'Two hundred and fifty dollars,' Topal told Evvie.

'Yes!' Evvie began to dance about, flopping her hands, running out into the open to turn a cartwheel, then back again to hug Topal. She slapped Topal a whack on the behind. 'Two hundred and fifty dollars! Two ——'

Topal swung her hand. It struck Evvie behind the neck and sent her tripping over the canes to the ground. Topal walked off behind the two men. Once she turned and looked at Evvie sitting on the ground. 'You know what we going to get from that money?' she asked. 'We're going to get this!' She clutched her wrist and flipped her thumb sharply upward. 'Watch what I tell you.'

23

POUR SOME WINE
FOR JUARELLE

IN THE afternoon, Topal on the front porch folded her arms and brooded, her face turned away from her mother sitting on the swing. The men were loading the last of the Easter lily buds on the lugger in the river. It was raining, a bright shower, soft and sunlit. The rain was good for the lilies. It would crispen the buds for shipment.

'Anyhow, you got no time to get no dress goods and make a dress for tonight,' Mrs. Crochet said to Topal.

'Okay, okay, okay.'

'So don't pester me. Is my lily money a Community Chess? I could throw it in the river. My mind's tangled up to decide what we gunna get firss that we need so bad.'

Topal kept her hard dark face turned away, her eyes fixed on the orchard and the green flashing of dripping leaves.

'Anyhow, where we gunna get change?' Mrs. Crochet asked. 'You couldn't buss a ten-dollar bill on this whole livin Margin. I defy you.'

'I said I'd walk to Venice to get change. I want to make that dance tonight. They're having one of those marathon dances. Okay, let's drop it.'

'All by yourself to Venice with ten dollars? Sacré nom. Listen, I don't know if the money's counterfeit, before hell.

It might be counterfeit. I'm a hitchin post. I'm a ole hitchin post for this family, but I ain crazy like your gibbetin din-widdie of a father, trussin every stranger the river washes up.'

'Papa went and paid Shoepick's taxes with some of it.'

'Maybe the ress is counterfeit. How do I know who's Beaumont Crochet from Adam, and your father's arready claimin him for a fiff cousin? I don't care if his firss name is Saint Simon Stylites. He's Crochet right on. Far as me, by his looks he oney needs the horns and fitch-fork to be name Lucifer, and a harpoon on his tail. Them Crochets! I like to know what scattered them aroun the country, me.'

'Jule would let me have the goods on credit.'

'Who? What on credit? God dog it, don't start that, Topal Crochet! You'll never see no credit come in my house again. After ——'

'Is the thanksgiving Mass you ordered a while ago paid for?'

Mrs. Crochet snatched off a shoe. She stood over Topal and waved it. 'Your sass is gunna get you mangled to smither-eens!' she cried. 'Get outa my sight, before ——' Topal backed away, sliding along the wall. 'How come it's oney *you* startin to wunna use the money and we jiss got it? Right away quick! Oney you! Nobody else axin for anything yet, and the chirren's hungry and naked, and your poor father rollin a wheelbarrel in the rain with no coat!'

Commodo, rolling a wheelbarrow piled high with lily buds on long stalks, plodded tipsily behind Beaumont Crochet toward the river. Beaumont Crochet had hired the lugger to take the flowers to Lacroix. Evvie was scrubbing the big front steps in the rain, wearing over her body an old piece of tarpaulin. She turned and looked at her father rolling the wheelbarrow, and noticed that now the seat of his pants did not make any funny faces as he walked, because they were wet and stuck to his skin. She returned to her work, rubbing hard with the broom. She loved the pale wood in the rain, the long reddish marks of its grain glowing like satin.

When Commodo returned from the river, he rolled the wheelbarrow up to the porch.

'Duck! I got a name for your lily farm!' he cried. 'The Great Southern Bulb Nursery, Grass Margin, Louisiana!'

'That's fine, sweedart,' Mrs. Crochet said. 'Oney thing I wish you quit drinkin home brew in the shed. Look the ole rangatang, he can't hardly stand straight, and the track of his wheelbarrel is crooked with the home brew. You don't see that Beaumont Crochet drinkin no home brew.'

'Wait when you see me tonight singin and cuttin up,' Commodo said. 'Woopy! I closed an importan deal for this family and I bought a stupendable house to go on the great big doorsteps today, me, an that's the importaness thing happened sense the invention of the wheel.'

'Say you! You wooden be sellin a livin lily ef it wasn't for my son that he was kicked out this house bodily. Don't start.'

'I was the one close the deal and I can take me a sip of beer when Beaumont paid for it.'

'You don't need to make a hog and a glutton outa yourself. Are you all finish haulin the lilies?'

'Pretty nilly.'

'Hurry, I'm honin to rub you againss the bronicle pneumonia with my rough bedspread quick as you done. Me, I dunno where to turn firss today, with the strangers trackin up my scrubbin and this one with her round shoulders plannin how to spend the money arready, if you please. Evvie's gunna take the road after and get us some can salmon and lovely raw onions for supper with vinegar, Duck.'

'Ummmmmm!'

'And poke sosssidge, Mama!' Gussie cried in the front room. 'Nice hot poke sossidge, huh, Mama?'

Topal burst into harsh laughter. 'Pork sausage! Go draw it on your tablet with a pencil, Gussie.'

Mrs. Crochet said, 'Me, I wish you send that round-shouldered gool to town with that udda Crochet out there. Listen, Duck, I'm worried about poor Juarelle. Who gunna go tell her we own her property? Goddle mighty, I dunno ——'

'Don't get excited,' Commodo said. 'I done tole her this mornin.'

'You didn't tell me that!'

'Aw, I been too busy.'

'What did she say? Tell me about it, you dinwiddie.'

'I stopped on my way home. Juarelle was all church-eyed because she's a-scared to stay there with no men aroun. I tole her we got the place.'

'Goddle mighty. Poor Juarelle. What did she say?'

'Aw, she jiss sat down. I tole her. I hadda tell her, Duck. It's awright. I tole her she can stay with us. She can stay with us, Duck.'

'Mais oui, she can stay with us, Duck.'

Topal said, 'At last a nigger, Evvie!'

'She almoss white, and so well raised,' Mrs. Crochet said. 'Poor Juarelle.'

'There's plenny lil things for her to do aroun the house and yard,' Commodo said. 'Leave her stay with us.'

Two men with wheelbarrows loaded with lily buds splashed through the front yard. The rain broke into vapor along their backs. Beaumont Crochet appeared over the rainy levee, and beckoned the men to hurry. He had on a suit of Commodo's ragged overalls for the rain, the legs turned up into great rolls, and the crotch hanging halfway to his knees. 'All right, all right, any time next week will do!' he yelled at the two men. 'I never saw people move so slow!'

When the clouds hid the sun, the rain turned pale, and it drummed briskly on the front steps. Evvie bent her muscles over the broom, and she thought of Bruce Holt in New Orleans behind the rainy miles, far up the twisting river. She remembered New Orleans in the rain from a newsreel view she had seen of a cornerstone laying — a glistening sea of restless black umbrellas, the square buildings without roofs, and the rows and rows of misty windows. Maybe Bruce at this moment was watching the rain from a dormitory window, as lonely people do. She saw his dark fine face staring through the gray slanting rain. She hoped he was having lewd thoughts about her.

Later, walking homeward on the levee with the supper groceries, she rolled the piece of tarpaulin under her arm, because the rain had stopped. The ruts in the road turned purple, and she straddled them playfully, squeezing the smooth cold slush between her toes. Now it was a beautifully colored evening, soft and fresh by the strong river. Cardinals and mockers on the wires shook their wet feathers and sang. Everything was lovely, and Evvie's throat was tight. The frigid slush licked under the arches of her feet. Now she would not have to tell Bruce her family had planted lilies in another man's canes, at least for a long time.

A girl passed by and said, 'Hey, Evvie.'

'Hey, Ernestine.'

'What you doin?'

'Nothing.'

'Yall sold yall's lilies. Yall got a big windfall, huh?'

'Pretty big.'

'Hey, Evvie. Mama got a dress for you. Blue with a white collar from Roebuck. It's too little for Loretta and too big for me. Come over tonight, Evvie, you hear?'

'Sure. Thanks.'

The lily buds had been loaded on the lugger. As Evvie crossed the front yard she noticed old man Dupré on the porch talking to Beaumont Crochet. Dupré's clothes were soaked with rain, glued to his body. Topal sat on the swing with the baby. Evvie crossing through the tense atmosphere on the porch heard Dupré say softly to the florist, 'I want my rights.' These grave low words were carried with her into the front room. She perceived that here was something she might want to write to Bruce about, some day.

In the front room, Mrs. Crochet had Commodo pinned in a corner, shoving against his belly. He was very drunk. His knees sagged. His big face wobbled round as he tried to focus his eyes, and shook his fist toward the porch, howling, 'The ole miser and nail-straightener! We'll get outa his house! We got a house! We'll get outa his house that we been holdin up with sticks and planks for ten year that Goddle mighty knows why it ain fell on these poor chirren's head!'

'Be quite,' Mrs. Crochet said. 'You makin a holy show.'

'Nail-straightenin mulatto chaser! It ain today I seen him poundin the road without a hat in the sun like a sneakin culprit from a mulatto's house!'

'How much do you want?' the florist outside asked Dupré. 'I've got to go.'

'They were not supposed to plant anything on my land.'

'Father Pennygrass said it was okay!' Mrs. Crochet shouted. 'Go talk to that lil saint of a priess! See what he says!'

'How much?' the florist asked.

Evvie looked out at Dupré. The man seemed to be shorter in stature, to have somewhat withered up since the Juarelle incident. Evvie was sorry for him. He stood working his lips and tongue, manipulating the bits of herb or bark to keep it between his nervously nibbling front teeth. 'The land's mine back there. Do you know anything about this — this irresponsible child of a man? He wants all he can get for nothing. I bought him cauliflower seed ——'

'Listen, Mr. Dupré, I've got nothing to do with these things.'

'Ask his wife. Years ago. I offered him land. The cauliflower plants wilted in the bed from no watering. He hit the ceiling when I passed here and asked about them. He thought he was doing me a big favor. Actually. Ask the people. I want them off my property quick and for good. Let them get off my property and leave me this front steps. We'll call it square and good riddance.'

Commodo emitted a savage roar. He stamped his bare feet. A candle on the mantelpiece fell. 'Over my dead body you'll take it!' he yelled. 'Them doorsteps was an act of Province! They ain't nailed on your house! Lemme go! Lemme show him they ain't nailed!'

Commodo staggered out to the porch. Mrs. Crochet, clinging to him, was dragged. He shook her off. He jumped down into the yard, falling to his knees in the mud. Rising, he took hold of the big front steps. With his teeth bared and his eyes blazing, he yanked the steps away from the house and turned it over in the yard to show it was not nailed to the house.

In the place where the steps had been, the ground was dry. Standing in this dry space was little Paul. He looked around with a scared expression, then put his finger in his mouth, and hung his head.

'Get inside and button yourself up!' Mrs. Crochet cried. She smacked the side of Paul's head. The boy stumbled over a lot of empty beer bottles which Commodo from time to time had hidden from his wife. She went to Commodo and backed him against the house. 'Quiten down, you! Look the neighbors!'

'I'll break his face! I'll stomp him! Jiss let him try to take my front steps!'

Topal was laughing loudly. Mrs. Crochet leaned against Commodo with all her weight. Her feet slipped like locomotive wheels, pawing for a hold in the mud. Commodo began to weep. There were people gathered on the levee. Unnoticed by anyone, a man descended the levee and came across the yard. He wore a yellowish linen suit. His pants were rolled high, exposing a pair of very thin, white, hairless legs. On the bottoms of his shoes were large thick pads of clay mixed with grass and clamshells. He stopped near the house with his mouth open, swinging his large, bulging eyes from side to side. In one hand he was balancing a big round package, a dish or a bowl wrapped in a colored comic supplement.

Beaumont Crochet abruptly took a checkbook from his pocket and said, 'Suppose we pay you rent for the use of the land, Mr. Dupré? How much would it be worth?'

'Twelve dollars.'

Commodo, squatting against the house, sobbed, 'Him, he oughta pay me for cultivating the lann, the chinchy ——'

'You keep quite, Duck,' Mrs. Crochet said.

The florist wrote the check.

Dupré said, 'They owe me house-rent.'

'You gunna get your house-rent!' Mrs. Crochet cried.

Dupré examined the check. He turned to leave. 'Tell them to get off my property and stay off,' he said.

The man in the yellow suit approached Mrs. Crochet, holding out the package. He looked at the ground. 'Miss Crochet,' he mumbled, 'Mimi say here some nice pea soup. Grammaw Jeanfreau made it. It's nice and hot. Papa an Too-too hadda go to the lighthouze, an it's oney gunna spoil ef somebody don't eat it.'

Everything was fine. Now the Crochets had a lamp in every room. Their first purchase had been two new lamps. Paul and Gussie were happy. They could play in any room they chose to. 'Mama, looka me!' Gussie cried, dragging his toy boat. 'I can see good everywhere!'

'Yes, darlin! Don't wake up the baby!'

Mrs. Crochet was waving a damp diaper over the hot kitchen stove. She had fixed her hair a new way. Evvie admired her mother's hair, a great black mass, very heavy for a small woman. Her mother's skin was nice, too — smooth and firm, and wrinkled in the right places. The fog and sun had preserved it.

'When them boys are playin nice, they look alike,' said Commodo. 'When they fightin, they look different. Tonight, they jiss as much alike as them two notes the fat man in a brass band plays on the big horn.'

'I wonder what Poison Ivory's gunna do with this house when we leave. I bet he leaves it rot. The place where my chirren was born, two twins and a chile.'

Commodo said, 'Forgit about the ole worm-goat, Ducky. Drink wine. Tonight I celebrate. Tomorrow I go to work on the place we gunna live.'

'Oui, I know your ole shovel is hungry to bite out that mud up there and do our drainin.'

'Who? Wait when I get up there with my shovel!'

'Eh bien! You gunna peel off the prettiess slices of clay and gumbo mud and pile it on the ditchbank one slice atop the udda all nice and even and pretty like you do.'

'Papa likes the mud,' said Evvie. 'I mean!'

Commodo said, 'I bet I know jiss what quality soil they got any place you point to unneat that-there land, and the color and the smell and weight, and how big is the crawfish holes and which way they run.'

'I wish you'd put down a pair of slacks for me on that list,' Topal said. She was sitting on the floor sewing a button on her pus-colored sweater. 'A pair of ninety-eight-cent slacks, if it won't use up all the money.'

'She means them pants the rich chippies is wearin in Hollywood,' Mrs. Crochet explained. 'She been sittin there sense supper thinkin and thinkin of things to buy. Me, I keepa wonderin what he's gunna do with this house. He'd leave it rot to spite me, jiss to see me pass every day and watch it fall to pieces.'

'I'd love the job of burning it down,' Topal said.

'Arsony would be a new sin on your soul for a change. I know noboddy gunna wunna live here. In a coupla years, oney the nail gunna be leff for Jewpray to pay a nigger to straighten. It's gunna rot and tremble on its knees, like, down and down a stick at the time. A house got to have people to stay alive, hot meals and voices . . . Eh, Lord! A lamp in the window and a man sleepin on the porch! Listen at Huey, crowin out there like he knowed we was movin soon and he gunna have him some hens to boss. A house dies and falls when the people leave. It's like they take away the strank of the house when they go. Even a boat dies, like, when the owner pulls it asho and forgits it, I notice. A sad thing to see.'

Commodo said, 'Put down a pair of oars, Duck. Somethin

I been needin six year and mine is worn to a pencil by the thole-pins, and that's a sad thing to see for sure. I'm gunna caulk and paint my pullin skiff firss thing.'

Mrs. Crochet sat by the kitchen table and wrote in Evvie's school tablet, 'Oars for pulling skiff.' There were about fifty items on the list of things to buy, two whole pages.

Commodo took a long pull at his bottle of raisin wine, smacked his lips, and winked at Topal, pulling up the entire side of his face to wink. He said, 'A outbode moada it oughta be, steada oars to pull at my age of life.'

'Go head and keepa tellin me more things, you all! Me, I'm scared to price these things and count it up. Jiss look at the size of the liss!'

'Mama, you can strike off my books and just get me the rocking chair I want for Papa,' Evvie said.

'A man's ridiculous like a woman on this Margin without a good boat,' Commodo said. 'People laugh behine my back. Where's a person gunna go and get fish without a boat? I feel like a ole sissy to stand on the groun watchin the clouds of fat ducks and geese flyin over. The sky is fulla meat, and I got no good boat to get to a pond.'

'But sweedart! You can't have a moada boat and a twenny-dollar plowin pony too. Some day you'll get a moada boat makin that okra you been crazy to plant for the market with the pony. Maybe you gunna need eyeglasses, too, Duck.'

'How, eyeglasses?'

'To see in the field so early in the mornin and late at night.'

'Hyanh-hyanh-hyanh! Crack her for me, Evvie! Before hell I feel like my ole self tonight! Woopy! Take wine, Duck! Why, I'll break ole Poison Ivory in half, he tries to take that steps. Pour some wine for Juarelle!' Commodo bellowed to Juarelle sitting on the floor against the wall, 'Hey! You wunt some wine?'

'Nawsa, thanks.'

Mrs. Crochet bent over the mulatto girl. 'Juarelle, will our shades fit your windows?'

'Nome, Ah don think.'

'You got shades to sell me second-hand?'

'We got um in one room.'

Commodo said, 'Whynt you wait tell mornin to count up your liss, Duck? Drink wine and forgit the ole money when we got us a home of our own to celebrate. Leave Evvie count it or Topal.'

'I'm bad in arithmetic,' Evvie said. 'I can't ——'

'Your maw's worse than bad.'

'Who?' demanded Mrs. Crochet.

'You! You can oney count nickels. Wait! How much is eighty-five apples and fifteen apples?'

'Don't bother me!'

'How much is eighty-five cents and fifteen cents?'

'A dollar, you dinwiddie!'

Everybody laughed except Juarelle. Evvie looked at Juarelle, sitting with her big rough hands folded in her lap. The fingers were thick as a man's. It was going to be curious — living with a strange, deaf, attractive colored woman. Juarelle was the only mulatto on the Margin who did not wear a large hat to keep from getting darker. Her head was round and small, her lips thick and curled like a horn. It was going to be difficult for Evvie to raise her voice for Juarelle always. But there would be plenty of the fine vegetables Juarelle was noted for raising with the hoe. No wonder Commodo was happy. His fine drainage would produce fine food.

There was a knock on the back door. Mrs. Crochet made a face. 'Who else is gunna buss in on me?' she muttered.

It was Mrs. Bob LaRoque. She did not stay long. She had

been to see the Crochets earlier in the evening, when other neighbors had been there. She had come now to bring a little toddler for T. J.

'Muncle Smiddy give it to Bella and she learnt to walk in it,' the woman explained. 'You jiss put T. J. in it and strap him, and he rolls it over the floor. Ain't it grand?'

'Oui, it's grand!' Mrs. Crochet said. 'Thanks very, very much. Evvie, get Miss LaRoque a slice of cake, darling.'

'Bob say we gunna call it a day,' Mrs. LaRoque said. 'Seven chirren's enough. Hello Juarelle! What you doin down the road so late?'

'She's a-scared to stay in that big house by herself,' Mrs. Crochet said. 'Topal gunna sleep with her up there tonight.'

Juarelle sat watching the women discuss her. Mrs. LaRoque smiled at her, and she returned the smile. 'Such a fine lady to work for!' Mrs. LaRoque shouted, pointing to Mrs. Crochet.

'Anyhow she gunna have a good home,' said Mrs. Crochet, 'And treated like the family, if possible. She gunna have a room right in the house with us.'

'I know you gunna fix it up nice, Miss Crochet. It's a pity the law says they got a right to redeem it back in a year.'

'Excuse me, Miss LaRoque,' Commodo said. 'Please don't get her started, because she done threw some hysterics about that today.' Commodo moved closer to Mrs. LaRoque and talked softly, 'I tole her nobody knows what can happen in a year.'

'Ain it the trute?'

'I tole her we gotta look on the bright side, and she promise not to get discouraged. Maybe Shoepick gunna get swallowed up in the city and never make no money, or maybe he gunna think the Drainage Bode done got the property and he can't redeem it. Maybe ef we treat Juarelle nice, she rather we have the worry of the property. I say I'll give her a home like she never had. I wunt this whole family to treat her nice.'

'She oughta be glad, like I told Bob. The house is too big for her. They couldn't sell it to no white people. No cullud people got the money to buy it. It worths a nice property for you all to take care of Juarelle and live on the cullud part of this Margin, Mr. Crochet.'

'If they redeem it on us, Miss LaRoque, maybe we gunna make enough in a year on lilies and oranges to make the down payment on anudda place. Listen, I got a fiff cousin a big floriss, Beaumont Crochet, that bought my lilies today. He gunna help us run a fine lily nursery.'

Mrs. Crochet said, 'They his lilies now, but they was my lilies when somebody hadda plant and mulch them on their bended knees. You better let that bottle alone. Beaumont Crochet gunna knock down a dollar for every dime he spend, and give you the dime.'

'Now, now, Duck. Take a blow. Remember you promised to turn a new leaf over and shun defeat. Eh bien! me, I'm gunna keep on in the drainage business tell we make a crop, Miss LaRoque. And we gunna live the same as we do now. Plain strong grub and clothes, huh Duck? Nothin fancy, in udda words.'

'I'm so glad, me,' said Mrs. LaRoque.

Topal was glaring at her father. She snickered, got up abruptly, walked over to stand brooding in the back door. Once she turned to look at her mother writing at the table, her lips curled.

'Nobody aroun here gunna be a spentriff,' Commodo said, glancing at Topal from behind the lifted bottle.

'Me, I got to be dragassin it up the road,' the visitor said.

'Don't you dare to forgit to come see me when you get settled, Miss Crochet.'

'And you muss come see me, too, Miss LaRoque.'

After the woman had gone, Mrs. Crochet snorted, 'The hipplecrite! "It worths a nice property to live on the cullud part of the Margin!" I can hear her standin in front of the church! "I see the poor Crochets is livin up amongst the niggers." I wouldn't go see her for Johnson, me. Soon as a person leaves her house, she startsa talkin about them. Again, you went and tole her all our business to scatter in the neighbors with your wine and your gubernatorial palaver.'

'Eh bien!' Commodo said. His eyes were getting glassy. 'Me, I got to celebrate all by myself, and you promised you wasn't gunna fuss any more. Nobody drinks with me.'

'Hush and lemme fish these prices from the Roebuck book.' Mrs. Crochet dipped the pencil in her mouth. 'Goddle mighty. It look like we can't get no ice-box, you all, and maybe no sewin-machine. My God.'

Topal looked over her mother's shoulder. 'Why don't you put the clothes on a separate sheet?' she asked. 'We just got to get the clothes. What's all those marks mean, the crosses and circles and subtraction signs?'

'*Will you get away!*' Mrs. Crochet screamed. 'Don't you see I'm gunna be a gibbetin maniac before I finish tryin to see what we get on a hundred and eighty-three dollars? The ice-box, the stove, the sewin-machine is importan as anything, and it looks like they gunna eat the money, Duck. Will you kick Topal Crochet some place for me? *I'll fling it in the river!*' she yelled, tearing her hair.

'Okay, okay. She's got a subtraction sign by some of my things.'

'Tope, whynt you go up the road with Juarelle like a good

girl and let your Mama work her sums to tell us what we gunna get,' Commodo said.

'I only want what I've got to have,' Topal said, 'and what I've earned around here. Why don't she make another list of the work everybody's been doing all these years. I want what I've *got* to have.'

'When you come to pullin the bung,' said Commodo, 'I've *got* to have a tractor and a stummick specialiss and a sprayin machine and ——'

'Tell that to her. I'm not dishing out the money.'

Juarelle left her seat on the floor. She wandered toward the front to sit on the big front steps alone.

The house grew silent, with only the sound of Commodo's occasional guggling.

Suddenly Mrs. Crochet slapped the pencil down, grabbed her hair, and groaned. 'Goddle mighty. Not even enough for the new beds and chairs and stuff!' She tore the list in half and crumpled it. 'I ain't buyin nothing! We ain got enough money for nothin!'

'Don't get excited, Duck. Whynt you jiss put down the importan things?'

'There's certainly things we've got to have,' Topal said.

'*We got to have everything!*' Mrs. Crochet screeched. 'We need ten thousan dollars! Every damn thing on that liss is jiss as importan as the thing nex to it, so we ain gunna get nothin, and we gunna take what we got here up to the new place. *And I don't wunna hear no more!*'

'That's all I want to know,' Topal said. She spun on her heel and went into the back shed. She made a bundle of her things. She went around through the side yard to the front steps. 'Let's go,' she said to Juarelle. They went up the road together to sleep in the big house.

Next morning Topal went to the back road behind the Shoepick place, and took the bus for New Orleans. She left a note with Juarelle telling her parents she was going to find work in the city, and stay with her Aunt Lucille on Tchoupitoulas Street.

Two days later they received a letter saying she had not yet located a job, but that her aunt had told her there was no hurry about finding work.

At the end of the letter was a note to Evvie: 'Hey, Evvie. I saw the street broadcast today. I am going downtown Friday and will be on the street broadcast myself. Tell all my friends to listen.'

Commodo said, 'Friday's tomorrow, sweedart, so you better tell all your little friends and Topal's friends. We'll hear it here on my set.'

'Mama, we'll be in Port Sulphur shopping Friday!' Evvie said. 'Maybe we can hear the street broadcast on the loud-speaker they have up there. It's a loudspeaker, a box that magnifies the voice!'

'She got nothin to say that I wunna hear,' Mrs. Crochet said.

She was finished with Topal.

After moving up to the new house all their belongings but the big doorsteps, Commodo and Mrs. Crochet took a morning off to go to Port Sulphur to buy the few things not ordered from the mail-order house. They rode the morning bus, and took Evvie with them, because she wanted to hear on the big loud-speaker the street broadcast and the voice of her sister in New Orleans.

In the general store at Sulphur while Mrs. Crochet was buying shirt and dress material, Commodo went about examining the tools displayed on the counters, and Evvie waited outside by the loud-speaker for the New Orleans street broadcast to come on. There was a lot for Evvie to see outside. Big things were being done in this little river community since sulphur mining had begun out near the sea. Evvie saw red girders in the air, paths paved with cement, piledrivers hammering down the piling for a big dock. Houses were being built for the families arriving from Texas. Soil had been pumped from the river bed to make a healthful townsite elevated above the surrounding lowlands. There was a new drugstore, a handsome post office. Evvie was amazed at the number of parked automobiles, at least fifty, all bearing Texas license tags.

A loud-speaker was a great novelty in the Delta. Idlers in denim, booted or barefooted, stood round listening, all looking up at the blaring apparatus. The braying words of the speaker, a minister addressing a gathering of Sunday school workers in Meridian, Mississippi, bounced back off the side of a huge warehouse across the road. One of the by-standers, Evvie noticed, had a big Western hat and high-heeled boots, but no horse. The words of the minister coming from the loud-speaker would sometimes collide with the echoes bouncing back off the warehouse. Evvie could not understand the words. Why were the people gathered round listening so intently? The words had no meaning.

'Ahmo tell yall sm wunnerful nyews ful nyews. Alla you good BYPU baw-woys n girls listenin daown n Creepmo Counny mo Counny. Ou ole friend Miz Cholly Awmstid's rot oucher on the platfawm the platfawm. Naow Ah thank yall go rememba Miz Awmstid's saw-woybean progum fum the fair at Jackson, an Miz Awmstid wawnts us to say a lil in behalfa her saw-woybean progum befo we git off the air

off the air. Creepmo Counny where some ou most progressive
people lee-uv hadden sen in any saw-woybean pledges fofo
yeahs han runnin I understand I understand. So folks Ahmo
talk plain talk plain. No munkey bidness key bidness. We
expeck alla yall BYPU people daown there to line up behind
Miz Cholly hind Miz Cholly. We wawnchalla promise you
go *taw-uk* saw-woybeans an *thank* saw-woybeans an *lee-uv*
saw-woybeans n lessall heppum putt this progum ova hundid
per cent caws Ahmo tell you ——'

At this moment the minister's words were interrupted by
a cheerful, rapid-fire voice, the street broadcaster in New
Orleans:

'—— daily noon street broadcast, Station WRIX, right
in front of the Creole Cafeteria today folks where today's
specials are broiled Spanish mackerel, lamb stew, curried
shrimp and hillbilly salad billy salad. Pardon me, brother,
don't lean on the mike on the mike. Free banana split at
the Creole Cafeteria and lovely weather today so many
pretty faces I see this little lady with the new shoes and the
sassy hat looking right at me and blushing and her boy-friend's
red-headed just like yours truly yours truly. Come closer,
little lady, come on hurry up don't be bashful I haven't got
all day come up closer that's it do you know who I yam I yam?'

There was the tremendous sound of a shy muttering.

'Speak up young lady and don't be afraid be afraid.'

'You're Tony Durel the announcer nouncer,' came the
voice of Topal and the echo from the warehouse side. Evvie
smiled. The great voice was loud as thunder.

'*Tony Durel* of course ha! ha! ha! and you young lady
you come from down the country and did you ever see me
before and tell our listeners how do you know who I yam
I vam?'

'You broadcast the pirogue races rogue races.'

'*The pirogue races* of course ha! ha! ha! and tell us come closer nothing's going to bite you tell us your own name own name!'

'Topal Crochet from Grass Margin Louisiana gin Louisiana.'

'Well well Miss Tople Croshay ple Croshay! And your boy friend . . .'

Evvie turned and dashed into the store to fetch her mother and father. They returned with her, and stood among the people listening. Commodo spied a man he knew in the group. 'What you say, Karl!' he called. He jerked his head nonchalantly toward the loud-speaker. 'My daughter on the broadcass in town!' he said.

'Shut up your mouth!' Mrs. Crochet whispered. 'I wunna hear the brazen imp.'

The announcer said, 'And you and the boy-friend come to town to eat at the Creole Cafeteria that wonderful lunch and the pie like Mama used to make to make!'

'You're telling me ling me!'

'Come to town for one day I guess I guess.'

'No sir, Dave's been in the hospital and I came to see him, and we're getting married this evening this evening.'

'*Married!* Hey folks just listen to this . . .'

'Goddle mighty!' Mrs. Crochet muttered. She walked away wringing her handkerchief. Commodo followed her.

'Don't get excited,' Commodo said.

'The brazen witch! At lass the round-shouldered limb got her a man.'

'Refined, and studdy as a jug,' said Commodo. 'That Mr. Tobin. Now she got something to straighten up for at lass! Listen, I wunt them to come to visit us right away. Come to pullin the bung, I like to have my son-in-law to live with us.'

'The brazen witch! The nerve, to marry a Protason!'

Evvie, standing under the loud-speaker, motioned her parents to come back. Mrs. Crochet was leaning on the fender of a parked car. She shook her head absently. She was deep in thought, angry or excited. Evvie saw the spokes of black light in her eyes.

'We can hear good right where we are!' Commodo called to Evvie. He moved closer to his wife, and held her round the waist, and they stood together with large listening eyes gazing away, both smiling when the announcer turned a jest. Once Commodo poked out his tongue and examined it in the window glass of the automobile.

The raw, earsplitting, nasal female voice of Topal blared forth like a one-note calliope: 'I want to say hello to my friends and my mother and father and little sister little sister!'

Then Dave Tobin was interviewed by the announcer, and told the listeners he considered himself a lucky man to be getting married to Miss Crochet. No, she was not his first girl-friend. He had had a girl-friend in France during the World War.

People who knew Tobin around Port Sulphur were stopping to listen. A larger crowd had gathered, and people were calling to others. Evvie looked at her parents and smiled, to hear Mr. Tobin's quiet voice magnified until it could be heard all over the town.

'YEAH, I would say we were glad to fight for our country in the World's War and we would do it again. I love my country, although I haven't seen all of it yet. And I would say we didn't quite understand some things that maybe need explaining to the average man, such as, why does a man get paid more for making bullets than he gets for stopping them? I would say this condition should be corrected in the next war, because far as I could see, soldiers is mostly always looking to bum a ride or a cigarette arette.'

Tobin told his listeners he was out of the hospital now and feeling fine, and hoped to return to his job with the sulphur company, and he considered himself a lucky man to be getting married to Miss Crochet.

The Crochets returned to Grass Margin on the bus. Evvie sat directly behind her parents, and she could hear every word they said above the rattling and squealing of the bouncing and plunging vehicle.

'Did you put the money back in the syringe?' Commodo asked.

'Oui, and I hid the syringe good. But I'm afraid for it, afraid of it, that money, it keeps me nervouser than when before we had any money.'

'Take a blow.'

'When are you going down to get the doorsteps for the new house? Can't you put down that window? I'm hot. Me, I'm worried about that money always.'

'You oughta never hide the syringe, sweedart,' said Commodo. 'It ain no use puttin money in the syringe unless you leave it where burglars and criminals could see it plain and think nothin ain in it.'

'I don't care, I'm disgusted. It ain enough money to half get what we need for our backs and all the rooms in that great big house, with a firss-married couple comin in with us like you wunt.'

'Take a blow, Duck,' said Commodo. 'Wait when we gunna make us a crop of oranges and lilies and stuff. Me, I don't pay no attention to your worriments. Everything gunna be lovely. Your tramp of a son Arthur's comin back today, and maybe he's down there helpin Juarelle right now. Your daughter that was a turrible ole maid's gettin married. You got a good nigger girl to leave the chirren with. Still you keepa worryin.'

Mrs. Crochet said: 'Of course the lilies was a good token for a start in life, sellin them for money, but what good is it? I was tellin Miss Gravier in the store, it look like everything a person buy makes them need somethin else to go with it, like. That great big house empty like a bladder, and it sound so scary when you walk down the hall at night, although it sure is solid. But it's gunna take me ten year to fill up them rooms. So I say things ain turnin out so grand. And again, things is movin too fass, entirely too fass. Goddle mighty. We got a orange grove and loss a daughter an got back a son, and you might as well say adopp a cullud girl. All that in a few days. I can't see where I'm gunna land.'

'Jiss hole on to me good,' said Commodo. 'Think about sweet things. We gunna have fun raisin things and lilies with Beaumont Crochet's fertilizer and booklets. Woopy, Duck! Think about all like that. You take right now, I remember we used to rassle when we was innocent boys in a great big cow pasture on a Sunday. You'd rassle and try to throw one anudda in the cow-mess piles. Anybody got throwed in cow-mess with his Sunday clothes on would get a terrible beatin when he got home, and that's why we learn to rassle good, and why we was strong. Them innocent days before the inventions come down the river, I tell you all the boys was innocent an treacherous. The reason I think of them days in the cow pasture is because I wunna get me a good bull some day if God spares me. I made up my mind. Pasture him on Jewpray's land next door.'

'For God's sake. A bull. Then you need a cow for him. Then you need a stable. Then you need a corn-crib ——'

'A bull. Of all the animals it's a singin bull to lead on a holiday by the nose down the road I wunt.'

'—— then a churn you'd need.'

'A great big bull! A big red dusty fella with cockleburrs in his tail stompin and huffin and pawin holes in the levee.'

'You nasty thing.'

In the afternoon Arthur came home to the big house, and he went into the vegetable patch to help Juarelle at once. He and his father avoided each other. Arthur and Juarelle worked together, hoeing the young sweet peppers, and Evvie, holding T.J., watched them from the ditchbank, enjoying this day off from school.

Later, when Commodo borrowed a pony and a sled, Evvie went down the road with her mother and father to the old house to get the big doorsteps. While Commodo loaded and tied the doorsteps on the sled, Mrs. Crochet and Evvie dug up their rosebushes.

'This groun gunna miss my diggin,' Mrs. Crochet said. 'And watch next week, the weeds. But what do I care, me? It ain nunna my business no more.' Evvie thought she detected a tightness in her mother's voice.

Commodo drove the pony dragging the sled across the front yard and up the levee slope to the road. Evvie and her mother followed with the rosebushes. They looked at the big doorsteps tied to the sled, now all shining in the red susnset, and they looked back at the old house.

'The ole house,' Mrs. Crochet said. Her clacking laughter was hard and bitter.

'Wait! I got to go out back a minute,' said Commodo.

'Hole him.' He handed the pony's reins to Evvie. 'I be right back, Duck.'

Commodo's fat, slightly knock-kneed legs hurried over the front yard and took the path that ran around the dwelling to the outhouse. Evvie and her mother sat on the levee side.

'The ole house,' Mrs. Crochet said.

'Aw, Ma,' Evvie said.

'The poor house.' Mrs. Crochet bowed her head. Her shoulders jerked.

'Shh! Here he comes, Ma!'

Mrs. Crochet turned away, turned her back on the house, wiped her eyes. Evvie watched her father stop at the rear corner of the kitchen, back up to it and begin to rub his back on the corner of the building.

'Look what he's doing, Ma!' Evvie laughed. 'Hey, Pa, are you telling the house goodbye?'

'One lass good scratch!' Commodo yelled, leaning hard against the building and wriggling. 'This the oney thing the ole house was good for! I'm gunna miss it bad, this place for scratchin, because it's sharp, but still got some *give* to it!' His eyes closed with delight.

Evvie was standing frozen, unable to cry out at what she saw. Behind her she heard her mother scream: '*Duck! Look out!*'

Commodo paused and turned, but too late. The house was falling, very slowly, like a tired animal lying down. The rocking of the kitchen from Commodo's rubbing had dislodged the old schooner-boom, and now, being without support, the kitchen teetered far over, swung for a moment, then sank, pulling the two other rooms with it. Commodo tore savagely out toward the levee, dropping his green derby and leaving it where it fell. Before he reached the road the house had entirely collapsed, folding slowly down sideways through a thin red mist of dust, settling into a jagged pile of rubbish curiously without crash or clatter — only a dull low rustle, like a sigh.

'Nobody seen me!' Commodo said in a low tone. 'Less go! Easy, now! Don't crack a bone!'

Mrs. Crochet grabbed Evvie by the hand. 'Don't stand there like a spink!' she hissed, slapping Evvie's head. 'Hurry while nobody's on the road!'

The sled moved off, Commodo speaking softly to the pony; the big doorsteps swayed, settled back, rode away securely.

Evvie and her mother hurried ahead, stealing along through the roadside weeds. Both were chuckling softly.

THE END

Afterword

By Eudora Welty

AS THIS novel opens, Topal and Evvie, the two young Crochet daughters, are out in frosty grass bringing down all the birds they can manage to hit with a slingshot, then wading through the marsh to trade the birds to a smelly old fisherman to use as bait in return for coffee coupons good for premiums redeemable at the store; and "Let me carry her," Evvie says when the statue of the Blessed Mother is handed over. "I killed most of the birds."

It is a strange opening scene, set in a part of the country most of us never saw, had never known was on the map. It is a scene which takes for granted the misuse of everything —birds—young girls—the Virgin—probably even the barter system. It is also true comedy, and is brought about to tell us how desperate life is on Grass Margin.

Grass Margin is the name of this narrow peninsula at the lowest fringe of Louisiana, running out into the Gulf of Mexico at the Mississippi's mouth, and *margin* is the word for their whole world, and the fact of their lives, for the people there; it is the exact substance of what they are clinging to to survive. It's where the verbal form for "go" is "take the levee," where crawfish breed under the house, where the vibrations from a passing boat cause the statue of the Blessed Mother to travel across the mantel shelf to the edge and need to be kept an eye on, and where the lone doctor arrives at his office in hip boots and carrying a pirogue paddle, direct from his latest confinement case in the marshes.

The novel has strong physical presence. How easy it is to *see* the family out on the levee, stooped under the great white clouds "as though hunting something which had fallen from the sky"—actually for wild greens on Good Friday to cook for dinner; the young girl fruitpickers in their tinted blouses up in the orange trees, being treated to a wrestling match on the ground between two furious young men, delighting in it even when a knife is pulled out; Jaurelle dancing on the sack of dried shrimps to remove their shells.

O'Donnell makes eloquent even the objects of everyday life: the old cypress pirogue, "hollowed from a root by Tony's great-grandfather, was filled with ancient cracks and holes patched over with rusty tin. Its bottom, which had been dragged over reefs and clamshell bottoms for nearly a hundred years, was worn thin as grocery cheese." Even when we can't see it, we know this world is there. At midnight, we can smell the lilies from a mile away. In the river fog, we hear the close bells of invisible ships.

When sentimental Uncle Dewey tells Topal, "Don't be downhearted, my lil Creole belle," she flares up. "Who's Creole? I'm Cajun and proud of it." So are they all, proud, passionate, and instantly assertive. They're a people temperamentally unsuited to working for others. (Remember poor Topal, trying it at the shrimp factory.) The grain of their character is independence. And in their hearts they can all be dreamers. There's only one who takes authority as a realist. "Me, I been fooled too much," says Mrs. Crochet to Commodo, her husband. "You got sixty dollar,

you ole rangatang of a fool walking all over your shoestrings with your sherry-wine ideas?"

O'Donnell writes with particular tenderness for the
youthful characters, and with one exception (Mrs. Crochet,
of course) they have been given more depth than their
elders. We see Evvie—vulnerable, sweet-natured, re-
sponding with fervor to life before she quite knows (and
nobody will tell her) where it can lead her—she can't help
calling back and forth with those unseen men on their
unseen boat in the fog—and at fourteen helplessly seduc-
tive, she is besieged simultaneously from four directions
with unwanted attentions, simply by occupying her seat at
the movie on bank night. Her dream, that of becoming a
Little Sister of the Poor, after first finding a lover to
renounce, is really only half hers, the first half being her
mother's. (Did O'Donnell playfully name his Evvie after
Evangeline, as a bow toward the original Acadians—
Longfellow's heroine who was parted from her lover, lived
out her life as a Sister of Mercy, and could only look
forward to being united with Gabriel in the grave? A
statue has been raised to her in Southern Louisiana.)
Topal the rebel is more brooding, more apprehensive in
one-sided competition with her beautiful younger sister
("You little feen!"), giving terser expression to her yearn-
ings: "I'm young, I oughta be out. Soft ball game at Port
Sulphur. At Venice a dance. I saw a lugger pass in the
river with a bass-drum on top." Her despair is realer than
Evvie's hopes, for being six years older; she is brought to
tearing up her precious Pen Pal letters and scattering
them from the window of a moving Greyhound bus.

And there is Dave Tobin, the sulphur man, trailing a
cloud of sulphur smells that cause Evvie's eyes to weep.
Laconic in his promises, physically unselfprotective to the

point of lunacy, he is a foreign element in this world—he is from Texas. "He's all right," says Topal, at the time not dreaming that she is to be his bride, "but he always wants people to please walk on him." We see what makes him a mystery on the Margin: he is the opposite of a Cajun.

Though the characters of the novel are all such clear identities, declaring themselves from the very first through act and speech, we don't make the mistake of supposing them simple. Even to be crude is not necessarily to be simple, and only Tayo Delacroix can qualify.

O'Donnell gives them a further dimension by his touch of irony. Shoepick, who knew how to write a song, gets caught stealing schoolbooks with which to help himself write a letter to the man who stole his first song, to ask why he'd never been paid for it; he can never write the letter. O'Donnell has embodied Mrs. Crochet's harsh defiance toward Commodo's "sherry-dreams" in nothing else than an Easter lily. Cultivating her illicit garden in the thick of the landlord's canebrake, toiling with her daughters behind her by night ("We got to use that moon"), she carries on in her own rival hope, secret scheme, of selling the bulbs one day to the market in New Orleans.

They have another dimension. Everybody in the novel is vocal. Even the baby, T. J. Crochet, too young to enter the conversation, can interrupt it by bawling in his bass voice; when he's offered his mother's breast discouragingly sprinkled with red pepper, he interrupts the louder.

O'Donnell's supreme gift may be his dialogue. He has uncommon versatility; he can even write in the agonized speech-sounds of Arthur with a pool ball stuck inside his mouth. Dave Tobin, who swears "Hells'far!" speaks pure Texas. "By rights I'm a athalete. I went to Texas A. & M.

A fally good school, but too strict for me. It like to broke my daddy's heart when I quit."

He just as precisely gives us Shoepick's unlabial speech and Shoepick's songs: those four or five words repeated over and over to the bonka bonk bonk bonk of the guitar, that come out sad enough to make Evvie cry. And there are the noises broadcast over the loudspeaker in Port Sulphur from the Baptist preacher in Meridian, Mississippi, together with echoes, addressing the B.Y.P.U. Evvie can't understand a word he says, but O'Donnell got him perfectly.

His ear is wonderful, but for a novelist this gift is only the beginning. In writing of his Cajun people, what seems to me extraordinary is that O'Donnell has taken a dialect highly distinctive in itself and flamboyant by nature and made it so thoroughly responsive, so echoing, to his needs. As he uses it, the dialect becomes an instrument of a pure sensitivity, and for expressing human feeling it has gained rather than lost range through passing through the modes of Cajun speech.

Recall the conversation in which Evvie tells her mother, "Suppose I didn't want to be a Sister. You'd still fuss if I looked at a man." Mrs. Crochet hisses:

> "Mais non! Mais non! I wooden fuss! I'd laugh, me, and tell you to go ahead and get married. Live in a rented house! Get you a trapper and skin muskrat the ress of your life and a band of kids pullin your skirt off with belly-ache from eatin kidney pills the sample man threw in the yard. Get married and turn your back on Jesus on the cross that he's beggin you to give up your life to the poor!"
>
> "Ouch! I don't even know why people get married."

"Broadcass it! Broadcass it on the road! They get married
to drip coffee through a undershirt sleeve."

It is through the outcry, and the battling, and the clowning
along with the dreaming that O'Donnell conveys the pressing realities of their lives. Commodo's wild bravado and
his wife's vivid scorn (while they're still calling each other
Duck) are what they fight poverty with when they give out
of everything else.

The ugliness and periodic brutality that are part of
Margin life are talked back to in the novel but are never
concealed. The wonderful long evening when Commodo
and Uncle Dewey get more and more inspired and tearful
over the Dago red ("Life is a tess") doesn't cause you to
forget the day of the poisoning of the whole skyful of
blackbirds, or the way it makes Evvie feel. The loneliness is
as palpable as the uncanny beauty of the Easter lily patch
in the moonlight. And as we watch Mrs. Crochet starting
her *roux* and going through the process and the ritual of
preparing her court bouillon, imparting her recipe to her
daughters at every step of the way, the coming feast lavish-
ly brings before us the hunger the family lives with on
ordinary days.

This comedy holds more than what is funny. It is filled
with the antics of survival, the relish of surviving. No-
where in *The Great Big Doorstep* appear the passivity and
the anonymity, the accepting and accepted *helplessness* of
the poor in our own day. Here alone the novel may be said
to date. Of course there is never anything funny about
poverty itself—what O'Donnell has written with humane
warmth and comprehension is a story of what people defy
its desperation with. Their folly and their courage both
overrun the pages.

AFTERWORD361

The comedy doesn't rule out the inclusion of any human endeavor. It accepts both dreams of future glory and prayers to the Virigin to please not send any more babies. It takes in dread and the ignorance of it, skepticism and credulity, fantasy, lies, Pen Pal letters, the tall tale about the green mule, the incessant promptings of love. There is one thing that comedy must always include, though— some living hope, misguided or not as the hope may be.

When there is nothing to start with, whatever is hoped for, like whatever is sent, may be tinged with the miraculous. As a gift delivered by the river, the doorstep is not unique on the Margin; the confessional box in the Negro Baptist Church had come down the river ahead of it, in the form of a telephone booth.

In *The Great Big Doorstep* it isn't the separate ingredients or the accumulation of them that make this comedy the triumph it is, but O'Donnell's comic vision. I wonder if he may not see the novel with every element of it dependent on all the others, closely related, and all bumping intimately and unceremoniously against one another, exactly in the way the Crochet family lives together in the house with the waiting doorstep.

That the novel advances by a plot as economical and teasing as a fable's is one of its charms. The river, now peaking, must fall, and then Emilien Perdu will drive his cattle out of the marshes and hold the meeting of the Drainage Board that will pass the resolution that decides the future of Shoepick's house—the house that would match the doorstep. It is a plot just right to channel a way—a shortcut—into the full, bounding life of the Margin; the story opens out to it and it brings us into view of everything.

O'Donnell's narrative doesn't proceed inductively from

event to event but winds suggestingly from scene to scene; each chapter is a further suggestion, rounded off. This is O'Donnell's special way of conveying to us the life on the Margin, from which we learn that the life of complete poverty is very rich. He has brought out its natural exuberance, its bitterness, its zest. He has tested it for cruelties without letting their harshness disguise the presence of tenderness or the aroma of youthful aspiration. There is the quality of the unexpected that streaks through the writing, a freshness, as though O'Donnell enjoyed improvisation. The novel is his court bouillon. O'Donnell had a beautiful redfish, caught on the scene, to make it with, but his secret was in his *roux*.

The Crochets are virtuosos, and the fact that they have nothing—or the fact that the check presented by Uncle Dewey will in due course be returned marked N.S.F.—can't keep them from making the grand gesture at the time it's called for. It doesn't keep them from the symbolic gesture, either, the most moving example perhaps being Topal's casting away the unwanted lily blooms on the river.

And there's the revolvement of the entire novel about the grand symbol of the doorstep itself. The doorstep is a symbol, but like any valid, working symbol it earns its way as solid fact. The novel demands that it be dealt with as both. It is here that O'Donnell makes (through the enjoined action of all the Crochets) a bravura gesture of his own. He allows their dream to come true.

Our first reaction may be to wonder ungratefully if they should have got their wish—literally got it, moved into it, taken up life there. Does the stroke of the wand that makes everybody happy destroy the perfection of the novel? The great big doorstep had its high value in being *without* the great big house to go with it, in being the basis for a continuing dream. Shoepick's house matched to it seems out of place because it's in a different category from that of a dream.

The Crochet house, propped up on its schooner beam, resembling a problem in long division, and bursting with living Crochets, has been the binding spell that was holding the story together. It is the story's frame that is lifted away from the characters. Does it take some of their identity with it? And a more serious question (for of course the identity of the Crochets is never in danger): has O'Donnell taken the deliberate risk of allowing his novel to be a lesser comedy for being in part sentimentality now?

Well, first, by his virtue of keeping everybody in top form and in positive character through the emergency of a contagiously happy ending—for other problems are settled in its wake—O'Donnell brings it off. The ending carries out the *spirit* of the characters. For this reason, we grant it all—every item of it; we believe that Topal is going to settle for marriage to a somewhat damaged Mr. Tobin when we hear her voice announcing the engagement in authentic Crochet fashion, over the street broadcast emanating from outside the Creole Cafeteria in New Orleans, for the world to hear.

And Shoepick, whose career has always run in the opposite direction, who has represented the other possibility the Crochets don't admit, defeat, fills in the pattern. In the end, after losing his song and his house, he beats his sister disgracefully in public, and, reeling drunk, is carried away senseless—also to New Orleans, which is of course the songwriter's proper destination. Shoepick at the end is on the way to his fulfillment too, only he goes there in perfect character: in spite of himself.

The novel ends, then, in giving us not a finality but the sense of coming change, of change already here. It was not only heralded by the street broadcasts that have been reaching from New Orleans to Port Sulphur; the climax of the novel depends on the connection made from Grass Margin to the lily bulb market in New Orleans—another miracle, I should think, since it was made *from* Crochet *through* Crochet *to* Crochet. With Arthur and now Topal broken away from the closest of home ties, we can foresee further change. At novel's end, the author's granting the dream of the house to come true is modulated, has been matched now, by his intimating that it is to be the dream of all the children, one by one, to leave it. We see the ending for what it is. There has been not a sentimental resolution of the novel but an ironic one.

There are characters that will last longer than the story, however, formed through O'Donnell's sharpness of vision, his sensitive touch. Commodo comes out in broad, gaudy strokes, while Evvie has been put in with a very delicate brush. The portrait of Topal is full of contrast, and shows that she got her intensity from her mother. And it is her mother, Mrs. Crochet, whose portrait is the finest in the novel; we shall see her for a long time to come as we see her now, assessing the worth of dreams.